TRINITY OF SOULS

To Christa

All the Best,

Carl Bugly

ABOUT THE AUTHOR

Tax writer turned storyteller, Carl Bayley, moved to Scotland in 1997 and fell in love with its landscape and history. The country ignited his creative passion and a desire to tell timeless stories that weave together the past and present. Pausing a mere quarter of a century to write a series of popular tax guides, he developed a skill for explaining complex concepts in simple everyday language. Now, he combines skills and passion to produce a series of fantasy novels unlike any other. And, don't worry… tax is only mentioned once!

TRINITY
OF SOULS

First instalment in the Souls Series

Carl Bayley

Troubador Publishing Ltd
Unit E2 Airfield Business Park,
Harrison Road, Market Harborough,
Leicestershire. LE16 7UL
Tel: 0116 2792299
Email: books@troubador.co.uk
Web: www.troubador.co.uk

ISBN 978 1805142 140

British Library Cataloguing in Publication Data.
A catalogue record for this book is available from the British Library.

Printed and bound in the UK by TJ Books Limited, Padstow, Cornwall
Typeset in 11pt Baskerville by Troubador Publishing Ltd, Leicester, UK

For Diana, who brought me into the light;
And for Linda, my She Wolf, who brought the sunshine back again;
Without you, this would never have happened

Thanks to Linda, Aleck, and Sarah for all your encouragement.
Wherever this takes me, I won't forget it

CONTENTS

PROLOGUE

THE END?

It was a horrible night, the kind of night sensible people stayed indoors, keeping warm and dry. The rain did not fall; it was hurled sideways on the wind. Only complete fools or those with urgent work to do would be out on a night like this.

A sports car was hurtling up the winding road clinging to the side of the glen, racing faster with every twist and turn. Its headlights tried in vain to push back the darkness as it shot past a sign bearing the silhouette of an animal and splashed through a stream that had burst its banks.

Ben barely noticed the triangular sign. He was in no mood to heed any warnings. The news he'd just received had shaken him to the core. He had to find her; had to save her from the horrifying fate that awaited her.

Looking back, he remembered how he'd dismissed the old man as a crank. But the stranger had persisted, calling time and again, refusing to take no for an answer.

He begged Ben to see him. When Ben finally agreed, the stranger insisted on meeting in a small hotel in the north-west of Scotland.

"Why so far away?" asked Ben.

"It will be safer; and it will help you remember."

"Safe from what; remember what?"

The stranger did not elaborate.

A dark winter's day was already turning to night as Ben arrived at the hotel. Walking towards the dimly lit building, he wondered how a man he'd never met, from a country on the other side of the world, could know what he dreamt. He found the stranger in the bar, anxious to begin. As the man started his story, Ben was sceptical; it all seemed too fantastic. But he began to waver as the stranger described recurring elements of his childhood nightmares as if he'd witnessed them first-hand. Eventually, Ben allowed the stranger to put him into a hypnotic trance. And it all flooded back… everything.

Coming out of the trance, Ben fired a barrage of questions at the stranger. It soon became apparent the woman he loved was in terrible danger. "I must go to her at once," he jumped to his feet, "I can't risk waiting a moment longer."

"But, how will you find her?" asked the old man as Ben headed for the door.

"I don't know, but I will. Somehow, I will."

As Ben sped around another bend in the treacherous road, a stag stepped out of the darkness, only yards in front of him. He stamped on the brake in desperation, but it was too late. The majestic beast towered over him like a monstrous demon, its fourteen-pointed antlers glistening in the headlights.

'I'm going to die,' he thought.

'Again'

1

HOPE

The music was loud, but beautiful, and strangely familiar. He was floating with it on a wave of emotion. There was joy and love but, oh my God, there was pain and sorrow, and aching despair. Strongest of all was the sense of loss.

He couldn't go on. The music stopped. He had stopped it. Silence fell, followed by darkness. The darkness deepened, becoming a void of nothingness. It was calling him, telling him this was where he belonged; welcoming him home. It was powerful, its pull strong. He was falling into it.

Another presence was calling him, something warm and caring, filled with love and light. He needed to find it; cherish and protect it. He tried to reach out to it. But the void would not let him go.

For a long time, he was held by a strange tug of war, neither falling deeper nor escaping the void. Then the presence above grew stronger. He began to rise, slowly at first, gradually faster, until he surged upwards. As he left the void behind, he could feel its anger. He knew it would be waiting for him, waiting for another chance.

It grew lighter: still dark, but no longer the void. He sensed pain, anguish, and fear ahead. But it was the only way to reach the presence he sought. So he allowed the lighter darkness to envelop him.

*

Susan hurried along the corridor, eager to see for herself. As usual, she'd woken early and checked the hospital intranet. After reviewing her other patients, she'd tapped the tab labelled 'Carlton, Ben', with little hope of seeing any change.

It had been over a month since Carlton was brought to Princess Diana Memorial. For days, they'd battled to save him while he hovered on the brink of death. Eventually they'd been able to stabilise him, and now his body was beginning to mend. But that was only part of the story. He'd suffered severe head injuries in the crash and been in a coma since, with no sign of recovery in brain function. Until last night, that was.

A single spike in his brainwaves, that was all, but it gave Susan hope. It was something she could build on, something she could use to fight his corner. The pressure had been mounting to remove life support and let him slip away, but that spike would buy her time.

She hated losing patients, any patient, but something about Carlton made her more determined than ever.

She'd never seen a case like his before. No-one could explain why he'd survived when, right from the start, her experience said he would die. Somewhere inside, there was a spirit, a force, a God-knows-what, defying the odds, and it wouldn't let go. Reaching the doors of the intensive therapy unit, she shrugged to herself. Whatever it was, she was going to do her damnedest to help it bring him back.

"My shift finished twenty minutes ago, but I thought I'd wait for you," said the nurse as Susan entered. She looked Susan up and down, "You're brave, Worthington won't be happy you're wearing scrubs."

"Screw Worthington; they're comfortable, hygienic, and they provide the added pleasure of pissing him off."

The nurse laughed, "Yeah, there's a lot to be said for that."

"So, any more news on Carlton?"

"No," the nurse shook her head, "only that one spike. Probably just a glitch, I reckon. You know how some of the monitors do that now and then. Minster got awfully excited though, started shouting, 'Look, he's alive,' like something out of Frankenstein."

"I take it you wrote the entry in Carlton's notes?"

"I had to, Minster hadn't got a clue. Some of these junior doctors are about as useful as a chocolate teapot. Honestly, I think he only bothered checking the monitors to try to impress me. I hope to Christ he doesn't make another pass."

"You shouldn't be so hard on him; he only wanted to take you out to dinner."

"Huh, I know what he wanted. Well, I'll be off anyway, unless there's anything else you need?"

"No, you get off home, Jenny. Thanks for waiting."

The nurse paused at the door, looking back, "How are things going with Ray by the way?"

"Yeah, good," Susan nodded; "we're both off next weekend, I'm gonna stay over at his place. He's promised to cook me something special."

"Sounds great; well, I'll see you tonight then, I expect."

Susan watched Jenny go then went to take a closer look at Carlton. She studied the monitors clustered around his bed, making notes on her tablet. With a sigh, she realised Jenny was probably right, that spike may have been no more than a glitch. Apart from that momentary exception, there was no indication of brain activity. They may have saved his body, but where was his mind?

Glitch or not, she wasn't ready to give up. There was still hope. Gazing down at Carlton, she felt a sense of wonder at how he'd defied the death that should have claimed him a month ago; how he'd hung on to life. She felt something else too: an odd feeling she couldn't put her finger on, but she sensed it every time she was near him.

Shaking her head, she started to turn away. Then, without really knowing why, she turned back and whispered, "Come on, Ben; come back."

*

Pain; terrible, agonising pain

8

For a time, the pain was the only thing he was conscious of. He was floating alone in the Universe with nothing but his pain.

There was a thick fog around him. He was floating in the fog, with his pain, but still he was a shapeless, ethereal being, unsure whether he was alive or dead, or even what the difference was.

Slowly, he began to take physical form. He became aware he had a head and he turned it to look at his body. Something was wrong, he knew that much, but he couldn't see past his waist, the fog was so thick he could only see a few inches.

At last the fog began to clear. Maybe it wasn't fog. No, it was smoke. He peered downwards. He could see a little further now, but there was still nothing below his waist. Then he knew what was wrong. There wasn't anything past his waist; his legs, his entire lower body, were gone. He flopped back onto the sand and waited to die as the others ran up the beach into the maelstrom of shells and bullets.

*

Susan was furious. She could barely concentrate on the rush hour traffic. How dare that bastard put her in such a difficult position! She could feel the anger seething within her. No doubt it was responsible for the thumping headache she'd woken up with.

She'd gone to Ray's place on Friday as arranged. Everything had been fine until they'd been relaxing after dinner, when he'd produced the white powder and started spreading it out on the coffee table, using a knife to divide it into neat lines.

"Er… that's not what I think it is; is it?" she laughed nervously.

"Yeah, just a bit of coke to give us a buzz before we hit the bedroom. You wait; you haven't experienced anything 'til you've climaxed on coke."

"I, er… I don't do drugs. I mean I smoked a bit of pot at university, but I've always kept away from anything harder. You never know what it might do to you. I'd hate to get addicted. We can't anyway, we're practising neurologists. It would be completely irresponsible, not to mention likely to get us struck off."

"Chill out, babe, it's harmless. I've been doing it for years; it's never done me any harm."

"Oh yeah, and what about your patients; don't tell me you've been at work with that stuff in your system?"

"Don't be such a square; lots of people do it."

"Well, I'm not doing it. Look, Ray, I think I'd better go, I'm not comfortable with this."

"Go? After I cooked you dinner, forked out for champagne and a couple of grams of top quality coke? No, you're not going, you're gonna snort some coke and have the fuck of your life."

"No, Ray, I'm going," she started to get up, but he grabbed her wrist and pulled her down. He pushed her back on the sofa and leaned over her, "You're not going, you're gonna stay and have some fun."

"Let go of me," she gasped, struggling against him. She was frightened by his reaction, afraid what he might do next.

He picked up some powder on the blade of the knife and held it under her nose, "Come on, babe, take a snort, you'll love it."

She turned her head to the side and took a deep breath. Turning back, she blew the powder into his face. He jumped back, coughing and spluttering, "What the fuck. You stupid bitch, that stuff costs a fortune."

"Well it's not gonna cost me my career," she snapped as she sprang to her feet and marched out of the room.

She should have known better, she'd never had any luck with men. She'd fled the flat and driven home. All weekend she'd struggled with the dilemma Ray had left her in. She knew she should report him to the hospital authorities, but would they believe her? Nobody likes a whistle-blower, and being associated with a drug user was going to reflect badly on her. Damn him; things were hard enough at work as it was. Not for the first time, she thought about quitting.

She used to love her job when she was at Queen Square. The work had been so fulfilling then, she'd felt she was making a real difference, caring for people like she'd always wanted. But, since her transfer, her patient contact had steadily diminished while the hours taken up by management duties escalated by the day. She wouldn't mind so much if she felt she was achieving something, but the harsh reality was she wasn't able to influence the quality of patient care anything like as much as she wished.

Pulling up in the staff car park at the back of the hospital, she walked towards the locker room; head down, deep in thought. Maybe she should volunteer for the Red Cross or something; go and work in Africa, or South America, anywhere she could feel useful.

Her thoughts were interrupted by a cheery, "Hello." She looked up, "Oh, hi, Jenny, how are you this morning?"

"Bloody knackered to be honest; it's been a long night, ruddy awful from the start."

"Why's that?"

"Well, the wannabe widow was in again for one thing."

"Huh," Susan grunted. She'd seen Carlton's wife visiting before. The woman didn't look particularly upset by her husband's perilous condition. In truth, she looked like her lucky number had come up; she wouldn't have to go through that messy divorce after all. Susan hoped the bitch was wrong. If she had anything to do with it, Ben Carlton was going to live.

She chatted to Jenny a while, then waved her goodbye and carried on towards the staff entrance. Her damn head was still thumping away. It seemed to be getting worse as she approached the building. She'd have to stop off at the pharmacy before she started her rounds.

Reaching the locker room, she remembered there was an alternative to resigning; a way she could have a real impact on how the department was run. For weeks, she'd been mulling over whether to apply for Deputy Head of

Neurology. She was sure she could do a better job than the other likely candidates, but Ray had been doing his best to talk her out of it, said she'd only humiliate herself going up against more experienced applicants. Like him, of course, he meant. Last week, he'd finally persuaded her not to apply. But that was last week. Things had changed.

She looked into her locker and considered her choices. She made her decision and reached inside.

*

The pain was back. It was bad, though not as bad as before. It wasn't all over this time, either; just down one arm.

The fog was back too. Quickly, he realised the fog was actually the smoke and dust from the artillery barrage. Why couldn't he move though? He needed to move forward, march on for King and Country, march towards the enemy trenches through the mud and chaos.

He looked down. There was barbed wire wrapped around his arm. That was alright, he could soon untangle it. He'd get the sarge to safety then go on with his pals, marching towards the German lines. Marching to the victory that, this time, finally, must surely be theirs?

There were several thumps across his chest, like an unseen giant had punched him. He staggered backwards then slumped to the ground, still held in the grip of the barbed wire.

Everything began to fade away.

Susan swept through the hospital, her white coat flowing behind her like a cloak. Despite her persistent headache, she was in a good mood. She'd made up her mind; she was going to apply for Deputy Head. Sod it, they could tell her she didn't have enough experience if they wanted; she was going for it. That's what her father would have told her to do.

There was also another reason for her good spirits. A couple of weeks ago, it looked as if Ben Carlton might never come out of his coma, but the report she'd just seen showed what initially seemed like a random glitch had, in fact, been the beginning of a cycle made up of brief spikes of intense brain activity followed by long, dormant periods… long, but getting shorter, and, while she wasn't exactly sure what that meant, it was definitely a positive sign.

She reached the I.T.U. and headed straight for Carlton, leaning over to examine the monitors around his bed. The readings confirmed what she had hoped: he was beginning to regain some degree of normal brain function. It was nothing short of a miracle. She smiled down at him, delighted with his progress, and felt the same strange sensation she always felt when he was close. It seemed to be getting stronger every time, but she still couldn't grasp what it was: a sense of familiarity, or belonging, or even…

'Susan!' she chastised herself. It was just sympathy that was all. What's more, it was totally unprofessional. Carlton was a patient, strictly off limits. And he was married; even if his wife was a total bitch. Double off limits!

She shrugged off her feelings and continued her examination. But later, as she walked back along the corridor, echoes of the sensation Carlton had evoked still lingered in her mind. Well, at least it had displaced that bloody headache.

*

The ferocious dark hordes were getting closer, the sustained volley fire no longer holding them back. Even the briefest pause to open a box of ammunition allowed dozens of native warriors to rush forward and threaten the line. The situation was getting critical. Basil wondered how much longer his company could hold their position.

A few yards to his left he saw a trooper hit in the chest by a flying spear. The man next to him fumbled and dropped the cartridge he'd been loading into his rifle. It was enough. Within seconds, the enemy reached the weak spot and began to pour through the gap. The line was breached.

Basil knew he must stem the ebony tide or the whole battalion would be under threat. It seemed unthinkable: these spear-wielding savages were poised to score a victory over the British Army. If the Zulus won here at Isandlwana, what next: the Natal Colony; the Cape itself?

He couldn't let that happen, he had to stop them. Quickly, he selected a few men from one of the stronger sections and ordered them to form around him. Leading his small force, he rushed at the infiltrators. He could see the intense, courageous expressions on the warriors' faces. Many were young, but he could see no fear in his adversaries. Fleetingly, and grudgingly, he had to admit a certain admiration for them. He wondered if England's children would defend her from a foreign invader with such ferocity.

The opposing groups came together and he had no time to think of anything but fighting for his life. The battle raged around him, some of his men fell, but his little unit seemed to be gaining the upper hand. He began to think he may have successfully repelled this fiercest of foes. Then he felt an assegai thrust into his gut.

He collapsed, gasping for breath, and lay spread-eagled in the dust. Staring up at the clear, blue, South African sky, a dreadful sadness stole over him. Not for himself and this sudden, violent death; he was a professional soldier, he had enough experience of the vagaries of war to know his number was simply up. 'Just bad luck, old chap,' he would have laughed if he'd had the strength.

No, his sadness was for the one he loved. Lying here, dying, he knew his love was real, no matter how indecent, immoral, or outrageously shocking, it might be considered. Here, at the point of death, he could see love was more important than society's judgement. The tragedy was he'd never be able to tell the person he loved how he felt; his realisation of the true nature of his feelings had come too late.

A tear fell from his eye as, with his last breath, he whispered, "Sebastian."

11

BACK AGAIN

Susan slipped quietly into the back of the room, hoping Worthington wouldn't notice. He was in the midst of one of his favourite diatribes.

"… simply will not tolerate this modern nonsense. I expect doctors in my department to wear appropriate attire. I did not spend eleven years at medical school so I could dress like a porter and I do not want to see my staff dressed like one either. White coats will be worn at all times unless you are in theatre."

Someone sniggered and muttered, "Eleven years." Worthington had inadvertently let slip the fact his own medical training had taken rather longer than usual. How he'd risen to become a professor of neurology was a mystery to everyone.

He scowled, scanning the room for the source of the snigger, but found another target for his verbal venom when he spotted Susan standing at the back. Despite the fact he'd gone out of his way to secure her transfer, their relationship had deteriorated from the start. He always seemed to be looking for ways to undermine her, make her look small in front of other staff. Today was no exception.

"You're late, Doctor Carpenter. I have made it abundantly clear I expect staff to give my weekly departmental meeting the utmost priority. There hasn't been any emergency as far as I am aware, and *I* would surely be aware if there had been, so, therefore, it follows you cannot possibly have a valid excuse for this lapse."

Susan blushed. After everything she'd been through, professionally and personally, there were few things that got her flustered. But, for some reason, Worthington was a different matter. Somehow, he was able to reduce her to feeling like a naughty schoolgirl. She could feel her throat drying up and she had the nasty taste in her mouth she often got in his presence, "But… but… it's Major Carlton, he's w-woken up. It's a…" she stammered before Worthington held up a hand that clearly demanded silence. "We will hear your report on Mr Carlton's condition later. Be assured, doctor, your miracle-worker reputation cuts no ice with me. Good, solid, well-established medical procedure is entirely responsible for any patient's recovery, nothing more. Now, will you please *sit down!*"

With the admonishment ringing in her ears, she searched for a seat in the crowded meeting room. To her dismay, the only empty space was in the front row, between Ray and a man with long, dark hair, who she didn't recognise. Reluctantly, she hurried to the front and sat next to her ex. She'd been avoiding him since the incident at his flat; it made her skin crawl to even be close to him, now she'd found out what he was really like.

Ray whispered something suggestive, but the details escaped her as her head reeled with the embarrassment of her dressing-down. How did Worthington do that to her? She was furious with herself for letting him get her in such a state; she was never like that with anyone else. 'Focus,' she told herself. She took a deep breath and concentrated on the meeting.

"So, now that everyone is finally here," Worthington stared down at her, "we can at last begin the meeting proper. Before we get on to reviewing the patients, it gives me enormous pleasure to introduce you to a new, but alas temporary, member of our team," he gestured at the stranger sitting next to Susan. Forgetting her own problems for a moment, she turned to look the newcomer over.

He had a strong, handsome face, spoiled only by a scar across his forehead. His skin was pale next to his jet black hair; and unusually smooth. Plainly, he wasn't a young man, but just how old he was seemed impossible to guess. Her attention was drawn to a large gold ring on his middle finger. She found it striking for several reasons. Firstly, he shouldn't have been wearing it, staff were forbidden to wear jewellery on hospital premises; secondly, it looked old, very old; and thirdly, it had the most amazing stone set in it. It looked like a ruby, but was shaped like a star, a seven-pointed star. She'd never seen a jewel like it.

In stark contrast to the ancient ring, the stranger wore

a very modern device on his wrist; like one of those new watches that does everything from telling the time to alerting you if your blood sugar is running low: except, unlike the others she'd seen, the casing was made of solid gold. He must be a wealthy man, Susan surmised.

Worthington was continuing to garner as much reflected glory as he could squeeze out of the stranger's introduction, "... and so, I am proud to announce that Professor Lord Mortimer has agreed to join us on a short-term assignment in the role of Director of Neurology. Perhaps you would like to say a few words to the staff, your lordship?"

As Mortimer stood up, Susan could see he was exceptionally tall, at least six foot six. He moved with a grace that suggested great age and yet had a steady, swift step as he walked over to stand in front of the assembled staff.

"Please, please, we're all colleagues here, just call me Professor Mortimer. No need for that aristocratic nonsense." Despite his assurances, Susan knew it would be hard to ignore his peerage. Perhaps that was why he was so dismissive of his title; no-one was likely to forget it. It explained why he was allowed to wear his ring anyway. Lords must be an exception.

He continued to outline his temporary role and assure the staff he wasn't here to interfere or check up on them. That was a sure sign he'd be looking over their shoulders all the time, Susan thought. She wondered why he was really here.

Her nagging headache flared up again. In an effort to distract herself from the pain, she turned her thoughts to the extraordinary events earlier that morning.

Carlton appeared to be sleeping normally as she was checking his chart and reviewing the monitors recording his progress. She was concerned to see some peculiar patterns in his heartbeat and, on a whim, bent to take his pulse, manually, the old-fashioned way, as she'd been taught in medical school years ago.

As she touched his wrist, he cried out, "Sarah," and every monitor around his bed fell silent. Instinctively, she recoiled, dropping his hand. As she released him, his heartbeat, breathing, and brain activity all resumed as normal.

She stood there, her heart pounding, her mind racing, as she searched her memory for any medical precedent she could think of to explain such a phenomenon. After what seemed an age, she realised she was holding her breath. She started to exhale. At that moment, Carlton woke for the first time in over eight weeks.

His eyes slowly focussed on her face. He gave her a weak smile. Hoarsely, with a voice he hadn't used in a long time, he whispered something that seemed to touch her deep inside. Then he fell back into a heavy sleep.

"Doctor Carpenter!" She was dragged abruptly from her reverie. Worthington was asking her to give her report.

The rest of her day was a whirl of activity. Three more RTA victims were admitted in the afternoon, all with serious head injuries. She had to move Carlton to a private room to make space; he seemed to be out of immediate danger now, although he still had a long way to go.

She didn't get back to her flat until late that evening. Exhausted, she headed straight for bed, pausing only to examine the old greeting card pinned to her notice board. The roses on front had faded to a dull pink and there was a worn spot where the picture had been rubbed away, but the handwriting inside was still clear. She touched her fingers to her lips then the card. "Love you, Dad," she whispered.

Leaving the kitchen, she prepared to turn in. As she lay down and switched off her bedside lamp she remembered Carlton's words. She knew she should take them as no more than the ramblings of a sick man, but they ran through her tired mind, and she couldn't help feeling it was no accident he'd said them to her. Four words that didn't make sense, but which had reached out to her with awesome power, "Hello, Sarah, I'm back."

*

It would have been Brian's ninth birthday next week. Would have been; but little Brian Shannon wasn't going to have any more birthdays, he was dying.

He wasn't afraid of dying. He'd died many times before. He could remember the last three clearly: he'd died on Omaha Beach, Normandy, on D-Day, 6th June 1944; he'd died at the Battle of the Somme in July 1916; and he'd died fighting the Zulus in 1879.

But he didn't want to leave Sarah. In the delirium of his terminal illness, he remembered how much he loved her, how much he'd always loved her. There was no point telling her though. She was the matron in charge of the ward, almost sixty years old, and he was a sick little boy dying of leukaemia. He could see so much, but was powerless to do anything about it.

He remembered her as the pretty little nurse at the field hospital in St Germaine where he'd been taken in the autumn of 1915. She'd come over from Ireland a few weeks earlier and was at the beginning of a long career in nursing that would lead her back to him here in London over forty years later. His own path from 1915 to 1958 had been more traumatic, he'd died twice along the way, and was about to do so once more.

He'd met her again in 1943, at the hospital in Totnes. She was Sarah Wilkes by then, a sister in the casualty department, married to an artillery captain who'd been taken prisoner at Dunkirk. He smiled as he remembered how he'd crashed his motorbike on the way back to camp after celebrating his sergeant's stripes. Lucky, in an odd sort of way, if he'd been caught 'DUI' by the MPs instead of being brought to the hospital he might have lost those stripes. His name had been Brendan O'Doyle then. He'd been Irish too, but his family had emigrated to America when he was a little boy. Their origins had given them something in common and they started chatting away, sharing stories about the old country, as she tended to the grazes on his leg and back.

"It's not too serious, sergeant, I think we can class you as 'walking wounded'. You won't need to go taking up any valuable bed space. You're a lucky man, you know, you don't want to go chargin' 'round these Devon lanes on your motorbike like that; 'specially not with a few pints of scrumpy inside you. You can get dressed now."

He grimaced as he got to his feet and began pulling on his uniform. He'd been trying to conceal his inebriated state, but it was clear she wasn't fooled. He could see the ring on her finger, and he guessed she was probably a bit older than him, but he found her very attractive. After all, it was wartime, and God only knew when they'd be sent to start the second front. He could be dead before Christmas.

"Shucks ma'am, it's not the cider that's got me in a whirl, it's having such a beautiful nurse looking after me."

She did her best to hide her smile; he could tell she was flattered, perhaps even tempted. She hesitated a moment, but then rebuked, "That's enough of that now, can you not see I'm a married woman."

"I meant no harm, sister. It's just you're the prettiest thing I've seen since they posted me down here."

"Oh hush, I'm a lot older than you think, you silly man. Come on with you, you're all fixed now," she pushed him towards the exit.

As he reached the door, he glanced back. She was still watching him. She looked sad; she looked like she was terribly lonely. He wanted to change that.

Fifteen years later, a tear fell from Brian's eye as he

recalled everything he'd learned about Sarah's life; all the heartbreak she'd suffered. He loved her so much, but they were always parted; why must they always be parted?

The room began to spin and he realised this latest, short little life was almost over. He spied Sarah coming towards him. The scar across her cheek hadn't been there when he last knew her, and the years since then had taken their toll, but to him she was as pretty as she'd been in 1915, as beautiful as she was in 1943.

He clung to his final moments in the hope of feeling her touch once more. As she took his wrist, he felt himself losing the battle. "Sarah," he whispered.

*

Sarah Wilkes, the lonely, twice-widowed matron, felt the little boy's pulse flutter and die beneath her fingers. They'd lost him. He wasn't the only one, the same dreadful disease was taking many children; but this boy had been special. Little Brian had looked at her with eyes far beyond his years. She felt the tearing sensation of unbearable grief, a sensation she'd felt just twice before, for the only men she'd ever loved.

She kept up her professional demeanour as she arranged for Brian to be moved to the mortuary and got his bed changed but, as soon as she could, she excused herself and went back to her room. She locked the door, closed the blinds, sat down and wept.

III

AWAKENING

Ben woke to find a visitor at his bedside. He was surprised to see someone in his room, but was transfixed by a remarkable sense of familiarity. Even before the man spoke, Ben felt sure he was Latin American. His clothes belonged to a warmer climate, and he was clasping a battered old panama hat, still wet with the English rain he'd braved to make his visit. His first words puzzled Ben enormously.

"Hello Bakara, it is good to see you again."

"Who-o-o-o- … who are you?"

The visitor bowed his head, "My name is Francesco Miguel Antonio Del Rivera, and I am here to help you, for your soul is in the gravest peril."

"My *soul?*" Ben laughed; "I'm not sure I've got one, to be honest."

"You have one, my friend, I assure you, and I want to help you save it."

Ben groaned inwardly. The man was obviously some sort of fanatic, hanging around the hospital looking for converts. He lifted himself up on one elbow, so he could look the visitor in the eye, "Look, pal, I'm not really religious, so if you're here to offer me eternal salvation, I'm sorry, but I'm not interested. My worries lie in the here and now. Try someone else."

"You do not understand, Bakara, the peril *is* here and now, you must listen to me, you…"

"What are you on about? How did you get in here, anyway?"

"Come, Bakara, surely you must remember something?"

"I think you have me mistaken for someone else. I'm not this Bakara guy. I've never seen you before in my life. Now please leave or I'm going to call the nurse."

"No, Bakara, wait. We have met before, but you have forgotten. Still, you are awake enough to see some truth, I think. You find me familiar, no?"

Ben's head was reeling. The stranger had a persistence about him that was hard to ignore. Despite his denial, he had a feeling they might actually have met, though he couldn't for the life of him think when. He fell back against his pillow with a sigh, "Yes, alright, you are a bit familiar. So what are you then, a long-lost relative or something?"

"Something… yes; perhaps this will help you remember," the visitor leaned forward and grasped the back of Ben's hand.

Ben gasped as the hospital room disappeared and he found himself no longer lying in bed, but standing upright in medieval armour, looking down at a blacksmith.

"But you *can* get it off her?" he hadn't been conscious of forming the words, but he heard himself making the demand and felt the anxiety behind it.

"I said I *may* be able to," the smith seemed to be speaking English, but Ben sensed it wasn't English as he knew it. He was aware they were in a small, dark, workshop, surrounded by the tools of the smith's trade. Somehow, he knew the man before him was Finnian Smith, the best locksmith in all England.

"I can surely try," continued Smith, "but I cannot promise anything, for it is the most secure piece of ironwork I have seen in all my years."

"Well, try then, in the name of all the Saints, for she will surely die otherwise," Ben heard himself say, just as the scene began to fade away and he slipped into deep, dark oblivion.

*

Two days later, Ben was sitting up in bed, eating his first meal without assistance from the nurses. He'd slept a solid eighteen hours after Del Rivera's visit then woken with a great sense of renewed strength. But he was bewildered by the experience. Who was Del Rivera; why had he come; what was his interest in him; most of all, why had he had that weird dream? It had seemed so real; he could even feel the heat radiating from the forge. He was becoming accustomed to peculiar dreams lately, but the fact they were growing steadily more vivid was disturbing.

He was still thinking about the dream when one of the nurses popped her head around the door, "Your uncle's here to see you again, shall I let him in?"

Immediately, he realised she was talking about Del Rivera, he must be posing as his uncle. The old man was a bit eccentric, but Ben was sure he meant him no harm. What the hell, it was something to pass the time, "Yeah, sure, send him in."

The visitor stood at the foot of Ben's bed, "Hello again, Bakara, you are looking a little better, I think, no?"

"Much better, thank you; I have an odd feeling I might have you to thank for that, although I can't understand how. But why do you keep calling me 'Bakara', what does it mean; who am I to you?"

The visitor smiled, "We will get to that, my friend, when you are a little stronger; I do not want to push you too fast. But, be assured, we have known each other before." He came forward and sat on the chair next to the bed. Looking into the distance, he sighed, "A pity we could not save her that time."

Ben frowned, "What do you mean?"

"Do you not remember? You were there, standing in your armour, talking to the locksmith, were you not?"

"But... but that was just a dream. How do you know about that?"

"That was no dream, Bakara; that was a memory. More than a memory, more like a... like a... oh, what is your English word... er, a recording? No, er... a *replay*, that is it."

"A replay; are you trying to tell me that was real? That I've lived before, in medieval times?"

"Of course," the visitor shrugged; "you have lived many times, Bakara."

"You're suggesting I've been reincarnated?"

"That is the modern word for it, yes."

Before his accident, Ben would have scoffed at the idea. But all those dreams had seemed so real. Could it be true? Had he lived before?

"What you say is fantastic, yet..."

"Yes, Bakara, you know it is true. You have seen your past as you have slept, have you not?"

Ben nodded, it was a relief to share his experiences with someone, "I have dreamt of death since I came to the hospital, many deaths. Were they real too?"

"Yes, my friend, they were real. You are achieving 'awakening', the awareness of your past lives... and deaths."

"But why do I only dream about death? Why can't I see anything else? Except when you were here, that was different, and it was clearer, more realistic."

"When I came before, I put you into kaetchemo, a sort of, er... a trance. Like hypnotism, but different, because it is real, a true, er... yes, replay."

"Hmmm," Ben frowned, struggling to comprehend

the enormity of Del Rivera's revelations. In truth, he wasn't sure how much to believe, but he knew how real it felt, and he knew he felt refreshed, renewed somehow, since his so-called replay. "Look, I'm not saying I'm convinced, but I am curious. If you genuinely can show me my past, I'd like to see more. Can you do it again?"

"Of course," the visitor nodded; "but we must proceed carefully, take it slowly. The experiences can be, er… er, they can take a lot out of you: although, ultimately, they will leave you stronger, when you have had time to recover."

"Yeah, I noticed that. I feel sort of… well, like I've been healed somewhere deep inside."

"That is because the rift between your present and your past is beginning to mend."

"I see. So when can we start visiting the past some more?"

"We will start tomorrow. It will be good for you, help you learn about your true self; prepare you to face your destiny."

"My destiny; what are you talking about?"

The visitor smiled, "All in good time, Bakara. We need to build your strength up first." He got up and started to walk away.

"Wait; you haven't told me why I always dream of death."

Del Rivera turned back. He paused for a moment, his expression turning grim, "I think, because, if we are not careful, it may still be close."

*

Del Rivera came every day for the next week. Each day, he put Ben into a trance, or 'kaetchemo', as he called it, and took him to a different time and place. At first, Ben's visits to the past were brief, lasting only a few minutes. But, as the days passed, the experiences seemed to last longer, although the time elapsed in the real world remained the same.

The sensations were astounding. It truly was, as Del Rivera said, like seeing a replay of a previous life. Not just seeing it though, Ben could hear, smell, and sense the world around him just as in normal life. The only thing he couldn't do was change anything. The events played out in their immutable way and, although he was part of those events, he was powerless to alter them. And there was a great deal he'd have altered if he could.

He found himself in England in the 1600s, dressed in the drab clothing of the puritan era. His name was Barnaby Robbins and he was in a tavern, talking to the girl serving him and his companions. "Good day, Mistress Parsons, do I find you keeping well?" he enquired.

"I am well thank you, Master Robbins, and how are you keeping yourself?"

They talked for some time and then the scene shifted. Perhaps a few days or a few weeks passed, it was hard to tell. He was waiting outside a church in glorious spring sunshine, pacing up and down in nervous anticipation.

The same girl emerged from the church. She too was dressed in drab puritan clothing, but this did not detract from her natural beauty. He felt his heart flutter with excitement.

"May I walk you home, Mistress Parsons?" he asked.

"Why thank you, Master Robbins, I should like that very much."

He was hugely relieved; he'd feared she might reject him. Samantha Parsons was by far the prettiest girl in the village. But more than that, she had an infectious smile and a warm personality; she seemed to sparkle with life. In short, as Barnaby Robbins, he wanted to marry this girl.

In his trance, Ben witnessed many scenes from Barnaby and Samantha's courtship. It was more than witnessing them though; he was participating in them, experiencing them the same as real life. Months passed in Barnaby's seventeenth century world while only minutes passed in Ben's hospital bed. He got to know Samantha better and learned she was an orphan, working in the tavern in exchange for room and board until she finished her training with Mistress Gibson, the midwife in the next village. Once her training was over, she could practise herself. "It is all I have ever wanted to do," she told him, "I just want to be able to care for people, help them whenever I can."

The seasons turned. Spring was almost upon them again before Barnaby plucked up the courage to propose. Once again, he was a bag of nerves. What would he do if she refused? He loved Samantha so much, she was so bright, so lovely, she was the centre of his world, being with her was all he wanted from life. If she said no, he'd be heartbroken. This was the most terrifying thing he'd ever done.

"Yes, of course I will marry you, Barnaby," she responded. He wept with joy. They both did.

In keeping with local regulations, they had to seek permission from the parish magistrate. They were both nervous. Matthews was a stern, forbidding, character, with a reputation for finding the most bizarre reasons why couples couldn't marry, or should have to wait several years; reasons that only made sense to him. Still, as his word was, quite literally, law, they had no choice but to approach him.

"I understand you have almost finished your training with Mistress Gibson?" he asked Samantha.

"Yes sir, I have just three months left."

"Excellent, then I shall allow you to marry a month after you complete your training."

They were disappointed by the delay, but it was only a few months. They knew Matthews had recently told a couple they were to wait three years, simply because he felt it would be appropriate. He had refused another couple permission altogether because the boy was slightly lame in one leg and the girl had a wart on her hand. "I do not feel it would be wise to risk propagating such deformities," he had declared.

Throughout the spring, Barnaby and Samantha prepared excitedly for their wedding. Samantha finished her training at the beginning of June and they went together to the little village church to book the date for their union a month hence, in accordance with the magistrate's instructions. As they spoke to the minister, Barnaby could not help noticing how he stared at Samantha, running his eyes over her.

"Yes, indeed, Mr Matthews told me to expect you," the minister said at last; "he and I both feel somewhat dismayed by the haste with which many young couples rush into marriage. We agreed you should wait a little longer."

"How much longer?" Barnaby frowned.

"Mr Matthews suggested the last Saturday in August."

Barnaby sighed in frustration, "But Matthews said we had only to wait a month, I do not understand why…"

Samantha took his hand and smiled softly at him, "Do not fret, my love, it is but a few more weeks, we have the rest of our lives to spend together."

*

There was a week left until the wedding when Samantha was called upon to put her skills into action. That afternoon, Matthews had visited an expectant mother in the village. She hadn't been due to come to term for at least a month but, shortly after he left, she began suffering labour pains. Samantha worked through the night as the poor woman endured an agonisingly difficult childbirth. Her struggles continued into the next day, the next evening, and on into the following morning. Finally, the exhausted mother delivered the child.

Samantha gazed down at the cold little bundle and sighed. She had done everything Mistress Gibson taught her, and she knew she'd done it right. She knew her craft and she couldn't have worked any harder. But, sadly, the child was still-born. Clearly, it was deformed. It never stood a chance.

Suddenly, the door to the bedroom burst open. Samantha looked up to see Matthews in the doorway, two yeomen behind him. The magistrate strode across the room and looked at the pathetic little corpse. Samantha was struggling to understand why he was there, or how he could have arrived so quickly; it was hard to think straight after working non-stop for a day and a half.

Matthews sniffed. "Witchcraft," he declared. He turned and pointed at Samantha, "Seize her." The yeomen grabbed her by the arms. Bewildered and exhausted, she staggered along between them as they marched her to Matthews' house and locked her in a dark, basement cell.

*

News of Samantha's arrest reached Barnaby later that day. He rushed to the magistrate's house and demanded an audience. Matthews kept him waiting over two hours before a servant ushered him into an ornate office.

"What is this nonsense, this is crazy. Samantha's not a witch, surely you can see that?" Barnaby's emotions were running wild, the fear inside him at fever pitch.

Matthews beamed with all the benevolence of a friendly uncle, "Calm down, dear boy, this is all routine procedure. She will receive a fair trial and I am certain the truth of the matter will soon emerge. She is a charming girl, absolutely delightful, no-one wants to see any harm come to her. But you must understand, in my position, I have to follow procedure. Procedure, dear boy, that's the thing."

"So, you agree she is innocent?" insisted Barnaby.

"Well, my boy, that's not for me to say, is it? That's what the trial is for. Nonetheless," Matthews winked, "I am pretty sure she will be acquitted. Just go home and relax. I will see you in court in the morning."

"The morning?"

"Yes, we start proceedings at ten o'clock in the forenoon. I expect you will want to be here to see her cleared of this unfortunate business."

"Can I see her now?"

"Ah, sadly, no, I am afraid that is not allowed: procedure again, dear boy. But you will see her soon. After all, you have a big day together on Saturday, do you not?" Matthews patted Barnaby on the back as he walked him to the door and showed him out.

*

Word of the trial spread quickly and, by nine o'clock the next morning, the great hall of Matthews' house, which doubled as the local courtroom, was packed with people from the village and surrounding area. Barnaby was lucky to get one of the last remaining seats.

At ten o'clock, Matthews entered through a side door, followed by a clerk and two burly yeomen. A hushed silence fell over the crowd. "Bring the prisoner forth," he ordered, and the yeomen left to carry out his command. A minute later, Barnaby heard the sound of laboured footsteps and clanking chains. Slowly, Samantha appeared on the steep spiral staircase leading up from the cells. Her hands shackled in heavy iron manacles, she was struggling to mount the steps under their weight. She blinked uncomfortably as she adjusted to the sunlight streaming through the windows. As she regained her focus, she stared around the crowded courtroom. From the back of the hall, Barnaby could see her eyes were sunken and dark, the rest of her features pale. When she reached the top of the stairs, he saw her bare feet were cut and bleeding. It broke his heart to see her in such distress, but he felt sure her ordeal would soon be over when she was proven innocent.

The yeomen pushed Samantha into the dock, where she would have to stand throughout proceedings. They took up position either side of her, and the trial began.

It was a sham from beginning to end. Matthews was prosecution and judge. There was no defence. The first witness was the woman who'd given birth to the still-born. "Can you please tell the court what types of witchcraft the accused used?" Matthews demanded.

"Begging your pardon sir, but I didn't see nothin' at all, I was in a good deal of pain."

Matthews turned and faced the woman with a steely gaze, "That is a great shame, madam, because in my experience of these matters, only another witch would fail to speak up in court when she has witnessed witchcraft in action."

The woman blinked, her face turning pale. She shot a sympathetic glance at Samantha, looked down for a moment, and then spoke again, "Well sir, I don't know what it was she did, but I know it was witchcraft, sir, I swear it."

"Thank you, madam, the witness is excused." The clerk ushered the woman out of court. As she went, she looked back at Samantha with a terrible, guilty, pity in her eyes.

Next, Matthews called a series of women who'd known Samantha as a child. He encouraged them to relate tales of her talking to animals and having an unnatural interest in matters girls should not be concerned with, like the true nature of the stars and how children were created in their mother's bellies. Barnaby watched with an increasing sense of foreboding. But he hung on to the belief justice would prevail. Matthews knew Samantha was innocent, surely? He wasn't going to let anything bad happen to her, was he?

Finally, Matthews brought the show to a close, "It is clear there can only be one possible verdict arising from these proceedings. Samantha Parsons, this court finds you guilty of practising witchcraft and it is my solemn duty to pass sentence upon you. I hereby decree you shall be taken from here to a suitable place of execution, where you will be burned at the stake."

Samantha stood in silence, a single tear rolling down her cheek. Barnaby stared at her, unable to believe his ears. He was reeling from the shock, like a prizefighter taking a punch to the head. He took a moment to recover his wits then leaped to his feet, "No, you can't, it isn't true; you said she would be cleared. Please, I beg you, you can't do this."

Matthews turned to face him, "Master Robbins, you forget yourself. This is a court of law. Restrain yourself or I will have you arrested for contempt." One of the yeomen took a step forward, his hand gripping the hilt of his sword.

Barnaby felt the strength drain from his legs. There was a horrendous ache in the pit of his stomach, a dreadful feeling of emptiness, as if someone had reached inside and pulled out his guts. He collapsed back into his seat in despair as the awful realisation began to sink in. Samantha's fate was sealed; there was nothing he could do.

Matthews made a show of consulting a few documents, "Well, by good fortune, it appears the church will now be free on Saturday. Better still, I do believe the tavern is prepared for a celebratory feast. We will dispose of the witch in the churchyard then repair to the tavern to toast our deliverance from this diabolical scourge.

"Take her away," he ordered the yeomen, and they led Samantha back to her cell.

*

Samantha was woken early on Saturday, before it was light. A group of women, the wives of the most prominent men in the village, burst into her cell, pulling her from her bed before she was fully awake. They began roughly stripping off her clothes.

"Please, I can undress myself, I…"

The largest woman slapped Samantha across the face and held up a knife, "Silence, witch, or I will take your tongue." Samantha recognised her; it was Mrs Wishbone, the minister's wife. She'd helped Mistress Gibson deliver their first grandchild a year ago.

The women marched Samantha down the passageway, to where a cold bath was waiting for her. They forced her into the icy water and scrubbed her until she bled. Pulling her from the bath, they took her back to her cell and made her kneel on the rough, stone floor while they shaved off her hair. She watched her pretty, blonde curls falling onto the grey stone and began to cry. Wishbone threatened her with the knife again, "Stop bleating; it is your vanity that led you here, witch. You think you are better than the rest of us because you have a young body and a comely face; because men look upon you with desire in their loins."

"No, I do not think that, I…"

"Silence!" Wishbone slapped Samantha hard with the back of her hand, splitting her lip; "God gave your beauty and He will take it away again. He knows how wicked you are. He will punish you for your sins before He sends you to the Devil."

When they had finished shaving her, the women dressed Samantha in a shift of coarse sackcloth and bound her hands with rope. "Stay there on your knees, and keep your head bowed, do not look at us with your evil witch eyes or I will cut them out," ordered Wishbone.

Samantha stared at the ground. She still couldn't believe what was happening; she felt like she was being swept along by a river of unstoppable madness, powerless to save herself from the lunacy of it all. It had to be some horrible nightmare. She'd tried so hard to help that poor mother and her baby, done her best, done everything she could for them. How could this be, why was she being punished?

The stone floor was cold, hard on her knees. She started to lose the feeling in her legs. The sun rose, casting a thin shaft of light into the passageway outside the cell. She watched it move slowly across the wall, marking the hours, until the messenger came and spoke to Wishbone, "All is ready, my lady, you may bring the witch now."

The women tied a rope around Samantha's neck and pulled her, staggering, to her feet. They led her upstairs, through the empty courtroom, and out onto the street. Jeering crowds lined the way as the women led her barefoot through the village. One in front held the rope, two others followed behind. Wishbone remained close by, knife in one hand, a heavy club in the other. Many of the crowd spat at Samantha as she passed, some threw stones, rotten vegetables, or animal waste. By the time she reached the avenue leading up to the church, she was covered in filth.

For the first time, she saw the stake in the churchyard. She could see the platform at its base, the firewood stacked around it. Until this moment, she had clung to the hope this was just a ghastly mistake, there would be a reprieve, the villagers would see reason, realise she was innocent. But now, with the vicious mob around her, and her gruesome fate before her, she finally accepted the truth. They really were going to burn her alive.

She went numb from top to bottom, as if emptying of normal feelings, having them replaced by a terrible, cold dread. "No, no, you can't," she moaned, trying to pull back. The woman holding the rope pulled her forwards while the two behind prodded her with sticks. "Please, no, I don't understand, I've done nothing wrong. Please, you can't," she was trembling as she shuffled along between her captors. "I wanted to help, to care for people, for mothers and their children, it wasn't my fault. Please, give me another chance. Please, I beg you, no…"

Wishbone clubbed Samantha on the side of the head. Stunned, she fell to her knees and almost lost consciousness, until the woman in front jerked on the rope, dragging her back to her feet. Wishbone brandished her knife in Samantha's face, "Be quiet, or you will know more pain than you ever thought possible. The fire will be nothing after I am finished with you."

Samantha stumbled onwards, shivering in fear and confusion.

*

For three days, since the trial, Barnaby had tried in vain to see Samantha, but the yeomen had barred his way. He couldn't eat, he couldn't sleep; his mind was a whirling hurricane of horror and bewilderment. He arrived at the churchyard on Saturday looking like a haggard old man. The yeomen tried to keep him out, but Matthews said, "Let the boy in. All good Christian souls must be allowed to witness God's work."

He waited for Samantha to appear, hoping that, somehow, she wouldn't, but knowing that, undoubtedly, she would. He didn't want to be here, he didn't want to see her die; but he had to be here to see her while she still lived… and for her to see him.

At last, he saw the procession coming up the avenue. To begin with, he didn't recognise the figure in the centre, but slowly it dawned on him the sorry, shaven-headed creature, coated in blood and dirt, was his beloved Samantha. Watching her suffering was more than he could bear. He forgot the armed yeomen beside him and, before he knew it, he was rushing down the avenue towards her.

The yeomen swiftly caught him and knocked him to the ground. Still, he struggled and managed to break free. Again, he rushed down the avenue towards his fiancée, but again the yeomen caught him. One held him down while the other tied his hands behind his back.

"Bring him here," Matthews shouted, "I want him to see justice at work. Make sure he has a clear view."

The yeomen dragged Barnaby back to the churchyard and threw him to the ground, a few yards from the waiting stake. The larger man sat on top of him, pinning him down. He squirmed beneath the burly yeoman, trying to escape. But it was hopeless, he couldn't move. He was powerless to intervene.

*

Every inch felt like a yard, every yard like a mile, her feet hurt more with every step. She could hardly see; there was blood running into her eyes from a cut on her forehead. Her back ached where the women behind were constantly prodding; the rope around her neck was tightening, threatening to choke her; the coarse shift rubbed harshly against her skin. She longed for the torment to be over... but she knew there was worse to come.

Eventually she reached the platform. The women led her up the steps and tied her to the stake. Each of them spat in her face as they left; concluding with Wishbone, "Burn, you filthy harlot."

Matthews faced the crowd, putting a bitter twist on the ceremony that, only a few days before, had been scheduled to take place in the same church, at the same time, "Dearly beloved, we are gathered here today to witness the union of this vile witch with her lord and master, Satan. May he take her soul to his bosom and continue her punishment in fire that we good people begin today." He took the waiting torch and lit the pyre.

The fire spread quickly through the dry wood. Samantha felt the temperature rising. She would soon feel the flames licking her flesh. She had never known terror like this. She was shaking uncontrollably, the tears rolling down her cheeks evaporating in the heat. She tried to prepare herself for the pain to come, but could not even begin to imagine what it was going to be like.

She could feel waves of hatred coming from the hysterical crowd, the very people she'd wanted to care for. "Burn, witch; burn," they clamoured. They genuinely believed she was evil; every one of them wanted to see her die. She felt so alone; shunned, abandoned, deprived of any human kindness, just so utterly alone. The loneliness was almost more unbearable than the heat.

But then she saw Barnaby. Through tears mixed with the blood and filth running down her face, she could see him weeping, struggling beneath the hefty yeoman, trying to reach her, his cries lost in the mad baying of the crowd. Helpless as he was, he was here for her. She wasn't alone, after all. A strange calm settled over her. She stopped shaking, looked him in the eyes, and whispered, "I love you."

She tried not to scream, she didn't want Barnaby to hear it. But, as the pain rose to a crescendo, there inevitably came a point when she could hold out no longer.

*

The screaming seemed to go on for hours, the horrifying sound tearing through Barnaby's soul; Ben's soul: it was more than he could endure. Finally, it stopped. The agony was over, she was gone.

The crowd drifted away and the yeomen released Barnaby. The heat held him back for a long time but, eventually, he managed to get to her. He cut her down and sat on the ground, her blackened corpse cradled in his arms. He held her tight, rocking back and forth, as if he could ease her suffering. "My love, my love, oh Samantha, my love," he repeated over and over again, his wailing punctuated by deep, painful sobs.

He was still there the next morning, holding her, rocking back and forth, moaning softly to himself, when the yeomen came. They had to prise her from his grasp. If he hadn't been so weak from days without food or sleep, they would never have got her from him.

They carried her to the village cess pit, and threw her in.

IV

THE RELENTLESS TIDE

Ben came around in his hospital bed with Del Rivera sitting beside him. The kaetchemo visions had been fascinating until now, but that had been horrific. He was stunned; he could still feel the trauma of watching the girl he loved perish while he was powerless to help. He couldn't speak for a long time as he tried to digest the feelings raging within him. What had seemed an interesting way to pass the time had taken on a darker aspect; he'd opened Pandora's Box and suffered the consequences.

"Why did you show me that?" he said finally; "I loved her and they burned her. Fucking burned her alive. And she'd done nothing wrong, nothing at all. How could anyone do that?"

"I am sorry, Bakara, I know that must have been hard, but I do not choose what you see. I only open your mind to the past. It is you that chooses. There will be a reason you saw that life at this time, but I cannot tell you what it is."

"You know what I saw though?"

"Yes, when I put you into kaetchemo, I see it too. For me, it is like, er... like watching a film. But for you, it will be real."

"Hmmm, yes, bloody real." Ben thought for a minute, "What happened to Barnaby... You know, afterwards?"

"You are Barnaby, just as you are Bakara."

"I don't know. It felt like it at the time, yeah. But he didn't act like me. For one thing, he went to church, and I'm not religious at all. Plus he waited ages to marry Samantha, just 'cause that bloody magistrate said so. There's no way I'd let some petty official stop me marrying the girl I love."

"You must understand, in every life your attitudes and behaviour are affected by your environment, by the values of the society you live in. Your upbringing has an impact too. A loving family might make you stronger in one life; a domineering parent could make you more timid in another, especially when you are young. But that is all for the psychologists. The point is you are the same person at heart, the same soul. The fact you know you loved Samantha proves that."

"OK, I get all that. It makes sense you'd have to adapt to your environment. And, yes, when I was dreaming I was Barnaby, I could feel I loved Samantha," Ben looked down for a moment, then up at Del Rivera again; "which is why I have to know. What did he do? How did he cope, after losing her like that? 'Cause, if it was me, which you're saying it was, I'd want to murder that bastard, Matthews. Burn him alive, preferably."

"No, you did not do that, although you may have thought about it. But, you are right; it was difficult for you to cope with what had happened. You moved to London. You helped many people during the Great Plague in the 1660s. You wanted to care for them in memory of the woman you loved, who'd been devoted to caring for others herself."

"How do you know all this?"

"I, er… it is a long story. I will tell you another time. Anyway, after the plague, there was the Great Fire…" Del Rivera paused, as if gathering his thoughts.

"And?"

"You were trying to help. You got trapped. You were burned alive."

*

"It looks like you'll be leaving us soon, Major Carlton." Susan was giving Ben a final examination before authorising his release. It was a routine matter, she should have got Minster to do it, but she couldn't resist a last look at her star patient. At least, that's what she was trying to tell herself. In truth, his astonishing recovery was only part of the reason behind her fascination. There was something else, something she couldn't understand. Whatever it was, it had compelled her to take this last chance to see him.

Physically, Carlton had achieved a complete recovery. The physiotherapists had never seen such powers of recuperation. But his mind was another matter. She knew he was having some awful nightmares. Jenny had told her about him crying out, shouting things like, 'So you have come to take me too, same as my beloved Samantha.'

His personal life couldn't be helping. That bitch, his wife, was almost beyond belief. Serving divorce papers to a man in his hospital bed, telling him he shouldn't bother coming home. Unbelievable!

At least he had his uncle. A strange man, but nice enough. He was oddly familiar too, although she couldn't recall ever meeting him before.

She reached across to check one of the monitors and accidentally brushed Carlton's forehead. As she touched him, she was overwhelmed by an incredible sensation, as if she was falling, or fainting. Her head span, her vision blurred, and suddenly she was somewhere else, far away, and long ago…

*

"Bakara, we must not lie together, we are sister and brother; it is a sin."

"But, Shebana, you know we are not sister and brother by blood."

"Yes, I know, but no-one else does, they will see only the sin."

"Mamboja knows the truth, our mother told him

52

before the sea chose her. He would speak for us if we were discovered."

She wasn't sure she shared Bakara's faith in their guardian, but she knew he was right, Mamboja did know the truth about them. "I suppose he would," she admitted; "he is our father by law now, since our mother was chosen."

"Anyway, Shebana, I do not want to be a man with you, I only want to hold you and protect you. You are precious to me, more beautiful than the waves. My love for you is as relentless as the tide."

As he spoke, she felt the same relentless tide in her heart, and knew another truth she could no longer deny. "Oh Bakara, I feel the same. I know we have been raised as sister and brother, and that is how the people see us, but I will lie with you this night because I love you as the fish love the sea, and I know I must care for you. We must be together."

They lay under a blanket of dried seaweed, inside a tent made from the skin of sea creatures. They held each other close, the warmth of their innocent love comforting them through the darkness. As she drifted into a peaceful, contented sleep, Shebana knew she was where she belonged. One day, when they were older, she would become Bakara's woman. But, for now, simply being in his arms was enough.

*

Outside, on the beach, the people drank their brews and danced around the fires as they sang in praise of the sea and gave thanks for the fruits it bestowed upon them. But the people knew the sea could be vengeful and it was always hungry. Every year, it would take many of the people, for its hunger was great. To appease the sea, the people had to make sacrifices.

Fujabi, captain of the first boat, sat by one of the fires, reflecting how the sacrifices had grown more frequent since Mamboja had become the voice of the sea, telling the people who had been chosen. The sea's choices were not always popular, but no-one dared argue any more. It was strange how often anyone who spoke against Mamboja would get chosen soon afterwards. Who was going to take that risk?

Turning to his old friend, Fujabi asked, "Where are Bakara and Shebana; surely they are old enough to join the feast?"

"Perhaps," responded Mamboja, "but they are spoilt children; their mother was soft with them. We are blessed the sea chose her. Now they will grow strong."

"Praise the sea for it is wise. But, surely the feast is important for them to grow? They will not be children much longer. Bakara must soon take his seat in a boat and Shebana will be taken by a man at the next spring tide."

"You may be right, my friend, I will send one of the women to bring them to the fire."

Mamboja despatched a woman to fetch the children. Moments later, she returned in a state of anxiety. She fell to her knees, "Oh, my lord, it is terrible; your children lie together as man and woman."

Mamboja sprang to his feet and marched to the tent. Following behind, Fujabi watched as he threw open the flap, revealing his children wrapped in each other's arms. "Abomination," shouted Mamboja, "this is an abomination, sister and brother shall not lie together; the sea will be angered." He reached down and grabbed Shebana by the hair, pulling her to her feet. Blinking and half asleep, she pleaded, "But, father, you know we are not…"

"Silence, abomination, I should have given you to the sea with your mother. It is bad enough I was burdened with you when she was chosen, but now you are worthless, no man will take you. There is only one thing to be done with you," he pushed her out of the tent, releasing her hair as she staggered back into the arms of the waiting crowd swiftly gathering outside.

He turned his attention to Bakara, kicking him in the stomach as he began to stir, "As for this piece of slime; he is not worthy of the people, he would be the curse of any boat he was placed in."

"Our father by law, we have not sinned," Bakara protested, "we have only slept, we have not lain as man and woman. And our mother told you, we are not sister and brother by blood, we…" he was cut short as Mamboja struck him across the face then pulled him to his feet and sent him stumbling after Shebana.

"Take these abominations to the place of the chosen."

The people took the children away but Fujabi lingered by the tent, troubled by what he'd just witnessed, "My lord, they are your children by law, are you certain you must do this?"

"Do you doubt the will of the sea, captain?" Mamboja spoke to him as though he were a stranger. The threat in his voice was clear, but Fujabi pressed on, "My lord, before the sea brought you to us there were stories Bakara was not your wife's child. Perhaps he speaks the truth?"

"I am the voice of the sea. I speak the truth. The sea chooses in many ways, captain. It may be choosing now, by allowing the chosen to doubt its word?"

Fujabi had no other option. Mamboja controlled the people for they believed he was the voice of the sea. Without another word, he left the tent and returned to his own. He packed his few belongings, took a boat, and paddled out to sea. The people never saw him again.

*

As dawn broke, the people were gathered at the place of the chosen, a small cove not far from the village. Shebana was kneeling on the sand next to Bakara, trembling with fear. Both of them were bound hand and foot, two hefty guards stood over them.

Bakara looked up at Mamboja, "Please, our father, punish me only, it was I that asked Shebana to lie with me. I was not a man with her, she is still a maiden. You can find a man for her yet. Please, father, I beg you, you need only choose me."

56

Shebana was almost petrified by the icy dread gripping her heart, but she could not bear the thought of losing the boy she loved. She spoke before Mamboja could reply, "No, Bakara, I would not live without you. If we must feed the sea, we will feed the sea together."

Mamboja nodded at the guards and they dragged the children across the beach to a set of pegs staked out in two adjacent squares. The pegs were long and heavy, extending deep beneath the surface of the sloping sand. It took two strong men to pull them out when they were replaced each spring tide.

The men forced them to lie on their backs inside the squares then tied their hands and feet to the pegs. Shebana tugged on the bindings on her wrists and ankles but they held tight, struggling only made the coarse material dig deeper into her flesh. Her fear swelled like the sea in a storm, overwhelming her senses. Looking up, she saw Mamboja standing over them, his arms open wide.

"The sea has chosen; now it shall feed. Let us hope this sacrifice may quell its anger."

"Praise the sea for it is wise," the people responded. Then they moved back up the beach to wait.

The tide came in, slowly but relentlessly advancing into the little cove. Shebana watched the hungry sea coming to devour them, her eyes wide with the terror raging within her. What would happen when the waves swallowed her and everything went dark? Would she just cease to exist? It couldn't be; there had to be more. Surely her spirit, and Bakara's, must endure somehow. But how would they find their way back to the land? How long would it take, how would they find each other again? Her doubts and fears whirled around her head as the water grew ever closer. The first time it touched her feet, she began to cry.

Bakara was crying as well, "I am sorry, Shebana, this is my fault. I should not have asked you to lie with me."

Sensing the guilt that burdened him, she stifled her sobs and, with an effort, raised her head so she could turn to face him, "No, my love, it is not your fault. I wanted to lie with you too. If you had not asked me last night I would soon have come to you. Do not blame yourself, we were always meant to be together." She lay back and stared at the sky, "We will feed the sea today, but one day the tide will wash us back to the land, and we shall lie with each other again."

Before long, the water was washing over their bodies. Then it started to cover their faces and they were gasping for breath between the waves in ever-increasing desperation, instinctively hanging on to life, but wishing the torture could be over; each more distressed by the other's suffering than their own.

Neither knew which of them died first. They fed the sea together.

*

Susan came to her senses in the midst of a coughing fit. What had just happened, some kind of hallucination? She looked at Ben, "Di-i-i-d... di-i-d you... wha-a-a-t, what..."

58

Before he could say anything, the door flew open. Mortimer marched in, Worthington following behind like a faithful puppy.

"Ah, the famous miracle in person; thought I would take a look for myself, see what all the fuss is about."

Susan was still reeling from the vision. She felt deeply disturbed. It had been so vivid, like she'd actually been there, drowning on some ancient beach. She took a step back and put a hand to her head. Wow, there was that bloody headache again, suddenly flaring up out of nowhere, worse than ever. This was seriously worrying. She would have to get checked out; hallucinations and headaches were not a good sign. As an experienced neurologist, she ought to know what it meant. But self-diagnosis is a tricky business. Lack of professional detachment, that's the problem. Christ, she hoped it wasn't a bloody tumour. Even a benign tumour could mean surgery or radiotherapy, and this wasn't a good time to be off sick. That would be the end of any chance at this promotion… Shit, what was Worthington waffling on about?

"… So his lordship and I thought you would be the perfect person to go with him. What do you think, Doctor Carpenter?"

"Er, sorry… go with him where?"

"To the International Neurological Conference next week. It will be an ideal opportunity to show there's more to you than patient care; you daren't really miss it if you're serious about the Deputy Head post."

Caught off guard, with a thumping headache, her throat drying out, feeling more than a little unsettled by Mortimer's towering presence, she found herself saying, "Oh, er... yes, er... that sounds great," before she'd given herself chance to consider what she was getting into.

"Excellent, that's settled then," Worthington was hopping gleefully from foot to foot beside Mortimer; "I'll get the office to sort your flights."

"No need for that," interjected Mortimer, "Doctor Carpenter will come with me on my Lear. It will be nice to have some company. I find modern air travel rather tedious."

He smiled down at Susan. Her headache got worse.

V

DISCHARGED

The stag filled his vision, towering over the car as it skidded out of control. He wrenched the steering wheel sideways. The car began to turn, the beginning of a spin, but still it slid on towards the startled animal. There was only one way to avoid hitting the beast. He released the brake, hastily changed gear, and stamped on the accelerator. The car shot sideways across the road, missing the stag by a whisker. It smashed into the rock face, which deflected it spinning back towards the steep drop on the other side.

Just as the front of the car left the road, the rear collided with a tree. It bounced back, reversing the direction of spin. The car turned around once more and came to rest facing the way it had come. The mangled wreck sat on the edge, half of it hanging over the side, hundreds of feet of open hillside beneath it.

He raised his head. His vision was swimming, distorted

and discoloured, like looking through a red waterfall. One of the headlights had survived and was enough for him to see the stag turn and run. At least one of us made it, he thought. The redness grew darker until everything went black.

*

Two days after Susan's final examination, Ben was discharged. Many of the staff were astounded by the speed of his recovery, almost unheard of for someone who'd been in a coma so long. Even Ben was surprised by the strength of his new-found vitality.

He was disappointed not to see Doctor Carpenter again though. He'd hoped to talk to her about the vision they'd shared. At least, he thought they'd shared it, her reaction suggested they had, but any discussion had been rendered impossible by Mortimer's arrival.

The vision seemed as real as those he'd experienced with Del Rivera. He wondered if she'd felt the same. And why had it happened with her? Had he also known her before, like Del Rivera? That could be possible, he supposed. There had been something reassuring about her; a warm, comfortable feeling, like coming home. Of course, that might equally be because she'd saved his life.

Leaving the hospital, he thanked Jenny Fletcher for all she'd done for him, and asked if she knew whether Doctor Carpenter was around?

"She's at home, preparing for her trip to the

conference. Doctor Minster is here, you could talk to him if you want?"

"No, er… it's a personal thing… I need to speak to her."

"Oh, I see… well, you'd be wasting your time, I'm afraid; she has a strict rule against getting involved with patients."

"No, no, it's not that, I just wanted to ask her something. Never mind, thanks anyway."

Jenny smiled to herself as she watched Ben walk away. It was hardly the first time a patient had fallen for Susan. Next time she spoke to her, maybe she should tell her every rule needs an exception. After all, he was an ex-patient now, and Ben Carlton looked like he might be worth breaking a few rules for.

*

With nowhere else to go, Ben checked into a hotel. He needed time to think things over, sort stuff out. Among other things, he had a large insurance claim to deal with, had to find somewhere to live, and, oh yes, a divorce looming soon. He also needed to get his business going again. Work as a security consultant was dull after his years in the army, but it paid well and he was good at it, even if he said so himself. Besides which, he'd better start earning his keep, this divorce wasn't going to be cheap, especially knowing what Maria was like.

He couldn't say he was particularly sorry. Things between them hadn't been the same since he left the army. He'd tried to make her happy, but she never seemed satisfied. She always wanted a bigger house, a better car; more exotic holidays with 'the girls', the other ex-models who made up her circle of friends.

She'd been working as a model when he met her. Moderately successful, you might say, not exactly in the big time, but doing well enough to have gained a taste for the finer things in life. Some very expensive tastes as it turned out. But the early days had been fun, he the dashing young major, she the glamorous model. Of course, they'd spent a lot of time apart owing to his tours of duty in Afghanistan. Looking back now, he could see it wasn't until he left the army they'd spent any significant amount of time together. That was when things started to go wrong.

There'd been a time when he thought he would never leave the army; he was set on a lifelong career. But when they withdrew from Helmand with the job half done, and everything started flaring up in Iraq again, he began to feel their efforts had been in vain. They were supposed to protect people, yet all they seemed to have done was bring more misery and suffering upon them. Disillusioned with it all, he'd resigned his commission.

He remembered calling Maria to tell her his decision. "Well that's marvellous, darling," she'd said, "you can do so much better than army pay." But when he'd told her he was planning to set up a college to train people from poor communities how to protect themselves, she'd had other ideas, "Oh no, darling, there's no money in that, how on earth would you make a profit?"

"Well, we'd take on private clients as well, to balance the books. There's loads of rich bankers, lawyers, and others who want to know how to protect themselves."

"No darling, you want to go into security. That's where the money is, private bodyguards and all that. You could do really well."

So he'd set up Carlton Security Services Ltd and had indeed done really well. Their turnover last year had been over three million. Not that he had much to show for it. He'd got his staff and contractors to pay, he was happy to do that; they were the ones who did the work. Then there was the taxman. He wasn't so happy about that, but he remembered his years in the army, getting paid from the public purse. Someone had to fund that, now it was his turn, so that was fair enough. What was left though, pretty much all went to Maria.

Not long after he'd left the army, she'd retired from modelling. "Quit while you're ahead, darling, I don't want to be some sad old bitch desperately touting for work after her looks have faded. Not that mine will ever fade, of course," she laughed. Later, he discovered offers of work had been falling off sharply and, in truth, her agency had let her go.

They'd always agreed to put off starting a family while she was modelling. Now she'd quit, he suggested they could try? "Oh, that would be wonderful, darling, but I must get Pictures up and running first." 'Pictures' was her new venture, an art gallery on the south coast. "I've always wanted to run a gallery after I finished modelling," she said, though he couldn't remember her mentioning it before.

To be fair, she'd started Pictures with her own money but, before long, she began asking for help. "I just need a bit more working capital, so we can have the right ambience to attract quality customers. Empty walls don't sell, darling," she laughed; "if you could just help me out a little, I'm sure the gallery will soon show a profit."

It had gone on like that for years. Between the gallery and her extravagant lifestyle, she'd used up the money he'd made in the security business. And it hadn't just gone on paintings. She'd spent a fortune turning the flat above the gallery into a luxury apartment. At first, she'd come home at weekends but, after a while, she was staying there full time. He hardly saw her and any possibility of starting a family was quietly forgotten. They hadn't spent a night together in over a year.

The last time he'd driven down to see her he'd arrived at four o'clock on a Tuesday afternoon to find the gallery closed. He tracked her to a local wine bar, where he found her dining on oysters and champagne with a guy in his early twenties. She sat laughing, her arm draped around the boy's shoulders. Seeing the expression on Ben's face, she said, "Don't be jealous, darling; Tony's been helping me pick out some pictures. He's got fabulous eyes... I mean a fabulous eye... for art, you know. I was just buying him a spot of lunch, it's the least I could do." She planted a sloppy kiss on the boy's cheek, "Thank you, Tony."

Ben wasn't jealous. He didn't care what her relationship with Tony was. He was past caring. The boy looked terrified anyway. Later, he found out Tony was an unemployed former art student living with his boyfriend. Not that it would save him from Maria now she had her claws in him. It didn't matter. No, he wasn't jealous, but he was outraged. The closed gallery, the oysters and champagne, the drunken laughter, the tens of thousands of pounds she'd talked him into giving her, enough was enough. It was the final straw.

His temper had got him into trouble a couple of times in his youth, but life in the army had taught him to control it. He simply turned around, left Maria and Tony in the wine bar, and drove home. That had been six months ago. The next time he saw her, he was lying in hospital and she was handing him a letter from her solicitor. Ironically, she'd moved back into the house while he was in a coma, and now she was demanding it as part of the divorce settlement.

So be it, she could have the house if she wanted. It was over.

*

By the next day, Ben had made some progress putting his life back together. He'd hired a lawyer to take care of the divorce, booked some viewings for a new apartment, and arranged a few appointments with potential customers for his company. He didn't have the stomach to face his insurance claim yet, but, by and large, he was getting back on track.

The events in hospital were starting to fade into memory. It had been fascinating for a while, all that past life stuff. But, after watching Samantha being burned alive, he hadn't allowed Del Rivera to put him into kaetchemo anymore. He never wanted to see anything like that again.

That vision he'd shared with Doctor Carpenter had been pretty disturbing too. His first instinct had been to talk to her about it, try to understand what it meant. But now, as he began to settle back into normal life, he was more inclined to just let it go. He was still getting weird dreams, he'd had one about being crucified last night, but what use was any of it? Even if they truly were memories of past lives, they had no relevance to him now. It was time to move on, get on with *this life*, here in the present. If he could revitalise the company, build it up a bit more, he'd soon be able to pay off Maria. Then he'd be able to start his training college, begin teaching people how to protect themselves. There were plenty of modern day despots like Matthews or Mamboja people needed protecting from, without delving into a past you couldn't change.

Having decided to focus on the present, he was irritated when he got a call from Del Rivera, insisting they meet up to discuss something urgent.

"What are you talking about, how can anything be urgent about the past? It's all very interesting, but I've got more important things to do."

"Please, Bakara, I must speak to you, I must warn you. This is not about the past, it's about the future: your future and Shebana's. You are linked together, entwined in ways you do not yet understand."

"You're right about that, I don't understand half of what you say. Alright, look, I'll meet you for dinner here tonight, but I'm not doing any more of those catchmos."

"Thank you, my friend, I will see you there at eight o'clock," Del Rivera hung up.

*

At seven-forty, Ben went to the hotel bar, ordered a drink and settled down to wait. He was already regretting agreeing to see Del Rivera; he genuinely did have better things to do with his time. The old man may have helped him see the past, but what could any of it have to do with his future? And where did that girl from the beach fit in? Surely she was long dead, what did she have to do with anything?

Del Rivera arrived looking flustered. He asked if Ben knew Doctor Carpenter was flying to the conference with Mortimer.

"Er, yes, actually; him and that guy Worthington came into my room when she was there and asked her to go. It was a pity to be honest, 'cause I'd just had one of those visions, like one of your catchmos, whatever you call 'em. I was being drowned on a beach with this girl. I had the feeling Doctor Carpenter saw it too. I wanted to ask her what she thought but…"

"Of course she saw it," blurted Del Rivera, "she is Shebana."

"What? You mean she was the one on the beach? I guess that would explain why she saw it. Bit of a coincidence though, I wonder how many people…"

"It is not coincidence, you are drawn together; you are always drawn together. She is Shebana, and Sarah Wilkes, and Samantha Parsons, and many others. She is the soul you are bound to; she is the one you are destined to be with forever."

"Well, wait a minute," Ben laughed, "she's very attractive, I can't say I'm not interested; but I'm not sure I want to sign up for eternity with her, I hardly know her."

"Bakara, you have known her almost twelve thousand years; you have met countless times, all around the world. You must be with her."

"Alright, so I guess we'll get 'drawn together' like you say then."

"No, you cannot wait. She is in deadly peril, we must go and find her; we must save her. It is imperative you bind your souls together before he… Oh, damn that accident of yours. I told you all this in Scotland, but you have forgotten."

"You were in Scotland?"

"Yes, Bakara, we met before your accident. I showed you everything. You believed me then, but I am afraid it was too much for you. You raced away and had that dreadful crash; you were almost killed. That is why I was taking it slowly in the hospital, showing you a little at a time, piece by piece. But now we are out of time, we need to…"

"Hang on… are you saying *you* were the reason I nearly died in the middle of nowhere?"

"Well, not exactly… but it is true that when I told you the danger Shebana was in, you rushed away to find her, though neither of us knew where she was, or even *who* she was."

"But now you know she's Doctor Carpenter?"

"Yes, I felt it last time I visited the hospital, when I was close to her."

"Oh, you *felt* it. Must be true then," Ben was beginning to tire of all the mystical fate and destiny talk; "look, I'm sorry, Del Rivera, the past life stuff was interesting, although some of it will haunt me for the rest of my days, but I have to get on with this life now. I don't have time to go on some crazy mission after a woman you *felt* was someone from my past."

"You must, you don't know what danger she is in."

"Well, why should I worry? According to you, she's been drowned, burned at the stake, and God knows what else, and she's still come back again. I can always catch her next time."

"But, you don't understand. Mamboja will destroy her; there will not be a next time. She will never be back and you will not be able to save us. You must be together. It is the only way to stop him."

"OK, that's it; I've had enough of this. Thanks for the visits in hospital, they were entertaining. Disturbing,

71

but entertaining. Maybe it's all true and, if so, thanks for showing me my past. But that's it now, the past is the past. I need to focus on the future, and I don't see what Bakara, Shebana, and 'mumbo-jumbo', whatever he's called, have got to do with it. Even if they're real, they're firmly in the past," Ben stood up and started to leave. After a few paces, he turned and confronted Del Rivera again.

"One last question, what's in this for you? Why are you so hell bent on saving my soul? Who are you anyway?"

The old man looked down, "I am Fujabi. I was the one who told Mamboja to fetch you from the tent that night. It was my fault he fed you to the sea. I have had to live with that guilt for nearly twelve thousand years."

He stared at his shoes as Ben walked away.

VI

DREAMS

Ben refused to see Del Rivera again, but the old man's influence remained strong. The dreams came every night, more vivid than ever and as powerful as kaetchemo.

He was a Chinese peasant living a life of hard work in the fields until he travelled at last, for the first time in his long life, to the neighbouring village. There, he met her. Her name was Shu Chen and, for over eighty years, they had lived just a few miles apart. Now, they had finally found each other. But it was too late. They met twice more, drank tea, held hands, and talked. That was as far as they got. Then he died.

In Greece, long before the birth of Christ, they met in their youth and fell in love. They lay together and enjoyed a loving relationship. In his dream he could feel her body as he caressed her, kissing her gently on the lips, touching her buttocks, her breasts, and her womanhood. He could feel her touching him too, the tender ecstasy as she kissed him back and caressed his buttocks, his breasts, and his womanhood.

He woke filled with a sense of bliss. On that ancient island, long ago, he and Shebana had been together a whole lifetime. It seemed a uniquely joyous memory. But, as the euphoria wore off, he began to feel unsettled. The fact he'd been a woman had come as a surprise. He wrestled with the strangeness of it, feeling oddly threatened by this revelation. He'd come to accept the idea of reincarnation, but being a woman was something he'd never expected. Up to now, he'd assumed he'd always been a man. It shook his notion of self, challenged his preconceptions. What was he: man, woman, or something between? He struggled with his emotions as he faced this new paradigm. He knew it was true, he *had* been a woman. Here and now, in this hotel room over two thousand years later, he could remember what it felt like.

After a time, he got over his unease. Instead of feeling threatened, he began to feel empowered. It had been a phenomenal sensation, being in the other half of the human race; and now he knew something very few men knew, he knew what it was like to be a woman. Did it affect his sexuality, change his identity? No, he was as masculine as anyone in this life. It just proved being male or female was purely physical, nothing to do with the person inside. Beneath the surface, there were no men or women, only people in different bodies. He laughed as he imagined what his old army mates would think. He remembered some of the bigots and misogynists he'd known. It would be fun to show them the truth.

This really did alter everything. If he could be a woman, what else could he be? As Basil Cunningham in the nineteenth century, he'd been in love with a man, but he'd never acted on it. Could he? He was straight in this life, but had there been other lives when he'd been gay? He'd been a lesbian in Greece, after all.

Anything seemed possible. He could be a man or woman, gay or straight, white, black, oriental, or anything else. Did he even have to be human? That was the most extraordinary thought of all. Maybe he'd been a bit harsh on Del Rivera. This stuff was amazing. Perhaps the past could show him how to build a better future?

Still, what he'd told the old man was true; he had a lot to sort out, here and now, before he worried about the past. Give it a couple of weeks to get things organised. Then he could give him a call.

*

Ben lay in bed feeling a new sense of adventure. The day belonged to the tiresome, mundane problems of the present, but his dreams belonged to the past. Not only could they take him anywhere, any time, he could also be just about anyone.

The only constant was Shebana. She had many faces, many names, but she was always there; sometimes he even sensed things from her point of view. He always recognised her, though his past self didn't. And he always loved her.

It all had to mean something. He began to wonder if he should get in touch with Doctor Carpenter when she got back from the conference. What would he say though, 'Hey babe, I think our destinies are entwined?' She'd think he was nuts.

He closed his eyes, letting sleep carry him away. He was almost disappointed when he found himself back in familiar territory, dressed in his sergeant's uniform, waiting outside the hospital in Totnes.

"Are you in need of medical attention again, sergeant?" asked Sarah as she emerged from the casualty department.

"No, ma'am but, er… I got a little lost. All these tiny roads here look the same and they took down all the signs. I, er… I wondered if you could show me the way to one of your country pubs. In return, I'll happily buy you a drink."

"I can't, I'm back on duty at midnight."

"Well, er, a coffee then… or tea?"

She held up her hand and wiggled her fingers, displaying her wedding ring, "I'm still married, sergeant."

"We can just be friends… please?"

"Now why would you want to 'just be friends' with a married woman?"

"Well, er…" he grinned, looking down at the ground, "we could see how it goes."

"It won't go anywhere, sergeant. I made a vow, in

church, to God, I'll not be breaking it; not even for the most handsome American in Devon."

He looked up and smiled at her, "You noticed, huh? Come on, it's just tea, ma'am."

"You can call me Sarah, and it will be one cup of tea, and that will be it."

But it wasn't, of course, and soon they were spending many happy days riding through the Devon countryside on his motorbike, stopping for tea, and laughing at each other's jokes about the English. As the months rolled by, friendship turned to love and, by the spring of 1944, they both knew it. But still Sarah held something back, her vows keeping her emotions in check. It was late May before they kissed for the first time. Afterwards, as they sat close together in the corner of a crowded pub, she put her hand on his, "Brendan, I warned you when we met; I'm older than you think. I don't want to lead you on without you knowing the truth."

"I don't care how old you are, a gentleman doesn't ask a lady that kind of question."

"I'm forty-three, Brendan; I'll be forty-four next month."

He took her hand in his, "It wouldn't matter if you were sixty; you're still the most beautiful girl in the world."

She smiled, a tear in her eye, "You're very sweet, Brendan. But you're in the prime of your life, only twenty-seven; I don't understand why you would want me."

"I want you because I love you, Sarah; you're everything I've ever wanted."

She sighed, looking down at their hands clasped together on the table, "I love you too, Brendan, and perhaps you're right; perhaps it doesn't matter how old I am. God knows, I want nothing more than to slip off me wedding ring, forget me vows, and take you into me bed; I want it more than anything. But I can't."

"Why can't you?"

"Because I made a promise to God I'd be faithful to me husband; I can't break me promise."

"I've seen the look in your eyes when we part; I know how lonely you are. Do you really think that's what God wants? You're practically a widow, you deserve some happiness. I... I want to make you happy."

She sighed, "You already make me happy, Brendan, but, I... I don't know if I can... I mean, I don't know if I'm ready, I..." She kissed him softly on the lips then sat back and looked into his eyes, "Give me some time, be patient with me, please?"

"Of course, take all the time you want, you're worth the wait."

But time was something they didn't have. June arrived a few days later and, with it, Brendan's destiny on Omaha beach.

*

A night later, Ben dreamed of Sarah again. But she was Sarah O'Shaughnessy, a nurse at the field hospital in Flanders. He was Billy Davies, a private in the Welsh

Fusiliers, wounded on the front line. He was a brave boy; as brave as anyone could be in the living hell he and his mates endured every day.

Some of the boys had taken their rifle, pointed it at their foot and pulled the trigger. In the early days, it often got them the honourable discharge they hoped for. But it didn't always work out that way. Owain Carter's foot became infected, complications set in, and he died on the operating table. Then there was poor Davey Halfpenny. The lieutenant had seen him shoot himself. Davey was put on a charge, court-martialled for cowardice and shot by a firing squad. They waited for his foot to heal first. What was it the general said? "Procedure, gentlemen; we must follow procedure."

Bloody madness, all of it: if you're going to shoot a man, what does it matter whether his bloody foot's healed? Still, what's another mad thing around here anyway?

He had to laugh when he remembered Tommy Cuthbert though. Missed his bloody foot six times he did. Then he managed to shoot Johnny Williams instead. Johnny got the honourable discharge, Tommy died at Ypres.

So, it was bad luck when a ricocheting bullet happened to hit Billy in the foot in almost exactly the same way as a self-inflicted wound. Bloody bad luck. It was bad enough his bloody foot hurt, but his mates saw it as a marvellous opportunity for a laugh at his expense. Still, they knew him well enough to know he'd never try to buy his ticket home that way. They were quick to leap to his defence when the officers started looking at his wound suspiciously. They were good lads really, all of them.

It probably helped his case that he'd fought on for another hour after being wounded. In the end, the officers realised it was just a bizarre coincidence and packed him off to the field hospital. The captain even gave him a note to show anyone who might doubt his commitment to King and Country.

And that was how he met Sarah.

*

Just fifteen years old and fresh off the boat from Ireland, Sarah had only been in Flanders three weeks, but had already seen unimaginable horrors. She had a strong stomach for a girl her age and coped well with most of it. It was only burnt flesh she couldn't stand. Something about it made her feel peculiar.

She could see why the young private was embarrassed. His wound did have a superficial resemblance to a man who'd shot himself in the foot. However, she'd seen enough bullet wounds to know this bullet had been fired from much farther away. Still, she thought she'd tease him a bit; a little banter always cheered the lads up, especially when it came from a pretty nurse, "Well now, decided we wanted to go home, did we?"

"No miss, no, it's not like that, honestly. See, I've got a note from the captain I have, it was…"

Realising she'd upset the boy more than she intended,

she quickly reassured him, "Hush now, I'm only joshing with you, even one of these idiot doctors could see this bullet didn't come from your own gun. It's still in your foot though; it'll have to come out."

"Oh, right."

He sounded nervous. She felt a strange affinity for him. It was plain to see he was in a fair amount of pain, but was trying to hide it, even from her. She decided to tell him a few facts of life about the field hospital. The poor boy deserved a chance.

"Right, I'm going to tell you something… er, what's your name?"

"Private William Edward Davies number 4126…"

"I'll not be needing your number, William, you're not on parade now."

"Er, yeah, of course… er, it's Billy; my mates call me Billy."

"Alright, Billy, well the thing is this. It's Butcher Bates on duty tonight. He's about the worst doctor in the hospital. I'd rather go to Mr O'Sullivan, the butcher in me village back home, than let Bates take a knife to me. One boy came in with a flesh wound last week. The bullet was lodged in his shoulder, but a simple enough job to sort out. Bates made such a mess of it, the boy lost his arm."

"Oh," Billy's face had turned as white as a sheet; "can I wait for another doctor?"

"No, Billy, you can't. As soon as Bates comes over to examine you, he'll have you up on the table and start hacking at you. The good lord only knows how much damage he'll do before he's finished."

"What can I do, miss?"

"Well, Billy, there's just one thing we can do. I can take it out for you before Bates sees you."

"Oh please, would you?"

"I will if you'll trust me?"

"I do, I trust you; but is it allowed?"

"No, it's not; it's against all the rules. I'm just a junior nurse; I'm not supposed to do anything like that. But I've helped me daddy on the farm since I was a little girl and I've seen enough in this place to know I can do a better job than Bates."

"Won't you get into trouble? I wouldn't want you to get into trouble for me."

"Oh, sure enough, they'd pack me off on the boat back home away from this awful place. I think that's the kind of trouble I can handle."

He grinned at her briefly, but then the pain swiftly returned to his face. "Alright then, can you do it for me, miss? Please?"

"There's just one other thing, Billy."

"What's that miss?"

"I won't be able to use any anaesthetic. You'll have to deal with the pain on your own, and you'll have to be quiet."

He gulped, "Alright, miss, I'll try."

She gave him a piece of cloth to bite down on and began work. Both of them tried to keep as quiet as possible.

The moans that did escape his mouth were stifled by the cloth and lost in the general hubbub coming from the other wounded soldiers in the tent.

Beads of sweat broke out on his forehead as he battled with the pain. She was sweating too as she battled with the bullet. It was trickier than she'd expected, the bullet had entered at a difficult angle and was lodged against the bone. She lost it twice as it slipped back into the hole, already held by the healing flesh around it. Finally, she pulled it free and disposed of it quickly, away from his cot.

"Well done, Billy, that's the worst over now," she began washing out his wound, glancing up anxiously every few seconds. She was almost done when she spotted Bates approaching. It was Billy's turn for the butcher's ministrations.

"How is this one, nurse? Looks like a bullet wound to the foot. Bit suspicious that."

"No doctor, he's a brave one this boy, he wouldn't be doing anything like that at all. He has a note from his captain, he showed me he did. Very brave he is," she stood up for her charge, protecting him like a lioness with a wounded cub.

"All right then, let's have him up on the table, I shall need to cut the bullet out. It'll be quicker if I use the large knife, plenty more men to see tonight."

"Oh there's no need for that, doctor, passed right through it has. I'm just cleaning out his wound then I can easily sew it up meself. He'll be fine as he is. Up and about in no time he'll be."

"Hmmm, well I'd better take a look at the exit wound," Bates took a step forward, but then he looked at the other men in the hospital tent: screaming, bleeding, crying for their mothers; dying. "Perhaps later though," he turned away; "this one looks like he's on the mend. I'll leave him in your hands for now."

Sarah and Billy looked at each other and breathed a sigh of relief. She finished cleaning his wound then deftly sewed it up and applied a fresh bandage. "There, that's nice and clean. It'll heal up nicely as long as you look after it. Don't trust the other nurses to change your dressing, some of them are silly girls from big houses who don't know how to look after you properly. Make sure it's changed twice a day. Insist on it, don't be taken in when they say there's no need, they're just lazy cows they are."

"Thank you miss, I'll be sure to do that. Thank you for everything."

She smiled at him then got up to leave, "Well, I think you'll be alright now. Just remember what I said about your dressing. Twice a day now, you hear?" she started to walk away.

"Miss?" he called her back.

"What is it now? Me shift finished two hours ago, I've to get to me bed or I'll be no use to you boys in the morning."

"What's your name miss?"

"Well, Private William Edward Davies number 4126, you are addressing Junior Nurse Sarah Elizabeth Louise O'Shaughnessy of County Cork, so you are."

"Blimey, that's a big name for a little girl."

"Not so much of the 'little' if you please. Don't be forgetting who it was pulled that bullet out of your foot."

"No, no, I won't, I would never... I'll never forget," he was obviously anxious he might have offended her; he looked more horrified than when he'd faced the prospect of losing his foot. "No, I'm grateful to you miss, truly I am. But I wondered if I could see you again? You know, after my foot's better, when I get my next leave?"

"Well, William Davies, aren't you the fast worker then?" she blushed a little, but bent down and spoke softly in his ear; "nurse's quarters, Rue de La Bouvier, St Germaine. Best to come about seven o'clock. If I'm on day shift, I should be back by then," she turned away and walked out of the tent, making sure he couldn't see the enormous grin on her face.

*

Billy visited the nurse's quarters every time he got any leave. It didn't always work out. One time Sarah was on a double shift for most of his leave then too exhausted to do any more than say 'Hello'. But, when it did work out, they grasped whatever time together they could get. Their love grew through the autumn of 1915 and into early 1916.

One fine warm day in April, they managed to go for a picnic. She'd saved up some food parcels from home and he'd got hold of a couple of bottles of beer. He needed the beer because it was time to be brave again.

He got down on one knee in the grass, took her hand and gazed up into the dazzling emerald-green eyes he'd come to love so much, "Nurse Sarah Elizabeth Louise O'Shaughnessy of County Cork, will you marry me?"

She looked down at him with tears in her eyes, "Yes, Corporal William Edward Davies number 41268955, I will marry you."

They hugged and kissed in the Belgian sunshine. It was a moment of heaven in the midst of hell.

Legally, they couldn't marry until her sixteenth birthday, on the Twenty-Eighth of June, but they didn't want to wait a minute longer, so the ceremony was arranged to take place in the little church in St Germaine that same day.

Billy managed to get special leave for the wedding and a couple of days afterwards. He asked Sarah's father for permission to take her hand in marriage through an exchange of letters. Her own letters contained enough tales of the handsome, courageous Billy to convince her father to agree to the union, so all was set.

On the morning of the Twenty-Eighth, Billy was getting ready to go off on leave when the captain called a parade in their trench.

Captain Smith was a fair man. Billy knew that what little he could do to make his men's miserable, and often short, lives better, he did. So it was clear to Billy that Smith delivered the news with a heavy heart, trying to sound as positive as he could.

"General Mortimer has ordered our brigade to the Somme sector where we will be taking part in a special operation. I can tell you no more, but the general did specifically request our brigade which is, of course, a tremendous honour to the regiment, so I'm sure all you men will be proud of that… er…" Smith faltered, taking a moment to gather himself before continuing, "we move out at 1600 hours. All leave is cancelled forthwith. Dismissed"

Billy couldn't believe his ears. The wedding! What was he going to do? How was he going to tell Sarah? This could not be happening. In a panic, he asked to see the captain. The officer let him into his makeshift office at one end of their section of trench. Smith spoke first, "I'm sorry, Corporal Davies, there's nothing I can do."

"But, begging your pardon, captain sir, the wedding… Sarah will be distraught; we were wanting to marry today. I want to do my duty, sir, I really do, but can't you just give me one day?"

Smith sat down and took off his cap. He sighed as he studied the message lying on his desk. Putting it to one side, he seemed to make up his mind. Looking up, he said, "I can't let you go to St Germaine, Billy, we would both be shot. But, if you can get Sarah here before four o'clock then, as your commanding officer, I can marry you here. It's the best I can do."

"Thank you sir, you don't know what this means to me sir," Billy bolted out of the office to get a message to Sarah.

She arrived just before three-thirty. The muddy trench ruined the beautiful dress her father had sent all the way from Ireland, but she clearly didn't care, "I'm marrying my Billy," she smiled, "that's all that matters."

Sergeant Jones gave her away, Corporal Henson acted as best man, and Captain Smith conducted the hasty ceremony.

"You may now kiss the bride," concluded Smith. Billy and Sarah kissed; the men cheered and clapped them both on the back. Smith smiled sadly, but warmly, at the newlyweds.

"Alright men, party's over, on the truck with you," Smith shouted. He turned to Billy, "You've got two minutes, son."

The rest of the men left. Billy held Sarah tight for a long minute, then he stepped back and gently took her hands, "I'll get back soon as I can then we'll have our honeymoon. The captain's promised me a seventy-two hour pass first chance he gets. He's a good man, the captain; he'll do right by us, I know."

"Oh Billy, if only you didn't have to go," she was holding back the tears. Just.

"Now then, Mrs Sarah Elizabeth Louise Davies of Trench 6, Section 21, stiff upper lip and all that, it's not like you to get all emotional on me now," he was barely holding back his own tears.

"Yes, my husband, off with you then."

He turned and walked to the waiting truck. This hurt more than when she'd taken the bullet out of his foot. Bless that wonderful bullet. It had taken him to her.

*

Thirty thousand men died on the First of July, 1916, the opening day of the Battle of the Somme. It achieved nothing, but the generals persisted with the same madness for weeks.

Captain Smith died courageously, leading his men. He was nominated for a posthumous Victoria Cross, but General Mortimer quashed it, claiming Smith had done 'nothing particularly out of the ordinary'.

Billy was trying to pull the wounded Sergeant Jones to safety. They'd nearly made it to a shell crater when they got caught in some barbed wire. Billy freed Jones first but got his arm tangled up in the process. He was trying to free himself when a stream of machine gun bullets hit him in the chest.

Jones crawled the last few yards to the crater. Thanks to Billy, he survived. Billy's body was never found.

Two months later, the sergeant was able to tell Sarah how brave Billy had been, how he'd saved his life. It was a small comfort to the sobbing virgin widow who'd had two minutes of married life with the man she loved.

After the war, she remarried. She was still young, after all. Gordon was a good man, but she never truly loved him. She did find love once more, with Brendan O'Doyle, many years later, but he was really too young for her. He hadn't even been born when Billy died. It was funny how alike they were though.

VII

TAKING FLIGHT

The moment Susan boarded the Lear Jet, a terrible feeling of dread came over her. She couldn't put her finger on why, or what had caused it, but she felt like she was going to her doom.

She was angry with herself for agreeing so readily to come on this trip. What had she been thinking? She'd been caught off guard, not paying attention, and her career ambition had taken control of her tongue, making her commit to this crazy venture before she'd had time to think about the consequences. Now she would have to endure a whole week in the company of the strange Professor Lord Mortimer, whose very presence made her uneasy.

He was an odd character alright. There was a peculiar air about him. It was more than the fact he was a lord, he seemed different to other people, as if he wasn't even…

'Stupid girl,' she chastised herself. Of course he's

human. He's probably perfectly normal for an aristocrat. How would she know what a lord was supposed to act like?

She sighed as she settled into the comfortable chair and fastened her seatbelt as instructed. She was here now; she'd have to make the best of it. The plane began to taxi. Her sense of foreboding intensified. The headache didn't help. Her head had started thumping the minute she boarded. She would definitely have to get checked out when she got back.

Take off didn't help either but, as the jet approached cruising altitude and started to level out, Mortimer's servant began serving drinks. A couple of large gin and tonics helped, although they probably wouldn't in the morning.

She tried to focus on something positive. This trip would certainly be good for her career, Worthington had hinted as much. When she interviewed for Deputy Head, she'd be able to answer those infuriating questions like, 'What else have you done apart from patient care?' Christ, what else was a doctor supposed to do?

She'd always wanted to be a doctor, ever since she was a little girl. Well, nearly always, there had been a couple of brief spells when she'd had other ideas. When she was seven, she'd decided to be an archer. She was quite good with those little toy arrows that had the suckers on the end. She always beat the boys when they played 'Cowboys and Indians'. Her father bought her a proper archery set for her birthday. She was overjoyed when she unwrapped it that morning until, minutes later, her mother made him take it back to the shop. She lost interest in archery after that.

At eleven she wanted to be a singer. She spent hours in front of the mirror wailing into a hairbrush, or dressed up as 'Baby Spice' with her hair in bunches while she tried to copy the dance moves and sang at the top of her voice. This fad came to an abrupt end one Saturday afternoon when her mother burst into her bedroom, "Will you shut the fuck up, I've got a monstrous fucking headache and you can't sing a fucking note to save your life, you stupid little cow."

She'd run to her father in tears. Ever the diplomat, he suggested she might try miming the words when her mother had one of her 'bad heads', "They always mime on Pop Toppers. You'll need to practise for when you're a big star." Despite his encouragement, she could never bring herself to sing again. Later that night, she overheard her parents shouting. Still later, she came to realise where her mother's 'bad heads' came from.

But, apart from these short-lived phases, she couldn't remember wanting to do anything other than be a doctor. From an early age, she wanted to care for all the sick people in the world and make them better. When she was very young, she even believed it was her destiny to save them and she was the only one who could. That grandiose notion had passed, of course, but, aside from the occasional distraction, her determination to be a doctor and care for the sick had grown stronger with each passing year.

She could still recall her father sitting patiently with his arm outstretched as she bandaged his imaginary wounds. He would grumble good-naturedly as he tried to eat his dinner with both hands swathed in bandages and they would laugh at his hopeless efforts to cut his food and lift his glass. Her mother would scowl at the mess he was making, but he would clean it up and keep the laughter going with a few well-placed winks and other tomfoolery. It seemed like she always went to bed laughing in those days and her father would kiss her on the forehead and say, 'Good night, Doctor Susie, thanks for making me all better again.'

Later came secondary school, GCSEs and 'A' Levels; vital to her dream of getting into medical school. He supported her every step of the way, often sitting up late at night to help her with her studies, even when he had an early start on site in the morning. When she got her acceptance from University College London, he handed her a bottle of Moet et Chandon and an envelope containing the keys to her first car and a greeting card with red roses on the front. Inside, he'd written, 'I always knew you'd do it Doctor Susie!'

She was on a voluntary attachment after her first year at UCL when she got the call that changed her life. Her father was a senior and well-respected Chartered Surveyor. He didn't need to do site visits any more, but he always liked to see things at first hand. It was the middle of a long hot summer, possibly the hottest day of all. Normally an absolute stickler for health and safety, he took his hard hat off for a second to wipe the sweat from his brow. Hundreds of feet above, a worker accidentally dropped a hammer. The heavy tool plummeted earthwards and struck her father's unprotected head.

They rushed him to hospital where he lay in a coma for three days, clinging to life by a thread. She hurried to his side as soon as she heard. One of the doctors found out she was a medical student and explained her father's condition in more detail. "We just know so little about brain injuries," he concluded, "it's frustrating, to be honest; if we understood more about the brain's physiology, we'd be able to save a lot more people like your father."

When he died, she thought she would just collapse into her grief but, with her mother in an almost uninterrupted drunken stupor, she found a strength inside herself she never expected. She organised the funeral as she hoped her father would have wanted. She could only guess because, at forty-six, it was something he hadn't thought about yet. One thing she knew for certain though: his favourite song. He loved to tell her how he'd seen it performed live for the first time the night he met her mother. He used to say, "Millions of people have come to love that song since then, and almost all of them have heard it played considerably better. But, you know what, that didn't matter; it was a moment of pure magic, musical history in the making. I feel privileged to have been there."

So she made sure they played 'I Have Loved You Since the Dawn of Time' by the Vomix. It was a bit before her time, but it was her favourite too.

As the familiar chords rang out, she almost managed to sing along. But she glanced at her mother standing next to her and remembered her screaming, 'you can't sing a fucking note to save your life, you stupid little cow,' and she just couldn't. She mouthed the words instead.

From her meagre savings, she bought a wreath that bore the words 'With Undying Love and Eternal Thanks – Your Doctor Susie'. When her mother saw it, she said, "You're not a doctor yet, Susie."

"Don't call me that," she retorted; "that's what Dad called me. No-one gets to call me that any more. From now on, my name is Susan."

She decided two other things that day. She would see her mother as little as possible and, when she graduated, she was going to specialise in the treatment of brain injuries.

In the years since then, she'd often wondered if she would have been as successful if her father hadn't died. Remembering his support, his undying faith, gave her the strength to carry on and overcome the obstacles in her path. Every hurdle she faced, every problem she encountered, she pushed herself onwards for him. Sometimes she felt he was still by her side, holding her hand, whispering, 'You can do it, Doctor Susie.'

She graduated first in her class and won a highly coveted post at the National Hospital for Neurology in Queen Square. She took a two year sabbatical to research the physiology of the brain and treatment of brain trauma, and gained a PhD. She could just imagine her father laughing, 'So, you're Doctor Doctor Susie now then,' while his eyes glistened with tears as love and pride overwhelmed him.

The usual sadness swept over her, as it did whenever she thought about the great days in her life she hadn't been able to share with him. She knew he'd be proud though and, as always, that gave her some comfort.

Sipping her drink, she returned to her recollections. She got her Certificate of Completion of Training at thirty-three, young for a neurologist. That qualified her for a consultant's position as soon as she could find a suitable vacancy. But it quickly became clear there would be no openings at Queen Square for some time. That was when she'd been offered her current post. She had some reservations about Princess Diana Memorial, but it had the largest, best-equipped, brain trauma unit in the country. In the end, she knew she had to accept. She owed it to her father, she owed it to the little girl she'd once been, the little girl who wanted to care for all the sick people no-one else could save. The further she progressed, the more she could help. It was as simple as that.

Except it wasn't, was it? Now she was stuck in a department run by an obsessive bureaucrat determined to resist change, blind to the benefits of new techniques that would save lives, ease suffering, and advance medical knowledge. For three years, he'd had her bogged down in a mire of administration, bureaucracy, and hospital politics, unable to pursue any of her own ideas. Could she really overcome all that if she became Deputy Head?

She shrugged to herself; she had to try.

With a grimace, she remembered she had another, more pressing, problem. She couldn't in all conscience just stand by and let Ray continue working in the department while he was taking hard drugs, but she'd held off reporting him so far. Now she'd decided to apply for Deputy Head, it could be misconstrued as a sneaky attempt to put him out of the running. He was bound to claim she was making it up so she could get the job. It was a real quandary; she'd have to think of a way around it.

The curtains separating the cockpit from the passenger cabin opened and in stooped the enormous figure of Mortimer. Looking up at him, Susan wondered again what he was really doing at Princess Diana. Would it be worth talking to him about Worthington's shortcomings? Probably not, the two of them seemed pretty close; she got the impression they went back a long way.

"Hello, my dear. I do apologise for leaving you on your own, but I like to handle take-off myself. Hans can take it from here though; he's an able co-pilot. Has Sun-lee been looking after you?" Mortimer gestured towards the attentive servant as he sat across the table from Susan.

"Oh yes, thank you. She's been marvellous. I'm on my second G&T already."

"Jolly good, you just relax. I am afraid you will find your time at our destination rather taxing, so I suggest you get a good rest on the flight. Just ask Sun-lee for anything you want and she will see you get it."

"That's very kind of you, your lordship. This is certainly a better way to travel than a commercial airline."

"Oh, indeed it is. But please call me Marcus. We have a long journey ahead of us; let's dispense with the formalities."

Susan did begin to relax; although she was concerned he thought she would find the conference so taxing. Maybe he felt she was too inexperienced, she'd be out of place? She had to admit the thought had crossed her mind.

Nonetheless, her feeling of dread subsided and she started to dismiss it as nothing more than a natural anxiety generated by unfamiliar surroundings. After the third gin and tonic, she drifted off to sleep. And she dreamt.

VIII

PRISONERS

Sally was the sixth child of a poor family. She was just eight years old when she was sent to work for the Mortimers. Not that she saw much of the Mortimers. She scrubbed floors, emptied chamber pots, did all the dirtiest, most menial tasks in the mansion. But she was happy. The old lord was renowned for treating his servants well, and he did. He looked upon the household like an extended family. She was the lowest of the low, but even she got a gift from him every Christmas.

As time went on, she learned more about the old lord and his family. The other servants told her how his first wife had died giving birth to Marcus, his elder son, in 1776, the year the American colonies had declared their independence. He grieved for many years, but eventually he married again. Her ladyship, his second wife, was known for her warmth and kindness; everyone loved her from the start. Except Marcus, who'd turned into a spiteful boy, and seemed to despise his step-mother. He seemed to despise everyone in fact. He was the sort of boy who enjoyed pulling the wings off flies. This cruel streak was not confined to flies, Sally was warned.

The older staff would always frown as they recalled Marcus's childhood. He was a strange boy, they told Sally. From an early age, rather than mix with other children, he preferred to spend long hours on his own looking at books and papers, tinkering with alchemy. Odd pursuits for such a young child; although, 'leave him if it keeps him happy,' was the old lord's view.

But they smiled when they talked about his lordship's other son. Bartholomew, or Bartie, as he was often called, was born in 1789; the year the French decided it was time for a change. The staff remembered how, almost immediately, it had been obvious he was very different to his half brother. He wanted to play outside in the sunshine and would even play with the village children; although Sally only met him after she started working at the mansion.

The years rolled by, a new century dawned. Sally worked hard, but was content with her station in life. In 1804, when she was thirteen, she was promoted to housemaid and began to see the family more often. She liked the old lord and she liked her ladyship, both of them were always kind to her. She liked Bartie a lot; he was really sweet and friendly. But Marcus frightened her; she remembered how the other servants had warned her about him.

On one of her first encounters with Marcus, he called her into his chamber and told her to look at the rug, "Do you see the stain?"

She looked carefully, but could see nothing, "No, my lord, I cannot see any stain."

"You must be blind, you stupid girl. There's a huge ugly stain on my rug. You must have spilt wine on it when you cleared away the glasses this morning."

"It wasn't me that cleared your things away this morning, my lord; that was…"

"Silence girl or I will have you whipped." She cringed and shut up immediately. "I expect you to scrub this stain out. Start now and don't stop until I tell you."

She hesitated; baffled by his insistence there was a stain she couldn't see.

"I said *now* girl, unless you want to feel the lash first."

She knelt down and began scrubbing. All she had was a wet cloth, but she was afraid to ask if she could fetch something more suitable. Suitable for what though? She still couldn't see any stain. How could she scrub a stain she couldn't even see? Was there a stain there and she was unable to see it for some reason? She was totally confused, but more scared of being flogged than anything else, so she kept her head down and scrubbed as hard as she could.

Marcus stood over her; she could almost feel him glowering at the back of her head. After ten minutes he declared, "Well, clearly you are so useless I can't be expected to waste my time supervising you. Any other maid would have had the rug clean by now. I'm going out. If you are not here scrubbing that stain when I return, I will see you get twenty lashes in the stable yard."

He left the chamber. Terrified by the threat of a flogging, she continued to scrub at the rug. After two hours, her fingers started to bleed. Now there was a real stain, but it wasn't wine, it was blood, her blood. It was just getting worse. Horrified, she scrubbed even harder. Her fingers bled even more. It was a vicious circle.

At six o'clock, she'd been scrubbing for four hours when Marcus came back. At last, it will be over, she thought; surely he will see this is pointless?

"I'm sorry my lord, but it's my fingers, they started to bleed."

"You stupid girl, don't you have the sense not to bleed all over the place? Honestly, I have never known such an incompetent maid in all my life. I think I really should have you thrashed to get some sense into you."

"No, my lord, please," she sobbed; "I will get your rug clean, my lord, I will."

"Oh stop babbling, girl, and get on with it." After another twenty minutes, he left again, "I'm going to dinner now. You had better have that clean when I return."

"Yes, my lord."

She kept scrubbing. Her fingers were raw, her back was aching. The last time he'd threatened to have her thrashed, she'd wet herself. She was mortified. She hadn't done that since she was a little girl. She worried her urine might stain the rug. She managed to squirm away a bit to prevent it, but her legs were getting chapped as they rubbed together.

Marcus returned at midnight. She could smell he had the usual carafe of port inside him as he bent down to examine the rug, "Well, I'm going to have to sleep somewhere else tonight then, aren't I, you stupid little bitch. Keep scrubbing and remember I might look in on you at any time. You will be whipped if I find you slacking."

She sobbed through the night as she continued to scrub. Eventually, her fingers stopped bleeding, although she couldn't feel them anymore. Without her blood staining the rug, she was finally able to get it clean, but now she had a bigger worry, she'd rubbed a hole in it. In effect, she was scrubbing the floorboards while slowly making a bigger hole in the rug. What would his lordship do when he found out? He'd have her whipped if she stopped scrubbing and he'd have her whipped for destroying his rug if she carried on. Fear and confusion whirled around her head. She wet herself again. Still she scrubbed.

*

It was just after ten o'clock in the morning. Bartie was walking along the corridor outside his brother's room. He wondered where that pretty little maid was. He liked her, she was nice. She was just a maid, of course, but father always said, 'All souls deserve our respect, my son, no matter how humble their place in the world.'

He heard the sound of sobbing. That was odd, Marcus wasn't known for his emotions. Well, only anger and sulky moods. But not crying; that wasn't his way at all. Some of those girls he smuggled in cried, especially when he made them leave. But this sounded different. He knocked cautiously at his brother's door, "Marcus, is that you?"

The sobbing stopped and then came a faint reply, "No, my lord, Lord Marcus has gone to sleep in another chamber."

"Who is that?"

"Miss Trigg, junior housemaid, my lord."

Sensing something was wrong he opened the door and stepped inside. For a moment, he watched the maid working. There was a frantic desperation to her movements that made him uneasy. Then he noticed the rug.

"Why are you scrubbing a hole in a perfectly clean rug?"

"Lord Marcus said there was a stain, my lord. He told me to scrub until he said I could stop."

He remembered the girl's name, "How long have you been scrubbing, Sally?"

"I don't know, my lord."

"Well, when did you start, Sally?"

"About two o'clock, my lord."

"What, two o'clock in the morning?"

"No, two o'clock in the afternoon, my lord"

He crossed the room and grabbed hold of her. He took away the tattered remains of the cloth she was desperately scrubbing at the floorboards with and pulled her to her feet. He looked at her hands. They were a dreadful mess; she must be in terrible pain.

She pulled away and tried to grab the cloth back, "I mustn't stop, my lord; he'll have me flogged."

At that moment, Marcus appeared, wearing a dressing gown and looking somewhat the worse for wear. His usual carafe of port was evidently exacting its revenge.

"What is going on here? What are you doing in my chamber, brother, you know that is forbidden?"

"I found this poor girl cleaning your rug. She's been working non-stop for twenty hours. That's ridiculous. What are you trying to do, kill her?"

"Nonsense, brother, the servants must learn to obey their betters. She will scrub until I tell her, a hundred hours if necessary. And then I will have her whipped for disobedience. I told her not to stop until I said so."

"No," screamed Sally, grabbing for the scrap of cloth in Bartie's hand; "no, my lord, please, I will clean it for you, I will."

But Bartie took hold of her and began to lead her, trembling and traumatised, from the chamber. Marcus blocked their exit; his six foot two inch frame almost filling the doorway.

"Let us through please, brother," Bartie asked quietly; "she needs to be seen by the physician."

"No," snarled Marcus, "the little bitch needs to get back to work and then you can leave."

"Let us through or…"

"Or what? What are you going to do, little brother?"

Marcus towered more than a foot over the top of Bartie's head as he stared down at him with a malignant grin on his face.

Bartie looked down and saw the cord tied loosely around Marcus's waist. Reaching out, he pulled it sharply and Marcus's robe fell open to reveal everything he had. Sally blushed and a distracted Marcus grabbed at his gown. Bartie seized the moment and pushed past, bundling Sally along with him.

It nearly worked; they got six or seven paces. But Marcus swiftly recovered his composure. With three large strides, he was close enough to grab a handful of Sally's hair. She squealed in pain as Marcus pulled her back. Bartie spun around and tried to hit his brother in the stomach, but Marcus comfortably batted the punch aside and grasped him around the throat. Dragging Sally along by the hair, he pushed Bartie towards the top of the staircase where there was a thirty foot drop beyond the low railings.

"You have no idea what you are dealing with, little brother. I have disposed of you plenty of times before and I can easily do it again right now."

As Marcus forced him backwards, Bartie glanced behind at the yawning drop and realised to his horror his brother genuinely was intent on killing him. At that moment, his mother appeared from another room further down the corridor.

Marcus released Bartie and Sally. His sneer changed to a warm, friendly smile, "Brother dear, this is all a foolish misunderstanding. I only asked the maid to scrub the rug until *she* was happy it was clean. I can't imagine why she kept at it all night. Look at her poor hands.

"Mother dear," he turned to his father's wife, who had reached the group at the top of the staircase; "this silly girl has worked her fingers to the bone. It is highly commendable but perhaps father should send for the physician?

"Please excuse me anyway. As you can see, I need to dress," he turned, went back into his room, and closed the door behind him.

Bartie led the sobbing Sally downstairs to his father's study. Her fatigue was so bad, she could hardly walk. The old lord sent for the physician, who attended to her injured hands. Bartie tried to tell his father his version of events, but the old lord could see no evil in his elder son, "I am sure it was just an unfortunate mistake. The girl obviously misunderstood what Marcus said."

*

Sally lost the top joints from two fingers on her right hand. It made her duties more difficult and she was a little clumsy until she got the hang of things again. Otherwise, though, she recovered from her ordeal. She was grateful when Bartie managed to get her moved so all her work was in the other wing of the house, far from Marcus, closer to him and his mother.

They saw each other frequently from then on and developed as much of a friendship as their different standing in society would allow. By the summer of 1807, he was eighteen, she was seventeen, and she was deeply in love with him, though she could never dare admit it.

Then tragedy returned to the Mortimer mansion. The old lord and his wife were coming back from church in their carriage when something spooked the horses. The crazed animals bolted straight for the river, in spate after a prolonged spell of unseasonably heavy rain. Her ladyship jumped from the carriage and broke her neck. His lordship drowned in the river. Nobody ever found out what had startled the horses.

The day after the funeral, Sally filed into the great hall along with the rest of the household staff to hear Lord Marcus address them for the first time as their master.

"No-one had more affection for my late father than I, but he was altogether far too lenient and ran this house extremely inefficiently. Accordingly, there are going to be a few changes." The new lord ran through a long list of revisions. He extended everyone's working hours; told some older staff his father had been keeping on as a kindness they had the rest of the day to pack their belongings and leave; re-assigned a weakling kitchen boy to work in the stables; and gave one elderly footman the job of replenishing the water jugs in the upstairs bedrooms: a job that would entail him having to climb four flights of stairs carrying the heavy jugs several times every day. He saved Sally's fate until last, "... And, finally, Sally Trigg, housemaid, will move to the east wing and serve as my personal chamber maid. That is all."

Sally stood, frozen in shock. She wanted to cry. The memories of her scrubbing ordeal came back to her. She looked at Bartie. He looked back at her with an aching sadness in his eyes. But there was nothing either of them could do.

After finishing her work for the day, Sally went back to the tiny attic room she shared with another maid. Solemnly, she packed her few possessions and took them to her new quarters. She got a room to herself now, a nice room; it even had a mirror on the wall. Technically, this was a promotion; although it felt more like a death sentence.

She could just leave of course, resign in the morning and work her notice. But what kind of future would she face? Her family couldn't afford another mouth to feed and she was unlikely to find another job without a decent reference. In reality, she was trapped as surely as if she were in prison. Then there was Bartie. He was the one truly good thing in her life. She knew she wouldn't see as much of him now, but she couldn't bear the thought of being parted altogether.

Standing in front of the mirror, she let down her chestnut brown hair. Long and wavy, it fell almost to her waist. She slipped off her uniform and undergarments then took a step back so she could see herself better. Her breasts had developed into two shapely, curving mounds, which she tried hard to hide from the men on the staff. On the other hand, she recalled, smiling to herself, she always pushed them out a bit when Bartie was near. Lately, she'd begun to daydream about him caressing her there while he kissed her gently on the neck.

She sighed as she reminded herself of the absurdity of her fantasies. He was the brother of a lord and she was just a housemaid. The friendship they had was all she could hope for. Still, it was enough to bring some light into her life, give her existence some meaning.

Turning around, she continued her self-appraisal. Her buttocks were firm and pert; her legs long and slim. She was a fine-looking girl, marred only by the two missing fingertips she'd lost after her night of torment at Marcus's hands.

And now she was in his hands again.

With that thought, she curled up in her cramped little bed and cried herself to sleep.

Two hours later, she was woken by a knock at her door. She got up groggily, pulled on her night gown and opened the door. One of the bell boys was there. "What are you doing, Jimmy, what time is it?"

"It's a quarter hour before twelve, miss. You are to report to his lordship's chamber at midnight."

"Midnight?" she questioned the boy.

"Yes, miss; those are his lordship's orders," the boy turned and ran down the corridor.

She hastily dressed in her maid's uniform and hurried downstairs to the master bed chamber where Lord Marcus had been ensconced since the night of his father's death.

"Come in, Trigg, stand over by the bed," he responded to her hesitant knock. She stood with her hands clasped in front of her and her head slightly bowed as he continued,

"I'm aware that a certain level of affection has developed between you and my brother, would you agree?"

"My lord, I don't mean no harm by it. Bartie… I mean Lord Bartholomew… he's always just been good to me, my lord."

"Well it has to stop. It is wholly inappropriate for a housemaid to be on friendly terms with the brother of a lord."

She choked back a sob, "Yes, my lord."

"As I cannot control my brother, I hold you responsible for putting an end to this dangerous fraternisation. Is that clear?"

"I'm sorry my lord, I don't understand what you mean?"

"I mean, Trigg," he sighed, "you are not to speak to my brother any more. Do you understand?"

"Yes, my lord," she responded, her voice choked up, and on the verge of weeping. The prospect of losing all contact with Bartie was burning her up inside but she was just about holding herself together.

"Will there be anything else my lord?"

"Yes, take off your clothes."

"My lord?"

"Take off your clothes. If I have to ask again, I will have you whipped."

She was terrified, but this was more than she could bear. Somehow she found the strength to stand up for herself.

"No, my lord, if that is meant to be part of my

duties then I shall leave your service tomorrow," she was trembling as she spoke. She knew this meant never seeing Bartie again, a probable flogging, and a life of poverty and destitution to follow. But she wasn't going to take her clothes off for this monster.

"Hmmm," Mortimer hummed to himself as he crossed to a small table and picked up a silver snuff box. "This went missing from my father's study a few days ago. It was found in your old bedroom this evening."

"I've never seen it before in my life, I swear it."

"Is that so? Would you like to tell that to the constable? Who do you think he will believe: Lord Mortimer, newly anointed member of the House of Lords, or little Sally Trigg, housemaid? Your old master's corpse barely cold and you stealing from him already; looks pretty bad doesn't it, Trigg? Fifty lashes and transportation to one of the Australian colonies: that would be about the size of it. I hear nearly a third of the convicts die on the ship. It's worst for the girls. If the men get hold of them… well, they're not gentle like me. So, shall I send for the constable or are you going to take your clothes off?"

She swallowed her sobs, lifted her chin and looked him straight in the eyes, "Send for the constable, I am not afraid."

Her response seemed to throw him off track. He put down the snuff box, turned away, and began to pace up and down, rubbing his chin. Then he chuckled to himself and turned back to her, "Brave girl. Yes, very brave indeed. All right then, I'll admit it, we didn't find it in your room, we found it in Bartie's, along with several other missing items and pawnbrokers' receipts for half the family silver. It looks very much as if he has been stealing from father for some time. Gambling problems, I believe, awfully sad. I have witnesses ready to swear they saw him taking the box during the reception yesterday. Atrocious behaviour; the court is likely to assume he's started to get desperate now I've inherited everything and he's not got father to go begging to for money. There's certainly enough evidence to convict him in any case... *if* I decide to press charges."

He smiled at her; clearly he knew he had the trump card this time. Staring back into her eyes, he continued, "Poor boy, he's not as strong as me. It would be a shame if he never got the chance to grow into a man. I don't imagine being chained up on a prison ship will suit him terribly well. He's quite a good-looking boy really. Some of the men prefer that, I understand. So, shall I send for the constable?"

She was crying as she began to take off her clothes. Marcus watched her placing them in a neat pile on the floor. Laughing, he gestured at her missing fingertips, "I can't understand why you're so upset. I would have thought someone with such a hideous deformity would have been grateful for any attention they got."

Naked, she stood before him, proud and straight, her hands by her sides, not trying to hide anything. She stared back at him, the light in her eyes undiminished, despite her tears.

"For Bartie," she said.

*

When he was done with her, he told her to leave but, in addition to her other duties, she would be required to attend his chamber at midnight every night he was in residence. If she failed to comply, or tried to leave his employment, he'd see to it Bartie was arrested and charged with theft, with the inevitable consequences.

His ability to keep finding new ways to abuse her body horrified and astounded her. Within weeks, she was looking pale, drawn, and sickly. Bartie tried to ask what was wrong, but she could only whisper, "I can't speak to you." It broke her heart.

In the summer of 1808, she realised she was pregnant. Mortimer seemed to know as soon as she did. He waited a few weeks then called for the constable and played out the snuff box charade. She protested her innocence, but it did no good. The constable put her in irons and sent her to London, where she was tried, found guilty, and, as Mortimer had predicted, sentenced to fifty lashes and transportation to New South Wales.

On the prison ship, she discovered she was listed as Smith instead of Trigg; Mortimer had bribed one of the guards to give her name to another woman. It came as no surprise; he'd taken everything else from her, why not her name too.

If you wanted to survive the voyage, you learned to sleep with one eye open. She found that out the hard way, in the first week, the night someone stole her rations. It was a tough lesson but, in the long run, the thief did her a favour.

She bartered another week's rations for a knife. It was a bargain well struck: she used it to fight off the men. Most of them backed down, but one simply laughed at her, "You ain't gonna use that on me; you're a spoiled little bitch what grew up in a mansion changing bed sheets. You don't know what real life's about, you dumb cunt. Now, drop the knife, lift your skirts an' don't give me no trouble, an' I won't hurt ya. Not much, anyway," he leered at her as he shuffled forwards, his breeches already pulled down to his knees, his pox-ridden dick standing to attention.

One swift slash of the knife, and he was curled up on the deck, screaming.

"I grew up in a mansion changing bed sheets soaked in my own blood. You're the one who doesn't know what real life is about," she picked up his severed member and threw it to him; "take this useless thing and go, before I take your balls as well."

The men left her alone after that. There were easier pickings who didn't fight back.

She lost the baby somewhere in the Indian Ocean. There was a great deal of blood. For a while, she feared she would soon join the others who'd perished, dumped over the side. But she recovered. By the time the ship dropped anchor in Sydney Cove, the frightened young girl, sobbing and pleading as she was arrested for a crime she hadn't committed, a crime that hadn't even taken place, had grown into a strong, determined woman.

Standing on the deck, gazing over the railing at the strange land that would be her home for the rest of her life, she felt ready to face anything. Whatever hardships lay ahead, she was certain it would be a better life than being Mortimer's plaything.

The ache in her broken, empty heart grew, as it always did whenever she thought of the world she'd left behind. She was certain of something else too.

She would never forget Bartie.

IX

DECISIONS

Someone was shaking her, trying to wake her up. She opened her eyes and saw Sun-lee. "We're coming in to land, Doctor Carpenter; you need to put on your safety belt."

Rousing herself from her sleep, Susan held up her hand to check her fingers, knowing it was a foolish impulse, but feeling compelled to do it all the same. Breathing a sigh of relief when she saw her digits were intact, she sat up straight and fastened her seatbelt. That had been one hell of a dream.

The little jet seemed to swoop to the ground alarmingly quickly, but soon it was taxiing to the stand and Mortimer came through the curtain from the cockpit. She looked at him feeling nonplussed. It was him, he'd been in her dream; he even had the same name. As he sat opposite, she couldn't shake off the seemingly all too real memories of what had happened, apparently with this same man, but over two centuries ago. She remembered being on her hands and knees by the fire, her mutilated fingers next to the rough patch in the rug, the pain…

"Did you get a good rest, Susan?" he asked, interrupting her thoughts

"Er, yes, not bad thank you, er… Marcus. Although I did have a rather strange dream," she sneaked another glance at her hand.

"How interesting, you must tell me about it some time. Right now though, we need to clear customs and immigration and then Hans will take you to my villa."

"You're not coming?"

"No, I am afraid I have some business to attend to here in Dubai first. But I will attend to *you* later, I assure you." A shiver ran up her spine. Was that a promise of support or a threat? It could be construed as either. She managed a weak smile.

"Don't worry, my dear, Hans is extremely dependable. He's very efficient, especially when it comes to, er… well, er… shall we say getting rid of problems. Been with me a long time, one way or another; I should call him the faithful Hans."

He smiled at his joke, which Susan failed to comprehend. Then he flashed a strange look at her that made her tremendously uneasy. For a horrible moment, she felt as if he was contemplating whether to eat her.

*

Despite Susan's misgivings, everything went smoothly for the next few days. As soon as they cleared the airport, Hans took her straight to Mortimer's villa, 150 miles south of Dubai, in the neighbouring emirate of Abu Dhabi.

This was desert living, luxury style. The lobby had an array of mirrors arranged around the walls, with frames of pure gold stretching from floor to ceiling. Beyond that, each room was filled with priceless paintings, antiques, and more gold everywhere you looked. The views outside were stunning, especially around sunrise and sunset, and the villa had its own water source, electricity generator, swimming pool, gym, games room, helipad... you name it.

As time went on, Susan began to relax and forget about strange dreams and the odd sense of dread she'd been experiencing lately. Her headache disappeared and she started to feel more like her old self. She worked on her presentation for the conference and her personal statement for her Deputy Head application. She felt pleased with the results of both.

She took to walking around the grounds at dawn and dusk, the most beautiful and hospitable times of day. On the last evening before the conference, she walked a mile or so out into the desert and turned her thoughts to Ray and his drug abuse. Walking had always helped her face her problems. It didn't fail her now. By the time she returned to the villa as the desert night was falling, she knew what she had to do.

The following morning, Hans drove her to the

conference venue in Dubai in Mortimer's gold-coloured Rolls Royce. She was scheduled as the second speaker that afternoon. During the buffet lunch, she stood with the other delegates, holding a plateful of food, but she could barely eat a thing. She hadn't realised how big the conference was, nor how many of the most senior and well-respected members of the neurology profession would be there. She felt completely out of her depth.

As one of the speakers, she was guided to a seat in the front row for the afternoon session. Her nerves continued to mount as she listened to the first speaker, Professor Benneyworth; one of the world's leading experts on epilepsy. He was a man she'd admired for many years and his presentation was superb. As he finished, she joined the rest of the audience in applauding him. Inside, she was thinking, 'I can't follow that, what am I doing here?'

When the applause finally petered out, the conference chair took the podium and began her introduction, "Our next speaker is Doctor Susan Carpenter from the Brain Trauma Unit at Princess Diana Memorial Hospital in the UK. She is going to update us on the latest advances in the treatment of brain trauma. Doctor Carpenter graduated first in her class at…"

As Susan sat listening to her own introduction, she wanted to run, to find any excuse not to go up on stage. She was terrified of failing, terrified of the awful embarrassment of being exposed as no more than a foolish little girl in front of the most prominent members of her profession.

"… Ladies and Gentlemen, Doctor Susan Carpenter," the chair led the audience in welcoming her with a round of applause. Slowly, she mounted the steps, feeling like she was going to her death. As she crossed the platform, a brief image flashed though her mind: a wooden stake with a pyre lying around it. For a moment, she felt she was being dragged towards it by unseen hands.

She reached the podium and stared at the audience. The room itself was intimidating enough, a purpose-built auditorium seating several hundred. But, worse still, among the delegates she recognised two of her university lecturers, the head of her old department at Queen Square, and many others of 'the great and the good' in the neurology world, including Professor Benneyworth. They were still applauding but, in her mind, it sounded like jeering and screaming. Did someone shout 'burn'?

Then, clear as a bell, she heard another voice, 'You can do it, Doctor Susie, sock it to 'em sweetheart.' She glanced down to see the toy bow from her childhood in her hand. She smiled. "Thanks Dad," she whispered. She blinked and the bow became the 'clicker' for controlling the slides in her presentation.

Raising her head, she faced the audience and clicked onto her first slide, "Well, how do I follow Professor Benneyworth? I feel like a pub singer following the Rolling Stones." A few delegates laughed. Encouraged, she began her presentation.

Nervous at first, she stuttered a little once or twice, but gradually her passion for the subject took control. Her nerves fell away and her confidence surged. She started to enjoy herself and could tell it showed. The allotted hour flew by and she knew she had the audience's full attention. Although she hadn't prepared it, she decided on the spur of the moment to end on a personal note.

"When I was a medical student, my father was in a tragic accident and suffered severe brain trauma. Three days later, we lost him. He's still with me in spirit, of course. In fact, just an hour ago, he told me to sock it to you lot." This time everyone laughed and she had to pause before continuing.

"But, with the help of these new techniques, it is my earnest hope that the next time a young medical student's parent, or any loved one, suffers severe brain trauma then, when the time comes for that student to stand here, petrified and humbled in the company of the giants of their profession, their loved one will still be with them, not just in spirit, but in body too. Thank you for your attention ladies and gentlemen."

She stood back from the podium and the auditorium exploded into applause. Some of the delegates began to stand and it turned into an ovation. Susan blushed. She hadn't expected anything like this. She'd feared the embarrassment of failure, but this was something completely different: the embarrassment of success perhaps? The conference chair shook her hand and, as she descended the steps from the stage, Professor Benneyworth rushed over to her.

"Blast that Doreen for getting in first," Benneyworth

looked at the conference chair, an old friend, and gave her a wink, "I wanted to be the first to congratulate you. Well, let me be the second anyway." He grabbed Susan's hand and shook it vigorously, clapping her on the shoulder at the same time, "Well done, young lady, that was magnificent, the best presentation I've ever seen I think."

"Er, thank you professor, that's really kind of you. But I don't think I'm in your league, or the other speakers', I haven't got the experience, or depth of knowledge, I'm just a..."

"Nonsense, you were brilliant. Your knowledge is excellent and experience will come. It's overrated anyway; even that idiot Worthington has experience. Not that he ever learns from it. But you've got something few others possess. Not just a passion for the subject, but an ability to convey that passion. It's infectious. You're infectious. And keep bringing in that personal stuff at the end; an inspired way to finish."

"Well, professor, that's so..."

"Oh and call me Ricky by the way. I'm just an ordinary bloke, you know."

"Er... OK, Prof... er, Ricky. You're very kind, I did my best. I'm just glad it wasn't a disaster."

He laughed, "It was far from that, Susan. May I call you Susan?" She nodded. "Well, Susan, why don't we go and grab a coffee."

They left the auditorium and made their way to the break-out area where afternoon refreshments were being served. It took a while to get there, many of the delegates wanted to congratulate one or both of them on their presentations. Mostly Susan, which seemed to delight Benneyworth enormously.

Once they had their drinks, Benneyworth led her to a quiet corner, "So, Susan, you know I chair the World Neurology Council don't you?"

"Yes, of course, Prof... er, Ricky"

"Well, we need more young people on the council, particularly young women. You tick a lot of boxes, Susan; do you think the council is something that might interest you?"

"Gosh, er, yeah, er... that's quite an honour. Umm, I don't know though, I'm not sure I could get enough leave to attend the meetings, aren't they held all over the world?"

"Yes they are, but I think I may have the answer to that."

*

Back at the villa that night, Susan lay awake, thinking about the remarkable day she'd had. She was glad the presentation had gone so well, couldn't believe it really. Then Professor Benneyworth's invitation to join the World Neurology Council: that was amazing. Best of all though was his other offer. Never mind applying for Deputy Head at Princess Diana, he'd offered her Head of Neurology at Shilling Club Hospital in Sydney. He'd said he would put in the word and the post was hers if she wanted. God, it was like a dream come true. It was a smaller hospital and a less well-known unit but, even so, her own department; that would be incredible.

She'd told him she'd have to think about it and to give her some time, which he'd graciously accepted. But, in truth, what was there to think about? There was nothing to keep her in the UK, certainly not the mother she despised, or her junkie ex-lover. She smiled to herself. That would help when she reported Ray to the authorities. No-one could accuse her of an ulterior motive if she was off to Australia.

There were a few friends and colleagues she would miss. She'd got to know Jenny Fletcher fairly well, and she had some good friends from university and Queen Square. But they'd all understand. And they could visit, that would be fun.

Suddenly, she found herself thinking of Ben Carlton. Why was he on her mind? He was fully recovered; she didn't need to worry about him. She had other patients still in residence, what was so special about Carlton?

She tried to shrug off her feelings, but she realised there was more to them than her responsibilities as a doctor. Why though? She'd only spoken to him a couple of times since he'd come out of his coma. Was this the fabled 'love at first sight'?

"I hardly think so," she scoffed. The last time she'd seen him had been pretty weird though, maybe that was why he was in her thoughts?

Turning over, she closed her eyes, and did her best to push Carlton out of her head. Slowly, the day's excitement subsided and she drifted off to sleep. And then she dreamt.

X

CAPTIVES

Moon Shadow had gathered every boy with fourteen summers, and every man with less than sixty. As usual, there were no women: except for She Wolf. No-one would speak against her inclusion; they all knew she was the best in the tribe with a bow. Apart from Moon Shadow himself, of course.

Other tribes were more tolerant of the white settlers, but Moon Shadow said the palefaces would steal all the land if they weren't stopped. He told the raiding party to kill the white men but capture the women and children alive if possible. The women would be put to work and used to breed sons; the children would be raised as part of the tribe if he deemed them young enough.

They approached the settlement in the darkness before dawn, creeping to within the length of four tree trunks from the perimeter, then crawling on their bellies to their final holding position to await the sunrise. As the first tiny sliver of sun appeared above the horizon, Moon Shadow gave the signal.

She Wolf ran forward with the others. Although she had only seventeen summers, she was an experienced warrior. She had been on many raids, and wasn't afraid to fight as ferociously as anyone in the tribe.

The raiders took the white men by surprise, killing more than half before they could reach their firesticks. Once they had their weapons, the startled settlers began to fight back, but their aim was not at its best. She Wolf rushed at one, standing beside a wooden shack. He hastily raised his firestick and it spat flame, but his shot flew wide. She put an arrow through his eye, leaving him twitching in the dirt. Running around the corner of the shack, she saw another white man standing in front of her. She raised her bow, ready to strike, but hesitated. Was this a man or a boy? There was no hair on his chin, as most of the white men had, and he was smaller than the others, with soft brown eyes that made him look like a girl.

She made a swift decision. This wasn't a man, this was a child. Her duty was to capture not kill. She lowered her bow but continued to run forward, pulling a club from a fold in her clothing. Reaching the frightened boy, she struck him unconscious.

As the boy fell to the ground, a woman ran from the shack. "Bobby!" she shouted, and rushed towards him. She Wolf struck her too and she fell to the dirt beside her son.

Returning to the middle of the settlement, She Wolf could see the last two white men were putting up a fight. They had killed three tribesmen and badly wounded another. The rest of the raiding party had them surrounded but were reluctant to approach close enough to get an accurate shot. Instead, they were firing a barrage of arrows at the settlers, inflicting many wounds, but lacking the skill to decisively end the conflict.

She Wolf glanced at Moon Shadow. He was smiling as he watched, seemingly content to let the struggle continue. She did not like this; a hunter would not treat a deer this way. She raised her bow, took aim, and shot one of the settlers straight through the heart.

Emboldened, the other warriors moved forward, concentrating their fire on the last man. Riddled with arrows, he dropped his gun and fell to the ground.

"Enough," shouted Moon Shadow, "take his firestick and let him bleed, he is finished."

Having dealt with the men, the raiding party began rounding up the women and children, threatening them with bow and arrow, spear and club. Most fell to their knees, huddled together in a group, crying and whimpering, offering no further resistance. But a small band, made up of three women and one of the older boys, made a run for it. Moon Shadow watched them go. She Wolf could tell he was toying with them, letting them think they had a chance. His abilities with the bow were legendary, both the range and accuracy of his shots famed among all the tribes within a quarter moon's journey in every direction. He waited until the runaways were climbing a hill, far beyond the reach of most archers, then raised his bow and loosed an arrow. It hit the running boy in the back, passed through his heart, and came out protruding from his chest, spearing him like a fish caught in the shallows.

Moon Shadow turned to three of his warriors and gestured for them to follow the running women, "Crazy Rabbit, Sleeping Bear, Dark Cloud, you will catch them and bring them back."

She Wolf watched the tribesmen swiftly gaining on the settlers, who were hampered by their cumbersome garments. One fell to her knees and begged for mercy. Crazy Rabbit grabbed her by the hair and pulled her behind a bush. Her screams lasted a few minutes more; then were silenced.

The other men caught the remaining runaways and dragged them back to the settlement. She Wolf asked Sleeping Bear if he would help her and they returned to where Bobby and his mother lay outside their home. They carried the unconscious settlers back and added them to the group of prisoners.

Nine of the white women had been captured alive. She Wolf and the others stood guard over them while Dark Cloud and Burning Tree pulled each one in turn from the terrified group then tore off her clothes and made her stand in front of Moon Shadow. The chief examined each woman and gave his verdict, awarding her to a tribesman who'd proved himself worthy in the fighting. After she had been allocated, Jumping Toad bound her hands behind her back then tied a rope around her neck and attached it to the last woman's hands, linking the women into a human train.

There was a great deal of joking among the men as each man who received a woman was teased by his comrades. They made cruel remarks about any imperfection, or the woman's age or size. "She will crush you in your bed, Sleeping Bear"; "She is so old and dry you will get stuck inside, Jumping Toad"; "She is so ugly you will have to shut your eyes, Burning Tree" …

One of the surviving runaways was a beautiful young woman with long, golden hair. This was a novelty for the tribesmen, a huge source of fascination. It was no surprise when Moon Shadow announced he would take her himself. He also took Bobby's mother. There was no joking when he made these awards; no-one questioned his right to take two women, even though he already had four others.

The last of the nine was an older woman, with perhaps around sixty-five summers. Moon Shadow examined her, reaching out and prodding her sagging breasts. She clearly didn't understand when he said, "A waste of food." He turned slightly, then whirled back around, club in hand, and she lay dead at his feet.

With all the surviving women now allocated, Crazy Rabbit demanded, "My chief, why is there no woman for me, did I not fight bravely?"

"I ordered the women to be captured but you disobeyed me. You chose to take a woman on your own and dispose of her so no other might have use of her. Be silent or I will take my knife to your shaft and make *you* a woman," retorted Moon Shadow.

Crazy Rabbit fell quiet. This was no empty threat. Moon Shadow's knife had a serrated edge that made it more lethal than any other known to the tribe. He'd taken it from a paleface three summers ago and She Wolf had seen him use it on both enemies and tribespeople alike.

Moon Shadow went to examine the children. There were six in total, ranging from a small baby to Bobby, the eldest surviving child by far. Moon Shadow picked the baby up by one leg and held it dangling upside down in front of his face. The baby began to wail. The woman who'd been awarded to Burning Tree started beseeching the chief, straining forwards as far as her bonds would allow. She Wolf could not understand her words, but it was clear she was pleading for the child's life. The baby's cries were suddenly cut short as Moon Shadow threw it through the air towards Crazy Rabbit, "Here, you can have this in place of a woman." The child's mother screamed. Crazy Rabbit hopped to one side and the baby flew head first into a rock then fell into the dirt, motionless and silent.

The mother collapsed onto her knees, dragging half the women down with her. Most of the tribesmen laughed, but She Wolf turned her face away. She was not afraid to kill when it was needed, but she couldn't bear to see a helpless infant slain for no good reason. Turning back, she watched Moon Shadow pulling the other children to their feet, either tugging their hair or grasping them by the neck. He pushed them towards the women. Three ran crying to grab one of the women around the leg. The fourth stood, forlorn and silent, nearby. Lastly, the chief came to Bobby. He ordered Jumping Toad to pull him upright. After looking the boy over, Moon Shadow turned to his warriors, "Why is this one alive when I ordered the white men to be killed?"

She Wolf stepped forward, "I spared him, my chief. He is but a child and you ordered the children to be captured."

"He has fourteen or fifteen summers, he is too old to join the tribe. You will dispose of this white man-child."

"Yes, my chief," She Wolf moved forward, ready to obey. But, as she approached Bobby, club in hand, she looked into his eyes and felt an overwhelming sense of empathy. She couldn't bring herself to take his life. Instead, she turned and, for the first time in her life, dared to question Moon Shadow.

"My chief, it seems unfair the other warriors are rewarded for their bravery, but I am not. Would it not be fair for me to take this boy as my reward?"

Many of the tribesmen laughed. One taunted, "She Wolf wants this boy to be her woman."

Moon Shadow raised his arms, "Silence." For a moment, he seemed to be considering her request. But, when he reached for his club, she knew he was about to strike the killer blow himself. Ironically, it was Crazy Rabbit's intervention that saved Bobby.

"She Wolf is promised to me. You have already made me wait until she has eighteen summers because of her skill with the bow. You cannot allow this white snake into her bed, she is mine. I will dispose of this poisonous creature." He moved towards Bobby, his club raised, ready to smash the boy's skull.

Moon Shadow moved so swiftly it was as if he disappeared from one place and reappeared in another. With one quick blow of his club, he left Crazy Rabbit lying stunned in the dirt, "I will decide who goes to who's bed, and when. If you dare try to usurp my authority again, you will go to your ancestors in the bellies of the ants." He was referring to the method of execution the tribe reserved for the worst traitors and wrongdoers and, in many cases, anyone else he thought should die the same way.

It was a horrible death. The condemned was tied naked to a post and left in the open through the heat of the day and the cold of the night, with no shelter and nothing to eat. They were given water, but this was not a kindness, it only served to prolong their suffering.

The ants were the worst part. The victim's legs were smeared with a paste that attracted the vicious red killer ants from their nearby nest. Once they began to feed, the victim's blood mingled with the paste and brought more of them. The last person Moon Shadow had sent to the ants had taken eight days to die as the insects gradually ate their way from feet to torso then head. The voracious creatures were working on their ears, nose and eyes by the time their heart gave out. After that, the ants consumed the corpse, picking it clean, leaving nothing but a skeleton to be bleached by the sun. Many of the tribe's clubs were made from the bones of such victims.

She Wolf was pleased when Moon Shadow turned to face her again, but he had a grim reminder for her too, "Very well, you are indeed one of the bravest warriors in the tribe. You may take this boy as your reward. But I expect you to keep him under control. If he disobeys, he will feed the ants. And, She Wolf," he fixed her with a gaze as deadly as the serrated steel blade of his knife, "if he goes to your bed, you will *both* feed the ants."

*

The party marched back to the tribal village. Jumping Toad led the weeping women. They stumbled along, several of them fell. Their bare feet, unaccustomed to going unshod, were soon cut and bleeding. They were in a sorry state when they reached their destination, but they all survived.

She Wolf led Bobby. As Moon Shadow had instructed, she had stripped the boy naked, tied a rope around his neck, and bound his hands behind his back, in the same fashion as the women. The boy followed meekly, but he did not stumble and she did not pull on his rope like Jumping Toad pulled the women. As a result, he arrived at the village in better shape than the others, although plainly still scared and shaken.

Following at the rear were Crazy Rabbit and the children. Moon Shadow had charged him with the task as a punishment, threatening, "For any that do not arrive, I will take a finger from your hand." The tribesmen laughed at his efforts to keep the youngsters moving with an almost slapstick combination of pulling, pushing, and sometimes even carrying them. Luckily for him, they wanted to follow the women anyway. His difficulties arose simply because they couldn't keep up the pace set by Moon Shadow. He was noticeably relieved when he finally delivered his charges to the village.

*

Over the next few days, the captives began to find out what lay in store for them.

She Wolf made a shelter outside her tent for Bobby and showed him how to gather berries and grubs, catch rabbits and fish, and wash her clothes. She took him to see the posts by the ants' nest and tried to warn him what would happen if he disobeyed, but she didn't get the feeling he understood.

The children were each given to one of the native women. Their desperate, heartbroken mothers only saw them if they happened to spy them from afar, across the village. There was little time even for that, as the captured women soon learned they were expected to work all day and do whatever their man wished at night. Life was not easy for any of them, but the way they were treated varied enormously.

*

Frances was petrified as Sleeping Bear led her to his tent. She'd seen how brutal the native warriors were, she was certain he was going to rape her. She wasn't going to fight; she knew it would only make it worse. She hoped if she was compliant, did what he asked, he wouldn't hurt her too much.

The unmarried, nineteen-year-old daughter of one of the settlers, her mother had died from a fever last year and she'd been living with her father and younger brother, Michael, before the attack. Moon Shadow's long shot had killed Michael. Her father had been the penultimate man to die, saved any further suffering by She Wolf's precision. Frances was grateful for that, it had been a mercy.

They entered the tent. Frances was surprised when the tribesman untied her and gave her clothes, food, and water. But then he gestured to the cot in the corner. She lay down, shaking in fear, waiting for him to force himself upon her. Instead, he left the tent for a few minutes and came back with a small container made of animal skin. The skin-bucket held cool river water, which he used to clean her bloody feet.

Later, he crawled into the cot beside her. Again, she began to tremble, expecting the worst, but he only held her, although she could feel he was aroused. He spoke softly to her. She couldn't understand his words, but she felt comforted by them and she was able to sleep.

The next day, he showed her what her chores were. Things were strange at first, but she soon found attending to his needs was easier than looking after her father and brother. Each night, he would touch her a little more as they lay in the cot together. He gradually explored her body, but he was tender and gentle, and he didn't rush her. On the fourth night, she began to reciprocate. When he climbed on top of her on the sixth night, she was ready. She wanted him.

Sleeping Bear treated Frances well. But she was the lucky one. Most of the women suffered days of endless drudgery and brutal nights at the hands of the men. The tribesmen were accustomed to being obeyed and many took this as an excuse to treat their women harshly. Their contempt for the captured settlers exacerbated matters.

Anna Jenkins was given to Burning Tree. As he led her to his tent, she was in a state of shock. Her baby Tommy's life had been snuffed out in a moment of senseless brutality, and her darling little Becky had been taken from her and given to one of the savages. She was beside herself with grief and worry.

The strain of horror and anxiety was compounded by the cruel treatment she was subjected to. For the next two days, Burning Tree kept her tied to his cot while he repeatedly raped and sodomised her. As he was leaving on the third morning, he spoke to one of his native women.

The woman untied Anna then sat her up and tried to give her some water. The liquid dribbled from Anna's mouth as she stared vacantly into space. The woman persisted in her attempts to help Anna. She bathed her injuries and dressed her in the simple garments the tribal women wore. She tried to feed her some fresh berries, but it was to no avail. The food fell to the ground while Anna sat unmoving, gazing blankly ahead.

When Burning Tree returned, he spoke to the native woman. When she replied, he began shouting. She raised her voice in response, trying to defend herself. The second native woman began shouting too. Burning Tree silenced the first with a vicious blow across her face, knocking her off her feet. The second woman fell quiet, cowering before him.

Turning to Anna, he grabbed her by her long, dark hair and dragged her from the tent. She didn't make a sound; her addled mind was in a place where he could no longer hurt her. He took her to Moon Shadow, like a dissatisfied customer returning a faulty purchase. The chief listened to his complaints, nodded, and then gave an order to his native women. Two of them took Anna to the clearing in the centre of the village. They forced her to sit on the ground with her back to a wooden post and tied her to it, beside another woman.

The other prisoner was Deborah Adams, the supposedly 'old and dry' woman given to Jumping Toad, although she was only forty-three. She was the wife of the settlement's leader, the last man to die, and one of the women who'd tried to make a run for it. She'd spent the long march from the settlement working to loosen the rope binding her wrists; they were raw and bleeding by the time she reached the village, but she'd done enough to be able to pull her hands free when the moment was right. As the savage took her to his tent, she knew what he was planning, it was written all over his face, evident in the way he leered at her. Once inside, he started groping her, squeezing her breasts, putting his hand on her naked crotch. Holding the rope around her neck, he led her to his cot. He leaned across, undoubtedly aiming to tie her to it. But he made the mistake of turning his back.

In a flash, she was on him. She scratched and tore at his face, nearly taking out his eye. He twisted around and grabbed her bleeding wrists. She slammed her knee into his groin, forcing him to release her then turned to run. But he still had a grip on the rope and yanked her back. He knocked her to the floor and started to climb on top of her.

She lay on her back, struggling on the dirt floor. Again, she scratched at him, clawing deep gouges in his cheeks, forearms, and back. He seized her arms and pinned her to the ground. As he fought to hold her down, he lowered his head. She jerked forward, clamped her teeth on his ear, and bit down hard. Wrenching her head to the side, she tore a piece away.

He screamed and fell off her, clutching at what remained of his ear. Spitting out the torn flesh, she jumped to her feet and, this time, was able to break out of the tent. She got about a hundred yards before Moon

Shadow's club came whirling through the air and struck the side of her head.

When she came to, she was tied to the post. She'd been there for three days without food or shelter by the time Moon Shadow's women brought Anna. As soon as the native women had gone, she tried to talk to the new arrival, keeping her voice to a low whisper. But Anna didn't respond and, eventually, Deborah gave up. Still naked, she shivered through the bitter cold of the long, dark night. She began to think the tribe was going to leave them there until they starved... or froze. But, as dawn broke the next day, two tribesmen came and untied them from the post. The men bound their hands behind their backs then took them across the clearing and forced them to kneel in front of a large wooden chair, beside the biggest tent in the village.

Deborah watched as the tribe slowly gathered around them. It looked like some sort of trial was about to take place; their fate would soon be decided. She didn't hold out much hope for their survival, but she prayed whatever happened would at least be quick.

The tent flap to her right was suddenly thrown back and the tribal chief stepped out. She stared at him for a moment until the tribesman standing behind her pushed her head down, forcing her to look at the ground.

*

Brown Doe came to She Wolf's tent just after dawn. "Everyone is to attend a gathering," Moon Shadow's woman said; "bring your prisoner and make sure he is restrained as required by tribal law."

She Wolf tied a rope around Bobby's neck and led him to the clearing, where Moon Shadow was already sitting in the big wooden chair. Brown Doe and his other women were taking up position around him. Bobby's mother and the golden-haired woman knelt on the ground, tied to the chair. They looked pale and tired. No-one knew what they had endured the last few days, but most of the tribe had heard the sounds coming from the chief's tent.

Bobby gasped when he saw his mother. He waved at her, trying to catch her eye, but she just stared at the ground. She Wolf tugged on his rope to keep him still.

Two more white women were kneeling in front of Moon Shadow, their hands bound, heads bowed. As she waited with the rest of the tribe, She Wolf felt sorry for them. She knew what was coming. They did not deserve it, whatever they might have done.

She was jostled as Crazy Rabbit pushed his way to the front of the crowd. Watching him licking his lips, she could see he was savouring the prospect of more suffering being meted out to the settlers. She hated this needless cruelty many of the tribesmen seemed to crave. Fighting an enemy with honour was one thing, but tormenting helpless captives was another. She looked around, hoping to see someone else who felt as uncomfortable as she did, and spotted Sleeping Bear standing at the back. He looked as unhappy to be here as she was. He was speaking softly to the white woman he held by a rope, apologising to her for having to treat her this way. She Wolf smiled as she saw the look on the woman's face. Clearly she couldn't understand a word Sleeping Bear was saying, but she seemed to understand his sentiment.

When everyone was finally gathered, Moon Shadow raised his arms. Silence fell over the crowd. Lowering his arms, he gestured towards the women kneeling in front of him, "These women are accused of disobedience to their men-owners." The word he used for 'men' also meant 'owners' in the tribe's language. "Who speaks against them?"

"I do," Burning Tree stepped forward. He pointed at Anna, "This woman was awarded to me for my bravery at the settlement. But she has withdrawn her spirit and refuses to give herself to me as a woman should. She does no work, no chores; she is of no value. I wish to be rid of her." As he made his accusations, Anna looked up. But she did not look at him, or Moon Shadow; she just stared into the distance.

Burning Tree moved on to Deborah, "This woman attacked our brother warrior in his tent. As you can see, she has inflicted grievous injuries upon him and he suffers greatly." Burning Tree gestured at Jumping Toad, who sat on the ground beside him, moaning softly to himself. Even from a distance, She Wolf could see his wounded ear was badly infected.

"And what recompense do you demand?" asked Moon Shadow.

"My chief, we demand these disobedient women be fed to the ants and their bones used to make clubs and other tools, so they might at last be of some use to us," Burning Tree recited the call for execution of a traitor.

"Does anyone speak for these women?"

The chief's question was part of the ritual. No-one was expected to answer. She Wolf was almost as surprised as everyone else when she found herself speaking up. But she had a new-found confidence since she'd saved Bobby at the settlement that made her want to try again.

"My chief, how can these women be punished for disobeying their men-owners when they surely do not yet understand they belong to these men?"

"She Wolf, you know the law as well as any. They belong to these men and they must obey, that is the law," Moon Shadow responded.

Undeterred, she tried again. She knew she wouldn't be able to persuade Moon Shadow to spare the women's lives, but she might at least save them from the ants, "My chief, that is true and the law is just and fair. I accept these women must be punished. But, my chief, these women are not part of the tribe, so they cannot be traitors. I demand they be given the clean death of an honoured enemy."

"No, they must be fed to the ants," Burning Tree objected.

Moon Shadow held up his hands for silence. He looked at Burning Tree, "These women disobeyed you. That is true. So they must be punished." Burning Tree smiled, gloating in triumph as he looked at She Wolf. But the smile was soon wiped from his face as Moon Shadow continued, "However, the women disobeyed because you,

Burning Tree, were too cruel and you, Jumping Toad, were too stupid. Without your cruelty and stupidity, we might have two more women to breed sons for the tribe. Now we shall lose them." He turned to face She Wolf as he rose from his chair and walked behind Anna, "She Wolf is right, these women are not part of the tribe and they should be given the clean death of an honoured enemy."

Taking out the vicious knife with the serrated edge, he pulled Anna's head back, and cut her throat. She didn't make a sound as her soul escaped to rejoin the broken mind that had left days before.

Deborah tensed, waiting for her turn. As Moon Shadow pulled her head back, she whispered, "I'm coming, Robert." A second later, she was lying on the ground, blood flooding through the gaping wound in her throat. As the light began to fade around her, she saw the events of the next few days with absolute clarity. She saw the infection to Jumping Toad's wound get a stronger grip, saw him getting a fever, slipping in and out of consciousness, and finally dying in unbearable agony. In her last fleeting moments, she actually managed to smile.

*

The surviving white women adapted to their new lives. Most of them found that as long as they obeyed their man-owner, day and night, life was tolerable. But the women Moon Shadow had taken were rarely seen, and the dreadful sounds kept coming from his tent.

Frances grew happier with each passing day as she got to know Sleeping Bear and began to feel more like his wife than his captive. She learned his language and, once they were able to speak, she discovered more about him. He'd only been with one other woman, and she had died giving him a son last winter. The boy died a few days later, leaving him alone again. Frances's heart went out to him as she realised how devastatingly lonely he must have been. As the months passed, she grew to love him very much, and knew he loved her back. She felt lucky to have found such a good man; she could not imagine ever being with anyone else.

She Wolf continued to train Bobby. He gathered food, fetched water, cleaned her clothes, kept her bows and arrows in good order, and attended to any other tasks she required of him. She began teaching him to use a bow and arrow so he could hunt rabbits but, when Moon Shadow found out, he forbid her from carrying on.

She was more successful teaching Bobby the tribe's language. She picked up a few words of English in return and, after a few months, they were able to communicate fairly well. The tribe had no name for a relationship like theirs, so he began calling her 'my chief' after he heard the tribespeople addressing Moon Shadow. "No, Bobbee," she tried to persuade him, "we only say 'my chief' to Moon Shadow; he is our chief."

"You *my* chief," Bobby replied, so it seemed she was stuck with it. She grew to like it though. She would never really be a chief, of course, but it was nice to have someone calling her chief, even if it was misplaced.

"Chores done, my chief, you want me do more?" Bobby asked one evening as she was staring into the fire he'd built for her, deep in thought. When she didn't answer after a while, he asked, "My chief sad?"

She looked up in surprise. She would never have expected a white boy to sense what she was feeling. "Soon it will be summer," she sighed; "I will have eighteen summers and I will be made to go to Crazy Rabbit's bed, as his father was promised by my father many moons ago. I would have gone in my sixteenth summer if I had not been skilled with the bow."

Watching him struggle to comprehend her words, she saw him frown as their meaning became clear. It took him a moment to formulate his answer, "My chief much big good with bow, I have seen. Maybe big chief let my chief stay warrior?"

She smiled. He genuinely did seem to care. "I had hoped so, Bob-bee. I have practised with my bow many hours every day since I have had you to do my chores. My arms are stronger and my aim is better, maybe even as good as Moon Shadow himself. But, today, when I asked if I could be released from my father's promise and stay in the hunting party, he just laughed and told me I must become Crazy Rabbit's woman at the next full moon."

She was as brave and fierce a warrior as anyone in the tribe, but now she looked up at him with tears in her eyes, "My life is over, Bob-bee."

*

A few days later, She Wolf was sitting among the trees by the river, making a new batch of arrows, when Bobby came to her late in the afternoon. Even without looking up, she could sense he was nervous.

"What is it, Bob-bee?"

"My chief, I have thoughts of my mother. I would see her if you can make it so. I beg, my chief?"

His command of the language was still pretty rough, but she understood well enough. She had seen the look on his face every time they were near Moon Shadow's tent, every time he heard the awful sounds. She knew how much he was yearning for his mother, how anxious for her he was. In fact, feeling some sympathy for his plight, she had already broached the subject with Moon Shadow. The chief's response had not been encouraging.

"That is not possible, She Wolf, you should know better than to ask this impossible thing. It only proves you are a weak woman in your heart, not a true warrior. You are skilled with the bow, but you are soft. It is indeed time for you to go to Crazy Rabbit."

Now she looked up at Bobby and delivered the bad news, "I am sorry, Bob-bee; Moon Shadow has forbidden the white women from seeing their children. Truly, I am sorry; I know how much it would mean to you."

He nodded and turned away, but she could see him fighting to suppress the tears welling up inside him.

*

148

Not long after their conversation by the river, Moon Shadow called another gathering. She Wolf took Bobby to the clearing, leading him by a rope around his neck, as before. While they stood waiting, she gazed around the crowd. A few changes had taken place since last time. Sleeping Bear and Dark Cloud's women had been accepted into the tribe and were allowed to walk freely; Jumping Toad was gone; and Burning Tree had only two women left to share the burden of his sadistic carnal appetite.

Crazy Rabbit was living up to his name, hopping around excitedly in expectation of another possible execution. She Wolf shuddered as she saw him staring at her lasciviously; she knew he was anticipating their union in a few days' time. The prospect filled her with dread.

Once again, Moon Shadow sat in the wooden chair with his women standing around him. But, this time, only the golden-haired woman was kneeling, tied to the chair. Bobby's mother was missing.

At a command from Moon Shadow, two tribesmen brought her out of his tent. She stumbled along, her hands tied behind her back, her head down, not making eye contact with anyone. The marks covering her skin told of the many torments she'd suffered at the chief's hands. The tribesmen led her to the spot where Anna and Deborah's lives had been extinguished, and pushed her onto her knees. She knelt there in silence, staring at the ground.

"Mother," Bobby shouted, trying to pull away from

She Wolf. He almost broke free, but she held on to his rope, her arms strengthened from training with the bow.

Moon Shadow turned to her, "You will keep your boy quiet, or you will share this woman's fate."

"Be still," she hissed at Bobby, "there is nothing we can do for her."

"But, my chief, you helped Mrs Jenkins and Mrs Adams. You can help my mother. I beg you, my chief."

"I will do what I can. But be quiet, it will not help if you create a disturbance." He fell silent, but continued to pull against his rope.

Moon Shadow continued, "This woman is accused of disobedience to her man-owner. I speak against her myself. I demand she be fed to the ants and her bones used to make clubs and other tools, so she might at last be of some use to us."

He then said the phrase that condemned Bobby's mother to a horrendous death, "Take her to the place of the traitors."

She Wolf shouted, "My chief, you do not ask if anyone speaks for this woman."

Moon Shadow glowered at her, but the laws of the tribe obliged him to hear her out, "Speak, She Wolf, what have you to say in this woman's defence?"

"My chief, as with the other white women, I would say to you this woman is not part of the tribe. She has not become one of the people, so she cannot be a traitor. I demand she be given the clean death of an honoured enemy, as required by our law."

The chief glared back at her. She feared for her life as she waited to see how he would react. She knew she was right, a captive who hadn't been made one of the people was still classed as an enemy, and tribal law demanded enemies be given a clean death. The chief was accustomed to flouting the law to suit his own ends, but would he dare to do so in the face of such a clear challenge?

He stared at her for almost a minute, as if he was truly seeing her for the first time, sizing her up, weighing her potential threat. She looked away, shivering slightly. She'd awoken something dark and vengeful within him, made herself a target. It felt like she'd started a war. Nonetheless, when he spoke, she had at least won this battle.

"Very well, She Wolf, your demand will be met in accordance with our law," he rose from his chair and started to walk towards Bobby's mother.

"You said you would do something," Bobby hissed.

"I have done what I can, Bob-bee, perhaps too much. I can do no more," now She Wolf stared at the ground, feeling sorry she was unable to save the poor woman's life. Bobby kept straining against the rope, but she had a tight grip. Looking up again, she saw Moon Shadow coming into position behind the kneeling woman. Bobby slumped and, thinking he'd given up the struggle, she relaxed her hold a little, "It is alright Bob-bee, she…"

He pushed her away and lunged forwards. This time, he broke free. In an instant, he was running through the crowd towards his mother. She Wolf swiftly regained her balance and ran after him. Some of the tribespeople grabbed at him, slowing him down.

"Let the boy come, let us see what he will do," commanded Moon Shadow.

The tribespeople released Bobby and made way for him.

She Wolf stopped in her tracks, a few paces behind, and watched.

*

No-one was holding him back now. He stopped trying to run and dropped to a walk, heading towards the native chief standing behind his kneeling mother.

He reached Moon Shadow. The chief towered over him, looking down from at least a foot above his head.

"So, boy, what are you going to do now?" said Moon Shadow in perfect English.

"P-p-p-please sir, p-p-please let my mother go."

"Or you will do what?"

Bobby looked up at Moon Shadow's enormous frame and summoned all his courage, "Or I will have to kill you, sir."

Moon Shadow laughed for a whole minute while Bobby stared up at him, wondering if his intervention would have any effect on his mother's fate.

"Oh, will you, boy," said Moon Shadow at last, still speaking in English, "I don't think so." He gave Bobby a vicious blow across the side of the head with the back of his hand.

Bobby went flying into the dirt and lay stunned and helpless as Moon Shadow took out the lethal knife and pulled his mother's head back. She turned her eyes to Bobby, just as Moon Shadow put the blade to her neck, "Be strong, my son. I'm proud of you. I will always…"

Moon Shadow pulled the knife across her throat and her lifeblood gushed into the dirt. It may have been his imagination, but Bobby thought he heard her finish, "… love you."

The chief stood over her in triumphant celebration. Bobby could tell he was milking every ounce of glory he could squeeze from the moment. This was an opportunity to display his strength and power, probably all the more important to him after She Wolf's challenge.

But Bobby had recovered from the blow quicker than the chief might have anticipated. Seizing his chance, he leaped up and lunged for the knife, still dripping with his mother's blood. He couldn't take the weapon, but he turned it in the chief's hand and plunged it into his side.

Moon Shadow was startled, but only for a moment. He grasped Bobby by the throat and began to squeeze. Bobby struggled and gasped. He started to lose consciousness. He thought Moon Shadow was going to kill him there and then.

It might have been better for him if he had.

XI

RECKONING

When Bobby woke he was tied to a post, naked. Two tribeswomen were smearing red paste on his legs. As his vision cleared, he saw Moon Shadow and most of the tribe standing around him. Almost everyone was there, although he couldn't see She Wolf.

The chief had a poultice covering the gash in his side. Disappointingly, it didn't seem to be causing him any discomfort. He raised his arms and spoke to the gathered crowd, "We give this traitorous boy to the worthy ants so they may feed and prosper and make for us the clubs and tools we need. In this way, may this traitor at last be of use to the tribe." He turned and marched back to the village. The rest of the people followed. A few, including Crazy Rabbit, paused to spit on Bobby before they left. Minutes later, Bobby was alone.

At first, the ants merely tickled as they ran up and down his legs, feeling his flesh with their antennae. Then a few began to bite. Each individual bite was no more than a minor irritation but, after a while, his legs were itching terribly. He longed to scratch them, but he wasn't yet in any real pain.

The sun went down. It started getting colder. His legs were sore now, like bad sunburn. About an hour after sunset, he heard a sound behind him. A voice spoke softly in his ear. It was She Wolf.

"Bob-bee, I am here. I will help you as well as I am able. I am sorry I could not save your mother, but I will save you if I can."

She moved in front of him. Smiling, she held up a small leather pouch, "This will stop them biting."

Crouching down, she began covering the tribeswomen's paste with her own. "My father was a medicine man," she explained; "he taught me how to make a paste to repel the ants and dye it so it looks the same as the one that attracts them. When anyone looks at your legs, they will not easily detect the difference."

"Thank you, my chief, I… I am sorry I have caused you so much trouble, I…"

"It is all right, Bob-bee, I understand. She was your mother; you had a right to avenge her. I tried to speak for you; I argued you could not be a traitor as you are not a member of the tribe, just as I did for your mother. But, as he was the target of your attack, Moon Shadow was able to overrule me this time. He had the backing of most of the tribe when he sentenced you to a traitor's death. I could not stop him, I am sorry."

She finished her work and stood up, "That will keep you safe until I work out how I can set you free. Do as your mother said, be strong. I will return tomorrow." Then she was gone, slipping silently into the undergrowth.

*

She Wolf returned each night with a fresh coating of ant repellent. She also brought food, water, and words of comfort. Apologetically, she explained she couldn't give Bobby clothing or shelter, as anything she provided would be seen; so he spent the days being burnt by the unrelenting summer sun, and the nights shivering in the cold.

Two of the chief's native women brought him water every morning. They also examined his legs, checking on the ants' progress.

"Moon Shadow will be displeased," said one, "the ants are not biting."

"It is not unknown for them to take one or two days to begin work," the other shrugged, "especially in the summer, when they are already well fed."

"Perhaps, but this is the third day we have brought water to the traitor, they should have started by now."

"I suppose you are right, it is strange they are not feeding yet. But I am sure the chief will know what to do."

*

She Wolf made her way stealthily towards the place of the traitors. She had made up her mind. In four days, she would be forced to leave the hunting party and become Crazy Rabbit's woman. She had nothing to lose, she would release Bobby tonight, and they would escape together. She could hunt and he could attend to her other needs. In time, they might perhaps even…

She heard a noise behind her and whirled around, her bow raised, ready to defend herself. Moon Shadow stood there. He was, indeed, casting a moon shadow and it fell upon her. She had the bizarre notion she could actually feel its cold grip tightening around her body.

"Take her," he commanded. Crazy Rabbit and Burning Tree appeared behind her and grabbed her arms. She struggled in their grasp, breaking free from Crazy Rabbit, whose very touch made her nauseous. But Burning Tree had a firmer hold; clearly well-accustomed to struggling women. She fought against him until Moon Shadow pulled out his club and knocked her out.

When she regained consciousness, she was back in the village, tied to the post in the clearing. So, she would be going to the ants too. At least she'd be reunited with Bobby. She'd grown very fond of him. No, it was more than that. He was from a strange land, far away, the land of the Great White King, yet he was familiar to her, as if she'd known him a long time, as if they were meant to be together. Trapped now, in this hopeless situation, she finally realised the truth. She loved him.

She felt angry with herself. If only she'd made up her

mind sooner and they'd made their escape the previous night. She'd been so stupid to delay. Now a gruesome death awaited them both. She racked her brain, trying to think of a way for them to avoid their dreadful fate.

Two tribesmen came to collect her shortly before dawn. As the sun rose above the horizon, they dragged her in front of Moon Shadow, her hands bound behind her back; and forced her to kneel before him. The tribe was gathered to hear the chief recite the usual execution ritual. Finally, he concluded, "Does anyone speak for this woman?"

"I speak for myself," She Wolf responded.

Moon Shadow laughed, "You are entertaining, if nothing else, She Wolf. In some ways, it will be a shame to lose you. Very well, let us hear what you have to say. Speak."

"My chief, I have broken no law of the tribe."

"You have given comfort to a traitor condemned to die. That is against the law of the tribe."

"My chief, the law of the tribe is no *man* may give comfort to a traitor condemned to die." Some of the tribe gasped. She continued for the sake of those who hadn't yet grasped the significance of her words, "But, I am *not* a man, my chief, I am but a *woman*."

There was a murmur among the crowd as they began to realise, once again, she had the better of him.

Moon Shadow hesitated. She knew he was considering how to overrule her. Before he could speak, she hit him again. She had not wasted her hours tied to the post.

"Also, my chief, I am promised to Crazy Rabbit at the full moon. If you feed me to the ants, I will not fulfil my father's promise, Crazy Rabbit will have only bones for a woman. But, if you do not send me to the ants, I will go to Crazy Rabbit's bed, I will be his woman, and I will breed many sons for the tribe."

Crazy Rabbit was ecstatic. Grinning from ear to ear, he shouted, "Yes, my chief, give her to me. I will make sure she is punished for what she has done. She will give up the bow, she will work in my tent; I will see she gives the tribe many sons."

She Wolf waited anxiously while Moon Shadow considered her proposal. She'd given him the excuses he needed to save face, a legal loophole and the prospect she might produce sons skilled with the bow. Mostly though, she was gambling on the dark, vengeful streak within him. He knew as well as she did Crazy Rabbit was stupid, sadistic, and violent; qualities that would make her life a living hell. He would know that instead of her being eaten by the ants in a few days he could relish her torment over many years, as her spirit was eaten away by a vicious, cruel husband.

When Moon Shadow smiled, she knew her gamble had paid off, but he was cautious at first, "How can I be sure you will fulfil your promises to Crazy Rabbit and not simply leave the tribe in the night?"

"I swear before all the tribe, gathered here now, on pain of death in the bellies of the ants, that I will fulfil this promise each and every day under your glorious leadership, my chief."

This was a strong oath; she was promising to go willingly to the ants if she were to break her word. Moon Shadow almost seemed satisfied, but he had a few conditions. He stared at her as he pronounced his verdict.

"She Wolf, you have not broken a law of the tribe. Furthermore, you have sworn an oath to obey your chief and become Crazy Rabbit's woman, go to his bed and give up the bow. For the benefit of the tribe you will not go to the ants so that you might breed many strong sons. But do not forget, if you break your oath, or disobey your man-owner, you *will* feed the ants."

Standing up, he continued, "We will return to the place of the traitors to make certain the white boy receives his punishment without further interference. When the white boy is dead, She Wolf will be given to Crazy Rabbit."

He ordered his women to untie her, and she got to her feet. "Yes, my chief," she said, "you are wise and just, and I thank you for it."

*

Bobby was worried. She Wolf had promised to come every night; she wouldn't let him down. When dawn came and there was still no sign of her, he knew something must have gone horribly wrong. His anxiety increased in tandem with the heat as the sun climbed higher in the cloudless summer sky. Where was she; what had happened to her?

Finally, he saw her approaching. He was immensely relieved to see she was safe, but concerned she was accompanied by the rest of the tribe. Then he saw Moon Shadow, and he was overtaken by an awful sense of foreboding.

When Moon Shadow arrived, he ordered his women to wash the ant repellent off Bobby's legs and replace it with the original paste. Then he told them to check the ropes holding Bobby to the post.

"All is well, my chief," said one of the women; "the traitor is secure."

"Good, his punishment can now resume. But, let us make sure," Moon Shadow took his bow, nocked an arrow, and pulled the string back so far Bobby thought it must surely snap. The chief held his aim for a moment, judging the wind, then unleashed his shot. The arrow flew further than anything Bobby had ever seen and landed right beside the path from the village.

Moon Shadow turned to She Wolf, "You will return to the village with the rest of the tribe. You are then forbidden to approach closer than my arrow until this white boy is dead. That shall be part of your oath. Break it and you share the traitor's fate."

He spoke to the grinning Crazy Rabbit, "You shall watch her, day and night. Make certain she obeys my command, report to me if she does not."

Moon Shadow led the tribe away. She Wolf was one of the last to leave. As she turned to go, she whispered, "I am sorry Bob-bee. You will not suffer long, I swear."

Bobby watched her walking away, hoping he would see her again, fearing he might not.

It was not long before the ants started to bite. It began as a tickle, then an irritation, then grew steadily more painful throughout the day and the night that followed. By sunrise the next morning, he was in agony, and it was getting worse every minute.

*

She Wolf left the village at dawn, carrying her bow and four arrows. Crazy Rabbit followed, grinning lustily at her, "I do not know what you are planning, She Wolf, but I look forward to the result. If you stray past Moon Shadow's marker, you will join the white boy in the bellies of the ants. If not, you will soon be my woman. Oh, the things I will do to you; things you cannot even imagine. Either way, you are going to suffer... and I am going to enjoy every moment."

She marched on, ignoring his threats, until she stopped an arm's length short of Moon Shadow's arrow. She gazed up at the place of the traitors, squinting to make out Bobby's figure. Could she do it? Moon Shadow was the greatest archer ever known. On top of that, the place of the traitors was further up the hillside, making her shot even harder.

Taking aim, she pulled back the string with every ounce of her fibre, and loosed off her shot. It seemed to take an age for the arrow to reach its target but, eventually, it sailed past Bobby, a finger width over his shoulder. He didn't seem to notice, he was probably in too much pain.

Calmly, she repositioned herself for another shot. She wet her finger and held it in the air, testing the wind. She nodded then lifted the bow again.

"You cannot do this; you swore an oath to give up the bow. I will tell Moon Shadow you have broken your oath," objected Crazy Rabbit.

"You are well-named, Crazy Rabbit. You are short on wits and as good a warrior as your furry namesakes. Now be quiet."

But the tribesman continued, "I order you to stop. You are my woman, you must obey me."

"I am not your woman yet, Crazy Rabbit. You cannot command me until I am given to you, and nor must I yet give up the bow. Be silent."

He wasn't giving up. He started to rush towards her, "I will stop you anyway; you must not do this." She turned swiftly and pointed her bow at him, "Just try." He stopped dead in his tracks and fell into a sulky silence.

Turning to face her target again, she raised her bow and aimed it into the sky. She pulled back with all her strength and loosed her second shot. She knew as soon as the arrow left the string. "Goodbye, my love, your pain is at an end now," she whispered.

The arrow flew high into the air, describing a long, graceful arc, until finally falling towards Bobby. It plunged into his heart. His suffering was over.

She Wolf turned and marched back to the village. She had two arrows left. She knew what to do with them.

*

As she threw open his tent flap, She Wolf saw what Moon Shadow was doing to the golden-haired woman. It turned her stomach, but she would not allow herself to be distracted from the path she'd resolved to take.

"Moon Shadow, I declare you unworthy to lead the tribe. I challenge you to the Reckoning."

For centuries, the tribe had used the Reckoning to challenge any chief whose leadership was in question. At the allotted time, chief and challenger stood on opposite sides of the clearing, each with their bow and a single arrow lying on the ground in front of them. Another tribesman would stand between and fire an arrow vertically into the air. When that arrow hit the ground, the contenders snatched up their weapons and fired.

Sometimes, in the face of a strong challenge, the chief would back down and relinquish power without the need for a contest; sometimes the challenger would triumph and the chief would be banished, or killed. And sometimes, more often than not, the chief would triumph. If the challenger was lucky, they'd be killed on the spot. If not, they'd be taken to the place of the traitors.

Moon Shadow was not going to back down, She Wolf was sure of that. This would be his sixth Reckoning. His first had been as challenger, many summers ago. He'd killed the old chief with an arrow straight to his heart. Four challengers had faced him since. Two had dropped cleanly, one bled to death, and one fed the ants. Moon Shadow had never been scratched. Many of the tribe said he deliberately avoided giving the last two a clean kill so he could watch them die in pain. She Wolf believed it. She wondered if he would give her the same treatment.

The tribe gathered to watch the contest. Moon Shadow and She Wolf took up their positions. Allowed only one arrow, she put the other to one side. She looked at Moon Shadow, studying him carefully. She knew her chances were slim. His speed was unparalleled, most saw nothing but a blur when he went for his bow; his aim was notoriously precise, even when firing in haste. She was almost certainly going to die.

But she would rather die here, like this, than live as Crazy Rabbit's woman. And this was her only chance to avenge Bobby. If she could at least injure Moon Shadow, he would lose face, and she might bring his cruel tyranny closer to an end.

Burning Tree stepped into the middle of the clearing. He leaned back and fired an arrow into the sky, then walked quickly to the side. A hushed silence fell upon the tribe. The onlookers hardly dared breathe as the seconds stretched into an eternity of waiting. All eyes were on the spot where Burning Tree had stood.

*

Frances stood in the crowd, near She Wolf. Now a fully-fledged member of the tribe, she was dressed accordingly, in a simple, short dress fastened by a single cord. She loved its simplicity because Sleeping Bear could take it off in an instant when they were alone together at night. There was nothing beneath the dress to delay their exquisite love-making by even a moment.

Under her dress, her body was blooming. The healthy diet and open-air lifestyle of the tribe suited her well; the surplus weight she'd been carrying when she came to the village had been burned away by days of simple chores and nights of passion. She was in the early stages of pregnancy and the changes this was bringing had turned her into a stunningly attractive woman.

She looked at She Wolf, standing tall and proud, ready to meet her fate. She admired this young girl-warrior; she'd seen how brave and strong she was, how she'd turned away in disgust when little Tommy Jenkins was killed, how she'd stood up for the women condemned to death, saved them from the ants. Now there were stories she'd saved Bobby from his terrible suffering with another act of mercy, like Frances's father.

She Wolf's acts of compassion meant a great deal to Frances. Bobby had been her friend; they'd played together as children. His mother had comforted her when her own mother died.

Frances watched She Wolf tensing in readiness, wishing there was something she could do to help her. As the tribe waited expectantly, she slowly took a couple of paces forward, positioning herself close behind She Wolf, a little to one side.

The arrow fell from the sky and embedded itself quivering in the ground. The signal was given. Frances pulled off her dress.

*

Moon Shadow moved like lightning. She Wolf couldn't match him. As she was straightening up, still nocking her arrow, he'd already raised his bow and was taking aim. Yet, at the last moment, something seemed to catch his eye. It was enough to pull his aim slightly off. His arrow flew across the clearing and hit her in the shoulder. An instant before it struck, she unleashed her own. Her aim was true; the arrow flew unerringly to his heart. The mighty chief stumbled and fell to his knees. He stared incredulously at her, disbelief in his eyes, "Next time, I…" He collapsed forwards into the dirt.

The crowd around her were stunned. Impervious to the pain in her shoulder, the blood dripping from her wound, She Wolf turned slowly through a full circle, so she could see all the tribe. She smiled when she saw Frances hastily pulling her dress on. Then she spotted Crazy Rabbit standing near Moon Shadow's body.

She retrieved her last arrow and marched across to the young warrior, bow in hand. He tried to back away, but stumbled and fell. Sprawled in the dirt, he began to plead, "But you swore an oath, you promised to be my woman, you cannot break your oath before the tribe…"

"I swore I would fulfil my promise each and every day under Moon Shadow's leadership. That leadership is ended," she gestured at the chief's body, "and my oath ends with it. I will not be your woman, Crazy Rabbit, and I do not wish to see you torment another." She raised her bow, her final arrow in place.

"No, please, my chief, I will not take another woman if you forbid it, please do not kill me."

She hesitated then lowered her bow. "Then go, you are banished. Leave before sunrise tomorrow and you live." She turned and began walking back to her tent. Behind her, Crazy Rabbit crawled to Moon Shadow's body and pulled out the chief's knife. He sprang to his feet and ran at her back, the knife held high, ready to strike.

She span around, her bow raised, and sent her last arrow into his eye. He dropped and lay twitching at her feet.

*

No-one had heard of a woman leading the tribe before, or any other tribe for that matter. But She Wolf's authority wasn't questioned. She had triumphed at the Reckoning, she was chief.

She stopped the attacks on the settlers and, when Frances had taught her enough English, she was able to negotiate with them to work out how their communities could co-exist in peace.

Speaking to the remaining white women, she offered

them a choice, "Worthy friends, you are welcome to stay if you wish. If you are not happy with your man, you may leave him and choose another, or live on your own, as you please. Those of you with a child may see them as much as you desire, you will share them with their new mothers and the child shall be loved all the more. Or, if you prefer, you may leave us and return to your own people. I have spoken to the leader of the new settlement and he will find you a home if it is what you want."

Frances elected to stay with Sleeping Bear. Two others with children in the village also chose to stay: they took up She Wolf's offer to leave their man and moved in with their child's adopted family.

The golden-haired woman had many wounds in need of attention. She Wolf took care of her, using skills learned from her father. She nursed her back to health. The woman was traumatised by her experiences with Moon Shadow. She Wolf spoke gently to her, knowing it was as important to heal her mind as her body but, as time wore on and the woman failed to respond, she began to fear she might never recover her wits.

One night, almost two moons after the Reckoning, She Wolf was trying out some of her newly acquired English, "I think we shall call you 'Golden Hair', for your hair is surely a rare and special sight to us, but I wonder…"

"Simone," the woman spoke at last, "my name is Simone. Simone Woodman."

"Simone," She Wolf repeated the unfamiliar syllables, "that is a lovely name."

After that, Simone recovered quickly. Within a few moons she had become a vibrant, beautiful woman once more. She Wolf asked her if she wanted to leave the tribe and join the new settlement. Simone looked at her with eyes the colour of a summer sky, "I cannot go back; the shame would be too much to bear. In any case, I do not wish to leave. You have shown me so much kindness; let me stay and I will do my best to repay you, even if it takes all my life."

Simone stayed as She Wolf's companion, fulfilling the simple tasks Bobby had once done for her. Over time, they became good friends. Some said they were more than friends, but the tribe respected their privacy.

The summer after Moon Shadow's death, one of Burning Tree's women miscarried. In the midst of her physical and mental suffering, she refused to go to his bed. He beat her senseless. The next morning he dragged her before the tribe.

She Wolf sat in the wooden chair, flanked by Sleeping Bear and Frances. Simone stood behind her. She listened while Burning Tree made his complaint and demanded his woman be fed to the ants. When he had finished, she said, "Even Moon Shadow warned you about your cruelty, Burning Tree. The tribe has already lost one woman because of you; we will not lose more. Your women are free; I release them from your ownership. They may choose another man if they wish. As for you, you are not worthy of any woman. You are banished from the tribe, be gone before sunset or forfeit your life."

Burning Tree stared back at her. She could tell what he was thinking. She smiled, "Think carefully before you challenge me, Burning Tree. There was none faster than Moon Shadow... and I beat him. Or, if you are considering stabbing me in the back, remember what happened to Crazy Rabbit."

He sneered at her for a moment. He opened his mouth to speak then seemed to think better of it. He spat on the ground then turned and walked away.

*

One white woman returned to the settlement. For the rest of her life, she would tell anyone who cared to listen about the courageous young woman who led a native tribe, a 'virgin queen' every bit as glorious as Old Queen Bess. Most of the white men dismissed her stories as nonsense; most of the women listened eagerly. And so her story spread... and grew.

XII

CELEBRITY

Susan woke feeling good; remarkably good. She'd had the most amazing dream. She felt full of confidence and vitality, strong enough to take on anything. It was as if her subconscious had decided to give her a boost. And, like the one on the plane, the dream had seemed completely real. It felt like it had lasted years, when obviously it had only been a few hours. It was quite extraordinary, it didn't seem like she'd been dreaming at all; more like she'd been living another life.

"I am She Wolf," she said to herself in the mirror, "don't mess with me!" She posed as if drawing an imaginary bow and smiled at her reflection. Silly nonsense, of course, but she did feel stronger.

She supposed her positivity was really more to do with how well her presentation had gone. Not to mention Professor Benneyworth's wonderful offer. She'd made up her mind, she was going to accept. Moving to Australia would be a massive upheaval, but it would be a whole new adventure. She was ready for that.

Going down to breakfast, she was surprised to discover Hans had been called away in the night to assist Mortimer with some urgent business. Sun-lee was as attentive as usual though, and arranged for another servant to drive her to the conference. When she arrived, she felt like a minor celebrity, with all the people congratulating her on her performance the day before. There was still no sign of Mortimer, but she was feeling more at home in her surroundings and, with her speaking stint behind her, she began to relax. Professor Benneyworth was continually engaged in discussions with other delegates, but they arranged to speak at the drinks reception before the gala dinner that evening.

The organisers had made a couple of suites available to delegates not staying in the hotel who needed to change for dinner. At six-thirty, Susan was putting on her evening dress when her head began to spin. A blurry, blue-grey image swam in front of her. Her lungs were burning, she couldn't breathe. Her arms were aching too, like they were being stretched. A darker shape emerged from the blue-grey. It came towards her, rapidly growing to fill her field of vision. It rushed at her and she tried to scream, but couldn't. Everything suddenly went black and she swayed on her feet, almost fainting. She steadied herself against the dressing table and took a few deep breaths until her vision cleared and she felt strong enough to stand again.

She looked in the mirror and saw her face, as pale as a ghost. What on earth was that? What just happened? This really was worrying. 'Sod's law,' just as life seemed to be going well in other ways, there was clearly something wrong with her. It was ironic. Many of the best neurologists in the world were in the building, but this was neither the time nor the place to get a diagnosis.

Recovering her composure, she headed to the drinks reception and her appointment with Professor Benneyworth. When she told him her decision, he was delighted. They made a toast and started talking about some of the issues involved in her move. She wondered for a moment if she should tell him about her headaches and hallucinations. Was it fair to take up a new post when she might be seriously ill? She didn't want to jeopardise anything though, it was too good an opportunity to miss. She decided she would keep quiet about her health issues for now. She would get herself examined when she got home. Hopefully, it wouldn't be anything too serious. If it was, she would tell him then.

Pushing her worries to one side, she started asking Benneyworth about the facilities at the hospital in Sydney. When they were called for dinner, they went to check the seating plan. To Susan's surprise, they were on the same table. They took their seats and continued their conversation.

"I can't tell you how much I'm looking forward to it, Ricky. I am curious about one thing though, why is it called Shilling Club Hospital?"

"Oh, that's because it was founded by the Shilling Club. You've probably never heard of it, but it's well known in Sydney. There's an interesting story behind it, actually."

"Do tell"

"Well, there was this girl sent to the penal colony in the early 1800s. They say she was innocent, which I do believe. That sort of thing happened often in those days. Rumour has it she was working as a maid for some English lord. When he got her pregnant, he accused her of theft and shipped her off to avoid the scandal."

"That's terrible," Susan frowned. This all seemed oddly familiar.

"I know. Anyway, when she got to the colony, she built a reputation for being hardworking and obedient; although she did blot her copy book once when she refused to inform on her fellow convicts. She got twenty lashes, but she still wouldn't say anything."

"Poor girl"

"Yes, it was a bit of a setback. Nonetheless, she kept working hard, served her time in the colony, and eventually earned her freedom. She'd done ten years by then, but she was still only twenty-eight. She got married, had three children. But it wasn't enough for her; she wanted to do something to help others suffering the same injustices she'd been through. So she set up a business retraining convicts for life on the outside.

"Like her, many of them were completely innocent, or had been transported for the pettiest crimes: things you'd get a slap on the wrist for these days. Apparently, she was a good judge of character and could tell who would benefit from her help, and who the real criminals were.

"She had a simple system; she found them a temporary home and arranged training in the skills that would help them find work. In the early days, the temporary home was her own house and she did most of the training herself. Later she rented rooms for them, but she kept up some of the training.

"As soon as her clients got a job, she helped them find a permanent home. She didn't demand payment, but suggested they give her a shilling for every pound they earned in their first year, so she could help other people in the same predicament. Most of them paid their shillings. Many insisted on paying for the rest of their lives. A lot of them said she'd saved their life. By the time she died, she'd helped over a thousand ex-convicts and her business was still growing. More than four hundred of her clients went to her funeral; it was one of the biggest events of 1845. Afterwards, they started calling themselves 'Sally's Shilling Club' and pledged to carry on her work. Over the years, the club grew, and expanded into other charitable activities, like founding the hospital."

"Her name was Sally?" Susan stared at Benneyworth, her eyes wide in astonishment. This was becoming too much of a coincidence.

"Yes, that's right. Remarkable story isn't it: a young convict girl becoming the founder of a philanthropic empire. Do you know one of her descendants even became Prime Minister of Australia? It's a pity the club changed its name to just the Shilling Club in the twentieth century, it would be nice for her to be remembered. Still, there is a street named after her."

"What street?"

"Trigg Avenue"

"You mean… she was… you're talking about Sally Trigg?"

"That's her. Why, have you heard of her before? There's not many people know about her outside Sydney."

"I… I…"

Before Susan could reply, the loud hubbub in the dining hall dropped to a low murmur. She felt the hairs rising on the back of her neck. Sensing something behind her, she turned to see Mortimer entering the room. His presence immediately dominated the hall, though it was filled with over four hundred guests. That's no mean feat, thought Susan, and he does it as if it's second nature, as if he's been doing it for… well, forever, really.

She winced as a sharp pain shot across her temples, that damn headache returning again. She reached for her wine glass and took a gulp, hoping the alcohol would dull the pain. Probably unwise, but it seemed to work, temporarily at least.

The rest of the evening flew by as she chatted with Professor Benneyworth about the World Neurology Council and her hopes for her new department in Sydney. Before she knew it, it was ten o'clock and Hans was there ready to take her and Mortimer back to the villa. By the time she got to her room, it was well after midnight. She felt exhausted, but Benneyworth's story was playing on her mind and she lay awake, trying to figure out how she could have dreamed of being someone she'd never heard of before. She'd thought Sally Trigg was just a figment of her imagination, a product of her subconscious trying to deal with her anxiety. But now it turned out Sally was a real person. How had a Georgian maidservant got into her dreams? It was bizarre. Maybe she'd seen a documentary about her or something? The story must have been there, deep in her memory, and she'd incorporated it into a dream about Mortimer. It was the only rational explanation.

Sighing, she turned off the bedside light and closed her eyes. Before long, she was dreaming again but, instead of being She Wolf, proud, strong, and free, she was back suffering the indignities of life at the mansion.

*

Despite her late night, Susan was up early the next morning. They were due to return home immediately after the conference closed and were going directly from there to the airport, so she needed to finish packing and be ready to leave by six-thirty.

Her dreams had been as vivid as usual. She could almost smell the stench of the prison ship. Her ankles even itched where they'd been rubbed raw by her chains. So weird what the mind can do. Was this her subconscious's way of telling her not to go to Australia? Surely not; she felt more like she was escaping than going into captivity. Still, it had been the same last time when she thought about it. Life at the mansion had been a worse prison than the penal colony.

What was she thinking, Sally may have been a real person, but her dreams about her weren't. Somewhere she'd heard the story and, for some reason, she was dreaming she was Sally. But those dreams were a fantasy, no more real than the idea of being a Native American girl who'd become a tribal chief. She snapped out of her reverie and continued her preparations.

It had been a nuisance being based so far from the conference, the long journey to the venue had eaten up a lot of time. Mortimer had insisted she stay at his villa though. It certainly was luxurious but, after almost a week, it was beginning to feel like a gilded cage. She was glad to be leaving. The house was surrounded by desert, there was nowhere for her to go, it was too hot to walk around in the day and pitch black at night. The only times she'd been able to venture out were sunrise and sunset. To travel further, she'd been reliant on the staff, mostly Hans. He was an efficient chauffeur, he was efficient at everything, but she always felt uncomfortable in his presence. There was something unsettling about him, as if he was constantly assessing her worth, deciding what to do with her. He'd got her to the conference punctually, but she felt constrained by her dependence on him. She was missing the freedom of hopping into her own car. If this was how the super-rich lived, they could stick it, she liked her independence too much.

Emerging from the shower, she turned on the gigantic television occupying almost an entire wall of the guest bedroom. A photograph flashed onto the screen. Recognising the face, she turned up the volume so she could hear the news presenters.

"… of Chinese tourists found the mangled body at the base of the Burj Khalifa around nine p.m. yesterday evening. The victim has been identified as Francesco Del Rivera, aged seventy-three, a retired history professor from Mexico City…"

Stunned, Susan put her hand to her mouth. She sat on a corner of the bed, staring up at the screen.

"… It appears Del Rivera may have fallen from the top of the world's tallest building, although apparently there are no witnesses, and police are currently unable to explain how he was able to gain access to the upper storeys. A statement issued by Commander Abdul al-Mansur of Dubai Police Force's homicide department confirms they are working on the assumption this was probably a suicide, as there is no evidence to suggest any other person was involved. However, other sources within the department report rumours of a strange black liquid found in the victim's throat, which the medical examiners have so far been unable to identify…"

The presenters moved on to other news. Susan switched off the television. A shiver ran up her spine, she had that same dreadful sense of foreboding she'd had when she boarded the Lear. She'd seen Del Rivera at the hospital, wasn't he Carlton's uncle or something? What was he doing here? It felt like death had followed her to Dubai.

She sat in silence, wondering if there was any connection to her visit, whether she might be in some kind of danger. But, after a few minutes, she decided that was ridiculous. She'd only passed Del Rivera in the corridor a couple of times; he probably never even knew who she was. He'd been an odd character; who knew what he was doing here, or what had driven him to take his life? It was an awful tragedy, but it was nothing to do with her.

She carried on getting ready. Mortimer wasn't due to give his closing address until after lunch, but he was adamant they should arrive in time for the beginning of the day's schedule. She didn't want to make them late; she had a feeling he was used to people doing as he asked.

*

Hans served her breakfast in her room and, at 6.25 a.m., he returned to collect her luggage. Minutes later, she saw her bags sitting in the lobby as she was on her way out to the car.

Mortimer's Rolls was sitting outside, the engine running, the air-conditioning keeping the interior pleasantly cool. She got in the back. A minute later, Mortimer sat next to her, "Good morning, my dear. I trust you slept well? No more strange dreams, I hope?"

She smiled back. She thought it better not to say anything about what she'd experienced. Not just dreamt, experienced. Her dreams, both as Sally and as She Wolf, had been that vivid. The memory wasn't fading either.

Dreaming about She Wolf had been far more enjoyable; it made her feel good, strong. She felt as though she'd really lived as a Native American warrior queen. But, like the other dreams, it felt as if Mortimer had been there too. Moon Shadow had seemed a lot like him; he didn't look like him, but there was something about his manner, the way he talked…

Still, it was perfectly normal for someone who featured in your life during the day to feature in your dreams at night. So what if her subconscious decided to turn him into a tribal chief. It didn't mean anything… did it?

Hans got into the driver's seat and the Rolls set off. "Hang on, you forgot my bags," she protested, but Mortimer intervened in a smooth, reassuring tone, "It's quite alright, my dear, I have arranged for someone to take care of your luggage. You won't be leaving without it, I assure you."

"Oh, right," she settled back in her seat. As the Rolls pulled away, she asked a question that had been puzzling her since she arrived, "Why do you have an American flag flying over your villa?"

"Ah, yes, it is a bit of a curiosity isn't it? Simple really, the US Army borrowed the villa for a diplomatic mission during the Second World War. I was happy to have them as my guests. After all, their nation shares my birthday. When they left, I arranged for the villa's diplomatic status to be continued. It comes in useful from time to time."

"Sorry, did you say you were happy to have them as *your* guests. Surely you can only have been a young boy at the time?"

"Well, my dear, I inherited young and I am somewhat older than I look."

Sitting back on the plush upholstery, she tried to make sense of his response. Let's say he's about eighty-five now, surely he can't be any more than that, so then he'd have been… She couldn't make it work. In the end, she gave up and decided to try another subject, "Did you see the news about that poor man they found at the Burj Khalifa? It seems no-one can figure out how he got there."

"Oh yes, I saw that. I am sure there is a simple explanation. There always is… in the end."

His replies never seemed to encourage further discussion, so she turned to watch the passing scenery. There wasn't much to see for the first couple of hours, but then the car started to approach the spectacular twenty-first century metropolis of Dubai. A huge spike sprouted from the desert in front of her eyes. As the miles rolled by, it grew taller, until eventually it dominated the skyline. In a city of towers, the Burj Khalifa towered above everything else. It pointed to the sky like a giant skeletal finger. The Americans had created the sky scraper but, here in the desert, this building didn't just scrape the sky, it pierced it.

Arriving at the conference felt mundane by comparison. Professor Benneyworth had left early that morning, but Susan threw herself into the routine of mingling with colleagues and discussing the theories presented over the last couple of days. Del Rivera came up in conversation and the other delegates were astonished to hear she'd known him before.

"So you actually met the guy?" a young Australian doctor asked.

"No, not really, I just saw him in the corridor a couple of times. He was visiting one of my patients."

"Still, bit of a coincidence," the Australian continued; "fancy him being here in Dubai."

"Yes, it did come as a surprise, I must say."

The Australian smiled, "You know, you remind me of my great-grandmother."

"Thanks, that's a real compliment; what is she, about a hundred?"

"No," he laughed, "I mean pictures of her when she was young; she was a beautiful lady. You know, I'm gonna be over in London next month. I was wondering if you might be free for…"

He was interrupted by the conference staff as they began ushering everyone into the main hall to begin the day's formal proceedings.

Susan smiled to herself. She knew what he'd been about to ask, she'd been there many times before. Her looks had always brought her plenty of attention, but never much happiness. Ray was just the latest in a long line of failed relationships. And though the young Australian seemed nice, she wasn't ready to risk putting herself through that again. Not yet.

She frowned. Why was Carlton suddenly on her mind?

XIII

REVELATION

It was dark, darker than anything he'd ever experienced. There were voices, faint at first, but growing louder. He tried to open his eyes to see where the voices were coming from, but his eyelids were coated in something sticky and he didn't have the strength to force them open. He tried to raise a hand, but his arm wouldn't respond. He focussed on the voices instead.

"… sorry, my lord, it should have gone over the side. It is just a lucky chance it has come to rest here."

"It's not very lucky from my point of view, Hans. We need to make sure he doesn't survive. It's right on the edge, see if you can push it over."

"Yes, my lord."

There was a grating, scraping, noise and the world seemed to sway for a moment, but then fell back into place.

"Try kicking it, Hans. I'm sure it will go over if you put your weight behind it."

A loud bang to his left and the world began to sway again. There was a second bang, then a third. The grating noise resumed, getting louder.

"That's it, well done. It's going now."

The world swayed violently and began to spin. The spinning went on for a long time until, suddenly, it stopped, and there was only darkness; darkness and silence. Then there was music. The music was loud, but beautiful, and strangely familiar…

*

Ben stepped out of the en-suite bathroom and turned on the television. He gazed, stunned and shocked, as a photograph of Del Rivera appeared on the screen above a caption reading 'SUICIDE AT WORLD'S TALLEST BUILDING'. Turning up the sound, he listened to the news item growing increasingly convinced the authorities had it wrong; this was no suicide.

The newsreader brought the piece to a close, "… was once considered a leading authority in his field, but an increasing obsession with some highly controversial theories eventually led to him being widely dismissed as an eccentric. There is speculation it may have been those theories that drove him to take his life."

Ben wasn't dismissing Del Rivera as an eccentric any more. The dreams had almost convinced him already but, with the news of the old man's death, he was certain everything Del Rivera had told him was true. He turned off the television and sat at the desk. He regretted his last encounter with the old man; he'd been too hasty ignoring his advice, he could see that now.

He picked up his phone. He needed to contact Susan Carpenter. But what would he tell her? If she *had* seen the vision of them drowning together, it would help, but how did he avoid coming across as a lunatic? How could he persuade her to believe him? He hadn't believed Del Rivera, and look how that had ended.

There was a knock at the door. He glanced at his watch. Strange, he hadn't ordered room service, and it was too early for housekeeping. He put down his phone, went to the door, and cautiously opened it. One of the hotel staff, a young man, was standing outside holding a thick envelope and a small clipboard with pen attached.

"Good morning, sir, I'm sorry to disturb you, but there was an urgent delivery for you," the young man held out the envelope. "Could you sign for it please, sir? Hotel policy" Ben took the clipboard and signed where the young man indicated. "Thank you, sir, have a good day."

"Er, yes, thank you, yes… you too." Ben was puzzled, who would send him a letter here? He'd only been here a few days; hardly anyone knew where he was. He looked at the envelope and read the address, written in the stylish handwriting of someone who'd grown up before the microchip took over the world, when writing with a pen was an important skill, 'Major Ben Carlton, Care of,' then the name of the hotel.

The envelope contained a large sheaf of closely

written paper. There were at least ten or twelve pages of handwritten manuscript, quite a rarity these days. He noticed the date in the top right corner, the day after he'd last seen Del Rivera.

He sat down and began to read.

My Dear Bakara,

I deeply regret I cannot convince you of the danger you are in. Since the time of the sea people, I have watched over you, from this side and the other. I have not always known I was there to look after you; I have only achieved awakening a few times. But fate has placed me where I needed to be, as it often does for many of us, and I have done what I could to help, even if mostly without knowing why.

You and I have walked the Earth since long before recorded history. I have been your father, your brother... many things to you; but always your friend. We are old souls, born many times, over thousands of years. Souls as ancient as you or I are rare; many of those you see around you are 'firstborns', new souls in their first life, many others are only in their second or third. Few have lived more than five or six times.

Shebana is another old soul. You and she have a special bond. You may have noticed you can sense what she is feeling, or thinking, when you experience your past. That is because you are bound together by your destiny.

She is an empathic soul; she has a natural ability to

care for others. As an empath, she may even experience other people's lives, as well as hers and yours, when she visits the past. You are a warrior soul, with an inbuilt desire to protect the weak and powerless. However, you are so closely linked it is not unknown for her to assume the role of warrior in your place.

Mamboja is older than all of us. He was thousands of years old already when he fed you to the sea. You and Shebana were firstborns then, but the bond between you was strong. He sensed the threat you posed, he had achieved awakening even then. That is why he came to our village, became the voice of the sea, and murdered Shebana's mother, Khulekani, a warm, kind woman. I knew her well, I wish...

But that is another story. What matters is this. Mamboja is the most powerful soul in the Universe. No *single* soul can challenge him. But when you and Shebana achieve your destiny, you will become a twin soul. Together, you may be strong enough.

He has always known this. He has stalked you through the ages, stopping you fulfilling your destiny, controlling your lives from this side and the other. He dare not leave you alone. He is drawn to you by his fear of what you might become. You have evolved into a 'Trinity of Souls' eternally bound together by love, hate, fear, and destiny.

I do not know which lives you have remembered, but you will always see his hand there. Sometimes it is obvious, like when he was Matthews the magistrate and charged

Shebana with witchcraft then burnt her at the stake. The witchcraft was his; he deformed the baby in its mother's womb. I know Shebana's death as Samantha Parsons was hard for you to witness, but I think it was something you had to see, to show yourself how evil he truly is.

Other times, he is more subtle. As General Mortimer, he sent your brigade to the Somme before you could have your wedding night with Sarah. He put you in the first wave on D-Day too. He could not be certain you would be killed in those battles, but he put you in the greatest peril and left fate to do the rest.

He has manipulated your souls from the other side as well. He made sure Shebana was reborn a man in Victorian England. You met and fell in love but could not even admit it to yourselves, especially not in the ranks of the British Army.

Until now, his aim has been to keep you apart, or find other ways to stop you fulfilling your destiny. He has often killed one, or both, of you. But that was only a means to an end; he always knew you'd be back. Now everything has changed.

For more than two hundred years, he has been Lord Mortimer, perhaps his cruellest, most abominable, incarnation yet. In that time, his powers, already formidable, have been steadily growing. He has achieved control of his life force, and no longer has to go through the process of death and rebirth. He can travel to the other side whenever he wishes, while maintaining the same earthly body in a state of perpetual life. 'Saves a great deal of time,' he told me once, before putting a dagger through my heart.

He has been using that time to pursue his plans. For over a century, he has been working on a potion to destroy a soul within a mortal body. I have seen this potion, or at least an early version, a thick black liquid unknown to anyone else on Earth. He made me watch while he tested it on some children: refugees and orphans he had tricked the authorities into placing in his care. Most of them suffered a horrifying death. Worse than death, it was utter destruction of both body and soul. But the test failed with one. She did not die, at least not while I was watching, and her soul, far from being destroyed, actually grew stronger. Mamboja was furious.

I expected him to give me the potion too, but he smiled and pulled the lever to open the trap door I was standing on. He made sure I was throttled by the rope; I did not get the mercy of a broken neck.

That was in 1948, the end of my last life. It has taken him a long time but, a few months ago, he perfected his potion. He has taken Shebana to the Middle East, where he will subdue and imprison her. He will force her to drink the potion and her soul will be destroyed. You will never achieve your destiny, there will be no-one to challenge him; he will become all-powerful, free to pursue his diabolical schemes. His ambition knows no bounds. He is without morality, without mercy, without remorse. He aims to take over the world and he will stop at nothing to achieve it. He has tried before. In the fourteenth century, he cultivated a new strain of bacteria, planning to use it to gain control over mankind. It mutated, thwarting his plans, and became the Black Death. Millions died, civilization teetered on the brink of collapse, but his only concern was to find another way to achieve his goals.

Now he has the power to destroy souls and he is ready to use it to establish dominion over Earth. I do not know the details of his plan but, without you and Shebana to prevent it, he will surely rain Armageddon on the world.

I cannot let that happen. I failed you before. I should have stopped him on that beach twelve thousand years ago. I was a coward then, but not this time. I have been unable to convince you we must act, so I am going alone. I will confront him and, if I have the strength, I will try to save Shebana.

My chances of success are slight. But perhaps I may delay him enough to give you the time you need. I am leaving this letter with a private detective agency, with instructions to deliver it to you immediately if, or more likely when, something happens to me.

If you are reading this, I have failed in my mission, and I must plead with you again to save Shebana; for her sake, for your sake, for the sake of all the souls in the Universe.

Please, my friend, you must.

Your eternal friend,
Fujabi (Francesco Miguel Antonio Del Rivera)

XIV

LAST DAY

By the time they stopped for the buffet lunch, Susan's longing to get home was fading. She was starting to feel rather sad it was her last day here. The conference had been nothing less than life-changing with the success of her presentation and the fantastic offers from Professor Benneyworth. She was almost sorry to be leaving.

Still, she had something to look forward to when she got back. She couldn't wait to see the look on Worthington's face when she handed in her notice. She'd have to wait until she'd had herself checked out though. Her headache had come on again in the car that morning, and those hallucinations were very concerning. But she was trying to be optimistic. Hopefully it wouldn't be anything serious, just stress or something. God knows, she'd been through enough of it lately.

She saw the young Australian approaching. She was

readying herself to turn him down gently when she felt a hand on her elbow.

"Come, my dear, I would like you to sit close by while I give my closing address," Mortimer led her to the auditorium and showed her to a seat in the front row. While his manner remained polite and respectful, his firm grip on her arm implied he expected her to obey. Releasing her arm, he gestured for her to sit, "There, I want to be sure you hear everything I have to say."

He spent most of his speech summing up the conference and praising the work of those who were pushing back the boundaries of knowledge in the field of neurology, all the usual things you'd expect. It was the last part Susan found odd.

"We have learned a good deal about the workings of the mind, but what about the spirit, or the soul? Some believe the mind and the soul are one and the same. Others believe, while the mind operates through a process of electro-chemical reactions, and in a way now well understood by science, the soul does not depend on mere chemicals for its existence. Most of the world's cultures believe the soul exists independently of the mind and endures beyond the death of the host. We must wonder if science and belief can, in fact, be united. If the soul inhabits the human mind for the duration of its stay here on Earth, might we, at some point, be able to identify its existence and divine the processes by which it operates?

"If so, then a whole new field of neurological science would open up. We might be able to cure the soul of sickness;

or perhaps, if unable to cure a diseased soul, we might find a way to control it, or even, like a diseased appendix, simply remove it. A man can function without many of the things with which he is born, is a soul any different?

"But all this is, of course, conjecture; at least until such time as someone can finally answer the question of what it truly is that lives inside our minds."

While he spoke, Mortimer gazed around the room, his eyes roaming over the gathered assembly. But, when he came to his concluding sentence, he stared straight at Susan, "Personally, as someone who has devoted a long life to studying that very question, I should dearly love to examine a living soul myself."

Susan shuddered; there was something disturbing about the way he'd aimed those words at her. Around her, the audience had launched into rapturous applause. She was astounded by their reaction. She wondered if many of them had understood the last part, or if Mortimer's voice had simply held them mesmerised. There was a tangible sense of euphoria and adulation in the room, he had them spellbound.

The chairman went through a few formalities then brought proceedings to an end, and officially closed the conference. Everyone began to drift away. Susan stood up and started making her way out of the auditorium. Once again, she felt a firm hand on her elbow. This time it was Hans.

"I have the car waiting, Doctor Carpenter. His lordship is eager for us to get going. We have a take-off slot scheduled in an hour and he does not want to miss it," his English was impeccable, his accent unmistakably German.

"Oh, er, yes, of course," she allowed him to lead her through the throng and out to the waiting Rolls. He opened the rear door and steered her into the back seat before getting into the front to wait for his master. Mortimer appeared a few seconds later and slid into the back next to Susan, "OK, Hans, off we go please."

Hans set off too quickly for her liking. This wasn't his usual sedate, dignified, driving style. He and Mortimer must be anxious about making it to the airport in time for the take-off slot.

She'd never been to Dubai before, and had just been to the airport, the conference venue and Mortimer's villa on this trip, but it only took a few minutes before she realised they were heading in the wrong direction.

"Where are we going, this isn't the way to the airport?" she was beginning to feel a sense of panic.

"There has been a change of plan, my dear. We are returning to the villa," Mortimer was using the smooth tone that somehow she no longer trusted.

"Why? When are we leaving? I'm due back at the hospital on Monday. I need time to unpack and... What's going on?"

"Let me explain," he reached over and placed a cold palm across her forehead. She passed out instantly.

And then it all came back to her.

XV

THE MESSAGE

He'd never imagined it could be this bad. He longed for it to be over, for the unbearable agony to end. His eyes were streaming with the pain spreading up his legs. But he saw it coming nonetheless. He watched it falling towards him. He knew she'd sent it… and he was grateful.

*

Ben woke with a start, clutching at the arrow in his chest. No, wait, there was no arrow. That had been hundreds of years ago, in a different lifetime.

His legs, the ants! He could feel the tiny creatures biting as they started to eat his flesh. But, after a moment, he realised he simply had 'pins and needles' caused by falling asleep in a cramped position. Looking at his watch, he saw he was about four hours into the flight.

After reading Del Rivera's letter, he had immediately tried to reach Susan Carpenter. He called Princess Diana Memorial but was given the run-around by the staff, who refused to give him any information. 'Sorry, hospital policy,' he was told, 'we're not permitted to give out details of staff members' whereabouts.'

There was only one thing for it, he would have to fly out to the Middle East and try to track her down. He could only assume she must be in Dubai, as that was where Del Rivera ended up, but he needed more than that to go on. What was the name of that conference she was at? They'd mentioned it when they burst into his room that time, just after he'd been dreaming about drowning on the beach. Well, not dreaming exactly but... 'Come on, Ben, think. Concentrate.' She was in the neurology department and they were going overseas, it was an international event... That's it, the International Neurological Conference. That was it.

He searched for the conference on the internet and found the venue, a hotel in Downtown Dubai. Damn, it was scheduled to finish today, at 3.30 p.m.

Looking at the time displayed in the corner of his screen, he realised the conference would end long before he could get there. He hesitated. Should he stay in London, or go to Dubai? What if she left Dubai before he arrived? They might pass in mid-air. It was certainly a risk. On the other hand, he felt sure she was in the greatest danger while she was overseas. He made up his mind, he would go to Dubai.

He booked onto the earliest flight he had any realistic chance of getting, 14.35 from Heathrow. Booking at the last minute meant an economy ticket was all he could get, and it cost a small fortune, but he wasn't concerned about money at this stage. He grabbed his passport, a few clothes and toiletries, ran down to the lobby, and jumped into a taxi. By the time the taxi had struggled through the traffic and he'd endured an agonising wait at airport security, he just about made it onto the plane by the skin of his teeth.

Initially, he'd planned to spend the flight researching some background on Mortimer. Could the wealthy lord really have been responsible for the Black Death, as Del Rivera claimed? It seemed improbable, but he was gaining more respect for the old man's claims by the hour.

But then he'd got to thinking how incredible his past life experiences were. He'd accepted the idea of reincarnation, of having lived multiple lives, but he was still grappling with the enormity of it. Since he was a boy, he'd admired the courage of the men who stormed the Normandy beaches, the stoic resilience of the British officers facing the Zulus, the grim determination of the soldiers in the trenches of Flanders. He'd always felt an affinity for these brave souls. Now he knew why: he was one of them. His perception of the nature of life was changing, and he was keen to discover more. So, rather than searching the internet, he'd decided he might learn more from his dreams.

Now, four hours later, he'd woken from something far more powerful than a dream, or even one of Del Rivera's kaetchemos. It had been the most vivid experience yet. And he hadn't just experienced being Bobby, he'd felt what it was like for She Wolf too, right up to the moment she ended his suffering. He felt certain they'd shared this vision, as if she'd sent it to him. But, if so, what was she trying to tell him?

It seemed there was only one way to find out. He lay back, closed his eyes, and went back in time again.

*

Bartie saw the lights burning in the mansion's windows. He was almost home. He spurred his horse on, eager for the long journey to be over.

He'd been away almost a week, up in London visiting the headquarters of the family's old regiment to arrange a commission, so he could go out to Portugal and join Wellesley. There was nothing to keep him at home. Mother and Father were dead and he saw little of Sally these days. He would miss her very much, but she hadn't been herself since she became Marcus's personal chamber maid. She was so quiet and withdrawn; the sweet, happy girl he'd once known seemed to have all but disappeared.

He still loved her though. He blushed at the thought. He knew any idea of a relationship between them was impossible. He was the brother of a lord, she was a housemaid. It could never work. Even so, he had thought about asking her to come to Portugal. It would be nice to have her around, see her pretty face every day and, more than anything else, talk to her freely, as they had when they were younger. But he knew she could only ever be his servant, wash his clothes, make his meals and, one day, watch as he took another woman for his wife. He loved her too much to let her suffer that humiliation.

Arriving at the mansion, he dismounted then led his horse to the stables at the rear. He found one of the grooms and handed over the reins, then walked back towards the entrance to the family home he'd known all his life, the home he was about to leave for a long time, possibly forever. As he walked, he weighed his purse in his hands. He'd already paid for his commission and most of the provisions he required for the journey. He'd need a few pounds in the months ahead, but he could spare enough to give Sally what she needed to leave the mansion and make a new life on her own.

Most people would think him crazy to give so much to a mere housemaid, but he didn't care. He loved Sally; even if he couldn't be with her, he wanted to make sure she was happy and safe. Above all, he wanted to get her away from his brother.

He walked through the main entrance and looked at the long case 'grandfather' clock in the hallway: a quarter past nine. Sally would hopefully still be awake. In fact, knowing his brother, she'd probably still be working. He pulled the cord beside the clock to ring for a bell boy. In less than half a minute, a boy appeared, panting after running up two flights of stairs. Marcus had the servants so terrified, instant obedience had become a way of life for them all.

"Yes, my lord?" asked the boy.

"Jimmy, isn't it?" Bartie smiled.

"Yes, my lord," Jimmy smiled back, visibly relieved to see Bartie instead of Marcus.

"Jimmy, would you be kind enough to fetch Miss Trigg for me. I'd like to speak to her."

"Oh, er… er, I'm sorry, my lord, I can't. I mean, er, begging your pardon, my lord, she's gone."

"Gone? Gone where?"

"The constable took her, my lord. Five days ago it was, just after you left. He put her in irons an' he took her away."

"What? But why? Why would he take Sally?"

"Because I asked him to, dear brother," Marcus's voice came through the open doorway leading to the mansion's great hall. Bartie stepped through the opening to see his brother striding towards him.

"What! What do you mean? Why on earth would you do that? What in heaven's name could possibly give you reason to have Sally arrested?"

"Well, there were a few missing items of some small value and one or two of them were found in her room. It is simple enough, dear brother. We cannot tolerate thieving among the servants. It must be rooted out and punished, swiftly and appropriately, before it spreads like the disease it is."

"But, what did she say? Did she admit she'd taken them?"

"Well, she claimed to be innocent of course, but she would, wouldn't she? I mean, she was only a housemaid. You can't trust them, you know."

"You can't trust them? That's ridiculous. She's worked here most of her life, never done a thing wrong; don't you think she deserved a chance to speak up for herself before you had her clapped in irons?" Bartie's tone had risen to a screech, he was shouting at the top of his voice. The commotion had attracted most of the household, but he was too angry to care about keeping up appearances.

"Calm down, little brother, the girl was a thief. She will get her just desserts. She was never a good maid anyway, so clumsy with that deformity of hers."

"It was because of *you* she lost those fingers. You've been an evil, cruel monster to her ever since she came to the house. She's a dear, kind, lovely girl and you've done nothing but ruin her life."

"Revenge is sweet, dear boy."

"What do you mean 'revenge', what did she ever do to you? She worked hard and served you faithfully for years, despite all the torment you heaped upon her."

"Ah, you will understand one day, little brother."

Bartie could take no more. He wanted to help put a stop to Napoleon's tyranny. But, before he could deal with the tyranny spreading across Europe, it was time to deal with the tyranny in his father's house. He crossed the hall to where the family's collection of weaponry was arranged along the wall, and took down one of the sabres. He turned to face Marcus, the sword thrust forward in the 'en garde' position, "Why don't you explain it to me now?"

Marcus smiled. He strode across the hall and took the sword's twin from the wall. "Very well, a duel it is then. En garde!" he held up his sword for the briefest pause then lunged at Bartie, almost running him through before the fight had even begun.

Bartie jumped back, evading the thrust. He'd only recently learned to use a sword, but he'd been practising. Not just for the sake of it, like his brother, he was getting ready to fight the French. He countered, attacking Marcus with intensity, passion, and determination, the thought of Sally protesting her innocence as she was dragged away in irons filling him with fury, driving him on.

But, despite his fervour, Bartie soon realised he'd made a mistake. His brother was an accomplished swordsman. Within seconds, it was clear Marcus was toying with him, watching him fight for his life, easily parrying his thrusts. Bartie was never going to get the better of him. In desperation, Bartie took a wild swing and got lucky for once, leaving a gash across Marcus's forehead. But he'd overextended himself. Marcus pounced forward, slashing Bartie's wrist and sweeping the sword from his grasp. The sabre went clattering across the floor. Bartie fell to his knees, clutching his hand, gasping at the pain. Marcus stood over him, his sword poised above Bartie's chest, "Goodbye, little brother, I will see you again soon."

The mansion's doorbell rang. Marcus took a step back and waved at one of the servants, indicating they should answer the door. A moment later, the servant led in the parish constable.

Duelling, although generally tolerated, was still, strictly speaking, illegal. As the constable entered, Marcus lowered his sword and smiled at Bartie, "Now, dear brother, you must get that nasty little cut seen to. Go and see Mrs Soames at once."

Bartie stood up, looking at the constable. He wondered for a moment if he should say something about Sally, assert her innocence. But he had no evidence, nothing to support his claim. Nothing except the fact he knew in his heart she was innocent. This was not the time, not in front of Marcus. If he wasn't careful, he might only make matters worse.

He made his excuses and left, heading towards the kitchen, ostensibly so Mrs Soames, the cook, who also acted as the nurse, could treat his wound. But, soon as he was out of sight, he doubled back to a secluded spot where he could watch Marcus while remaining unseen from the hall.

Marcus turned to the waiting official, dabbing at the blood dripping from his brow with a handkerchief, "A little sparring match, constable, my brother is keen to be ready when he goes off to tackle Bonaparte. He's quite enthusiastic, but sadly lacking in skill, I'm sorry to say. What news of the little thief?"

"As you ordered, my lord, she was taken to London and put on trial straight away. I just got word she'll receive the first part of her sentence tomorrow…"

"A hundred lashes as I requested?"

"The judge was adamant fifty was the maximum for a case of thieving, my lord."

"Hmmm, that's a pity. Carry on constable."

"The prison ship sails for the colony on Saturday. She'll be on it, my lord."

"Very good, constable; I must thank you for your assistance with this unfortunate business. Do please call again soon."

As the constable turned to leave, Bartie was already running down the stairs to the back of the house, where a rear door led to the stables. Fifty lashes! Australia! This was more than his heart could bear. He had to do something. But it was late Thursday evening, and more than a day's ride to London, he didn't have a moment to spare.

Readying his horse, he heard someone enter the stables behind him. Marcus stood there in the candlelight, "You will never make it in time, brother, the prison ship leaves on the tide, first thing Saturday morning. That gives you less than thirty-six hours. I don't believe anyone has done it in less than forty. And that was me, so I know what I'm talking about."

"I'll go after her. I'll take the next ship if I have to. I'll make the captain catch up. She's innocent, I know it. They'll have to listen."

"She's a convicted criminal, brother. No-one will listen to your ravings. But do run along after her if you must," Marcus started to leave but paused and turned around again; "oh, a couple of things before you go."

"Yes?" Bartie was frantically preparing for his desperate night-time ride.

"One, you will never return to this house, and two, if you do not report to your regiment on Monday, I will see you are court-martialled. I do believe they hang deserters? Awful way to go… Goodbye, brother."

Bartie reached the docks in just under thirty-four hours. He had to buy three new horses en route, using most of his money. It took him almost another hour to find the prison ship. He reached it just as the gangplank was being raised. He shouted at the crewmen, "Wait, you have an innocent girl in there, I must speak to your captain."

The sailors laughed. The largest and ugliest among them shouted, "Don't worry, sonny, there's plenty more whores ashore what'll lift their skirts for half a crown, 'specially for a pretty boy like you."

The ship cast off, taking Sally with it. Bartie fell to his knees on the dockside, knowing he would probably never see her again.

*

With almost no money, and Marcus's threats hanging over him, Bartie had no choice but to take up his commission. The life of a soldier suited him. Courage in battle came easily. He'd lost everything that mattered, he didn't fear death. He rose up the ranks as he fought his way through Spain and into France. He was a major when they beat

Napoleon the first time and sent the little emperor into exile on Elba.

For the next few months, he drifted aimlessly around Europe, visiting Vienna, Venice, Naples and Rome. He felt oddly at home in Rome and lingered there a while. He was there when the news reached him Napoleon was on the march again. Quickly, he returned to his regiment and renewed his commission, gaining a promotion to colonel. He led a brigade at Waterloo and was in the midst of some of the fiercest fighting. After the war, he returned to England. Unable, and unwilling, to go back to his ancestral home, he couldn't settle anywhere. He gathered his savings together and booked passage to Sydney.

Landing in New South Wales almost eight years after Sally had been transported he set out to track her down. His status as Colonel Bartholomew Mortimer, a respected war veteran, ensured the co-operation of the authorities. He found out there were six women named Trigg in the penal colonies. He visited every one, some of them on the harsh, isolated island of Van Diemen's Land; but none of them were Sally. After a long, fruitless, search, he established a female convict listed as 'S. Trigg' had died during the voyage in 1808. He came to the despairing conclusion Sally was dead.

He didn't want to stay without her and he couldn't face the idea of returning to England, so he booked himself onto a ship sailing for the Oregon territory on the west coast of America. In 1818, he became one of the first Europeans to cross the North American continent on horseback. He spent many years exploring this wonderful land, learning about its native people and their ways. In the autumn of 1824, he heard the story of the 'Indian Virgin Queen' who'd led her tribe into battle during the American War of Independence over forty years before. He found the village where she was rumoured to have lived and was allowed to see the chief, an old man called Sleeping Bear. The chief sat by the fire in his tent, gazing into the embers. He could only speak a few words of English, but his devoted wife, sitting by his side, spoke it fluently.

"I have been Feathered Dove for over sixty summers, but my name was once Frances, and I was of your people."

"How did you come to be here?" asked Bartholomew.

"I was captured in a raid and given to Sleeping Bear as a reward for his bravery in battle."

"My God, that's terrible."

"No," she smiled, shaking her head, putting her hand gently on top of the chief's, "not for me. Sleeping Bear was a handsome young warrior then, and he was kind. I fell in love with him, and he with me. He never took another woman and we had four beautiful children together, three boys and a girl. My life here has been a good one, I have no regrets."

"Well, I am pleased to hear that," nodded Bartholomew; "although it does not excuse how you were taken."

"Being taken led me to the greatest happiness of my life. Sometimes our path takes unexpected turns, yet still we reach our goal. How can we help you reach your goal, colonel?"

"I, er… I wondered if you know of this Indian Virgin Queen I have heard talk of in the town?"

Feathered Dove smiled, her old eyes twinkling. Fond memories were playing out behind them, Bartholomew could tell. "Yes, I knew the woman of whom you speak," she said, "and all you have heard about her is true. Her name was She Wolf and she was the bravest warrior, the noblest, fairest chief, the tribe has ever known."

"Is it true she fought in the revolution?"

"Sixteen summers after she became chief, the white settlers rose in rebellion against the Great White King across the water. At first, she kept the tribe out of the white man's war but, in time, she saw the rebels' cause was a just one. She asked for volunteers to go into battle with her. Most of our warriors went."

"But why, it wasn't their fight?"

"She was so well-loved the tribe would have followed her to Hell if she asked."

"What happened to her in the end?"

"She died as she lived, fighting for what she believed in. We grieved for her for many summers, we still do. She will never be forgotten. We believe she has become a star in the heavens and she will watch over us until the end of days."

"Is she buried here? I would like to see her grave if I may?"

"It is not our way to put the dead in the ground. We burn our honoured dead."

"Oh, I see," he frowned; disappointed there was

nowhere he could go to pay his respects to this legendary warrior queen.

"But, if you wish, we can take you to the place where we gave her ashes to the wind so she might find her way to the heavens."

"Yes, I should like that."

*

The walk to the place of the traitors took a long time. Sleeping Bear insisted on joining the expedition, but he was no longer the man he'd once been. Feathered Dove's gait remained firm and strong, however, and she helped the man she'd loved for over sixty years as he shuffled along the path to the tribe's most sacred place.

As they walked, Feathered Dove told Bartholomew how She Wolf had saved the white women from the ants, ended Bobby's suffering, and challenged and defeated Moon Shadow. She smiled as she told him her own part in that. "She never faced another Reckoning," the old woman added, "no-one in the tribe would ever challenge her."

They arrived at the ancient execution site and Feathered Dove indicated the fire, explaining the tribe kept a perpetual flame burning to honour all those who had died here unjustly. The posts that had stood for centuries had been taken down long ago. No-one had fed the ants for many summers, Bobby had been the last.

Bartholomew had a strong sense of déjà vu. He felt

certain he'd been here before. But that was impossible; he'd never been in this area until a few weeks ago. Still, as he knelt and touched the ground, he felt firmly connected to this place, as if it had some kind of message for him.

The little group sat around the fire; the ants didn't bother them, they had abandoned their nest and moved on many years ago. As the sky began to darken, Sleeping Bear took out a pipe and filled the bowl with a mixture of dried herbs. He lit the pipe and drew the smoke deep into his lungs. He went into a trance-like state and started to hum softly.

Bartholomew watched, slightly bemused. But he was more than happy to spend time in the company of these fascinating people and their age-old rituals. After a while, Sleeping Bear turned to him. The chief's eyes stared straight at him, though his gaze lay far beyond, "Your spirit searches for another, you are compelled to seek her but she is hidden from you by shadow."

He means Sally, thought Bartholomew. He believes her spirit still exists but we are separated by the shadow of death.

"You will search a long time," continued the chief, "and journey great distances. You will cross the ocean and fly like an eagle across the sky. You will find her among the sick and you will find her in a great hall filled with music. At last, in the end, you will find her in the desert beneath a marriage of stars. Many times you will find her, but seven times you will lose her."

Ben woke to find the plane starting its descent into Dubai; time to fasten safety belts, stow tray tables, and all that stuff. His journey was almost over, but what he would find at his destination, he had no idea.

For a moment, the sceptic in him took over. This is madness. What am I doing here, thousands of miles from home on some crazy fool's errand to save a woman I hardly know from a peril I can barely comprehend, and all because of a few dreams.

But then he remembered Del Rivera's sudden, violent death. If nothing else, that was a mystery worth looking into. As for the rest, he knew for certain now his past life experiences were real. They had to be, he'd never heard of anyone having dreams like that. The feelings he was experiencing were stronger than anything he'd ever known. Most of all, the love he felt for the woman who inhabited those dreams was far beyond anything he'd felt before... in this lifetime, anyway.

Of course, she wasn't always a woman; she'd been a man at least once. And, while he was usually a man, it wasn't always the case. He wondered what it was that determined their gender. It couldn't just be random, not based on what he'd seen; they both had a definite bias.

But, regardless of whether they were born a man or a woman, she was certainly the soul he loved. And, having seen what Mortimer was capable of, there was every reason to believe all Del Rivera said was true, she genuinely was in grave danger. So, how was he going to find her?

'You will find her in the desert beneath a marriage of stars,' the old chief's words came back to him across the centuries. As the plane touched the ground, he felt sure this was the message she'd wanted to send. But what did it mean? There was plenty of desert here… but what on earth was a marriage of stars?

XVI

SEARCHING

Ben landed at Dubai International just after one in the morning, local time. He'd been here a few times before, but he never failed to be impressed by the size of the place. A built-in railway took passengers from the gate to arrivals; the journey took more than ten minutes, so goodness knew how far it was. After a short delay at passport control, the rest of the airport was extremely efficient and he was soon walking through the green channel at customs and out into the baking heat, to the taxi rank.

"Where to, sir?" the driver asked.

Ben hadn't thought this part through. He'd meant to work out his plans on the plane, but ended up spending most of the flight reliving the past. Quickly, he remembered where the conference had been held, as good a place to start as any, "Kaiserplatz Hotel, please."

"Which Kaiserplatz, sir, there are several?"

"Oh, er… the one in the Dubai International Finance Centre, please"

"DIFC, of course, sir," the driver set off for Downtown Dubai.

Arriving at the Kaiserplatz just before three, Ben went to the desk and started questioning the receptionist, demanding to know if they had any idea where Susan Carpenter had gone. Tired, hungry, and growing increasingly anxious, he began to get irate, "But you must know something. She was at the conference. You know, the International Neurological Conference, right here, in this building, just this afternoon… er, yesterday afternoon, I suppose now."

The polite Indian girl was clearly struggling to deal with his demands, "Let me speak to my manager, sir."

The duty manager was a young Filipino. He did his best to calm the situation, "I'm sorry, sir, but we cannot give out details regarding conference delegates, it's against…"

"Hotel policy," Ben finished with a sigh, "yeah, I know. But, look…" he glanced at the young man's name badge, obviously not his real name, but what the hell, "look, Simon, it's really important I get hold of Doctor Carpenter. Please, I need your help," Ben fixed the younger man with a desperate stare.

"Well, er… I was on duty during the conference. I remember her. She was a very striking woman," Simon shrugged. "But all I know is she left with the keynote speaker. A strange man," Simon gently shook his head;

"I believe they left in his car and headed straight for the airport."

Ben recalled the conversation in his room at the hospital, 'Doctor Carpenter will come with me on my Lear,' Mortimer had said. "Do you have an office with Wi-Fi I can use?"

"Well yes, of course, sir, please follow me."

For the next two hours, Ben worked away in Simon's little office, trying to find some way of tracking down Susan Carpenter or Professor Mortimer. With his background in security, he was able to access most government databases without too much difficulty. His first idea was to locate Mortimer's Lear Jet. He found details of recent arrivals at Dubai International. There was one that seemed to fit the bill. It had arrived a few days before and been due to leave yesterday, but had now been booked to stay a few more days. That must be it, now he just needed the address it was registered to. Sadly though, the Lear's registered address was a company in the Cayman Islands; a dead end.

Next, he got Simon to show him the CCTV footage of the hotel's main entrance for the day before. Sure enough, there was the gold-coloured Rolls. Ben watched the chauffeur manhandling Susan into the back seat. Mortimer joined them a moment later and the car set off. Ben hit pause and took a note of the vehicle's registration. But, when he checked, it led him back to the same Cayman Islands' company.

By this time, it was after five. Ben was having difficulty focussing on the computer screen. He needed a break.

Simon found him a vacant room; he went upstairs, flopped onto the bed, and fell into a deep sleep… a sleep filled with dreams of an earlier time.

*

Lieutenant Bertin Duvall picked up his captain's sword and moved forward to crouch behind the low stone wall beside the leader of the natives attached to his platoon for the assault.

"Your captain was a fool standing up and showing himself to the enemy. He asked for death," the chief said in English. Ironically, their only common language was the language of their adversaries.

"He was unfortunate. Muskets are not usually so accurate at such a distance. We are lucky it is not a unit of riflemen up there."

"He was still a fool. If there are enough muskets, one of them finds the target."

Bertin shrugged, the way Frenchmen often do, "The captain was a courageous man. He believed fortune favours the brave. He encouraged us to fight with 'elan', believing our very bravado would shield us."

"And what do you believe, lieutenant?"

"I must admit I prefer a more tactical approach. I would like to see France again. Nonetheless, our orders are to take this hill at any cost."

"Your orders, you mean. I do not take orders, I fight for what I believe in," the chief smiled and placed a hand on Bertin's arm, "and perhaps for handsome young Frenchmen too."

His head span at the chief's touch. The captain had told him about this remarkable ally, leader of the tribe for twenty years, victor of numerous battles, a truly formidable warrior. And yet now, as he knelt beside her, what impressed him most was what an incredibly beautiful woman she was. As She Wolf spoke again, he tried to focus on the task ahead.

"The British are well defended on all sides and we cannot wait for nightfall. We have no choice but to make a full-frontal assault. It will cost us dear but we must rush them as fast as we can. They are only perhaps eight or ten men at most. Your captain threw away all chance of surprise; the only advantage we have left is our numerical superiority, although we shall lose much of that as we charge the hill."

Despite his youth, Bertin had seen a great deal of action, but he'd never seen anyone as confident and assured in battle as this amazing woman. Without a second thought, he immediately allowed her to take command, heartened by her calm authority.

She peered over the wall at the British position on the summit, "As we reach the top, our way will be barred by the rocks that defend them. I will break left with my warriors and attack from that side. You will lead your troopers to the right and attack from there."

Bertin nodded, "Bon, are you ready?"

"Just give the order, lieutenant."

He jumped to his feet and raised his sword, "Allez!"

French troopers and native warriors alike sprang to their feet and charged up the hill.

Bertin and She Wolf ran side by side at the head of their men. She screamed a war cry that was sure to put fire into the bellies of everyone in the platoon. Bertin had an overwhelming sense of admiration for her. He felt honoured to be fighting at her side.

The British kept up a steady stream of fire and the musket balls whizzed past their heads. One grazed Bertin's arm but he ran on unchecked. It was a small hill, but the ascent seemed to take an eternity and he was dimly aware of the ever-reducing number of troopers and native warriors following them as they ran towards the British guns. He fully expected to fall at any moment but at last they were only a few feet from the rocks sheltering the British position. He saw She Wolf break left at the head of her warriors, her bow raised ready to strike. He turned right and circled around the rocky outcrop, his sword held high.

As he stepped onto the higher ground beyond the rocks, he saw the British soldiers lined up behind their defences, still aiming their muskets down the hill at the rest of his platoon. He fell upon them with his sword, taking down two before they had chance to turn. Looking up, he saw the British officer bringing his pistol to bear. He rushed at the man, feeling something hit him as the distance between them closed, but soon reached his opponent and put his sword through the officer's chest.

Turning around, Bertin saw the skirmish was already over. His men had taken out another two British soldiers and She Wolf stood proudly before him with five of the enemy lying behind her, each with an arrow protruding from their chest, neck, or eye socket.

She smiled at him momentarily but her expression changed to a frown as she gazed at his chest. He looked down to see what she was staring at and saw the crimson stain spreading across his tunic. His strength began to fade, his legs crumbled beneath him. She Wolf rushed forwards and caught him as he fell.

"Merde," he exclaimed, "I really did want to see France again."

"You will, my friend, you will. Even if not with these eyes, you will see France again. I promise you," she brushed the hair from his forehead.

"The flag," he remembered, "it is the signal we agreed. We must raise our allies' flag to show we have taken the hill. Please hurry, I must see it before I die."

She laid him down gently, with his back against a rock, then stood up and demanded in heavily accented French, "Ou est la banniere?"

A trooper ran forward and handed her the flagpole. As she grasped it, the banner that united the rebel colonists and their allies fluttered in the breeze. She climbed the last few paces to the summit and held it high in the air.

Bertin felt an enormous sense of pride as he gazed up at the magnificent warrior queen. Her long, dark hair flew behind her in the wind, in parallel with the banner above her head. He looked at the flag as his vision started to fade.

Its red and white stripes began to blur, but the stars in the corner seemed to grow more vibrant. The last thing he saw as the darkness closed in was the outline of She Wolf's triumphant figure beneath a field of glowing white stars.

*

Ben woke with the image of She Wolf still in his mind's eye. Suddenly, he knew what the 'marriage of stars' was. A marriage was a union; the flag represented the union formed by the American colonies. Susan was being held captive somewhere in the desert beneath the Stars and Stripes.

Simon was off duty now, but Ben connected his laptop to the hotel Wi-Fi. He searched for US embassies and consulates in the UAE, but none of them fitted the bill. Next, he tried American corporations with offices registered in the UAE. Again, none of them were what he was looking for. All of them were in urban areas, nothing at a remote location in the desert. Having exhausted other possibilities, he decided to call in an old favour.

"Ben, great to hear from you buddy. What a terrific surprise. How's it hanging?" Colonel Jack Foster was an old friend from way back.

"Jack, I need a favour," Ben got straight to the point.

"Hey, anything buddy, just name it. I owe you big time for Basra." Ben had saved Jack's life a few years ago and the American had sworn, 'Any time I can do anything for you, anything at all, you just let me know.'

Ben told Jack what he wanted.

"Buddy, you'll get me court-martialled. Look, I owe you, Ben, we both know that. I wouldn't be here if it wasn't for you, but that's gonna take some organising."

"I need this, Jack. I can't explain why right now, but it's a matter of life and death, I promise. Please Jack?"

"OK buddy, give me twenty-four hours. I'll let you know what we find," Jack hung up, leaving Ben wondering what the hell he was going to do with himself for the next twenty-four hours.

XVII

NIGHTMARES

Susan slowly came to, feeling like she'd slept a ridiculously long time. She'd had some sort of awful nightmare, hadn't she? No, several nightmares, burning and drowning, other horrible things. A long series of dreadful nightmares playing one after the other like someone was showing an all-night 'nightmare special' in her head. God, she was definitely going to have to consult with one of her colleagues when she got back to the UK, there must be something wrong with her. And her bloody headache was raging again.

'This bed isn't very comfortable,' she thought. Then, as consciousness gradually returned, she realised she wasn't lying down, but standing up, sort of slumped, hanging from her arms. What a weird position to sleep in. She tried to move and the pain in her wrists jolted her wide awake. Her eyes snapped open and she saw, to her horror, she was chained to the wall. She stood upright to ease the strain on her arms and took stock of her predicament.

The manacles on her wrists looked like steel, or maybe chrome; some sort of grey-silver metal, anyway. They appeared to be fastened by a simple screw mechanism. There was another band of the same material around her waist, like a metal belt, holding her to the wall by a chain at the back.

She was standing barefoot on a small platform, raised a foot or so off the floor, still in the same blouse and skirt she'd been wearing at the conference. Her jacket, shoes, and tights were gone though; and she also seemed to be wearing some sort of girdle. She couldn't see it under her skirt, but it was pretty uncomfortable. She shivered, feeling uneasy. Had she been violated while she'd been unconscious? It didn't feel like it, but it was disturbing to know someone had taken her knickers off and replaced them with something else.

A low humming sound reverberated around the room; either air-conditioning or a number of computers, perhaps both. She spotted a few monitors on the other side of the room, arranged at desks with chairs placed in front. They looked like a scene from mission control at NASA during one of the old space shuttle launches.

There were no windows, just a solid iron door with three large keyholes: top, middle, and bottom. Probably a basement, she supposed. Despite this, it was brightly lit. Fluorescent lighting built into the ceiling added to the feeling of a mission control command centre. CCTV cameras were positioned in each corner. She was being watched.

She felt oddly calm. So calm, she surprised herself. She

should have been terrified after waking up in a position like this. 'I've been through worse,' she said to herself; then tried to think when, exactly, that was supposed to have been?

For a moment, she wondered if this was another nightmare. She pulled on one of the chains holding her to the wall and felt the pain in her wrist. No, it's real enough.

Casting her mind back, she tried to recall how she got here. She remembered leaving the conference in Mortimer's Rolls. The car had headed in the wrong direction, then he'd reached across and put his hand on her forehead... and everything had gone black.

Then all the nightmares had come, one after another. But they'd been so real, just like those bizarre dreams she'd been having that always seemed to have Mortimer in them; and that strange vision she'd seen in Carlton's room at the hospital.

Carlton. He was in her nightmares too. Only it wasn't the Carlton she'd met, it was another version of him; lots of versions, at different times, in different places. And she'd been in love with him every time. But it never worked out. One way or another, something kept getting in the way... something, or someone?

Oh, this was crazy. What was she saying to herself? Past-life regression through visions and dreams, could she really allow herself to believe that was what was happening? It was preposterous.

But, was it more preposterous than waking up chained to the wall in someone's basement?

'Come on Susan,' she told herself, 'there's a rational explanation to this, even if it isn't a very pleasant one. Now, think, why would someone hold you captive?'

Given that her last waking memory involved Mortimer, she could only assume he was the one holding her. He must have drugged her. A chloroform-soaked handkerchief in his palm when he'd reached across perhaps? Yes, that must have been *how* he did it, but *why*?

Ransom? No, that couldn't be it. He had more money than anyone could ever need, what would be the point?

Modern slavery? That wouldn't make any sense, she'd soon be missed. There must surely be other girls who'd make easier, less traceable, targets. Plus, that kind of scum liked them young and she was nearly thirty-seven.

Did he want her for himself? Some sort of sex slave? That made sense after what he did to her when she was Sally. No, wait a minute, if she actually was Sally, then we were back to reincarnation and 'rational' was out the window. No, that's crazy, think again, Susan.

Organ harvesting? Hmmm, that was a possibility. Maybe her DNA was a good match for some rich bastard who needed a transplant; or Mortimer himself? Oh shit, that must be it. It was the only thing that made sense. Fuck!

That would explain the computers: detailed DNA analysis to find a match for Mortimer and his cronies. That was probably what he did out here in the desert, assuming the basement was under his villa, which seemed logical. God, yes, he was prolonging his life by stealing other people's organs. That was how he'd been around in the war. He could be over a hundred years old, like some modern-day Dracula, only he steals organs instead of drinking blood.

So, now she knew what he was up to, she had to figure out how to get out of it. She couldn't believe she was so calm, she should be shitting herself. She supposed that would come later; she was always calm when they went into battle with the rebels. No, stupid, there she went again, that was just a dream, it wasn't real.

She pulled on the chains holding her to the wall and winced at the pain. No escape, she was stuck here for now. She'd have to wait for an opportunity to make a break for it. Oh God, what if she never got chance. He was going to cut her up, take what he wanted, leave her for dead. Christ, it could be even worse; he might keep her alive for years, take bits one at a time so they were fresh when he needed them. Talk about a fate worse than death. She had to find a way out of this. She scanned the room, looking for clues to Mortimer's intentions, or any kind of weapon she could use. She came up blank on both counts; the answer wasn't in the basement.

Well, dreams are sometimes a way to tell ourselves something we need to know. Maybe there was a clue in one of her dreams? She closed her eyes and tried to recall anything, any detail, which might help her now.

XVIII

LADY OF THE MANOR

She was born in 1168, in the reign of King Henry II, the eldest child of Charles and Maria de Brune. Christened Charlotte Maria, after both her parents, she had three sisters: Florence, who arrived in 1173; Isabella, who followed in 1177; and Margaret, the youngest, born in 1180.

Her mother finally gave birth to a boy in the spring of 1184, but the family's joy was short-lived; she died a few days later. The boy was never a healthy child and joined his mother in the family burial plot shortly after his second birthday.

With no sons, and four daughters to care for, Charlotte's father struggled on as best he could. He was a proud, noble man, a baron, but a poor one. His lands were not yielding sufficient crops or livestock for his subjects to pay him the rent he needed to maintain the estate. Unlike many other barons, he never evicted those who couldn't pay, but often accepted half rent or payment in kind. His generosity meant he was well-loved. But you can't eat love, or mend castle walls with it. By the beginning of 1187, more than half the castle was uninhabitable and he simply did not have the money to pay for the necessary repairs. The situation was becoming desperate.

He had another pressing problem too. Charlotte was almost nineteen. He had to arrange a match for her soon, or she would be branded an 'old maid', fit only for a convent. She had been betrothed to Baron de Villiers' son, but de Villiers was unable to take her on without a significant dowry, far more than he could realistically afford.

He knew where he could find a better solution. Lord Marner had had his eyes on Charlotte a long time and had offered to pay a substantial sum to 'take her off his hands'; enough to keep the estate going for years to come. It was the perfect answer to the family's problems. Except that Marner was more than twenty years older than Charlotte. He might have come to terms with that, but Marner also had a reputation.

The old baron spent many sleepless nights worrying. He knew what the sensible thing to do was, but he feared for Charlotte's happiness, he did not want to see her suffering at the hands of a cruel husband. Like many people struggling with a difficult choice, he put it off as long as he could. But, in March, things came to a head when the roof of the great hall collapsed. With a heavy heart, he finally made his decision. He summoned Charlotte to tell her the news.

"Come in, daughter, I have wondrous news for you," the baron responded to her knock.

She entered the cramped little room he was using as his audience chamber, and stood in front of his desk, "Good day, father, it is good to see you looking well. What is this wondrous news?"

"I have decided you shall marry Brentley de Villiers. We will arrange it as soon as possible."

Her first reaction was joy, a huge smile spread across her face. But her smile turned to a frown as she thought things over. She knew all too well what dire straits her father was in, and de Villiers was not a wealthy man either.

"Father, I am indeed gladdened by this news, but what of the dowry? Baron de Villiers has many repairs of his own to attend to, and the harsh winter has blighted his lands as well as ours. Can you afford the dowry he will want yet still have enough to restore our home and give you back the comforts you have lost these past few years?"

"Now, my daughter, it is not for you to worry about such things. Off with you now, I must get a message to de Villiers," he rose to his feet and tried to usher her out of the room.

She wasn't having it. Hands on hips, she stubbornly stood her ground, "Father, I will not move until I hear the truth of this."

He sighed and sat down again behind his little wooden writing desk, "I will offer de Villiers all the money I have in the hope it is enough, even though, my dear, sweet, daughter, you are surely worth much more."

"Well, my father, if I am worth more, surely you should get something in return for me. Is there no other who might provide a better bargain?"

"No, daughter, there is no other."

As he demurred, she noticed he couldn't look her in the eyes. She'd run her father's household since her mother's death, she knew when he was lying, "Tell me, father, I know you have a better offer; who is it?"

He sighed again and stared at the ground. He spoke in a low mumble, as if he didn't want her to hear, "It is Lord Marner."

"Then you must accept his offer and I shall marry Lord Marner."

"He is too old for you."

"What is he then, perhaps twenty years my senior? Were you not almost twenty years older than mother? Yet she married you willingly all the same and your time together was happy."

"Only eighteen years lay between us; Marner is twenty-two years your senior. It is too much. I cannot let you sacrifice your happiness for my sake."

"There is hardly any difference, and you know it, father."

"My child, it is not just his age. I have heard tales of his manner, his behaviour, his… er, his er… Well, let us just say he is a hard man with a harsh temperament. I cannot let you be his wife."

"What are these tales? Just that, tales! A man can be softened by the love of a good wife, it is well known. I am your eldest daughter; it is my duty to serve you. I shall serve you by my softening of Lord Marner, and you shall have fine grandchildren to please you in your old age."

"No daughter, I cannot… you do not understand… He… We will manage. I will let the servants go, look after the girls myself. We will live here in the west tower, just we four; it is almost intact, it does not leak much. We will be fine," he lowered his head.

She could see he was ashamed he could no longer look after his children properly. She came around to his side of the desk, knelt beside him and put her arm around his shoulders, "Father, you must think of Flossie, Bella, and Mags. You must let me do this for you, all of you. Please, father, I want to help you."

He was sobbing now. He could no longer speak. He simply nodded.

*

Charlotte was married to Lord Marner in his castle a few days before her nineteenth birthday. She looked resplendent in the elegant wedding gown her sisters had made. The feast went on late into the night. She was astounded at the amount of food and wine her new husband consumed. She was also struggling to get accustomed to being called 'Lady Marner'. Her new title felt strange, like a new dress that did not quite fit.

Among the gathering was a young man not much older than her. "Let me introduce you to Brentley de Villiers," her father said, leading her to him. "Young Brentley has joined Marner's company as his squire, so you will be seeing a fair amount of each other after all."

She chatted politely with Brentley for a few minutes until propriety demanded she resume her place at the top table beside the groom. She felt a pang of regret at what might have been. Young de Villiers would have made a fine husband, rather charming and very handsome.

'No use in that,' she told herself. Duty to her family came first. She would make the best of it with Marner, and that was that.

She took a proper look at Marner for the first time since the ceremony. He was certainly tall, dark and… yes, she supposed, handsome in a rugged sort of way. He was a lot older than her, it was true, but he wasn't *old*, not like her dear father was old. She was sure the tales of his cruelty must be exaggerated. And, besides, he wasn't going to be cruel to *her*, his wife, was he? 'Yes,' she thought, 'I am sure I can make this marriage work.'

Her wedding night was not what she hoped for. They retired to the master bed chamber a little after three o'clock. She stood in the centre of the room in nervous anticipation. Marner grunted at her, took off his clothes, clambered into bed and fell into a drunken stupor. It was a large bed but with Marner sprawled in the middle there was no room for her. She spent the night curled up on a chaise longue beside the fire. Never mind, she was certain it would be better tomorrow.

The following morning, Baron de Brune and his daughters were preparing to depart. The old baron was choking back the tears as the time came to leave his eldest daughter behind. "Remember, we are only a day's ride away, come and visit us when you can," he reached out and touched her gently on the cheek; "so like your mother, so beautiful, strong and brave, what will I do without you?"

"You will manage just fine, father, you do not need a young girl like me to look after you," she helped him into the new carriage bought with part of the money he'd received from Marner.

She turned and lifted her two youngest sisters into the carriage. Laughing and giggling at the fun of it all, they settled on the bench opposite their father for the long journey. Finally, she turned to her eldest sister, "Darling Flossie, I hope this same joy will find you in but a few short years. Until that happy day comes, please take care of father. He will need your support more than he admits. I know I ask a great deal of you, but please, my sister, do as I ask?"

"Of course, Charlie, I shall care for him as you have always done. Do not worry for father. But I worry so for *you*, my sister."

"Oh, I shall be fine, Flossie. I will soon have his lordship under control." The sisters laughed and Florence stepped up into the carriage to take her seat beside the baron, assuming the role of the lady of the family, as Charlotte had done the last three years.

Marner was busy with the affairs of his estate for the rest of the day. Charlotte tried to get to know some of the servants, speaking to a few of them when she had chance. They were all very respectful, but she could not get more than two words out of any of them.

On her second night as a married woman, she sat on the chaise longue by the fire writing a letter to her father while she waited for her husband. It was almost midnight when Marner arrived. He took off his sword and outer clothing, "Let me see you then."

She stood in front of him, "I hope my lord is pleased?"

He stepped forward and grasped the front of her nightgown. "I said, let me see you," he ripped off the gown, leaving her naked. "So this is the prize I paid so much for," he grunted, looking her up and down.

She was taken aback, but still determined to be a good wife, "How may I best please you, my lord? Forgive me, for I am a maiden and have no knowledge of what passes between a man and his wife in the bed chamber." This was not entirely true: her mother had told her much about the bed chamber before she died.

"Just lie on the bed," he ordered.

She lay on her back. He kneeled above her, looking down. "I do not need to see your face," he reached beneath her and flipped her onto her stomach; "lift up your arse, woman."

It hurt that first time. He took her in an act of raw lust. There was no finesse, no tenderness; most of all there was no love. It was the same most nights, nothing like the tender, exquisite act her mother had described. In time, she realised his drunken state on their wedding night had been a blessing in disguise, and she came to long for those nights when he fell asleep before he could do anything else. But it was bearable, just, and she reminded herself constantly she was doing this for her dear father and sisters. What was worse in many ways was her isolation during the day.

A few days after the wedding, she had a long conversation with Peter, a new stable boy, who had just arrived at the castle. That night, Marner demanded to know what she thought she was doing.

"I only wanted to get to know some of our servants a little better, my lord. In my father's castle, I always…"

He stopped her with a brutal slap across her face. He ripped off her nightgown and grabbed her by the back of the neck, forcing her into a kneeling position across the chaise longue. She raised her head to speak, but he pushed her down again, "Silence, bitch, you need to learn your place. This will teach you not to meddle where you are not wanted." He took off his leather belt and beat her across the buttocks until she was sobbing in agony. After the beating, he grabbed her by the hips and forced himself inside her.

When he was done, he stood up. Glaring down at her, he snapped, "You do not fraternise with the servants. You will speak to them only when necessary to pass on my orders or carry out your duties. Is that clear, woman?"

"Y-y-yes… yes, my lord," she sobbed.

The next morning, she ate breakfast standing up. When she went into the courtyard, she gasped in horror. Peter's corpse was hanging from the portcullis.

After that, she was wary of speaking to anyone. Even the occasional exchange of 'good day' with Brentley de Villiers filled her with anxiety. To compound her sense of solitude, Marner refused to allow her any involvement in the running of the estate. Her only duties were to supervise the kitchen and arrange entertainments for visiting guests. And there were not many guests.

Her days settled into a long, dull routine, and her nights were hardly anything to look forward to. Her only escape was the time she spent writing to her father. She wrote long, loving, letters, painting a far rosier picture than the harsh reality she was enduring. She did not want him to worry. His replies were all too brief. He had never been much of a correspondent, she had written most of his letters for him when she was at home. But, a few months after her arrival, she received a letter that filled her with joy. Her father and Florence were going on a tour of the de Brune estate to check on the renovations he was having carried out. He suggested they might pay her a visit at the end of their tour. She smiled when she recognised the writing as Florence's, despite her father's signature at the bottom. Overjoyed at the thought of seeing her family, she showed the letter to Marner and asked if she could start making preparations to entertain the guests.

"Out of the question, I am not having your useless family languishing here at my expense. Your father has been paid in full, you belong to me now. You will write back and tell him it is not convenient for him to visit."

"But, my lord, I have not seen my family in months, can I not…"

"I have spoken, woman. Do you wish to feel my belt?"

"No, my lord, I only…"

"Enough of this insolence, you will do as I command. See that your letter is on my desk first thing tomorrow, I wish to review it before it is sent. I shall be inspecting all your correspondence from now on."

Even her letters fell under Marner's control. Her last bit of freedom was snuffed out. She was nothing but a possession, a slave in all but name, with no chance of escape. Despair took hold of her as she realised her hopes of softening Marner were futile. She knew suicide was a mortal sin but she began to wonder if Hell could be any worse than the life she was leading. It was her children that saved her.

She gave Marner a son towards the end of 1188. She asked if Florence, now fifteen, could come to the castle to help with the birth, but he flatly refused and the cook was the only assistance she got. It was a long, difficult labour, which left her physically and emotionally exhausted. Marner gave her two days to recover before he started work on his next offspring.

When she gave birth to a little girl in 1190, Marner did not attempt to hide his disappointment it was not another son. This time, he did not even give her two days.

Her children became the one source of happiness in her life. She was completely devoted to them, adored them more than she had ever thought possible. They had a nanny to take care of them, but the nursery was just across the passageway from the master bed chamber, so she was able to see them whenever she wanted, or at least whenever Marner had no need of her. Satisfying his demands remained as unpleasant as ever, but she resigned herself to putting up with him. It was worth it to be close to her babies.

King Henry had now been succeeded by King Richard and, at the beginning of 1191, the Lionheart called for his nobles to join him on a crusade to the Holy Land. Marner was one of the first to sign up for the expedition, evidently relishing the prospect of using his sword on Saladin's hordes. But he needed someone to run his estate in his absence. Charlotte was quick to volunteer, "My lord, surely it is my duty as your wife. Let me take on this burden for you."

He laughed in her face, "You? A woman? I should like at least some of my castle to be standing when I return. Do not be so foolish." Instead, he appointed Brentley de Villiers to take over the running of the estate. He made it clear the boy was too soft in his opinion, but he acknowledged he had proven himself loyal.

The afternoon before he was due to leave, Marner summoned Charlotte and led her to the blacksmith's workshop in the grounds outside the castle. He told her to enter and stand in the middle of the floor. "Is it ready?" he asked the smith.

"Yes, my lord."

"And you have made it to my precise specifications?"

"Of course, my lord, just as you asked."

"Good, let us proceed," he turned to Charlotte, who was puzzled by her husband's behaviour. He was always cruel and brutish, but this was odd even by his standards.

"Undress," he commanded. She was well accustomed to his demands by now, but he had never asked her to bare herself in front of another man. Was this some kind of test, to check she would be faithful? She looked at the smith: not much of a test. Now, Brentley, *he* would be a test.

"Are you certain, my lord, should he not avert his gaze?" she gestured at the smith.

"Yes, woman, I am certain. Do as you are bidden, or you will feel my belt."

She stripped off her clothes and stood naked in front of Marner and the smith. The smith retrieved a strange-looking object from behind his workbench: a type of metal belt, with an additional loop extending downwards. She stared at it in horrified disbelief as she realised it was intended for her.

The smith put the belt around her waist, with the downwards loop around her groin. With a loud metallic 'clunk' he fastened it in place. He turned a key in a small hole in the belt's side and there was a further 'click' as the device was locked. He handed the key, hung on a fine chain, to Marner, who placed it around his neck.

"There," announced Marner, "that should keep my

property safe from interference. A belt of chastity one might say. You may dress again, woman." He walked away, leaving Charlotte standing naked in front of the smith, staring aghast at the contraption locked around her body.

She pulled her clothes on and walked awkwardly back to the castle. The metal belt rubbed against her hips and the tops of her thighs. By the time she reached the master bed chamber, each step was growing more painful than the last. But her ordeal had only just begun. Marner sent word she was to move to new quarters in the east tower immediately. No-one was sent to help her. When she had finally finished moving her belongings, there was blood running down her legs.

It was cold, draughty and damp at the top of the tower. There were few adornments and only the most basic amenities. Marner had left orders she was not to leave her chambers except to fulfil her duties supervising the kitchen. There would be no entertainments to organise while he was away. Worst of all, she would only be permitted to see her children once a week, for an hour.

She lay down in bed that night and started to cry. Her hips and thighs were throbbing where the awful metal belt had chafed. There was rain dripping through the roof and she was shivering under the thin piece of sackcloth she had been given for a blanket. Far from being lady of the manor, she was a prisoner in her own home, treated no better than a dog. She longed for her real home, with her father and sisters.

But all this was nothing next to the unbearable ache in her heart. Her babies had been taken from her. They were her world, what she lived for, now she would hardly see them. Being parted from her children was the cruellest torture of all.

Cold, lonely, and desolate, she sobbed long into the night. Marner left early the next morning, taking the key to the wretched belt with him.

XIX

TRAPPED

The first few weeks were hard on Charlotte. She struggled to cope with the cruel device locked around her waist and missed her children so much it hurt. Seeing them was the single ray of light in a life of unending darkness. But the hour passed so quickly, and the time apart was a torment. No doubt Marner had allowed their brief visits as a ploy to keep her under control. Nonetheless, the pitifully short weekly interlude gave her something to live for. She was grateful to see the children at all.

Brentley was settling into his new role. He started to organise the estate so everyone could accomplish their tasks more efficiently. Soon he was able to reinstate Sunday as a day of rest, after Marner had abolished it many years earlier, yet still increase the estate's productivity. He followed Marner's orders to the letter; it would be a foolish man who chose to disobey the lord, even while he was away. But he could interpret those orders a little more generously perhaps, especially when it came to Lady Marner?

He felt enormous sympathy for Charlotte and was appalled by the way Marner treated her. He had heard about the horrid belt she was locked in and how she was kept away from her children. If his father had been wealthier, they might have been married and he would have given her a much happier life. That was not to be, but he could still make her life a little better now.

Although he was acting lord, he had no direct authority over the household. Marner had left a governess in charge of the nanny and other domestic servants, with strict instructions regarding Charlotte and the children. Even Charlotte's supervision of the kitchen was nothing but a sham, as the governess made all the decisions. However, it did provide an excuse for her to leave her quarters. Two weeks after Marner's departure, Brentley sent a note, 'My lady, it occurs to me, in order to fulfil your duties and ensure the kitchen is functioning to your satisfaction, you should sample the food and report your findings to me. To enable you to do this best, I suggest you attend supper with me.'

They began to have supper together most evenings. Slowly, they opened up and started talking freely about their families, the servants on their home estates, favourite animals, their hopes and dreams, and so on. Their fathers were always an amusing topic. Each of them loved their father dearly, but the two old barons had plenty of interesting foibles, which generated much hilarity.

Brentley arranged to have the roof repaired in Charlotte's chamber and smuggled in a thick eiderdown to replace the sackcloth she'd been given by the governess. When she saw the eiderdown lying on her bed, she felt so grateful she broke down and wept.

A guard named Higgins was responsible for fetching the nanny to take away the children after their allotted hour with Charlotte. Every week, Brentley would find Higgins a task that took him far from the castle and the poor man had to rush back, perhaps an hour late, even two. But Higgins soon learned that, far from punishing his failure, the acting lord seemed more pleased the later he was. So, he stopped rushing back and began to linger in the tavern. After a few weeks, Charlotte was getting most of a day with her children.

The next couple of months were the happiest time she'd known since leaving home four years before. But her happiness was short-lived. She had a growing problem and, about ten weeks after Brentley first invited her to supper, she realised she could ignore it no longer.

From the moment she was locked in the belt, she had some practical concerns. Firstly, there was the problem of using the toilet. For a while she got into a horrible mess, but eventually she learned how to avoid that.

Her next concern was how to deal with her monthly 'visitor'. Luckily, she had received such a visit about a week before Marner left. She remembered it well because he slapped her across the face for getting blood on his sheets.

The first month came and went without any sign of the visitor. She was not unduly concerned, the pattern of her visits had been disrupted since she gave birth to her son, and it was not uncommon for her to miss a month. But, when the second month passed without a visit, she began to worry. A month later, when she started getting sick in the mornings, she knew the truth. She was with child.

What could she do? She couldn't give birth while she was stuck in this monstrous device. What would happen when her belly grew? The baby! It would be trapped inside her. The baby would die. She had to do something. She thought about trying to get a message to Marner, begging him to return the key before it was too late. But it would be no use, she had sent messages before and they had been returned with the seal intact. In desperation, she sneaked out to see the smith and asked if he had another key to the device.

"No, my lady, his lordship was most insistent he should have the only key. There were to be no copies made."

"But, can you make another?"

"I am sorry, my lady, he made me break the mould and melt it in the forge so there was no trace left of it, there is nothing I can do."

With a sense of hopeless desolation, she realised she and her unborn child were doomed.

*

Brentley began to notice his supper companion was not her usual self. He tried to cheer her up with a few humorous stories about his father, but to no avail. She was probably enduring her monthly 'visit', he concluded. In an effort to lighten the mood, he decided to tease her a little.

"I will have to cut down your portions, my lady, you are growing fat," he laughed, pointing at her stomach.

She stared back at him aghast and burst into tears.

Mortified that he had upset her, he quickly retracted, "I am sorry, my lady, I did not mean to offend you. I only meant you are looking healthy and well, less thin than usual, you are not fat at all, I apologise most profusely."

With great tears running down her cheeks, she tried to speak between the dreadful sobs racking her body, "It is not that, I… I… I… am… I… am…"

"You are what, what is it Charlotte?" in his concern, he forgot the usual etiquette.

She choked back her tears, "I am with child, Brent. With child and trapped in this terrible device. What will I do?"

He struggled to comprehend the seriousness of her predicament. Then the realisation she was in mortal danger hit him. Immediately, he despatched a message to Marner, imploring him to send the key for the sake of his wife and unborn child. But it would take months for the message to reach Marner and, even if he sent the key straight away, it would take many more for it to return. Very likely, it would be too late.

The next morning, Brentley went to the smith and established for himself that making a copy of the key would be impossible. He demanded the smith saw the belt off. The man was reluctant to help, fearful of Marner's retribution but, when Brentley explained the enormity of the situation, he agreed to try.

After an hour of work with his best saw, the smith collapsed, exhausted. Charlotte had been cut in several places, but the belt bore barely a scratch.

"I am sorry, my lord, it is the finest steel. Nothing will cut through it."

"Surely you can pick the lock then, you made the wretched thing, did you not?"

"Most of it is my work, my lord; that is true. But Lord Marner made the locking mechanism himself and, in truth, I am unable to comprehend its workings. I cannot help you my lord. Have you considered an alternative solution?"

"What alternative?"

"There is a woman in the village. Some of the girls go to her when they are in trouble. There is a risk, but she may be able to…"

"How much of a risk?" Brentley interrupted.

"From what I have heard, maybe one from each five will perish. But, for those that survive, she usually succeeds in disposing of the problem."

"No!" exclaimed Charlotte; "I will not countenance such a course. This is an innocent child growing inside me. I will not murder my child. Surely there is someone who can get this contraption off me?"

"Well, there is perhaps one who might."

"Who?" Brentley demanded.

"Finnian Smith, my lord, the best locksmith in all England; you will find him in London."

London was at least a five day journey, probably six, and Brentley could see Charlotte was already in distress as her growing belly pressed against the metal belt. "We must go at once," he announced; "we leave at first light tomorrow."

Charlotte turned to him and put her hand on his arm, "My father's castle is just a day from the road to London. I have not seen him or my dear sisters in four long years. Please, I must see them before we go to London. If our mission does not succeed…"

There was no need for her to say the rest. Brentley nodded his agreement.

*

Breaking with Marner's orders, Brentley instructed the nanny to take the children to Charlotte's chamber and leave them there the rest of the day. Charlotte held her baby girl for over an hour, singing lullabies and speaking softly to her as she watched her little boy playing on the floor with his toy soldiers.

When the girl was fast asleep, she hugged and kissed her son for as long as the little boy's patience would allow. Finally, she held him at arms' length and looked into his eyes, "Mommy has to go on a journey now. Will you be a brave boy while I am gone?" The child nodded. "That is a good boy. And when you grow up, Mommy wants you to be brave and strong, but also kind. Will you do that for Mommy?"

"Yes Mommy," the little boy answered and returned to his toys.

*

They left first thing in the morning with Higgins and two other guards in escort. A fourth man drove Charlotte's coach. She watched the castle disappearing behind them and choked back her tears. Leaving her children was a tremendous wrench but she knew they were safest at home with their nanny. Safe from harm and safe from what they might witness if things did not go well. She had spent the night praying she would see them again, but she knew it was far from certain. Turning forwards, she lifted her chin. Whatever fate had in store, she would face it for their sake, and for the sake of their unborn sibling growing inside her.

The journey was hard. The metal belt pressed into her belly every time she was jolted by a bump in the road; and there were many bumps. But, as the light began to fade, the de Brune castle finally came into view, and she could see three girls running out to meet them.

She barely recognised her sisters. Bella had shot up, she was nearly as tall as Charlotte, although as thin as a rake; little Mags was far more composed than the urchin she remembered; but the biggest surprise was Florence.

At seventeen, she had blossomed into a beautiful young woman. Charlotte felt a pang of jealousy as she spied Brentley looking at her. 'But why not,' she reminded herself, 'I am married to another after all.'

"Father will be thrilled to see you here at last. With such a handsome companion too," Florence looked back at Brentley with obvious interest; "but where are the children?"

"They are too young for the rigours of the road, my lady. They are safe at the castle in the care of a nanny," Brentley answered.

Charlotte was grateful to be saved from the awkward question as Florence climbed into the coach and sat beside her. They embraced warmly, kissing each other on the cheek. Florence smiled, "Oh, Charlie, it is wonderful to see you again after so long apart, I have missed you so. You must tell me all about the delights of married life," she winked mischievously. Sitting back, she studied Charlotte carefully, "Well, goodness, if I am not mistaken, you are with child again. Oh what joy, sister, to be blessed thrice in but four years. What do you think this time, another boy, or another darling girl?"

"Er, er... I... I do not know, sister, there is no way to tell," Charlotte stammered; she had not expected to have to discuss her condition so soon.

"Well, cook claims she can, although she does not always get it right," Florence laughed. She looked at Charlotte again, "But, sister, you have your corsets fastened too tight for a lady in your condition. Here, let me loosen them for you," she reached under Charlotte's skirt then suddenly recoiled in shock, staring at her with a look of horror in her eyes; "what is that?"

Charlotte looked down at her feet. She spoke softly, fighting back the tears, "Marner locked me in it before he left for the Holy Land. It is a device of his invention; he called it a belt of chastity."

"But why? Why would he do such a thing?"

"He said he wanted to keep his property safe from interference."

"His property?" Florence's voice rose in anger.

"Yes, I am his property, like his cattle and his horses, but loved even less. He feared I would be unfaithful," she looked up and the tears started to flow; "I would never have done that, Flossie, I am a good wife. I only ever wanted to be a good wife."

"But what about the baby, how will it…"

"I do not know, I…" Charlotte put her head in her hands and began to sob. Florence put her arm around her shoulders and pulled her close. They rode on in silence, Florence holding tightly onto Charlotte every inch of the way.

Just before they arrived at the castle, Charlotte straightened up and wiped away her tears, "Do not tell him yet please, sister. Let him have a moment of joy." Florence nodded, forcing a smile onto her face for the benefit of their father.

The old baron greeted them beaming from ear to ear, clearly delighted to see his eldest daughter once more. He moved slowly towards the carriage, leaning heavily on a walking stick, "My darling Charlotte, what a splendid surprise; it brings great joy to your father's heart to see you again."

"Mine too, father," said Charlotte, stepping down from the carriage and hugging him close.

"Have you been crying, my dear?" the baron frowned as he stood back, looking closely at her face.

"Tears of joy, father," Florence responded on her sister's behalf as she came to join them.

"Well, I am near to it myself, I must confess," the smile returned to his face; "do come in, I cannot wait to hear all about life as Lady Marner and how my grandchildren are doing. There is so little in your letters these days, you hardly tell me anything."

Charlotte looked away to hide the tears welling up in her eyes again. She saw Brentley striding towards them and seized the opportunity to change the subject, "Father, you remember Brent de Villiers do you not?"

"Of course, yes, welcome my boy, thank you for escorting Charlotte, very good of you. Please tell your men to get some supper in the kitchen; cook will look after them. But you must join us for dinner in the great hall; this calls for a celebration."

Brentley's response was interrupted by Bella and Mags, hopping and skipping across to their father, begging to be allowed to stay up late so they could join the rest of the family at dinner. Looking down at them, the baron smiled and nodded, "Of course, my darlings, of course."

Florence hooked her arm through Charlotte's, "Come along, dear sister, let us go inside." Together, they led the way to the great hall, where the family sat around the large oak dining table. The baron sent a footman to instruct the cook to serve the best food she had in store, and then to fetch the finest wine from the cellar.

"I am glad to see you spent my husband's money wisely, father," said Charlotte, admiring the newly restored room.

"Oh, er, thank you my dear," the baron smiled. Florence coughed into her hand and he quickly continued, "Ah yes, well, er, we have Florence to thank for that, of course. She has run the house well since you left us, looked after all the boring money matters and kept the servants in line. An excellent household manager she has become indeed. But I cannot keep you here forever, can I, my dear," he looked at Florence; "it will soon be time for you to take a husband too, eh?"

"There is no hurry, father, I am happy here with you a few years yet," she was evidently in no mood to discuss the subject. She turned to Brentley, "What about you, my lord, are you promised to anyone?"

Brentley glanced at Charlotte. He was blushing, something she had never seen before. The normally confident, composed young man stammered, "Er… ah… er… well… er, no, I am not as it happens, but… er…"

Looking up, Charlotte saw Florence studying them both. Her sister gave Brentley a sympathetic smile, "Well, my lord, I sincerely hope you find happiness soon."

Light dinner conversation continued until it was time for Bella and Mags to leave. Before they went, they hugged Charlotte around the neck and kissed her on the cheek, then politely shook Brentley's hand. Charlotte watched them go, smiling fondly at them. As soon as they were out of sight, Florence turned to her, "Now, Charlie, you must tell us everything."

Fighting off the tears once more, Charlotte took a deep breath to compose herself then began to explain the truth about life at Marner's castle and how she had been treated since the beginning. Among the many indignities she had suffered, she told how Marner had controlled her correspondence, "Every time you asked if you could visit, or begged me to come visit you, he insisted I refuse. It broke my heart to turn you away. I tried to drop hints you should come anyway, but he always saw what I had done and destroyed my letters. He made me watch as he burned them then stood over me while I wrote what he said instead. Afterwards he would punish me for my disobedience."

"Punish you? He punished you? What did he do to you, my darling, what did he do?" the baron's face was turning red with the anger rising steadily inside him.

"He, er... he... he would... he..." she cast her eyes downwards, too embarrassed to continue, and began to cry.

Florence moved next to her and took hold of her hand, "It is all right, Charlie; you do not need to tell us the details. We do not need to know. Your tears alone tell us enough. Be brave, sister, carry on with your tale. Tell us what happened next."

Charlotte lifted her head and stifled her tears. She smiled briefly at Florence, gripping her hand tightly then went on with her story. As she reached more recent events, she told how she had been locked in the metal belt, separated from her children, and practically imprisoned in the damp, cold room at the top of the tower. She described how she was shocked and horrified to discover she had an unborn child trapped inside the awful contraption with her. Then, incredibly, she began to smile as she finished by saying how marvellous Brentley had been. "I think I would have jumped from the top of the tower if it had not been for him," she turned to him, the smile on her face growing brighter still.

"Well, my sister, I am at least heartened to see you have found a protector to care for you in the midst of your trials," said Florence.

But the baron was not heartened; he was shaking with rage, his face almost purple now, "Oh, my precious daughter, that man is a monster, how could I have allowed you to marry him? I am filled with anger and shame; I feel as though I had sold you to the Devil in exchange for his gold. I will never forgive myself. But, what can be done about this calamity? What can we do?"

Brentley explained they had sent a message to Marner, but it was unlikely the key could be returned in time. Then he told how they had tried in vain to cut the belt off and how Charlotte had rejected the smith's suggested alternative. "I understand how she feels," he smiled at her; "and besides, it is too risky in any case. That is why we must go to London to find this Finnian Smith, and hope he can remove the ghastly device."

"Yes, yes, we must go at once," the baron tried to jump up. He stumbled and almost fell, but Florence swiftly caught him. She steadied him then gently lowered him back into his seat. "No father, you must stay to look after Bella and Mags. I will go with Charlie in your stead."

Baron de Brune nodded reluctantly. There was no point arguing with his daughter. There never was, not with any of them.

*

The party set off again at first light. Charlotte was grateful to have Florence sitting beside her. Not only was she good company, but her sister was able to steady her as the carriage bumped along over the rough road, easing her discomfort a little. They passed the time catching up on the events of the last four years, and discussing many other things besides, but tried to avoid the subject of Marner or Charlotte's perilous condition. Florence laughed when Charlotte mentioned their father's quest to find her a husband, "Everyone he suggests is either a stupid boy or an old fart; I cannot take any of them seriously. I would rather wait for a real man. Actually, talking of real men," she inclined her head towards Brentley, who was out of earshot, riding twenty yards ahead, "you know he is in love with you, do you not?"

"Sister! That cannot be, I am a married woman."

"Oh please, Charlie, you do not fool me, you are in love with him too."

Charlotte sighed, "Yes, sweet sister, but it is no use. I am married to Marner and that is my lot."

"Perhaps… But not every knight who goes to the Holy Land returns to his castle. Fortune may smile on you yet." The sisters looked at each other then collapsed in a fit of giggles.

A minute later, Brentley rode back to ask what the ladies found so amusing. "Nothing my lord," Charlotte assured him, "just some stories from our childhood; that is all."

*

It took six days to reach London. Most nights they were able to find an inn, but one night they had to camp beside the road. The sisters settled down inside the carriage, each of them curled up on one of the bench seats. Just after midnight, Florence slipped away quietly, and went to find Brentley sleeping beside the fire. He woke at her approach. She sat opposite and spoke directly, "I am no fool, Brentley, and there are two things I know well."

"Oh, and what are they?"

"The first is my sister may die. And it may be soon."

"No, I am sure we will succeed, the smith will…"

She hushed him then continued, "I know you have done everything you can, and I am grateful to you. But fate will decide the outcome and it remains a fact Charlie may die."

"Yes, I know," he stared disconsolately into the fire. After a moment, he asked, "And what is the second thing you know so well?"

"You and my dear sister are in love. Do not waste your breath trying to deny it; I see it as plainly as the nose on your face."

He smiled and looked into the fire, then looked up and spoke again, "Yes, it is true, I do love her. But she has never spoken of loving me and, in any case she cannot, for she is married to Marner."

"Brentley de Villiers, I have known my sister all my life. She loves you, I can assure you. As for her marriage to Marner, I pray Saladin will take the monster's head and mount it on a spike. But whether such fortune favours us or not, my sister loves you just the same. Now, go to her. I will stay here to make certain you are not disturbed," she gave him a look that said she would not be argued with, and nor, in truth, did he wish to argue anyway.

As he entered the carriage, Charlotte woke from a fitful sleep filled with frightful nightmares, "Is that you, Flossie?"

"No, it is I, Brent," he sat beside her on the bench, took her in his arms and kissed her passionately on the lips. After a fleeting moment of hesitation, she kissed him back with equal fervour. They kissed for a long time. Then he lay down beside her and held her close until the sun rose and ended the happiest night of their lives.

Two days later, they were in London. They tracked down Finnian Smith at his workshop by the river and begged him for help. Smith dismissed his apprentices before politely asking Charlotte to undress, using the same deferential tone gynaecologists would use in centuries to come.

"I should go too," Brentley turned to leave.

"No, please stay," Charlotte begged, "you and Flossie both."

She stood, anxious and embarrassed in equal measure, as Smith knelt in front of her to examine the complex device she was trapped in. After several minutes, he declared, "I may be able to remove it, although there is a part of the locking mechanism that is unknown to me. Its purpose is not clear."

"But you *can* get it off her?" Brentley demanded.

"I said I *may* be able to," Smith insisted; "I can surely try, but I cannot promise anything, for it is the most secure piece of ironwork I have seen in all my years."

"Well, try then, in the name of all the Saints, for she will surely die otherwise."

"My lord, before I do, I must warn you there may be a danger to the lady. I have heard tell of devices that may do great harm if one opens the lock without the proper key. I fear Lord Marner may have installed such a mechanism."

Charlotte looked at the others uneasily, a cold dread creeping into her belly.

Smith continued, "Perhaps you might consider another approach. There are women in the town who offer a discreet service. It would be later than usual," he glanced at Charlotte's growing belly, "but I am sure it would still be possible."

"Yes, Charlie, perhaps you should consider it," urged Florence; "I know it would grieve you to lose the child, but think of your other children. Think of us, your family, we love you, we do not want to lose you."

"Both paths carry much risk," Brentley added, "it is hard to say what is best. The smith at the castle said one from each five perished when disposing of the child. What are her chances if you take off the belt?"

"I cannot say," Smith responded, "as I have said, part of the mechanism is unknown. I cannot predict…"

"Enough, all of you," Charlotte interrupted, "I know you are trying to help but I will not take an innocent life. There is only one choice. Go ahead, good smith, remove the belt if you can. No-one shall blame you whatever the outcome. If any harm should come to me it is my vile husband who has done it."

"As you wish, my lady," Smith turned back to the belt and began to work. It was an intricate task, only he could comprehend what was involved. Charlotte tried to keep as still as possible, suppressing the impulse to shake with the fear that gripped her. Brentley took one hand, Florence took the other. She held onto them with all her strength, thankful for the love she could feel from both.

For almost an hour, Smith struggled, using tiny metal

implements to manipulate the locking device. "Nearly there," he muttered as he turned one of his minute instruments. There was a click and the lock finally opened. Everyone relaxed. Feeling an overwhelming sense of relief, Charlotte turned to smile at Brentley. A moment later, there was a second click. She winced in pain, her smile changing to a look of horror. A trickle of blood ran down her thigh.

"Do not worry, my love," said Brentley, "it is just a pinprick; you will be fine."

"Brent, I…" the world was spinning; she swayed and fell to her knees, losing her grip on Florence's hand. She started to collapse but Brentley swiftly caught her. "Poison," he exclaimed.

She stared into his eyes as the light around her began to fade, "I wish I could have stayed with you, my love. We had one night together at least, that was more than I had dared to hope."

Reaching out, she groped for Florence, "Sweet sister." Florence stepped forward and took her hand again, "I am here, Charlie."

"Thank you for… uh… sending him to me… uh, that… er… night. P-please… er… my… chil… dren… uh… they… will… er… need…"

She was struggling for breath; the darkness was closing in fast. She looked up at Brentley, "I… uh… I… er… uh… uh… love… you."

The light faded from her eyes and she was gone. He began to weep. "I love you too," he whispered into her hair as he held her tightly to him.

Smith removed the horrible device and asked if he might keep it for study. Without a word, Brentley grasped the belt, carried it to the river's edge, and hurled it into the Thames.

Florence bought the finest silk to wrap her sister's body in; then they took her back to her father's castle. When they broke the news to the baron, he seemed to age twenty years before their eyes. Despite Florence's clearly reasoned arguments why only Marner was to blame, the baron never forgave himself. He died a few weeks later.

Brentley had already returned to Marner's castle; Florence followed shortly after the baron's death, taking Bella, Mags, and the family's servants, with her. The de Brune castle was abandoned and fell into ruins.

A week after she arrived, Florence dismissed the governess and took over the running of the household. The governess threatened to write to Marner, claiming he would exact his retribution for this act of disobedience. Brentley was way past caring about Marner's orders. He personally marched her off the estate.

Next to go was the nanny. She had been recruited by Marner and shared his cruel streak. Bella and Mags cared for the children from then on, showing them the love and kindness they had missed since their mother left.

It was five months after Charlotte died before Brentley finally received a reply from Marner. The brief letter concluded, 'So I shall not be sending the key, for it is clear to me that, in all likelihood, this is nothing but a deceit designed to enable the harlot to fornicate with other men. When I return, I shall reckon with her; and with any man who has designs upon my property.'

Brentley threw the letter on the fire and wept for Charlotte again.

As time passed, Florence took on more duties and worked alongside Brentley to ensure the Marner estate became renowned for its efficiency, a model for others to follow. It was five years before their grief for Charlotte subsided enough for them to find solace in each other. On their wedding night, Brentley looked down at Florence, "My love, I cannot deny your dear sister is still in my heart. I hope that is something you can accept?"

"Of course, my love, she will live in both our hearts forever."

*

In the autumn of 1197, they received news Marner was on his way back to England and expected to return to the castle by Christmas. Brentley rode out, taking only Higgins, now captain of the castle guard. They returned two weeks later. The following day, news arrived that shortly after landing back in England Lord Marner had been thrown from his horse and killed.

The castle 'mourned' the lord's passing with three days of feasting. Even his nine-year old son was happy: he missed his Mommy. In time, he grew up to be brave and strong, but also kind, just like she had asked.

XX

INVESTIGATIONS

Ben decided the best way to kill time while he waited for Jack was to investigate Del Rivera's death. He owed the old man that much after he'd doubted him and driven him to come out here on his own.

He tried to examine the spot where Del Rivera's body was found, but soon discovered it was a private area, with no public access. Next, he tried to get to the top of the building, but was told there was a two-day waiting list for a trip to the observation deck. It would also cost 500 Dirhams: over a hundred pounds at the exchange rate he was getting. He could afford it, but it was a bit pricey for a ride in a lift. It would still leave him fifteen storeys short of the top in any case.

Exasperated by the lack of access, he returned to his hotel room and did some research into the reports on Del Rivera's death. He found the details for the police officer in charge of the investigation and decided to give him a call.

"Al-Mansur." He'd struck lucky; the commander had answered the phone himself.

"Er, yes, look, I'm calling about the Del Rivera murder."

"That's very interesting, Mister, er...?"

"Carlton, it's Carlton, *Major* Carlton to be precise," Ben seldom used his military rank, but it came in useful sometimes.

"And what makes you so sure it was murder, Major Carlton? Do you have something you would like to tell me?"

"Look, I knew the guy; it's a mysterious death and I don't buy the suicide theory. It looks like murder to me, that's all. I don't actually *know* anything, I was hoping *you* did?" Ben wasn't being entirely honest, but telling the truth would get him thrown into a lunatic asylum. He didn't want to end up on the hook for Del Rivera's murder either.

"Well, major, perhaps we can help each other. Why don't you come to the station and we can talk?"

Ben didn't like the idea of being interviewed in a police station. He made a counter proposal, "Why don't we meet at the scene of the crime? You must be able to get access to the top of the building?"

Al-Mansur hesitated. Ben could almost hear him considering his request, trying to decide whether to go along with it. "Alright major, meet me at the Atmosphere reception desk tomorrow morning at ten," the police commander hung up.

With nothing else he could usefully do, Ben turned in for the night and dreamed, once again, of a life lived long ago.

*

As he tripped through the dark passageways, using the wooden key he carried on a rope around his neck to open the gates, Bak-Ra thought back over his life as a slave.

He could still remember being roped together with Garma on the ship bringing them from their homeland, shivering in fear, terrified of what was going to happen to them next. Amenemhat had bought them both as houseboys and at first they'd undergone the same depredations and hardships. But, before long, their master had noticed Bak-Ra's keener intellect. Soon, he was given more responsibility; he was put in charge of the other boys, even given his own cell to sleep in. It wasn't much, but it seemed to be enough to start a raging fire of envy burning within Garma. It saddened him to realise his childhood friend had formed a jealous hatred for him, but he didn't know what he could do to make amends.

Since then, Amenemhat had placed ever more trust in him, granting him further privileges and freedoms with each passing year. He had a far better life than most other slaves, yet still he felt an aching emptiness inside; something was missing. And it was only now, in his seventeenth year, that he had finally come to understand what it was.

Her name was Su-Chi; she was from a distant land, far to the east. He had heard she'd been taken into slavery as a young child and brought to Memphis for sale. Amenemhat had bought her because she was exactly the sort of oriental he was planning to breed. Orientals had become fashionable in recent years; the men had a reputation as excellent house slaves, the women had a good reputation in other ways.

Like many of her race, Su-Chi was small and very pretty. Her dark, almond-shaped eyes and light brown skin set her apart as an exceptional beauty. She was about fifteen years old, almost ready for breeding. She spoke no Egyptian but, through eye contact and gestures, Bak-Ra had learned to communicate with her. He had developed a great affection for her and was sure it was mutual. Frustratingly though, he was only allowed in the compound when he was sent on an errand. For many months, he'd had to be content with the occasional stolen moment: special glances, secret smiles, and, once or twice, a delicate brush of his hand across her cheek. But tonight, at long last, he had seen an opportunity for them to be alone.

Pharaoh had just returned from a victorious campaign in the south. All the great houses in the city were throwing parties in his honour. Amenemhat could not shun this responsibility. His party was less extravagant than most, but a party was being held nonetheless. The festivities had reached their peak and the master and his guests were lying around the main salon in various states of drunken debauchery. Seizing his chance, Bak-Ra had slipped into the compound.

*

After winding his way through the dark passageways for what seemed like an age, Bak-Ra reached dormitory seven. He paused for a moment, his mind racing, formulating the last details of his plan. Satisfied, he knocked on the door, the final barrier between him and the object of his desire. Summoning every ounce of his courage, he shouted, "Open up dormitory-keeper, I am here on the orders of our lord and master, Amenemhat."

A sleepy old matron opened the door's rectangular peephole, "Wh-a-a-a-t you want, boy?"

"Master Amenemhat wishes to inspect one of your charges."

"Which one, boy?" the venom in her voice betrayed the hatred and distrust between the compound and house slaves. As a house slave, Bak-Ra outranked her and he knew he'd have to assert that authority to make his story believable.

"Less of your tongue, old hag, unless you want to lose it; though short in years I may be, I am surely not your 'boy'. Give me the respect the house is due or your insolence will reach the master's ears this night. Then your head will surely part company with your neck in the morning."

"Forgive me, young master, your commands disturbed

an old woman's sleep. Tell me which girl you require and I will fetch her for you at once."

"The master wishes to inspect Su-Chi."

"Su-Chi?" the woman was visibly surprised; "does he think the little one ready?"

"The master has spoken; it is not for you to question."

"No, no... of course not," the woman demurred, "I only wondered..." she trailed off into silence. Bak-Ra was relieved she was backing down, hopefully convinced further debate was both futile and dangerous. If she had known the truth of his mission, things would have been different.

"Shall I bind her for you, young master?"

Bak-Ra hesitated. He hadn't thought this part of his scheme through. The woman's question was a natural one, he should have anticipated it. Amenemhat had a particularly harsh method for restraining the breeding slaves if they were taken out of the compound: he demanded it was followed without exception. The thought of his lovely Su-Chi trussed up in the cruel bonds sickened him, but if he wanted to convince the woman he was genuinely here on behalf of their master, he had to order her to do it.

"Yes, of course," he felt terrible as he said it, but it would not be for long, he would release Su-Chi as soon as he could.

The old woman turned away from the peephole and waddled off, deep into the recesses of the underground cavern. Thick layers of fat wobbled beneath her dark brown skin as she moved. She'd probably been a breeder herself. Bak-Ra imagined she'd mothered many children only to see Amenemhat sell them off like cattle. Now past breeding, she was one of the few to survive so many childbirths and be allowed to see out her days as warden to her young charges. Speculating on the life she must have had, he couldn't help feeling some sympathy for her.

While he was waiting, Bak-Ra used his houseboy's key to unlock the dormitory door. He wished he could just go straight in, take Su-Chi by the hand and lead her out, spare her the painful humiliation that was coming. But, as well as the outside lock, the door was bolted on the inside; he needed the keeper's co-operation to open it.

A minute later, the woman led Su-Chi, blinking sleepily, to the entrance. The girl smiled when she saw Bak-Ra through the open peephole. But her smile disappeared as the woman produced a length of rope and tied it around her neck. Bak-Ra could see she was frightened as she stared back at him, pleading with her eyes. He wanted to comfort her, tell her everything would be alright. But he didn't dare.

The woman roughly pulled Su-Chi's hands behind her back, and started to bind her wrists with the loose end of the rope hanging from her neck. Su-Chi began to cry. "Stop fussing, child," the woman snapped, "no harm will come to you if you obey the master." She pulled the rope tight, cruelly twisting Su-Chi's arms upwards. This was how Amenemhat liked to see his breeding slaves, the tighter the bond, the more the slave had to strain to keep from choking themselves, rendering them helpless while he did as he pleased.

Su-Chi squealed in pain, Bak-Ra could see she was struggling to breathe. He could contain himself no more, "Please, er… not so tight, she is not being punished, the master only wishes to inspect her, see if she is ready."

The old matron frowned. For a moment Bak-Ra feared she may have seen through his deception. Then she shrugged, "As you wish, young master." She loosened the rope a little and Su-Chi breathed more easily. Pulling back the bolt, she opened the door, and shoved the frightened girl out into the passageway, "Will that be all, young master?"

"Er, yes… er… yes, that is all; for tonight."

"Good," the woman pushed the door shut, slammed the peephole closed, and rammed the bolt back into place.

Bak-Ra chuckled to himself, the old matron was obviously eager to return to her bed. He locked the door and retrieved his key. Then he turned to Su-Chi, a massive grin on his face. She scowled back at him, muttering something in her own language. He stepped forward, his hands raised in supplication. He tried to embrace her but she stepped back, shaking her head, speaking angrily, almost spitting out her words.

"Please, I am sorry, I had to let her do it so we could be alone," he stepped forward again and lightly rested his hands on her shoulders. She relaxed a little. He gently turned her around and began untying the rope that was causing her so much distress. Once she was free, he turned her back again and put his finger under her chin, tilting her face up so he could look into her eyes.

"I am sorry, Su-Chi; I had forgotten you would have to be bound before I could get you out of there. But I had to see you, I… I want you… I need you… I…"

Suddenly, she smiled, and it was like the sun was shining in the dark passageway. She reached up and pulled his lips down to hers, kissing him so softly, so sweetly, delicately probing inside his mouth with her tongue. He pulled her to him, holding her close, their bodies pressed tightly together. She murmured something in her own language and he spoke back to her in Egyptian. Neither could understand the other's words, but their feelings were beyond doubt.

Lowering his head, he began to kiss her neck, working his way slowly back up again, across her face, until he returned to her lips. The excitement welling up inside him threatened to overflow and upset his careful plans, but a voice in the back of his head reminded him of the danger out here in the passageway. Reluctantly, he gently pushed her away, then took her hand and led her back the way he had come.

For several desperate, anxious minutes, he guided her through numerous twists and turns, past four other dormitories, each housing at least twenty breeding slaves. Twice he stopped, frozen in fear, when he thought he heard footsteps behind them. He listened intently, but the only sound was a distant snoring. They pressed on and finally reached a storeroom. Opening the door, he was pleased to see it still empty, apart from a single wooden table, as it had been since yesterday, when a dozen barrels of wine had been taken to the house to fuel tonight's festivities. He led Su-Chi inside and pushed the door closed. They were alone at last.

They kissed with passion and intensity, held each other tight, and began to explore each other's bodies. His manhood was straining beneath his cloth skirt, she was creaming in readiness for him. She lay back on the table and gazed up at him in anticipation. He started to move towards her…

The door crashed open with such force it came off its hinges. Splinters flew across the room. Bak-Ra recoiled in shock. Su-Chi sat up quickly.

Amenemhat stood in the doorway, two guards behind him. Behind them, Garma was hopping from one foot to the other with glee, "I told you, master, I told you."

The slave master ordered the guards to seize the would-be lovers. A minute later they were kneeling on the floor, hands bound behind their backs, the rope tight around their necks.

"You were my most trusted houseboy," Amenemhat snarled at Bak-Ra, "I treated you well. This is how you betray me. Breeding slaves are not to be tampered with." He pulled Su-Chi to her feet and bent her over the table. Roughly, he probed her most intimate area. "Good, still intact, that is something to be thankful for; ready for breeding too. But this act cannot go unpunished," he turned to Garma; "fetch the Impaler."

Su-Chi was shaking with fear. Bak-Ra felt the blood drain from his face. The Impaler was Amenemhat's chief overseer. He had a brutal reputation, but that wasn't all. Rumour had it the Impaler was so-named because he possessed an exceptionally large phallus and, on occasion, this weapon was put to use.

Minutes later, a giant of a man, at least four cubits tall, appeared outside the storeroom, "You called for me, master?"

"Yes, I have a job for you, come in here," Amenemhat ordered.

The Impaler stooped to squeeze his enormous frame through the doorway. He had to keep his head bowed to stop it hitting the ceiling. Seeing Su-Chi bent over the table, he smiled and began to loosen his leather skirt.

"You want me to punish this one, master?"

"Just show it to her."

The Impaler removed his skirt to reveal the monster that lay beneath. He stroked it a few times and soon it reached full size. The rumours were justified; it was the length of a man's forearm, and as wide as his wrist.

Amenemhat pulled Su-Chi to her feet and spun her around so she could see the engorged weapon. She stared wide-eyed at it, quivering in terror. He turned the shaking, petrified girl around once more, bent her over the table and ripped off her tiny cloth skirt. A stream of urine ran down her leg as she waited to be impaled.

"No master, please," Bak-Ra begged, "she is innocent, this is my fault; I took her from the dormitory and…" He was silenced as the guard standing behind grabbed him under the chin and clamped his mouth shut. He watched in horror as the Impaler moved towards Su-Chi. Oh, why had he taken such a stupid risk? He couldn't bear to see her being terrified and abused like this. He'd been a selfish fool to put her in such danger.

Amenemhat held up a hand, "I think that will give her enough of a scare to stop her getting involved with any more house slaves."

The Impaler stopped, "You don't want me to punish her, master?"

"No, that will do. I don't want her damaged, she's good stock," he turned to Garma, who had returned with the Impaler; "take her to dormitory two and tell the keeper I want her put with his best breeding male at once. Tell him to leave her in her bonds; she's not to be trusted."

Garma led Su-Chi away to begin her life as one of Amenemhat's breeders; a life that would eventually see her end up like the old crone in dormitory seven... if she was lucky. Bak-Ra was relieved she had been spared any more punishment, but he felt an awful desolation as he watched her being taken away. Their eyes met one last time. Then she was gone.

"Now, I want you to punish this one," Amenemhat pointed at Bak-Ra.

A cold dread gripped him as the Impaler pulled him to his feet, pushed him face down across the table, and tore off his skirt. The giant overseer kicked at the inside of his legs, forcing him to spread them apart. Leaning on his back, pinning him down, the Impaler took a moment to position his weapon... then thrust forwards.

Bak-Ra screamed in pain as he was torn open. The shock of the first intrusion was followed by the repeated trauma as the Impaler rammed into him time and again. The agony in his lower body became his whole world, forcing all other thoughts from his head. The torture seemed to last for hours but, finally, he felt a hot stream of liquid burst inside him, mingling with the blood flowing from his ruined body.

The Impaler withdrew and Bak-Ra collapsed onto the floor. He watched as the Impaler wiped himself clean with the tattered remains of his skirt then replaced his own skirt and stood waiting for the master's next command.

"Now take away his stones," Amenemhat ordered.

"No, please…" Bak-Ra begged. But there was nothing he could do as the Impaler pulled out a knife, leaned down and grasped his testicles, then swiftly castrated him. The sharp sting as he was cut was compounded by the emotional anguish of his loss, but both were soon subsumed into the throbbing pain from his rectum.

"You may go now," Amenemhat told the Impaler; "take two women from dormitory nine, I am pleased with you." The Impaler smiled. It was well known he preferred women.

Turning to the other guards, Amenemhat indicated Bak-Ra, "Take him to the sales pens."

*

The next day, Bak-Ra, still bleeding from his mutilated scrotum, was sold to the owner of a salt mine. He spent the rest of a short, miserable, life working in the baking heat of the desert. He never saw Su-Chi again.

XXI

THE BASEMENT

Susan had no idea how long she'd been imprisoned. She was getting hungry. Her thirst was building to a concerning level. Worst of all, that damn headache still wouldn't go away. Come to think of it, it was getting worse.

She heard footsteps outside, muffled voices, the rattle of keys, and the sound of locks turning. The door swung open and Mortimer marched into the room, with Hans, Sun-lee, and Worthington following behind.

That bloody worm, Worthington. He was bloody well in on this, the horrid little turd. He was obviously the one who'd stitched her up; probably sent details of her DNA to Mortimer. No doubt the lord would be paying him a fortune for helping him find someone he could carve up to use what he wanted.

"Good evening, Shebana. Have you worked out why you're here yet?" Mortimer asked.

"Who's Shebana? What are you talking about? You won't get away with this, you bastard, I'm not some poor East European orphan you can just make disappear; I will be missed you know."

"Oh, Shebana, I shall miss you very much myself; I have always enjoyed our times together, especially poor Charlotte de Brune and little Sally Trigg. Such a pity I cannot risk keeping you a while longer, I'm sure we could have had a great deal of fun. Well, at least, *I* would have had fun, anyway."

"You… you… you know about Charlotte… and Sally? But those were just dreams… How… how can you know?"

"You disappoint me, my dear, I expected you to have worked it out by now. Those weren't dreams, they were memories; memories of the times we have shared. More than memories actually; you have been experiencing some of your previous lives. Lives I managed to make a little more interesting from time to time."

She shuddered as she began to realise the truth. A truth that, deep down, part of her had known all along. He was right, her dreams were real. In fact, she hadn't been dreaming at all, she'd been reliving her past.

The moment she accepted this simple truth, her entire history came flooding back to her in all its glory, pain, anguish, triumph and despair. Her head span as she tried to cope with it all. It was an incredible, potentially wonderful, revelation, but it also meant this vile creature threatening her now had abused, violated, and murdered her many times before.

"You fucking creep, you raped me, burned me alive, drowned me on the beach, locked me in that fucking booby-trapped chastity belt, you…"

"Yes, yes, now you're getting it. Now you see, Shebana. And you must also see your situation is hopeless. It is inevitable I will triumph every time; that is the way it is always destined to be."

She looked him straight in the eyes, "Oh really, Moon Shadow, have you forgotten our Reckoning, have you forgotten my arrow striking you in the heart? Have you forgotten how Brentley de Villiers broke your neck? Fuck you; you do not triumph every time."

For once, he lost his composure. In three quick strides he crossed the room and struck her across the face with the back of his hand, his ruby ring stinging painfully as it left its mark on her cheek. He grabbed her by the throat and started to squeeze. She gasped for breath; she could feel herself beginning to lose consciousness. She tried to stay calm, if he'd wanted to kill her, he'd have done it by now.

"No," he released her and took a step back, "no, I need you alive for what I have in store for you. Your insolence always did infuriate me. No matter, this time I will ensure you do not return to trouble me anymore." He tore open her blouse and reached inside, vulgarly squeezing her breast, "A shame though, it would have been nice to have you again."

She shivered at his touch. His hand was cold and strangely smooth. She was relieved when he withdrew it and moved away.

He turned to Sun-lee, "Bring the potion."

Turning back to Susan, he regained his usual calm, authoritarian demeanour, "Have you ever wondered how much more a man could achieve if he wasn't restricted to a pathetic mortal lifespan? I told you once the great nation of the United States of America shares my birthday. And so it does. We were both born on the Fourth of July, 1776.

"In the past, I have struggled to bring my plans to fruition within the constraints of a normal human existence. Seventy or eighty years is simply not long enough, especially as much of it is taken up by the tedium of childhood. Time and again I have come close to realising my goals only to be frustrated by my own mortality; often being reborn with little effective power and having to expend huge amounts of time and effort simply to regain any sort of useful position from which I might even begin to pursue my plans. It really was most annoying.

"Finally, I managed to engineer a birth into the British aristocracy, giving me a good head start and a guaranteed position of power. I had been a lord before, of course, but I always had to fight to get there. Learning from the lessons of the past, I concentrated first on eliminating the problem of my own mortality.

"After I had you transported to Australia, I began work on an elixir that would extend my lifespan. It took me over thirty years but, by 1840, I had a formula that worked. As a result, I have been able to remain in the same body for almost two and a half centuries, no longer aging or decaying and no need to endure the lottery of rebirth."

Susan's curiosity got the better of her. She couldn't help but ask, "But if you've been around for nearly 250 years, doesn't anyone get a bit suspicious? Don't people wonder why you never die?"

"Oh, that's easy. I simply become my own 'son' every now and then, fake a death, stage a mock funeral, and leave everything to myself. I've always maintained friends in the Government to help me keep my true identity hidden. I've helped them with their careers and they've seen to it my privacy isn't disturbed. It's been a mutually beneficial arrangement, even involving several Prime Ministers over the years. Churchill was difficult though, that's why he had to lose the election in 1945. You see, I..."

He was interrupted as Sun-lee returned to the basement. She was carrying a tray bearing a conical glass flask filled with a thick black liquid, like crude oil. Next to the flask was a glass funnel.

"Is this from the new batch?" he asked.

"Yes, my lord, just as you ordered."

"Good, I don't want any more mishaps. I need to feed.

"You see, my dear," he turned back to Susan, "the elixir only sustains the mortal body. Eventually, it becomes necessary to refresh the soul. Normally, of course, the soul is refreshed through the process of death and rebirth, but I needed to find a way to bypass all that messy inconvenience. Years of research led me to the conclusion I could refresh my soul by consuming another. I was already working on a potion to destroy a soul within a living body, so I decided to adapt it to serve a dual purpose. For a long time it was rather hit and miss, I could destroy some souls, while others grew stronger than ever, but none of them were fit for consumption. Through many decades of painstaking study and experimentation, I gradually refined the potion, increasing the proportion of souls destroyed, but still my original goal eluded me. Then, suddenly, just over a year ago, I made a critical breakthrough. Within months, I had perfected my potion. Finally, after over a century of work, I had what I needed. I can rip out a person's soul and consume it. At last, I am able to feed, and true immortality is mine."

"God, you *are* a monster," Susan exclaimed; "I thought you were going to harvest my organs, but this is a thousand times worse."

"Indeed it is, my dear, indeed it is; as you will soon find out," he stood in front of her, staring deep into her eyes, as if he was looking into her soul. As the seconds passed by and his unblinking gaze never wavered, she felt like he was draining her somehow. She began to wonder if this was part of how he did it. Was he feeding on her already?

"But perhaps not yet," he smiled and, with a flourish, turned and faced away.

"I am particularly keen to consume *your* soul," he continued; "I expect it to be an especially nourishing one. So I need to be certain. Fujabi's soul escaped me, a fault in the last batch of potion meant it perished too rapidly. I do not wish to make that same mistake again. Worthington," he turned to his henchman, standing grinning at Susan, clearly enjoying her ordeal.

"Yes, my lord?"

"I need a volunteer to help me test the new batch, you'll oblige won't you?"

"Er… er… you want me to find a volunteer for you, my lord?"

"No need for that, you'll do just fine," Mortimer nodded to Hans. The big German grabbed Worthington from behind, pinning his arms back, forcing him down onto his knees.

"My lord, no," Worthington pleaded, "I've served you faithfully. I found Shebana for you; I helped you last time, I… I… You can't do this, my lord; I am your loyal servant."

"Of course you are, Worthington," Mortimer smiled at the kneeling man, "and how better to prove your loyalty. Now open wide," he nodded at Sun-lee.

Sun-lee put on a pair of thick, black, elbow-length gloves. She pulled Worthington's head back and forced the end of the funnel into his mouth. She held it in place, nodding at her master, "Ready, my lord."

Mortimer had donned a similar pair of gloves. He took the flask and poured the black liquid into the funnel, pinching his victim's nostrils closed, forcing him to gulp it down.

As soon as Worthington had swallowed the liquid, the others released him. They stepped back a few paces then stood in a circle: Mortimer, Hans, and Sun-Lee, all silently watching.

Worthington spat out the funnel and tried to get to his feet, but collapsed back onto his knees, gasping and clutching at his throat. Slowly, his face turned red. Not the red of a blush or a sunburn; this was the bright red of a traffic signal; brighter, in fact. His eyes burned the same colour, so did his hands. His clothes began to smoulder with the heat. He was burning from the inside out.

The flesh on his face started to melt away. He opened his mouth and Susan expected him to scream but, instead, only smoke emerged. The smoke accumulated in a small cloud that began to glow and pulsate as it moved slowly towards Mortimer. 'Oh, my God, it's Worthington's soul,' Susan realised.

Mortimer stepped forward, "Come unto me lost soul that I may be replenished." He gazed upwards, his arms outstretched. The glowing, pulsating, cloud of smoke drifted closer. He opened his mouth and the cloud was sucked inside.

As Worthington's soul disappeared, his body collapsed onto the floor, where it continued to smoulder. Mortimer lowered his arms and looked down again. "Most satisfying," he declared; "the new batch seems to be working well." He turned to Susan and smiled, "So, your turn next, my dear."

She stood transfixed with terror, her previous calm completely gone. What she'd just witnessed was beyond comprehension. Mortimer hadn't just killed a man, *he'd eaten his soul!* An hour ago, she hadn't even been sure she believed in souls. Now, she faced the imminent prospect of having hers destroyed by this deranged madman. She felt a paralysing sense of dread as she waited for him to act.

"But not just now," Mortimer continued, "I shall need twenty-four hours before I can feed again. Sun-lee, give her food and water. I want her to be healthy when I consume her."

Mortimer left the room. Sun-lee followed, carrying the tray bearing the empty flask, and the funnel she'd carefully retrieved with her gloved hands. Hans lingered behind. He watched Susan with his usual emotional detachment, as if she was a piece of meat he was waiting to be ready to serve to his master. She thought about trying to reason with him, but somehow she knew it would be pointless. His devotion to Mortimer was total, his compassion non-existent. After ten minutes, he knelt down to touch Worthington's body, nodded in satisfaction, then picked him up as easily as if he were a scarecrow filled with straw. As she watched Hans leave, she realised he'd been waiting for the body to cool.

Finally she was alone. Her fear had begun to subside as soon as Mortimer left, and her strange sense of calm was starting to return. Even so, she was in a dreadful predicament. She had a little time but, a day from now, Mortimer would be back to destroy her forever.

Her head was practically bursting with the things she'd witnessed, the revelations she'd seen. In a single moment, she'd suddenly grasped a new paradigm: the true nature of life, the reality of eternal souls and reincarnation. Then, minutes later, she'd seen reality shift again, Mortimer had burned out, and consumed, another living soul. She'd never liked Worthington, but watching his destruction had been horrific. No-one deserved that.

And the same fate awaited her, unless she could find a way to escape. She'd had a look around the room before, there was nothing that could help, but now she realised she had another resource at her disposal, a vast resource. She had twelve thousand years of memories, every experience of every life she'd ever lived. She understood every language she'd ever spoken, even when her past self didn't; she knew how to use a bow and arrow, like She Wolf; she knew how to deliver a baby, like Samantha Parsons; she knew how to remove a bullet, like Sarah O'Shaughnessy. She smiled. She'd studied babies and bullets in theory, of course, but now she could actually remember doing those things. Surely somewhere in her memories was the knowledge she needed to escape?

Why did Mortimer want to destroy her anyway? Sure, he needed to feed, but that could have been anyone. He'd gone to a lot of trouble to bring her here. Was it because she was 'especially nourishing', as he'd put it? No, there had to be more to it. Was she some kind of threat to him? They did seem to be bound to each other somehow, meeting again and again in life after life. Ben too, as if they were an inseparable trinity of souls joined together forever. But Mortimer always went out of his way to ruin their lives. What was that all about? There must be some purpose behind the horrors he'd put them through?

Searching her mind, she could see her entire history laid out, from her innocent childhood as Shebana to her most recent past. Like normal memories, it took a bit of thought to recall some of it, like trying to find a book in a gigantic library, but it was all there if she looked hard enough. She tried to focus on some individual lives. She could see the broad sweep of the events that shaped them, but soon realised her conscious mind was incapable of experiencing the past as vividly as she'd done in her dreams. She needed to sleep to truly see. What's more, in her dreams, she could sometimes experience events from other people's perspective, especially Ben's. She had no idea how that worked but it was useful, like being able to switch camera angles to get a better view. She closed her eyes and surveyed her memories, looking for a life that might give her the clues she needed. She felt herself beginning to drift away…

The sound of approaching footsteps brought her abruptly back to the present. She opened her eyes to see Sun-lee entering the basement carrying another tray, this time bearing food and water. For a moment, she contemplated refusing to eat or drink, just to defy Mortimer; but she quickly concluded she should take what was offered. If there was ever a chance to escape, she would need all her strength… and her wits.

Sun-lee placed the tray on the floor and began to feed her pieces of chicken and fruit, squirting water into her mouth between each morsel. Susan wondered if Worthington's execution might provide an opportunity to find an ally. She tried to start a conversation between mouthfuls, "You realise he will do the same to you one day, don't you?"

No answer from Sun-lee, who simply squirted more water into her mouth.

Susan swallowed and continued, "I mean, if he can do that to one of his most loyal servants, then he could do it to anyone. You must see that, surely?" Sun-lee put a piece of chicken into her mouth.

She tried to speak again as she chewed, but Sun-lee put a hand over her mouth, "Worthington not needed any more. His lordship needs Sun-lee. You are wasting your breath, Doctor Carpenter."

Susan pressed on regardless; Sun-lee seemed her best hope of escape, "What makes you think he needs you? Is it your body he needs?" She remembered Mortimer's sexual appetite when she was Sally over two centuries before, maybe he was still the same?

Sun-lee blushed. 'Bingo,' thought Susan, "He likes you now, Sun-lee, but what happens when you grow old?"

"Sun-lee not grow old; his lordship promise. When he find suitable soul for me to consume, I join him in immortality," she finished feeding Susan, picked up the tray, and started to walk away.

"Is that what he's told you, Sun-lee?" Susan called after her. "Has he even given you any of the elixir yet?"

Sun-lee paused. She half turned her head back towards Susan. Then she straightened up and walked out of the room, pulling the heavy iron door closed behind her.

Susan heard Sun-lee locking the door and then she was alone again. Time to look for clues, but where did she begin? Was it possible to navigate between lives? Could she pick which life she experienced, or was it all just random? 'Well, here I go anyway,' she closed her eyes and thought of another place… in another time.

XXII

HUNTERS

O n most days, the hunt would leave the village at dawn. They would return later in the day, sometimes in the afternoon, sometimes in the evening, and sometimes after dark. It depended how successful the hunt had been. When they returned in the afternoon, they would usually pass the village girls out gathering food. That was when she would see him.

Baako was one of the younger boys on the hunt and Serwaah had had her eyes on him for some time. She thought he was the most handsome boy in the village. Whenever he was near she made certain he saw her. She would smile at him then swirl her little grass skirt around so he got a good look at her pert round buttocks, and she would jiggle her firm young breasts up and down for his benefit. She could tell he was interested, but was too shy to make the first move. One afternoon, as she saw the hunt returning, she decided to make it easier for him. As he passed close by, she dropped her basket. Fruit and berries rolled across the ground in his path and he was forced to a halt.

She knelt down and began collecting the spilled food. He knelt beside her to help. The two of them made quick work of the task and were soon able to stand up, the basket filled with fruit once more.

"Thank you, Baako," she said.

"You are welcome, er… I am sorry, but I do not know your name."

"I am Serwaah," she smiled sweetly then waited for him to continue. The silence drew out for an uncomfortably long time until they both spoke simultaneously, "Would you…"

They laughed and she gestured for him to continue.

"Would you like to have supper with my mother and me in our hut one night?" he asked.

"I would like that very much, Baako, how about tonight?"

"Er…er…ah…er… well I need to check with my mother. She will need to…er…ah…"

"Perhaps tomorrow night might suit your mother better?" she put him out of his misery.

"Er, yes, I think that would be best. I will see you then, Serwaah."

"I look forward to it, Baako."

The following night, she arrived at his hut a little after sunset. His mother, Amba, was preparing supper and Serwaah rushed to help with the final few bits and pieces that remained to be done. "You just sit there and wait to be fed, great hunter," Amba said to her son then turned to give Serwaah a wink. Serwaah had to fight to suppress her giggles.

When the food was ready, they all sat on the floor around the low table in the centre of the hut. Amba started the supper conversation, "You are one of Kwabena's daughters are you not, Serwaah? I have often seen you with your sister, I think?"

"Yes, lady, that is my older sister, Fremah, we go everywhere together when we can. I also have an older brother, Danquah, a younger brother, Kofi, and our little sister, Oppong."

"Oh, my dear, it was such a tragedy when your poor mother died giving birth to Oppong. She was a delightful woman, so full of warmth; much respected in the village. And please call me Amba, there is no need for 'lady'. But don't you have two older brothers, Serwaah? Wasn't Addae your father's first son? I haven't seen Addae in a long time."

Serwaah looked down, "Addae has disappeared; we haven't seen him in almost a year. Father thinks the white hunters took him."

The group fell silent at the mention of the hunters who frequently came into the area and snatched their people. No-one knew what became of those who were taken, but there were many terrifying stories. Some said the white hunters fed them to their god who would chew them up and spit out the bones. Others said the hunters could suck out their spirits and leave their empty bodies to roam the Earth. There was even a story that the white men put them in a giant canoe and rowed them to another world on the far side of a great lake.

Amba lightened the mood by bringing out some sweet grubs, a tasty delicacy to round off their meal. After another hour, it was time for Serwaah to go.

"You must walk her back to her hut, Baako; that is the proper thing to do. You will probably take a long time, so I will go to my bed now. Good night, my dears," as Amba rose to leave she turned and spoke softly to Serwaah; "please be patient with him."

The young couple strolled slowly towards Serwaah's hut. "I like your mother," said Serwaah.

"I think she likes you too."

"And how about you?"

"Well, she has to like me, I am her son."

"No, silly," she smiled and looked down, feigning shyness, "you know what I mean."

"Oh... er... yes... yes, er... of course I like you. Er... I like you a lot."

"And what do you like about me?" she moved closer, jumped up on tiptoes, her hands clasped behind her back, and grinned impishly up at him. She was teasing him, but with affection. She wanted to draw him out of himself.

"Er, well, er, you are very pretty and, er... you have a beautiful smile, and, er..."

"Yes?" she encouraged.

"Oh, and I *really* like your eyes," he seemed to suddenly remember.

"That's nice," she dropped back onto her feet, faced down towards the ground, and looked coyly up at him. Then she put her hands under her firm little breasts, pushing them upwards. "Do you like these as well?"

"Oh, er, yes I do, er, they are lovely. I, er…"

She laughed at his discomfort. Perhaps she had teased him enough for one night.

They walked on. Soon, they had almost reached their destination. She stopped a little distance from her family's hut, "Well, we are nearly there."

"Er, yes, we are. It only took a few minutes; I do not understand why my mother thought we would take a long time."

"Perhaps she knew we would like some time to do this," she reached up and gently pulled his face down to hers; kissing him on the lips, then the neck, then back to his lips again. She was soft and tender at first but, as he began to respond, they both grew more passionate.

Amba smiled to herself when she heard her son return to their hut an hour later.

*

Serwaah became a regular visitor. To begin with, she went to Amba and Baako's hut every four or five days but, after a couple of months, she was having supper with them almost every night. Amba played the role of chaperone, but always left Baako to walk her home. One night as they walked together in the moonlight, he turned to her and took her hands in his, "Once you asked me what I like about you, and there are many things. You have the most dazzling smile; you are clever, smart, and pretty, you are more fun to be with than anyone I have ever known. Even before we spoke, I could not help but notice the cute, sweet girl who always smiled at me whenever she was near. But it was the first time I looked into your eyes, those wonderful, deep brown eyes that seem to pull me towards you with a power I cannot understand, that I knew I wanted you to be my woman. Will you, Serwaah, will you be my woman?"

Serwaah felt her heart might explode with delight; this was the moment she had been waiting for, hoping the shy, but charming, handsome Baako would find the courage. She looked back at him, her smile almost splitting her face in two, "I will, Baako, for I have long known I want you to be my man. Let us celebrate our union as soon as we are able. You can ask my father's permission tomorrow."

"Must I, can you not ask him?" Baako frowned.

"No, Baako, it is tradition, you must ask him. Do not worry, he will not bite you."

"But he always seems so stern and strict. I fear he will refuse."

She laughed, "You do not know him; he is not always what he seems."

"Sit down, my boy," the older man commanded; "what do you want of me? Speak up."

"I, er… I would like…" Baako began, barely speaking above a whisper.

"Speak up, boy, I said, I cannot hear you."

Baako gulped, trying to quell his nerves, "Sir, I would like to take your daughter as my woman."

"Which daughter do you mean? I have several. There's Oppong, but she is very young, you would have to wait a long time before she could be your woman. Still, if you are willing to wait until her moon flowers then I suppose…"

"No, no, it is not Oppong, good sir; I wish to take…"

"Oh, then you must mean Fremah, my eldest girl. I am not sure about that, I think she may already have a man. Well, I suppose if you were to give me a better offer, I could…"

"No, sir, I do not want Fremah," Baako snapped, exasperated by the older man's apparent inability to simply *listen* to what he was trying to say.

"What do you mean," Kwabena got to his feet, acting as if he had just been deeply insulted; "are you saying my beloved Fremah isn't good enough for you? What are you trying to say, boy? How dare you come into my hut and start telling me my… er… my daughters are not… er, ahem, er… er… worthy… you do me a great… a great…"

Kwabena bent over double, roaring with laughter. Serwaah and Fremah burst through the grass curtain behind him, giggling hysterically. Baako stood in stunned silence, staring back at the mirth-stricken trio.

"I am sorry, my love," Serwaah chuckled, "we could not resist having a little fun with you."

Kwabena straightened up and looked at Baako, an enormous smile lighting up his face, "Of course you may take Serwaah as your woman; I have never seen her so happy. Welcome to the family, my boy." He grabbed Baako and swallowed him up in a massive bear hug.

*

Following village tradition, the ceremony to confirm their union was set for the night of the next full moon. As tradition also dictated, they were forbidden to spend any time alone together until then. Serwaah watched from a distance as Baako spent the next ten days building the hut that would become their home while she spent the time with Fremah, making the headdresses they would wear for the ceremony.

On the eleventh day, a dark shadow cast a pall over their plans when grave news reached the village. The white hunters had raided a neighbouring settlement. The white devils had brought their firesticks and many had died trying to fight them off. When the fighting was over, the raiders had taken the surviving adults, leaving only old people and children behind. This was a catastrophe for any village. With only the elderly and young children left, the community would soon wither away and crumble to dust.

In their own village, the elders gathered to discuss what they should do. After many hours of debate, three of them left. Serwaah heard a rumour they had gone in search of the white hunters, hoping to make some sort of bargain to save the village. The next day, the remaining elders summoned everyone to a meeting. Serwaah stood among the crowd with her family. She saw Baako a short distance away, standing beside his mother. He smiled at her and she felt a yearning in her heart as she longed for their union. But her feelings were tempered by the apprehension that filled her as she wondered what the elders were going to say.

Safo, the most senior among the elders, stepped forward and addressed the assembled villagers. "Men on the hunt and women whose moon is flowering will stand here," he gestured to his right; "the rest will stand over there," he pointed to the left.

The village divided up with everyone from around thirteen to fifty years old on one side and young children and older people on the other. Serwaah lost sight of Baako, but followed Fremah and Danquah as they joined the other young adults, leaving her father and Amba behind, among the older adults and children.

She watched Safo slowly moving his finger, speaking quietly to himself as he counted the young adult group. Then he counted out some grass straws, cutting some in half before placing all of them in a basket. Lastly, he covered the basket with a cloth and gave it a thorough shake. He turned to face the young adults, "Each of you will reach under the cloth and take a straw. If you take a long straw, you will join the old people and children; if you take a short straw, you will kneel in front of me. You will kneel in two rows, men and women separately, one person behind the other. Now, begin."

The young adults started to take straws and lines of kneeling men and women began to form. Serwaah saw Baako draw a long straw and return to his mother's side. A minute later, Danquah was walking back to their father. Now it was her turn. She had no idea what this all meant, but she had a bad feeling about it, she was sure something terrible was going to happen to the people kneeling on the ground. With mounting anxiety, she reached into the basket.

She held the straw up for the elders to see then dropped it on the ground. She turned around and slowly made her way back to her family. Baako and his mother were standing close to Kwabena now. Baako smiled at her as she came to stand between him and her father. But she could not bring herself to smile. She had seen many of her friends kneeling in the lines; she was frightened what was going to become of them. Then, as she looked back towards the elders, her heart froze: Fremah had drawn a short straw. She stared at her sister in dismay as Fremah joined the women's line. Looking up at Kwabena, she asked, "What is happening, father?"

"The elders are wise. Giving up half our young people is the only way to stop the white devils taking you all. I have already lost one son to them, and it will hurt beyond measure to lose Fremah too. But you and Danquah have emerged safely from this lottery, and Kofi and Oppong are too young to be included. I am grateful you will be saved by the others' sacrifice."

"But, father, we cannot just let the elders give Fremah to the white devils."

"I am sorry, my child, we must accept Fremah's fate. There is nothing we can do. It is for the good of the village, be thankful the rest of you are safe."

The tears were running down Serwaah's cheeks as she watched her beloved sister. Safo ordered some of the men to fetch grass ropes from the stores and bind the kneeling villagers' hands. Fremah knelt with her head bowed, quietly waiting, while many of the other women and younger men were crying as they began to suspect what was in store for them.

A few hours later, the elders who'd gone to barter with the white hunters returned. As they reached the village, they joined Safo in front of the kneeling men and women. Then the white men arrived, sitting on giant beasts with long, thin faces. More of the strange beasts pulled a heavy wagon behind them. Serwaah felt a cold dread descend upon her as the strangers surrounded the villagers, carrying their firesticks in their hands.

The leader of the white men was a tall man with long, dark hair. He spoke to his men in a language the villagers couldn't understand, "Well, it seems the bargain was well struck. Good of them to make it easy for us. This might be enough to fill the hold." He dismounted and came to examine the kneeling villagers, walking first along the row of men, occasionally pinching an arm, or pulling back a head to get a look at the teeth. He moved across to the line of women, where he also took a look at a few teeth, as well as squeezing some of the younger girls' breasts. Serwaah was horrified to see him taking a particularly close interest in Fremah. She felt sickened and fearful for her sister as she watched him callously groping her like she was no more than a piece of meat.

At last the white man turned and called out a name. A black man wearing the same style of clothes as the white men ran forward. The tall white man spoke to him, holding up four fingers and pointing at Fremah.

The black man dressed as a white man was not from the village, or even one of the nearby villages, but when he spoke, he was just understandable. "My chief, Captain Maxwell, must have that you give four more. Most pleasure comes from any that are sisters or brothers to this one," he indicated Fremah.

Serwaah's blood ran cold. She and Danquah were supposed to be safe; surely the elders would not give them to the white devils? She took Baako's hand, squeezing it tight. "Please don't let them take me," she whispered. He opened his mouth to reply but was interrupted as the elder who'd led the negotiating team answered the white man's demand, "That was not our bargain. We promised you half our young people and half is what you are getting," he gestured at the prisoners in front of him.

The translator relayed this to the white leader. "Hmmm," Maxwell hummed to himself. He pulled something that looked like a small stick out of his belt and pointed it at the protesting elder. There was a flash and a loud bang. The elder collapsed to the ground, blood streaming from his stomach.

"Tell them they will give us another four, including this one's brothers and sisters, or we will take all the young people, kill the old people, and leave the children to starve."

The translator spoke to the remaining elders. Safo stepped forward and pointed at Serwaah and her brothers, "Serwaah, Danquah, Kofi, you will join the line."

Serwaah was mortified. Little Kofi wasn't even in the hunt yet but, in his haste to avoid more bloodshed, Safo had either forgotten this or chosen to overlook it. Before she or her brothers could move, Kwabena stepped forward, "You cannot give them all my children but one. I will not allow it. I will kill any man who tries to take them."

"What did the old man say?" Maxwell asked. He nodded as he listened to the translation then spoke again, "Sergeant Reynolds, we have a trouble-maker. Deal with him for me, will you, I have not had the opportunity to reload my pistol yet."

One of the other white men raised his firestick. Another flash, another loud bang and Kwabena lay on the ground, grasping at his side. "Father," Serwaah screamed. She dropped to her knees beside him, pressing her hands to the gushing wound, but the blood kept pouring out of him. Behind her, she heard Safo issuing more orders.

Rough hands grabbed her arms, hauling her to her feet, spinning her around. Baako reached out for her, trying to pull her away from the men who held her, "No, you cannot, it is not fair; she drew a long straw…" One of the men lashed out, punching Baako in the face. He fell back, sprawling across the ground, blood running from his nose.

The men dragged Serwaah to the back of the women's line, forced her down onto her knees, and bound her hands behind her back. Looking to her side, she saw other men doing the same to Danquah and Kofi. Beyond them, Amba crouched beside her father, pulling soothing leaves from her pouch and putting them over his wound. But she couldn't stem the bleeding.

Then Serwaah saw Baako scrambling back to his feet. He shouted to her and started to rush forward. The man who'd shot her father raised his firestick. Baako stopped in his tracks. He gradually raised his arms above his head then slowly walked towards the line of kneeling men. Serwaah watched in astonishment, along with the rest of the village, as Baako knelt at the back of the line. He looked at her and gave her a wry smile, "If I cannot save you, I am coming with you. At least we will be together."

Behind him, Serwaah could see Amba still busy doing what she could for her father. She obviously hadn't seen her son making his extraordinary sacrifice. But, as another man was binding Baako's hands, Amba glanced their way. "No!" she screamed and tried to jump up, but Kwabena held onto her. Serwaah heard him whisper hoarsely, "No,

307

Amba, you will only die too. We must trust the spirits to take care of our children now."

"Good," the white leader announced, "I think we have our quota. Secure the merchandise, Sergeant Reynolds."

The sergeant gave some orders. The white men went to their wagon and returned with two sets of iron rings linked together by heavy chains. Serwaah watched in horror as they dragged these to where the captives knelt and started to put the rings around their necks, creating two trains of prisoners. When they reached her, and she felt the iron collar close around her throat, she was so scared she thought she might die of fright.

Far in front of her, one of the white men fixed a chain to the first woman's collar and used it to haul her to her feet. He pulled her towards the wagon. One by one, all the women were forced to stand and stagger forward after the others. Serwaah was afraid her neck might snap as she was abruptly jerked off her knees and onto her feet. She stumbled along at the end of the line, following the rest, until the white man at the front attached the chain to the back of the wagon. Looking to her side, she could see another white man doing the same with the male prisoners.

Now the white men pulled more iron rings from the wagon, smaller ones, chained together in pairs, and fixed these around the prisoners' ankles. As the heavy metal shackles were fitted to her legs, Serwaah gazed across at Baako, overwhelmed by a hopeless despair. He gave her a half smile, "It will be alright, Serwaah, I am sure we will…"

He was cut short as a whip fell across his shoulders. "Silence, slave," snarled Reynolds; "you will not speak unless you are told to." The villagers couldn't understand the words, but they all understood the whip. No-one in either line spoke again for a long time.

The white leader remounted his thin-faced beast and led the party out of the village. The wagon trundled along at the rear, dragging the villagers behind it. Behind them was Sergeant Reynolds, his whip always at the ready.

*

The pace was relentless. The chains on their legs forced the prisoners to adopt an uncomfortable, shuffling gait. Baako watched Serwaah as they marched through the hot afternoon. It made him ache inside to see her enduring such torment. Her pretty smile had disappeared; her lovely face was etched with pain and sorrow. But, despite the anguish she was suffering, whenever he caught a glimpse of her beautiful, deep brown eyes, he could see the light within them burning as brightly as ever. His love for her grew stronger still. He would do anything he could to protect her, whatever dreadful fate might lie in store for them.

Serwaah looked back at Baako and saw the determination written across his handsome features. Occasionally, he'd give her half a smile: as much as he could manage, she supposed. She knew he was watching over her. She could feel his love like she felt the warmth of the sun. It gave her the strength to carry on.

In front of Baako were her brothers. Danquah, the eldest, marched along easily, seeming almost untroubled by the straits they were in. He'd always been strong. Behind him was Kofi. He was the youngest boy taken prisoner and was struggling to keep up. She could see him crying and longed to speak to him, to ease his pain and fear, but Reynolds and his whip were not far behind. She gasped as Kofi stumbled and looked about to fall, but somehow Baako was able to jerk his head back and pull the boy upright using the chain linking their collars. She silently mouthed, "Thank you."

She looked ahead, hoping for a glimpse of Fremah. Her sister was in the middle of the line, separated from her by twenty other women. She could only see her occasionally, when there was a turn in the path, but she was tall and strong and seemed to be coping well with the arduous journey. As well as any of them were anyway.

After what seemed an eternity, they finally made camp. The white men pushed the two lines of prisoners to either side, so the men and women were kept apart. Still chained to the wagon, some could only kneel. Others lay on the hard, stony ground. When darkness fell, a few people started to whisper, until the white men found the culprits and beat them with sticks. Everyone stayed silent after that.

Serwaah managed to lie down but the rocks beneath her dug into her side. Lying in front of her was a girl called Afia. Her moon had flowered for the first time a month ago. Serwaah could hear her weeping and worried the white men would come to beat her. In the moonlight, she could see the little girl's back heaving with her sobs. Slowly, with great difficulty, she wriggled forwards. The rocks left painful scratches across her skin, but she eventually manoeuvred herself alongside Afia. She tried her best to curl around the little girl, her front pressed as close to Afia's back as possible, although the girl's bound hands were caught between them. She kissed her on the neck and softly whispered, "Shush, little one, shush." Afia's sobs gradually subsided and she fell asleep.

Serwaah lay awake a long time. She thought she would never sleep but she must have because, the next thing she knew, it was daylight and a white man was kicking her in the back, shouting at her. She realised he wanted her to get up, so she stumbled to her feet as quickly as she could. The chain on her collar pulled Afia up too. Woken abruptly, the little girl cried out in alarm. The white man raised his stick but Serwaah stepped in front of him and the blow fell on her shoulder instead of Afia's head. The man grunted and moved on, kicking and beating the other women to force them to their feet. On the other side of the wagon, more white men were doing the same to the men. Serwaah searched for Baako and her brothers but they were hidden from view.

The white men were laughing and joking as they moved among the captives, as if the villagers' appalling misery was nothing but a game to them. What were these creatures, Serwaah wondered, some kind of demons? Were they taking them to Hell?

The wagon started moving and the tortuous journey continued. As the lines of prisoners were pulled forward, they moved closer, and Serwaah was able to get a look at Baako. He looked tired and drawn but, as he saw her looking at him, he lifted his head and smiled. He glanced behind to check Reynolds wasn't watching then mouthed, "Be strong, my love."

"You too, my love," she responded silently.

She switched her attention to her brothers. Danquah marched on, as strong as ever. Kofi was another story. There was a large bruise on the side of his face, where he'd obviously been beaten, and his eyes were bloodshot and streaming. She was deeply troubled by the state he was in. She and Fremah had looked after the smaller children since their mother died and Kofi was very precious to her. She tried to smile at him, but he was staring at the ground, she couldn't catch his eye.

The pace was even harder than the day before. The white men forced them to march until dusk. When they made camp, most of the prisoners simply dropped to their knees and fell asleep on the spot. In the morning, the white men gave them a little water, the first they'd had in almost two days. The grass rope binding their hands was starting to come loose so Maxwell ordered his men to replace it with iron manacles. Each villager was now carrying the weight of an iron collar, a pair of heavy manacles, and a pair of leg irons. The burden was taking its toll, especially on some of the women and younger boys. As they set off on the third day, Serwaah looked at Kofi. She was horrified: he was pale and sickly; the bruise on his face had turned an ugly, greenish colour; and he was limping badly. He couldn't go on much longer. How much further would they have to walk? Surely it must end soon?

Three hours into the march, Kofi collapsed. Baako tried to pull him up as he had before, but to no avail. His limp little body was dragged along until Reynolds shouted at the wagon driver to stop. The sergeant walked over to Kofi and began whipping and shouting at him. It did no good. Kofi was just too sick and exhausted to move.

Reynolds spoke to the driver then went to the front of the column. He returned with Maxwell. The leader spoke to Reynolds, who whipped Kofi some more. Still he failed to respond. "Get up, sweet brother, please get up," cried Serwaah. She tried to go to him but the chain on her collar held her back. Reynolds glanced at her, but he was too preoccupied with Kofi to do anything.

The leader spoke again. Reynolds stopped the beating and stood back. Maxwell pulled out his pistol and pointed it at Kofi's forehead. "No-o-o-o," screamed Serwaah. There was a flash and a bang. The back of Kofi's head exploded. Bone, flesh, and blood flew in all directions. A sharp chip of bone sliced through Reynolds' cheek and fresh, bright blood ran down his face.

Serwaah turned away. She felt the grief rising inside and thought she would burst with the agony of it. But she couldn't. The shock and pain sat inside her like a rock. It ached, like a bad stomach after eating spoilt food, but she couldn't let it out.

Kofi's blood was spattered across Baako's face. He wanted to kill the white devils, to pound on their heads until they split open. But there was nothing he could do. He looked at Serwaah and wished he could comfort her, wished he could have saved her brother and spared her the horrendous pain she was suffering. But he was useless; he hadn't been able to do anything. He hung his head in shame.

The white men removed Kofi from the line. They took the iron rings that had dragged him down and put them back on the wagon, then tossed his lifeless body to the side.

After that, anyone who stumbled got straight back up before Reynolds could even begin using his whip. The rest of the day passed without further incident, but it was clear the prisoners couldn't take much more.

*

That night, Serwaah lay curled around Afia. She wanted to weep. She was desperate for the release of tears, desperate to let the turmoil inside drain away. But something wouldn't let her cry; something inside was telling her she had to stay strong, not give in to her emotions. Not yet.

Afia spoke softly, "I am sorry for your loss, lady. Kofi was my friend. I am so sorry for you. You are a great lady."

It was the first time anyone had given Serwaah the respect of calling her 'lady'. She didn't feel she deserved it. She was about to tell Afia not to use the term, but she changed her mind. "Thank you, Afia," she said.

Around noon the next day, they emerged into a clearing and came to a halt. The villagers stood frozen to the spot, gripped with fear by the intermittent 'whooshing' sound they could hear. None of them had heard anything like it before. Some began to whisper that it was the breathing of the white men's monstrous god, and they would soon be fed to it. The sense of unease was compounded by the sound of moaning and weeping coming from the cages in the centre of the clearing. Each cage held forty to fifty people, packed in closely together. Like their own group, the captives had iron collars, manacles binding their hands, and shackles on their feet.

The white men disconnected the prisoners from the wagon and led them to two empty cages at the back of the clearing. They pushed the men into one and locked it shut, but kept the women waiting outside the other. Maxwell walked over to the line of women. He gave some orders and two white men removed Fremah from the line then started to lead her away. She was shaking with dread, her eyes wide in terror, "No, no, please… anything else, please, I beg you… please do not feed me to your white god."

Serwaah cried out, "Sister, oh sister." Reynolds raised his whip and moved towards her, but Baako shouted, "Do not be afraid, Fremah, your mother's spirit will be there to meet you," and the sergeant turned and used his whip on him instead, striking at him through the bars of the cage.

After Fremah had been led away, the white men pushed Serwaah and the other women into the second cage and locked them inside. It was hot and uncomfortable in the cramped cage, they only had room to stand, but it was still a relief from the long march. Serwaah tried to peer through the mass of women in front of her to get a glimpse of Baako or Danquah in the men's cage, but she couldn't see either of them. At dusk, the white men came to give them a little water and a strange type of porridge. Some of the villagers feared they were being poisoned by the unfamiliar food, but they were so hungry they ate it anyway.

Serwaah leaned against the side of the cage. She let Afia rest against her, her head on Serwaah's chest. While Afia slept, Serwaah thought about Fremah; she was worried sick, wondering what had become of her. Then she thought about Kofi; he'd been full of life and laughter. He'd had the cheekiest little grin. She missed him so much. It ached inside to think about him. She missed her father and little Oppong too. She missed her village and the friends she'd left behind, and dear, kind Amba, who'd been like a mother to her the last few months. She knew she'd never see any of them again and it made her want to weep. But the thing inside that wouldn't let her cry took control again. 'Not yet,' it seemed to say, 'not yet.'

The moon rose above the trees and flooded the clearing with light. She stared up at the bright orb in the sky. It was the night of the full moon. She and Baako should have been celebrating their union tonight. She sighed then closed her eyes and whispered the words she had been looking forward to saying in front of the whole village, "Baako, son of Baako, I swear before all those present here tonight that I shall be your woman this night and all nights until we are parted by death."

She opened her eyes and watched as the moon was swallowed up by dark clouds, just as their union had been swallowed by a more diabolical darkness. She added another vow of her own, "Only death shall part us, my love, not these white devils."

*

In the morning, the white men began taking the men out of the cages and leading them towards the whooshing sound coming from behind the trees. Many believed they were being fed to the white god and wailed in desperation, terrified of the fate that awaited them. Soon it was the turn of Baako and his fellow villagers. He stole a glance at Serwaah as he was led away and tried to give her a reassuring smile. Watching him go, she felt more pain in her heart to add to the sorrow that already filled it.

The white men now began moving the women, but it was another hour before Serwaah's group were making their way towards the trees and the whooshing sound beyond. She was at the back of the line when the group came to a sudden halt. She bumped into Afia in front of her. The women at the head of the line had stopped and were gazing in astonishment at what lay before them. They began wailing and moaning, until the white men used their whips and the line moved forward again. At last, Serwaah could finally see what lay beyond the trees.

In front of her was a gigantic lake, so large it stretched farther than she could see. The lake moved backwards and forwards and, as the water crashed onto the sand, it made the whooshing sound. In the water was a giant canoe with enormous white sheets standing above its hull. As she watched, she saw the white men leading a group of women over a wooden walkway connecting the canoe to the sand.

Serwaah's group marched on, heading for the canoe. Minutes later, they crossed the walkway into the belly of the vessel. She followed the others down steep wooden steps. The shackles on her ankles made the descent awkward and she feared she would fall, but she was forced to move quickly as she was pulled onwards by the chain on her collar.

After negotiating the steps, they reached a long, wide room. Serwaah had to bend her head beneath the low ceiling and shuffle forward in a crouch. It was dark inside the canoe, especially after the bright African sun beating down on the beach outside. It took her eyes a while to adjust before she was able to see what the white men were doing to the women ahead of her.

They began by tearing off the woman's skirt, as well as any necklaces or other adornments, which they either pocketed or threw away. Then they used her manacles to shackle her to the woman in front. As she was dragged forward, more men forced her to lie on the wooden floor, pressed close to the woman who'd gone before. As each woman lay down, the chain on her collar pulled the next one to her knees. After every fourth woman, the men passed the chain under a metal hook set in the floor. The men worked quickly, getting each woman secured in a matter of seconds. They were clearly well-practised. Eventually, it was Serwaah's turn. They roughly manhandled her into position and fixed her in place with the others: one hand shackled to Afia, the other chained to a metal ring set in the deck. They chained her collar to the same ring, leaving her unable to raise her head more than a few finger widths. She had less than two spread hands' worth of space, between a wooden beam and Afia lying next to her.

The white men left. For a few minutes, all was quiet. Serwaah stared up at the ceiling and wondered what would happen next.

XXIII

A TERRIBLE JOURNEY

The women around her were weeping and wailing, crying out in desolation and terror, "The white demons are gods. They have put us in the belly of their beast. It will eat us like the spider eats the fly in its web. Oh, woe is us, we are doomed."

Fighting to suppress her fear, Serwaah spoke up so all the women on the deck could hear, "My sisters, this is no beast, it is a vessel made of wood. The white men are flesh and blood like us. They are not gods or demons. I have seen them bleed as we do. I cannot tell you what they mean to do with us, but you will not be eaten. Do not let them hear you moan or cry, for they will know you are frightened. Stay calm, my sisters, and we shall prevail."

The weeping and wailing subsided. Some of the women shouted 'great lady' in response. To her surprise, Serwaah realised she had become their leader.

Afia asked softly, "Is it true, great lady, do the white men really bleed like us?"

"Yes, little one, they bleed. I saw the one called Reynolds bleeding from his face. They bleed and, if they can bleed, they can die too, or at least they can be beaten. We are not beyond hope, little one, we shall survive this horror."

Lying back on the wooden floor, Serwaah became aware of the vessel bobbing gently up and down. She recalled a word she had heard the white men say many times as they were being brought inside: ship. That must be the name for this giant canoe with its huge white sheets and its deep belly where they were being held prisoner. But where would the white devils take them in this so-called 'ship'?

After a few hours, there was a lot of muffled shouting from the white men and the ship started to move forwards. Gradually, the bobbing grew more pronounced as they headed away from the shore. After another hour, the ship began to rise and fall with a violent motion, pitching fiercely from side to side. Many of the prisoners started throwing up. The stench of vomit soon became overpowering, which in turn caused more to join the chorus of retching.

Some had taken fright and urinated as they were chained in place on the deck. Soon everyone was forced to do the same, unable to wait any longer for relief. When darkness fell, some began to defecate. Many were suffering from diarrhoea and, before long, there was filth running over the wooden decking. Serwaah was lucky to be on the end of a row. Those in the middle had it worse.

In the morning, the white men came around with a wet sponge and dribbled water into each prisoner's mouth. This was followed by a morsel of bread, their daily ration. Wary of being bitten, the men dropped the bread into the captives' open mouths. Occasionally, a piece would fall onto the filth-soaked decking. The white men picked it up and dropped it into the next hungry mouth.

Apart from feeding time, they saw little of the white men. One would come to check their chains were secure every few hours, but that was all.

On the third day, Afia fell ill. A mixture of mucus, blood, and vomit streamed from her mouth and nostrils. Then her bowels opened and it seemed her entire insides were pouring onto the deck. She was moaning in agony. Serwaah held her hand, trying to comfort her. "Hush, little one, it will be alright," she whispered. Afia didn't respond. She started shivering then fell into a deep sleep. Her skin turned cold, her breathing grew more laboured then gradually shallower until, in the middle of the night it stopped altogether.

Once again, Serwaah wanted to weep. Dear, sweet, little Afia was gone. The grief inside was unbearable. It ached like she'd been kicked in the stomach. She longed to let it out, to dissolve in a torrent of tears, and sob her pain away. "Not yet," she said. This time, she said it out loud.

She was chained to Afia's body for another day and a half. As time went on, she felt her grief changing into something else. Partly it was anger at the white devils who had taken Kofi and Afia from her but, more than that, it was a determination to survive. She would not succumb, she would not give in to despair; she would get through this, whatever happened.

On their fifth day in the ship, the white men started to take batches of prisoners up to the main deck. Those who had died were unchained and dumped over the side. Serwaah watched Afia's body disappear beneath the waves and thought about her cheery smile, her pretty eyes, and her lovely little face. She turned her head away and whispered, "I will never forget you, little one." Her feelings of anger and determination grew stronger.

The black man who'd spoken for the white leader at the village stood in front of the prisoners and began jumping and dancing. The white men pointed at him and started shouting and whipping the captives until they realised they were meant to copy him. It was difficult with the shackles on their wrists and ankles, and the iron collars linking them together, but they all complied.

Most of the prisoners were terrified by the vast expanse of open water, with no land in sight. They couldn't understand how the white men's canoe could still be crossing the immense lake after so long. But Serwaah found her trips up on deck a welcome relief from the conditions below. She longed to see Baako, Fremah, or Danquah, but none of them were anywhere to be seen… until the twenty-second day.

Late that afternoon, she was up on deck for her

exercise period. She saw the white leader holding her sister by a rope around her neck. He spoke to Reynolds. The sergeant smiled and bowed his head, then took the rope and led Fremah away. Serwaah was relieved to see her sister alive, but dismayed to see her being passed between the white men like a tame goat.

One night, many days later, Serwaah lay staring at the ceiling, trying to sleep. She was startled by a faint noise. Looking to her left, she saw a familiar silhouette, "Fre…" Her sister quickly stifled her with a hand over her mouth. She spoke in the faintest whisper, holding her mouth close to Serwaah's ear, "Be quiet, my sister, if they hear us, we will both surely die." Fremah released her grip and continued, "This new white monster they have made me lie with is more stupid than the other. I have been able to escape for a short time. I have brought you some food, here," she began to put small pieces of fruit in Serwaah's mouth. Serwaah swallowed and listened to what her sister had to tell her.

Fremah explained she'd been taken to the captain's cabin where she'd been kept until the white leader tired of her and handed her over to Reynolds. She had seen a young boy being taken to the cabin in her place. "It would make no difference," she shrugged; "he always took me the way the men of the hill villages take their boys."

At first, Reynolds was as brutal as Maxwell, but the sergeant liked more variety. After a few nights, he released her from her chains and told her to 'get up'. She soon realised he wanted her to get on top of him. She found if she gave him much pleasure, he would fall asleep before putting her back in chains. The first two nights this happened, she lay on his bunk next to him and waited to see if he would wake before morning. He didn't. Tonight was the third night and she had finally plucked up the courage to sneak away and find Serwaah.

Fremah gripped Serwaah's hand and squeezed it tight, "I will be this white devil's woman until I find a way to free you. I will save you from this hell, my sister, I swear it. I will protect you as I have always done. Even in my sleep I dream I am hiding you from your enemies. Now, I must go. I will return when I can," she disappeared into the darkness, her ebony skin quickly merging into the shadows.

Three nights later, she was back, with more to report, "I have worked hard to keep the white devil happy. It is working. Now he is leading me on a rope during the day, like a symbol of his power. It is humiliating, but I see everything he does, how he keeps everyone in this terrible place. He has a ring of metal sticks to unfasten the chains holding our people. My sister, I am ready. In two nights, I will take the monster's ring of sticks as he sleeps and I will return to set you free. You must tell the others to be prepared. Remember sister, two nights."

In the morning, Serwaah began to pass on the word. She whispered to the woman next to her, who whispered to the next woman, who whispered to the next, and so on. When they were taken for exercise, they whispered to the others they met. In this way, the word was passed and, two nights later, most of the prisoners were ready.

Serwaah lay awake, thinking how good it would feel to be out of her chains, out of the stinking hold, able to walk freely and breathe the fresh air for more than a few minutes. She couldn't wait for Fremah to come and set them free. She strained her ears for the first sign of her sister's approach, expecting every little creak to be followed by Fremah's voice and the blessed relief of being released from her horrible confinement. The hours passed slowly, seemed to stretch into days. As the first light of dawn began to filter through the walls of their wooden prison, she realised, with a dreadful sense of hopeless resignation, her sister wasn't going to come.

The next day, there was more whispering among the rows of prisoners. What had happened? Why had Fremah not come? Some complained to Serwaah that her sister had let them down. That afternoon, Serwaah's row was taken on deck for their exercise. With a massive sense of relief, she saw Fremah being led around by Reynolds, just as she had said. Her sister was safe, but what had stopped her coming to free them?

Once again, Serwaah lay awake. In the darkest part of the night, Fremah appeared beside her, "I am sorry, my sister, the white devil fell asleep on top of me last night. I could not move from beneath him. This night I gave him much pleasure, and it was he who fell asleep beneath me," she snorted derisively; "I took the sharp blade from his cloak and held it to his neck. I shook him until he woke and stared him in the eyes. 'For our father and brother,' I said, and pulled the blade across his throat then watched the blood flow out of him. He grabbed at me, trying to throttle me, but his strength soon ebbed away. I took his ring of metal sticks, now I am here to free you."

She produced Reynolds' metal sticks and began trying them on Serwaah's collar. On her fourth attempt, she had it open. Then she separated one of the smaller sticks from the ring and released Serwaah from her shackles. Handing the stick to her sister, she said, "This will unlock the iron bands on our people's hands and feet. There is only one metal stick for the collars, but the chains that join them can be removed." Swiftly, Fremah demonstrated how to unfasten the chain from the next woman's collar, "Do you see?"

"Yes, I see," Serwaah nodded, still rubbing her aching wrists.

"Free the others here, sister; I will go to the next deck."

"Sister," Serwaah hissed. Fremah turned back to face her.

"Release the men first, they are stronger. Start with Baako and Danquah if you can."

Fremah nodded then disappeared into the darkness as she made her way further down into the ship.

*

Baako was at the end of a row of prisoners, on the first deck of men. He knew he was four decks beneath Serwaah; he had seen her once when they were being taken up to the main deck for exercise. Like the others around him, he had heard the whispers telling that someone was coming to free them: a great lady with metal sticks that could unlock their chains. She had been supposed to come last night, but she had not appeared. Now he wondered if it had just been a story someone had made up. If so, whoever had started the rumour was as cruel as the white men. To have hope then have it snatched away was more bitter than to have no hope at all.

Unable to sleep, he lay awake, listening to the familiar sounds of the ship: the creaking of the wooden walls; the splashing of the water beyond; the muffled sound of the white men's footsteps far above. Every few hours, one of the white men came to look at their chains. Sometimes one of the captives would cry out for water, but the white man would either just ignore them or, worse, beat them with his stick.

In the middle of the night, shortly after one of the white men's inspections, Baako heard new, less familiar sounds. Someone was moving on the decks above, but it didn't sound like the white men. What was happening?

Suddenly, a figure emerged from the darkness, seeming to materialise out of thin air at his side. "Hello, Baako, I have come to free you," she whispered.

"It is you; you are the great lady with the metal sticks."

Fremah smiled, "Well, I have the sticks at least." She held them up to show him then started work on his chains. "Where is Danquah?" she asked.

"He has made friends with one of the white men. He is with him."

"How did he do that?"

"First he smiled at him when we were on deck, then he danced next to him and let him touch him. Yesterday, he kissed the man on… Well, anyway, the man took him away."

"Ha! Danquah has always looked after himself. I am not surprised. He is not that way by nature, but he would do anything to gain favour."

Fremah swiftly released Baako. Once he was free, he helped her release more of the prisoners. They had liberated about forty men when there was a loud cry of alarm from above. Almost immediately, they heard the white men shouting and running along the decks overhead.

The men who'd been freed had already started to make their way up towards the main deck, but now it turned into a stampede. "This is our chance," shouted one; "we must kill the white devils before they can put us back in chains."

Baako turned to Fremah, "You carry on here, keep releasing our brothers. Free as many as you can so they can join the fight, get some of the younger boys to help you. I will go up with the others."

"Be careful, Baako, the white men will arm themselves with swords and firesticks."

"Do not worry, Fremah, there are many more of us than there are of them, we will prevail."

Baako began to climb, following the rest of the freed men upwards. As they ascended, they were joined by the women. He looked for Serwaah but couldn't see her in the press of bodies scrambling for freedom. He heard shots ahead, followed by shouting and screaming. Coming out onto one of the upper decks, he was able to see some of the fighting. The white men had shot a few of the escapees before they could reach them, but their firesticks were useless now the two sides had come together. The chains that had kept the prisoners captive had become weapons; several white men had been beaten to death. The others were being pushed back by the steady assault, in danger of being overwhelmed by the mass of humanity surging up from the decks below.

"Fall back and form two lines on deck," Maxwell shouted from above. The hand-to-hand fighting came to an end as the white men retreated, keeping the escaped prisoners at bay with an occasional shot or swing of a sword.

Baako was swept along by the rampaging mob as they followed the white men upwards. As he reached the open deck, he peered over the shoulders of the men and women ahead of him. The white men were lined up in two rows in front of Maxwell. They were rattled, some were shaking, but they were standing their ground, their firesticks at the ready. "Wait for my command," ordered the captain. Baako felt the cold grip of a paralysing dread descend upon him as he saw the weapons pointing at his fellow escapees. He was pushed forward as more prisoners forced their way onto the open deck behind him. Those in front began to spread out; he was getting ever closer to the white men's guns.

"Front rank, fire!" shouted the captain.

Half a dozen men and women fell to the deck in front of Baako. The survivors tried to rush forward, but their progress was hampered by the bodies of the fallen. "Reload," shouted the captain, then a moment later; "Second rank, fire!"

Another half dozen fell. The dead and wounded were beginning to form a human wall, hemming in Baako and the others. Just as a few managed to break through, the captain shouted again, "Front rank, fire!" Yet more escapees dropped. The rush forward came to a halt and the rebels began to fall back. Baako was exposed to the guns now; everyone in front of him had been struck down. The captain ordered another volley. Baako closed his eyes, waiting for the firesticks to speak, waiting for the fireball to tear into his flesh. He heard the blast of the guns, the others falling beside him, but somehow, he was unscathed.

"Advance in formation," shouted the captain. Baako opened his eyes and saw the white men moving forward, muskets raised, ready to fire. The captain followed at the rear, his pistol drawn. Some of the people at the back of the mob were retreating inside the ship. Most of those caught in the open fell to the deck, cowering in front of the guns. Baako glanced behind him, his way back was blocked. He got down on his knees and raised his hands in surrender.

A few of the rebels remained standing. The captain aimed his pistol and shot one in the chest, then pointed his finger at another. "Biggs," he commanded. One of the sailors shot the man in the head. Now the rest of the escaped prisoners fell to their knees. The white men surrounded them, beating them with the butts of their muskets until everyone was subdued.

The captain ordered the dead thrown overboard then dispatched some men to fetch manacles and leg shackles, which they used to secure the surviving rebels. They replaced any missing collars and reattached the chains linking the prisoners together. One of the older crewmen examined the wounded: if he nodded, the sailors chained the injured prisoner up with the others; if he shook his head, they were thrown over the side.

As he was put back in chains, Baako felt an awful despondency overtake him. Their rebellion had failed. However bad things had been before, they would only get worse now.

*

Serwaah had remained below decks throughout the fighting, trying to help more prisoners escape. When she heard the captain bellowing orders, the loud roar of the guns, and the sound of bodies falling to the deck above her, she began to fear for her fellow escapees. A minute later, when she saw some of them hurrying back down the wooden steps, she knew all was lost. She looked around, searching for somewhere to hide, but there was nowhere. She sat on the deck, leaning against one of the wooden beams, and waited for the white men to come.

From where she was sitting, she could see a group of escapees clustered beside the staircase. Suddenly, she heard the stamp of boots thundering down the steps towards them. As the white men came into sight, she saw the captain at the front. Before the escapees had time to move, he shot one in the head and put his sword through another. The rest fell to their knees, their hands in the air. The sailors dragged them away while the captain continued down the steps. Serwaah jumped when she heard another shot, fearful who the target might be.

The sailors returned a few minutes later. Two of them rushed over to Serwaah. One was shouting at her; he raised the butt of his musket above her head. She scrambled to her feet, holding her hands over her head in an attempt to protect herself. He smashed the musket into her temple. The blow was softened by her hands but still sent her dizzy. The sailors grabbed her arms and dragged her up the wooden steps, out onto the open deck, where they chained her at the back of the group of cowering prisoners.

As her head began to clear, Serwaah searched for any sign of Fremah, Baako, or Danquah. She caught a glimpse of Baako at the front of the group and was relieved to see he seemed unhurt. A short time later, she saw the sailors dragging Fremah to the front. Her sister hung limp in their hands, blood running from a gash on the side of her head, but at least she was alive… for now.

The recaptured prisoners were left on the open deck the rest of the night, guarded by two white men with muskets. Serwaah shivered in the cold. She longed to be with Baako and Fremah, but she was separated from them by the huddled mass of their fellow captives. Their hopes of escape had been dashed and she felt a tremendous despair descending upon her. She wanted to break down and weep for her lost brothers and sisters, but that inner voice was there, whispering in her head once more, 'Not yet.'

Just after dawn, the captain stood on the quarterdeck, surveying the prisoners. He walked down the steps to the main deck and pointed at Fremah, "That one." Two sailors disconnected Fremah from the others and dragged her to him.

The captain grabbed a handful of Fremah's hair and pulled her head up so his crew could see her clearly. She blinked in the morning sun, her eyes wide, filled with terror. Serwaah felt a cold chill sweep through her body as she waited to see what the white men would do to her beloved sister.

"This is the one that started it," said the captain; "she killed Reynolds and released the others. That's murder and mutiny, men. You know what to do."

The sailors took Fremah to the side of the ship where a rope hung from a pulley high above. They tied the rope to her leg shackles then went to the other end and began to pull. Serwaah watched helplessly as her sister toppled forwards onto the deck, and was then lifted by her feet until she was dangling upside down over the ship's side. Even from across the width of the deck, she could see the pain and fear on her sister's face.

Another two sailors took a long length of rope to the bow. They carefully looped it under the figurehead adorning the prow then walked slowly back, one man paying out rope on either side of the ship. When they reached Fremah, the man on her side tied the rope to the manacles on her wrists. Meanwhile, the man on the other side passed his end over another pulley. When they were done, both men stood beneath the pulley, holding the free end of the rope.

"Good, we are ready," said the captain. He looked at Fremah, "For the crimes of inciting rebellion and the murder of Sergeant John Reynolds, I sentence you to death by keelhauling." He turned to the men on the far side of the ship, "Begin pulling, dead slow."

It took a few seconds to take up the slack then the rope holding Fremah from above began to pay out and she descended head first towards the water. Serwaah stared in horror as she saw her sister disappear. She could see Baako silently clenching his fists. There was nothing either of them could do.

Several minutes passed before Fremah reappeared on the near side of the ship, closer to Serwaah, pulled upwards by the manacles around her wrists, her outstretched arms straining in their sockets. She was coughing and spluttering; blood streaming from dozens of gouges ripped into her flesh by the barnacles covering the hull as she was hauled across them.

"Again!" bellowed the captain. The men on his side of the deck heaved on their rope, pulling Fremah down towards the water to repeat her terrible journey beneath the ship in reverse. The men were tiring and it took longer before she resurfaced this time, back on the side where she'd begun. She gasped for breath as she was pulled feet first up the side of the ship. The men kept pulling until she was hanging high above the deck, her head level with the captain's.

She turned, looked her tormentor in the eyes, and spat a huge glob of blood and mucus into his face. Serwaah saw the tiniest flicker of a smile play across her sister's lips as the missile struck its target. The captain wiped his face then shouted, "Again."

The men started to pull Fremah beneath the ship a third time. A couple of minutes after she disappeared beneath the waves, they were pulled forward by a sudden, violent tug on the rope. Then, just as suddenly, they fell back. The captain looked at the other rope, hanging freely in the ship's wake. "Keep pulling, quickly as you like now," he ordered.

A minute later, Fremah's head appeared above the ship's side. Some people fainted; others, including two of the white men, threw up. Serwaah gasped. She almost collapsed, but, after a moment, she recovered her strength and stood upright. She stared at her sister's remains. One manacle held a disembodied hand; what little was left of her hung from the other. Her head was intact but most of her body was gone. Her tattered flesh dripped with blood where the enormous bite of some giant underwater creature had torn the rest of her away.

Serwaah felt as though part of her had been torn away too. Of all her family, Fremah had been the one she could always rely on, always confide in. They were more than sisters, they were best friends, partners in crime, they shared all their secrets, their hopes and dreams; as children they had done everything together, they'd been inseparable. Now they'd been separated by death: by death, and by the white devils. She wanted to scream and wail, to dissolve in a weeping mass of grief-stricken anguish. But still her tears wouldn't come. "Not yet," she whispered.

"Throw it into the ocean," the captain ordered; "the sharks can have the rest as well. Now then," he turned to the prisoners, "how shall we ensure there is no further trouble without losing any more cargo?

"Biggs," he demanded, "select five of the men and bring them over here." He pointed at Baako, "Start with that one."

The sailors separated Baako and four other men from the rest, took them to the captain, and forced them onto their knees in front of him. "Robinson," the captain called for an older crewman and spoke quietly to him. Robinson turned to another man and gave some instructions, then went below decks. The second man lit a fire in the brazier by the ship's wheel. This was the first time the brazier had been lit on the voyage; there'd been no call for it so far. Serwaah was puzzled and anxious as she watched the crewman stoking the fire. Its purpose wasn't clear, but she was certain it would not be a good thing.

Robinson returned with a long, sharp knife. He stood behind one of the kneeling prisoners and pushed him forward until his forehead touched the deck. Reaching between the man's legs, he grasped his cock and balls then, with one quick slice of the knife, removed them all. He threw the man's parts to the side, like scraps being tossed to a dog.

The castrated prisoner screamed and fell sideways onto the deck, blood spilling from his groin. The purpose of the fire now became apparent. Robinson pulled a poker from the flaming coals and applied its red hot tip to the man's wound. The man screamed again as his flesh burned, then lay weeping on the blood-stained deck.

Robinson did the same to each of the kneeling men. Baako was the last. As Robinson sliced through him, Serwaah looked up to see the captain break into a broad smile and say something she couldn't understand. But she remembered it.

*

More than three centuries later, Susan woke up and recalled what Maxwell had said, 'You won't trouble me this time, Bakara.'

And then she knew what she had to do.

XXIV

THE HIGHEST ROOM IN THE WORLD

en woke in a cold sweat, grasping desperately at his groin. With an immense sigh of relief, he realised everything was still in place. Some of these past lives were pretty unpleasant. Most of them seemed to end rather badly. He grunted to himself; that was Mortimer, of course, 'Wait 'til I get my hands on him; he has a lot to answer for.'

How did he always get the better of them? He always seemed to be there ahead of them, in a position of power; sometimes before they were even born. How was that possible? Was it destiny, fate, whatever you call it? Del Rivera had said he and Shebana were destined to be together but, if that was what the Universe wanted, it had a funny way of showing it. From what he'd seen, it always seemed to be on Mortimer's side. Was this what 'faith' was all about? Enduring the injustices meted out on innocents like Samantha and Bobby by evil bastards like Mortimer in the belief good would triumph in the end? He'd never bought that philosophy. Why shouldn't good prevail all the time, why should anyone have to suffer? He shook his head. He could get the idea of reincarnation, although it still seemed fantastic, but there was obviously much more to the workings of the Universe than he realised.

The soldier in him took over. He had a mission to fulfil. He was here to rescue Susan and, with Jack's help, he would find her soon. The mysteries of the Universe would have to wait. Meantime, he had an appointment to keep.

A few hours later, he was waiting in a reception area at the base of the world's tallest building. Al-Mansur took him a little by surprise. He'd expected the commander to have some sort of police uniform but, instead, he arrived wearing the flowing white robes of an Emirati official.

The commander flashed an identity card at the receptionist then gestured at Ben to join him. "Come with me, Major Carlton," al-Mansur indicated the lifts behind the reception desk.

"How did you know I was Carlton?" Ben asked as they walked towards the lifts; "there were a dozen other men waiting in reception."

"You are not the only one who knows how to use the internet, major. You are a decorated war hero." The policeman showed his card to the lift attendant and spoke to her briefly in Arabic. When the next lift arrived, the attendant held up a hand to stop the other waiting passengers and al-Mansur waved Ben inside. Pressing a button at the top of the control panel, the commander continued, "You won a medal for killing some of our Muslim brothers in Afghanistan, I believe?"

"Well... er... we were, er..."

The commander smiled, "Relax, major, the Taliban are no friends of ours here in the Emirates. We take a more tolerant view of you westerners."

"Right, yes, er, good." Ben realised he was in the hands of a man expert at catching people off guard.

The control panel displayed the numbers of the rapidly passing floors as the express elevator took them towards the sky: 70, 80, 90, 100, 110... the lift began to slow down... 120, 121, 122... Finally, it halted at 123. Ben couldn't help being impressed.

Al-Mansur led the way as they exited the lift. They were at the top of a staircase leading down to the 122nd floor where there was a luxurious lounge bar and restaurant. The policeman began to make his way down the stairs, past huge picture windows, through which Ben could see the city stretched out below, and far into the desert beyond.

"Not a good place to be if you have vertigo, eh major? Strangely, we must go down before we can go further up. Follow me," the policeman led them down to the restaurant and spoke to a member of staff who returned a moment later with the manager. Al-Mansur showed his ID and the manager led them through the kitchens to a service elevator at the rear.

"The less glamorous side of the Burj, major; now we go to the top," the policeman ushered Ben into the tiny lift then followed him inside and pressed the top button on the panel, marked '160'.

The service elevator was much slower. It was a couple of minutes before the doors opened on the 160th floor to reveal a room filled with pipes, machinery, and electrical ducting. Al-Mansur led Ben to a small metal staircase and began to climb.

After ascending three floors they appeared to reach a dead end, nothing but a plain white wall in front of them. Al-Mansur pulled out a key, inserted it into a barely visible slot, and a small section of wall opened to reveal another staircase beyond. They stooped through the narrow opening and continued their climb. Eventually, they reached the 166th floor, where the staircase ended at another plain white door. Al-Mansur opened it and they stepped into a surprisingly dull room.

"I thought the 163rd floor was the top?" Ben queried.

"Officially, it is. These top three floors do not officially exist. You won't see them in any architect's plans, or on any websites. But someone knew about them," al-Mansur crossed to one of the windows. Unlike those on the floors below, it wasn't designed for tourists to gaze out at the amazing views from the world's tallest tower. It was fairly ordinary; only two feet square… the view was still amazing though.

"We think he fell from here. Although it was sealed, and we missed it at first, we later realised it had been opened."

"So, it must be murder then? I mean, he can't have jumped and then sealed it behind him, can he?"

"Precisely, major; our conclusion exactly... But there are no fingerprints, no sign of any struggle; there is no blood. If he was pushed, it is almost as if he went willingly. Furthermore, given the shape of the building, the way it tapers, to land where he did... it is more like he flew. So, my question to you is this," the commander turned and stared Ben straight in the eyes; "what do you know?"

Ben's mind raced. How much could he trust al-Mansur? How much could he tell him without having his sanity questioned? On the other hand, the commander could be a valuable ally, he might need his help. He decided to risk telling him at least part of the truth.

"Del Rivera believed there was a woman in danger here, a British woman, a doctor, here in Dubai for a conference. He believed the man she was travelling with intended to harm her, probably kill her, in fact."

"I see. Do you know the names of these people your friend was pursuing?"

"Her name is Doctor Susan Carpenter. The man she was with is Professor Lord Mortimer."

"A professor *and* a lord; he sounds quite formidable. And you think he is responsible for Del Rivera's death?"

"I do, commander, yes, I do. Look, I get the sense you don't know whether to believe me, but can you at least help me find Susan? Er... Doctor Carpenter, I mean?"

Al-Mansur's eyes narrowed, "Who is this woman to

you, major? Are you, perhaps, romantically attached in some way?"

That was a hard one to answer. Ben kept to the facts as best he could, "She treated me in hospital after a bad car accident. I nearly died. I was, er… attracted to her, yes. But it was Del Rivera who was convinced of the danger. I didn't believe him at first, but when I saw the news of his death, I thought there might be something in it, after all. Now I'm sure of it."

Al-Mansur was pacing up and down in the small, bare, room; in a way, the highest room in the world. Each time he turned, he stopped and gazed at Ben, as if studying him, weighing him up. Suddenly, he seemed to make up his mind. He stopped his pacing, looked straight at Ben, and came to the point.

"You know, Major Carlton, meeting you here was highly irregular, but I had a strange feeling it might be the right thing to do. Now I am certain. I think you know a great deal more than you are telling me. I also think you have good reason not to tell me, and I do not blame you. Perhaps, if *I* tell *you* some things, you may feel able to speak more openly.

"A curious black liquid was found in Del Rivera's mouth. Our forensics team worked on it for two days solid. None of their usual tests indicated it posed any danger; no acidity, no known poisons. Thankfully, they continued to take every precaution, but they could not establish what the liquid was composed of. Some parts were recognisable, of course, but there were elements they could not identify.

Let me be frank with you, major, our department is well funded; we have an excellent forensics team. If they could not identify these substances, they are not known to science. A positively stunning conclusion, wouldn't you say?"

"Er, well, yes, I would say so."

"Indeed, major, indeed. But every test we did told us the liquid was harmless. Then, last night, one of our technicians got careless. It seems he picked up a vial of the liquid without using gloves. A little later, he must have touched his lips, or that, at least, is what we think he did. He died within a minute, his mouth and throat blackened and burned beyond recognition. And there was something else…" the police commander hesitated.

"What?"

"His colleagues reported a strange kind of smoke coming from his mouth. It lingered in the air a moment then drifted back inside him, just as he was dying."

"Hmmm, all very strange, but what does it prove?"

"On its own, nothing, but there is more; will you trust me enough to come to the station and I will show you something extraordinary."

"Do I have a choice?"

"Not if you want to know what is going to happen to Doctor Carpenter, no, I don't think you do."

*

An hour later, Ben was in al-Mansur's office. The commander had ensured the other officers in the department were all away. He produced a laptop computer, which he sat in the middle of the desk, and began looking for the file he needed, a video file.

"In this country, major, we have rules about how prisoners may be treated, just as you do in Europe. But I have a friend who works for the security services in another country not far from here. In his country, they have more leeway in these matters. There are prisoners there who will never see the light of day again. Most of them, I think, deserve that fate, a few, perhaps, do not. Nonetheless, when I wanted to conduct a live test on the substance that killed Del Rivera and my lab technician, I knew where to turn. I had a sample couriered across late last night and this is what took place this morning. Please observe."

Al-Mansur opened the file he'd been looking for and pressed 'play'. Ben saw a small, bare, room, an interrogation room by the look of it, with a large table in the centre. A policeman sat at the table with his back to the camera. The door opposite opened and two more policemen led a prisoner into the room. The prisoner was handcuffed and blindfolded. The policemen pushed him into the chair facing the camera, attached his handcuffs to a chain set in the table, and removed his blindfold. The prisoner blinked a few times and began speaking, but there was no sound on the video.

Seconds later, a technician entered the room carrying a tray bearing a glass flask filled with black liquid. The phrase 'dark black' would normally be something of a tautology, but it seemed appropriate. Ben had never seen anything so black.

The technician wore elbow-length gloves, like an abattoir worker. He carefully set the tray down on the table and handed out similar gloves to the policemen. Once they'd all donned the protective gloves, the two men who'd brought the prisoner held his head, pushing it back, and forcing his mouth open. The technician picked up the flask and poured the dark black liquid down the prisoner's throat.

The prisoner gulped and gasped then began to give off smoke. His eyes stared wide and unseeing at the camera; they turned a bright red, like the stop signal in a set of traffic lights. More smoke emerged from his mouth. It began to accumulate above his head and formed a small cloud. Moments later, he gave one last inaudible, but visible, shriek, convulsed, and then fell still. The cloud of smoke drifted back into the dead man, through his nostrils and open lips.

"We cannot be sure what any of this means, major," al-Mansur summarised, "but my theory is that your countryman, Professor Lord Mortimer, has developed a poison so powerful it somehow rips out a man's very spirit. Or a woman's," he added ominously. "We must not forget my technician got only the smallest taste. And this man here," he tapped the laptop screen, "drank second-hand fluid that had already been used to kill Del Rivera. We can only surmise the fresh, new poison will be considerably more effective.

"So, major, whatever it is you know; I can assure you I will be far more receptive than you might have imagined."

Ben opened his mouth to speak. Just then, his phone buzzed to indicate an incoming call.

"Do you mind if I take this?" Al-Mansur waved his acquiescence. Ben looked at the screen then tapped the icon to answer the call before putting the phone to his ear, "Jack. What have you got for me?"

XXV

SINCE THE DAWN OF TIME

Eight hours later, Ben was in the back of an armoured personnel carrier on its way to the neighbouring emirate of Abu Dhabi.

Jack Foster had come up trumps. At Ben's request, he'd diverted a US military reconnaissance satellite a few hundred miles off course so it could scan the desert south of Dubai.

"A villa flying the Stars and Stripes somewhere out in the desert, are you nuts?" Jack had objected. "What on Earth makes you think there is such a place? What the heck are you looking for, buddy?"

But Ben had pressed his old friend and eventually persuaded him to help. Twenty-four hours later, Jack had called back with the GPS co-ordinates for Mortimer's villa, "I have no idea how you did it, buddy, but there it was, like you said; 'Old Glory' flapping in the desert breeze, clear as day."

"Thanks, Jack, we're even."

"Oh no, buddy," Jack chuckled, "I still owe you, court martial or not. I'd be rotting in the ground if it wasn't for you. I don't know what you're up to, but good luck. Let me know if there's anything else I can do."

"I'll tell you all about it over a couple of beers," Ben hung up. Given that his friend was in command of the satellite reconnaissance section, a court martial seemed unlikely, but he was grateful to him nonetheless.

Ben passed the co-ordinates to al-Mansur, who found the location on his computer, "It's a remote area south-east of An Nashash, in the far south of Abu Dhabi, almost in Saudi Arabia. One might say the classic refuge of a scoundrel, miles from anywhere and close to an international border."

The police commander set about organising transport for them and suggested they set out after dark, "This Mortimer is a powerful man; he will have contacts everywhere. It is best we are not seen. I can come with you, but I will have no official jurisdiction in Abu Dhabi. Technically, it will be no more than a training exercise. I would not be surprised if Mortimer even has informers in my department, so we will only take one other man, my driver, Sergeant Kassab, he is trustworthy."

Just after eight o'clock that evening, the three of them set off from the basement parking area beneath the police station: Kassab driving, al-Mansur riding in front next to him, and Ben in the passenger compartment at the rear. With nothing else to do, Ben found his mind turning to

Sleeping Bear's prophecy. The 'marriage of stars' part seemed to have paid off, so there was obviously some substance to it, but what about the other part? 'Seven times you will lose her,' the chief had said. That was worrying. How many times had he lost her already? He counted the lives he'd seen: definitely more than seven. Sleeping Bear must have meant seven *more* times. How many had it been since then? He started counting again. Not enough. Try again. When had Sarah died, did that count?

His thoughts were interrupted as al-Mansur opened a shutter in the partition separating the passenger compartment from the driver's cabin. The police chief shouted over the noise of the speeding APC, "It will take us two hours to reach An Nashash, then at least another hour to get to Mortimer's villa. Why don't you get some sleep before we get there; you could probably use the rest."

Rest? Sleep had hardly been restful lately... filled, as it was, with the horrors of Mortimer, Mamboja, or whoever he was this time, attempting to kill, maim, or otherwise incapacitate him and Shebana. Or Susan, or whatever her name happened to be. God, this stuff was confusing.

And some of it was pretty gruesome, even compared to what he'd seen in the army. The hardest part was seeing Shebana suffer. Watching her being burned at the stake as Samantha Parsons was the worst thing he'd ever seen. Every time he went to sleep, he worried he might see something equally harrowing, or even worse.

But there were positives to his past life adventures too. He never knew who he'd be, where he'd end up...

or when. He always learned something, often something useful, and he found some of the experiences deeply fulfilling. To know he'd saved lives in the Great Fire of London, fought Napoleon at Waterloo, helped liberate the American colonies, it was incredible. What else might he have done?

He relished being so many different people from around the world and across the ages, protecting the innocent when he could, fighting evil and tyranny in all its guises and, of course, meeting Shebana and falling in love. On balance, it was worth the risk.

Doing as al-Mansur suggested, he lay down on the bench. He wasn't sure he'd be able to sleep, but the motion of the APC started to lull him. The speeding vehicle had a rhythm to it, a rhythm that reminded him of a time when harsh, mechanical sounds had been music to his ears. He began to doze off.

*

Bazza was having the time of his life. Punk was everywhere, it was taking over the world, and he was going to ride the wave to stardom. The Pistols were finished without Johnny Rotten, everyone knew that. It was time for someone new, that's what Billie said. Billie knew what was happening; he was mates with Malcolm McLaren's cousin. Just a second cousin, mind you, but that was good enough, Billie knew what was going on. Someone was going to be the 'next big thing', so why not Bazza and his mates?

Tonight was Vomit's biggest gig so far. They were only third on the bill, behind the main act and Mucus, another local band. But it was at the town hall, and there could be almost five hundred people there. Best of all, a guy from Skank Records was coming to see them. 'Fuckin' A,' thought Bazza, 'we'll get a record deal and we'll be outta here.'

Bazza played rhythm guitar. More importantly, he sang lead vocals. Lead vocalists got the most girls and, even though Vomit weren't exactly stars yet, there were already loads of them hanging around. Most of them came with hair and makeup copied from one of the big punk or new wave stars. There were always a few Siouxsie Siouxs, Debbie Harrys, and Poly Styrenes, even the odd Kate Bush; although they were a bit out of place in a punk audience.

He liked the Debbie Harry lookalikes best, even if some people claimed Blondie had sold out with their so-called 'disco album'. Secretly, he wasn't exactly a punk purist. Punk was a means to an end as far as he was concerned. God help him if his mates ever found his Abba albums hidden in his bedroom cupboard. He hadn't played them for a while, but he did occasionally get them out to look at. That Agnetha was something else.

His best mate Spunk went for the Siouxsie Sioux types. Spunk wasn't his real name, of course, he was actually called David, but that wouldn't do for a punk guitarist, just as Bazza didn't dare call himself Basil. He'd never forget the derision he suffered at school because his parents had given him such a fucking pathetic name.

Spunk was a brilliant guitarist, too good for punk really. They wrote the band's songs together. Most were strictly punk: lots of screeching, almost no melody, and simple guitar parts. One day though, they'd started experimenting, just for a bit of a lark. They ended up writing a song with a sweet melodic chorus and a fucking ace guitar solo. It still had a fucking good beat, mind you. When they'd finished, they looked at each other and a moment of recognition passed between them. Deep inside, they knew they'd created something special. Then Spunk laughed and screwed up the piece of paper they'd scrawled the song down on, "Well, we're never gonna be able to play *that* are we? Come on, let's finish 'Spit in Your Face', we need something new."

Later, after Spunk had gone, Bazza picked up the paper, straightened it out, and put 'I Have Loved You Since the Dawn of Time' in his desk drawer. 'You never know,' he said to himself.

Spunk was probably right though, it wasn't Vomit's kind of song. Perhaps they should be grateful for Dog and Gun, the band's rhythm section, who were good at making sure they kept their punk 'edge'. They achieved this basically by being completely crap. Dog, the band's drummer had chosen their names after a local pub. That was Dog's sense of humour alright. He wasn't very funny but, as a drummer, he was a good comedian.

Still, at least Dog could keep a rhythm going. Nothing fancy, but he could bang out a beat. That was more than could be said for Vomit's bass player. Known to his parents as Kevin, Gun plugged away at his instrument with only the slightest notion of which string did what. "That's alright," Billie said, "Vicious can't play either, he's just what you need."

Billie was supposed to be their manager, although he had to fit this around his job as a management trainee at Tesbury's. "Well, Brian Epstein was a store manager, you know," he always said.

"Yeah, but that was a record store, Billie," Bazza often replied, "not a supermarket, mate."

Still, to be fair, Billie had got them this gig. And he'd persuaded the guy from Skank Records to come and see them. So he was doing alright.

Bazza was last to arrive at the town hall. Billie and the rest of the band were crammed into a dressing room backstage. It was small and cramped, but still a considerable step up from what they were used to. "Did you hear," Spunk asked as he entered, "the Rats are number one. I tell you man, punk's taking over."

"Yeah, I heard the charts. The Rats are great, but there's a lot of crap around still."

"Yeah, like the fookin' Bee Gees," a rare comment from Gun. Putting on a mock falsetto voice with a heavy midlands accent, he mimicked one of the superstars' recent hits. "Fookin' disco."

Everyone murmured in agreement that punk was, of course, a purer and better form of music than disco. No-one dared disagree, although Bazza blushed slightly. He had a copy of the Saturday Night Fever soundtrack hidden with his Abba albums. John Travolta wasn't as nice to look at as Agnetha though.

"OK guys," Billie said, "you're on in twenty minutes. Georgie Grey, the guy from Skank Records I told you about, should be here just before you go on. I'm gonna take him with me and we'll watch from the side of the stage. I need you to put on a good show. I don't have to tell you what it could mean if Grey decides to sign you up."

"Yeah, lots o' pussy," Dog was sticking his tongue out, rolling his eyes and thrusting backwards and forwards with his groin just to make sure no-one was left in any doubt as to what he meant.

"Yes, I'm sure, Cyril," Billie used the drummer's real name, "but I think there might be other benefits as well. Anyway, just do your best, guys, eh? What are you going to play?"

The set list was usually chosen by Bazza and Spunk. They had a twenty minute slot and all their songs were fairly short, so they reckoned they could fit in seven or eight. Spunk listed the songs they'd chosen, "… then we'll do 'Spit in Your Face' and then, if there's time, we'll do our version of 'Anarchy in the UK'."

"Hmmm," pondered Billie, "sounds like a good set, but I think you should do 'Anarchy' before 'Spit in Your Face'. It's your best song and we want to be sure Grey hears it."

"Sure, whatever," Spunk shrugged. It wouldn't be cool to display any interest in what their manager or the visiting A&R man wanted.

They'd done two songs before Grey turned up, but that was OK, they still had a few to go. The audience were loving it, although most of them were so pissed they wouldn't have cared what the band played. There were plenty of sexy girls in the crowd but, during their fifth number, Bazza's eye was drawn to a pretty Indian girl who came in and stood near the back, next to Simon Carpenter, an old school chum who always came to their gigs. Not many Asian girls came to punk concerts, so she stood out from the crowd. Although she swayed gently in time to the music, Bazza could see she was uncomfortably out of place. She wasn't his usual type, but there was something special about her. He hoped he might get chance to speak to her later.

The sixth number should have been one of their best, but Dog and Gun botched it up and it sounded atrocious. Bazza saw the A&R man speak into Billie's ear and turn to go. Billie held onto his arm and Bazza could see him saying, "One more chance." It seemed to work, the man stayed.

"Right guys," Bazza turned to the others; "come on, let's do 'Anarchy' like we've never done it before. We can do this, guys." Totally uncool, but he had two reasons to want to look good: he wanted that record deal, and he wanted to impress the Indian girl.

Dog and Gun weren't too bad. Spunk was terrific. Bazza was in such a state of excitement, he had no idea how he was doing. But it felt like it was going well and the audience were lapping it up. 'We've cracked it,' he thought.

The band brought the punk anthem to a climactic finish and turned to look at Grey. The A&R man applauded, "Very good, that was very good lads, a genuinely exciting performance. But, the thing is, it was just a cover. We need original material. And I'm afraid we need something a lot more original than what you've played tonight. There are hundreds of bands who can screech those kinds of songs. We need something different. Sorry lads, best of luck to you though."

"We've got another one, it's different; it's not like the others. Give us a chance," Bazza blurted.

"Sorry son, I really do need to hear something different. I have to go…" Grey turned to leave.

"Please, two minutes. It really is different, I promise you."

Grey looked at him and shrugged, "Alright then, two minutes."

"Great, you won't regret it," Bazza stepped across to Spunk. His co-writer was surprised by his display of determination, "OK, well, er… er, well done, yes, but do you honestly believe he's going to think 'Spit in Your Face' is that different?"

"We're not gonna do 'Spit in Your Face'; we're gonna play this," Bazza pulled out the wrinkled piece of paper with the words and music for 'I Have Loved You Since the Dawn of Time' scribbled on it.

"We can't do this, we've never rehearsed it."

"Come on man; don't tell me you don't remember it as well as I do? Anyway, you can use this to remind you," he gave Spunk the piece of paper, "I know it off by heart."

"What about Dog and Gun?"

"Leave it to me." Bazza turned to Dog, "Same beat as 'Lick my Arse', start on my signal, OK?" Dog nodded, looking bamboozled by this turn of events.

Placing his guitar on the floor at the back of the stage, Bazza went over to Gun. Gently he took the bass from him, "Take a rest, Kevin, I'll take it from here." He strapped on the bass, stepped up to the microphone, and signalled Spunk and Dog to start.

It wasn't the best performance. But Bazza put his heart into it and, despite Dog's basic bashing, the band's lack of rehearsal, and the lukewarm reaction from the punk audience, the song shone through. It was different enough for Grey. As Bazza finished singing, the A&R man came over and handed him his business card, "Come to my office tomorrow, son, you've got yourself a record deal."

Grey walked away. Bazza punched the air in delight. He turned to the audience to say, "Thank you, and good night," but his euphoria was tarnished when he saw the Indian girl had gone. At first, he thought she must have left with Simon: his old school friend had got quite good at chatting up girls since he'd started that surveying course. Then he spotted Simon talking to a heavily made-up blonde in a leather jacket. She looked like she was drunk, but Bazza could tell she was keen from the way she kept touching Simon's arm. So where had the Indian girl gone?

Their set finished, the members of Vomit went back to their dressing room, where they started to celebrate with a few cans of beer. Billie had left with Grey and, after a few minutes, Dog and Gun went to watch Mucus. Bazza and Spunk were left alone. Slowly they began talking about their hopes and dreams, what the deal with Skank Records could mean to them, and the kind of music they *really* wanted to make. Bazza confessed to his Abba collection, although he swore Spunk to secrecy. His friend just laughed, "I've got 'The Kick Inside', 'Out of the Blue', 'Hotel California', 'Rumours'… you name it, man. Punk's just a phase, it's all music. We can write any style we want."

They talked for over an hour until the main act finished their set and Dog and Gun drifted back to the dressing room. Shortly afterwards, Billie returned with a bottle of something fizzy to continue the celebrations, "On me, guys, you did well tonight."

No band party would be complete without female company. Billie found a few girls waiting outside and invited them in. Among them was the Indian girl Bazza had seen in the auditorium. He was pleased to see her but she seemed out of place among the Siouxsie Siouxs (Spunk grabbed two), Debbie Harrys (one each for Billie and Dog), and a Poly Styrene (Gun's choice). Wearing a plain white blouse, navy blue skirt, and almost no make-up, she looked like a schoolgirl.

The other girls happily jumped onto the guys' laps, seeming content to let their roaming hands do as they pleased, cupping and squeezing as the kissing grew more passionate between gulps of cheap sparkling wine and beer. It was only a couple of minutes before Dog and his

'Debbie Harry' disappeared into the cupboard at the back of the room.

The Indian girl stood in front of Bazza, clearly feeling awkward amid the drunken debauchery around her. Gun took a break from groping 'Poly Styrene' and reached out to grab her bottom, "Come on, darlin', why don't you join the party?"

She whirled around and slapped his hand away, "I'm not that kind of girl."

"What you doin' 'ere then?"

"Uuughh, I don't know, you're just a bunch of drunken louts," she started to leave.

Gun stuck his leg out, blocking her path, "Well you're 'ere now, darlin', let's 'ave some fun. I've never done it with a wog." He began to run his hand up the back of her thigh beneath her skirt.

"No, please, no," she was trying to push his hand away, starting to panic.

Then Bazza was on his feet, gently pushing Gun away, "Come on, Kevin, don't be greedy, this lady's here to see me, aren't you?" he smiled reassuringly at her. She nodded; he could see she was scared, fighting back her tears. He took her hand and, leading the way, pushed past Gun's outstretched leg. He led her past the heaving masses of Billie and his 'Debbie Harry', Spunk and his brace of 'Siouxsie Siouxs', then out into the corridor.

"There, you'll be alright now, er…"

"Samaira… but my friends call me Sammie," she was brightening up, putting on a brave face, although she was still shaking. "Thank you. I was frightened what I'd got myself into in there."

"Oh, don't worry about Kevin, he didn't mean any *real* harm. Like you said, we're just a bunch of drunken louts," he shrugged, "we're harmless really."

"Oh God, sorry, no, I didn't mean you. I only meant... I mean I was nervous, worried, I..."

"It's alright," Bazza laughed, "I've been called worse things. But why did you come anyway? I get the feeling that wasn't your kind of scene?"

"No, I... I came to see you. That song, it was just so... so special; it was like you were singing to me... right to me, just me. That's why I had to come and see you."

"Really?" he was delighted. The lyrics were all his work and they'd felt pretty special to him too, "But you left, I thought..."

"I had to leave, I was so moved; I just had to go and... and just... just cry with joy!"

"Wow, that's brilliant... that it touched you like that, I mean. Never thought I'd be able to write something that good to be honest. 'Cause, Dave... er, I mean Spunk... he did a lot too. He's fuckin' ace on the guitar, you know. But what were you doin' here in the first place? You don't look much of a punk fan?"

"My brother's the drummer in Mucus, I came to see him. He helped me sneak out so my parents didn't see. That's why I'm still in my uniform," she shrugged, "I didn't dare change into anything else, or they'd have been suspicious." She looked down at her watch, "I'd better go, it's really late; I'm going to be in so-o-o much trouble."

"Wait a second," he pleaded, "can I have your phone number? I'd like to see you again."

She smiled and stood on tiptoe to whisper a number in his ear. She turned to leave, but paused, then turned back to give him a quick kiss on the cheek, before running off down the corridor. As he watched her go, he touched the spot where she'd kissed him and grinned to himself.

*

The next day, the band trooped along to Skank Records' offices in the centre of town. Billie wasn't with them; he had a shift at the supermarket, so he'd had to leave them to their own devices. Most of them were suffering raging hangovers, so they were a bit subdued. Except Bazza, he was too excited: he'd got a record deal *and* he'd got Sammie's number. Best night of his life.

After a bit of debate with security downstairs, they were eventually shown into Grey's office. Dog and Gun collapsed onto the sofa at the back of the room; Bazza and Spunk stood waiting nervously.

It was half an hour before Grey swaggered in. He glanced briefly at Dog and Gun, then addressed Bazza and Spunk. "Hey guys, good to see you, take a seat," he gestured at two chairs in front of his desk.

"So, great show last night, I think we can do business," Grey was looking at Bazza as he spoke.

"Er, yeah," Bazza responded, "we was hoping we could, yeah."

"But, er… Basil, er that is your name, isn't it?"

"Yeah, but I kinda like Bazza."

"Alright, Bazza it is then. Well, the thing is, Bazza, Skank Records is interested in *you*. But, er… well, er… just *you*, if you get my meaning?"

Bazza blinked as he took a moment to digest this, "But, we're a band, we're all together."

"OK, Bazza, let me be perfectly blunt. You're the star, you're the one we want; we don't need the hangers on."

Bazza was shocked. This guy wanted him to betray his friends. He was still trying to work out what to say when Spunk stepped into the fray, "Hey look, mister; I don't know what the fuck you think is going on here, but let me tell you…"

"Oh, I'm sorry," Grey interrupted, "it's, er… 'Spunk' isn't it? I wasn't referring to *you*, er… Spunk: now *you*, I think, should definitely have a place in Bazza's band."

"Oh… well, er… alright then, er… well, that's OK, I suppose."

"Although it might be better if we could call you David perhaps?"

"Dave," Spunk retorted, "I'd rather be Dave," he looked across at Bazza and shrugged.

"OK then," Grey concluded; "it's Bazza and Dave. So, what will we call your new band?"

"We're called Vomit," Bazza replied; "and what do you mean, *new* band?"

"My boy, you won't get anywhere with these talentless morons holding you back," he gestured at Dog and Gun, who were sitting nursing sore heads, seemingly unaware of what was going on. "You will need a new band: a drummer who can hit the drums in time with your music and a bass player who can... well, who can play bass. Mind you, you did a decent job on bass yourself last night; maybe you could manage as a three piece?"

"Shit man, this is a lot to think about," Bazza was reeling in disbelief at it all, "I don't know if we can..."

Spunk, who'd decided he wanted to be called Dave again from now on, put a hand on his arm and interjected on his behalf. "That's fine, Mr Grey, we'll 'ave a word with the lads," he indicated the band's semi-catatonic rhythm section, barely conscious on the sofa behind him, "and me and Bazza will be happy to sign up for you. We're very grateful for the opportunity. Where do we sign?"

"Hang on; shouldn't Billie be here before we sign anything?" Bazza queried; "he's our manager, isn't he?"

"You snooze, you lose," Dave shrugged; "should've been here, shouldn't he?"

Minutes later, Bazza and Dave signed the recording contract that would change their lives and consigned Dog and Gun to the obscurity they deserved.

XXVI

THE ROAD TO STARDOM

The next day, after a long night of celebrations with Dave, Bazza called Sammie's number.

"3-6-2-1," answered a mature male voice.

"Er... er... could I speak to Samaira please?" Bazza asked.

"Who is this?" demanded the voice.

"It's er... it's, er... Basil... me and Samaira met the other night at the concert."

"Oh yes, you're that English *punk* she met, aren't you?" The word 'punk' was spoken with as much contempt as anyone could put into a single word. "Let me tell you, boy, I don't appreciate young thugs like you trying to lead my daughter astray. She's only just sixteen, I'll have you know. She's been punished for her disobedience and grounded for a month. You won't be seeing her again, goodbye."

"Hey man, don't take it out on her, she only..." but

Bazza realised he was talking to thin air, the man had hung up.

He tried to call Sammie many times over the next few weeks. Mostly, he got her father, who simply hung up on him but, one time, a woman answered, "Hello?"

"Hey look, this is Bazza… er, I mean Basil. Look, I really want to talk to Samaira, just talk like. I know she's only sixteen, but we had a real connection, you know? I don't mean her no harm, I just want to see her again, or even just talk to her like. Please?"

"Oh Basil, how nice to speak to you, Samaira has told me all about you and your lovely song."

"Er, that's great, yeah. So, can I talk to her then?"

"Oh, I'm sorry, Basil. Samaira's father won't allow that. I am sorry. But it was nice to talk to you," the woman hung up, leaving him more frustrated than ever.

In the meantime, while he was failing in his efforts to speak to Sammie, things at Skank Records were moving rapidly. Two weeks after the meeting with Grey, he and Dave were in the recording studio laying down tracks for their album. 'I Have Loved You…' was the obvious single, although Grey decided it should be their second release. "We should warm them up with something else first," he advised.

'Spit in Your Face', 'Lick My Arse', and their cover of 'Anarchy in the UK' were all deemed acceptable album tracks by the record company but, the week before Christmas, Grey packed Bazza and Dave off with instructions to write at least six new songs, including something worthy of their first single they could record early in the New Year.

They found themselves in a small rented farm cottage in the middle of nowhere, trying to write songs to order, something they'd never had to do before. They had three they reckoned were good enough, another that might just about do, but they were struggling with the last two. One afternoon, after they'd demolished a bottle of whisky between them, the conversation turned to the night at the town hall.

"Whatever happened to that pretty Indian girl who was hangin' around?" Dave asked.

Bazza told him how much 'I Have Loved You...' had moved her, and how he'd been trying to get in touch with her ever since.

"Wow, that's a real bummer, man. Her dad sounds like a fuckin' control freak and her mum's under his thumb. That's a shame, man, she sounds like a cool chick. She really dug us."

"Yeah, wish I could see her again," Bazza paused, then repeated the phrase, with more hesitation and a lilt in his voice; "Wish I co-o-ould see-ee-eee her ag-ain. That's it, I've got it!"

By the beginning of March, 'Wish I Could See Her Again' was number fourteen in the charts and The Vomix were on their first UK tour. Bazza played bass and sang lead vocals, Dave played lead guitar, sang backing vocals, and occasionally had a go at keyboards. Grey had found a new guy called Toad to play drums, and they had a session player on rhythm guitar. They were pretty good as a punk band, but when they played 'Wish I Could See Her Again' and 'I Have Loved You...' they were something else.

The next week, they were back in their home town. The town hall was sold out, with a capacity crowd of over two thousand. Outside, tickets were changing hands for ten pounds. Small wonder really, 'Wish I Could See Her Again' had cracked the top ten and was sitting at number eight in the charts.

But Bazza was feeling down. Being back here reminded him of Sammie. After he and Dave got back from their song-writing sojourn, he'd carried on phoning her house every week, but he always got the aggressive rebuff from her father or the sympathetic, but firm, rejection from her mother. The last call had been with her mother, "Look, can you at least just tell her we're back in town this week, back at the town hall. Please?"

"I'll see what I can do, dear, but you know how her father feels about you."

*

Out of a sense of loyalty, or perhaps guilt, Bazza asked Grey if he could hire Dog and Gun as security for the town hall gig. Dog told Grey to 'go fuck yourself', but Gun took the job. On the afternoon before the show, Bazza led him to one side.

"Hey, man, I'm glad you agreed to come an' work for

us tonight. I was afraid you'd be too bitter about getting dropped from the band."

Gun stared at the ground, shaking his head, "Nah, it's no bother; I weren't cut out to be no bass player. You and Spunk was always the talent; I'm glad you're doin' so well, honest I am."

"That's good you feel that way. Listen, I'll talk to Grey, try to get you some more work."

"Yeah, that would be great."

"Meantime, can you do me a favour?"

"Sure, what can I do for you, man?"

"You remember the Indian girl who came to see me last time we were here?"

"What, that little wog cunt what was too stuck up to join in?"

"Please don't call her that. Her name's Sammie and I really like her."

"Aaah, you wanna shag her, don't ya?"

"No… I mean, maybe… one day… but not until… Look, I just want to talk to her, alright?"

"If you say so," Gun chuckled.

"Can you just watch out for her tonight please; bring her straight to me if you see her. No messing about, just bring her straight to me. Please?"

"Sure, alright, you're the boss," Gun shrugged.

Now The Vomix were chart-busting stars, they were considered worthy of a proper dressing room. The manager's office had been hastily converted and made available for the evening. It had a small ante-room where

Gun could vet any would-be visitors. He soon made it his little empire, obviously enjoying his chance to lord it over everyone who entered.

The gig went alright, but Bazza couldn't get Sammie out of his head. Being bigger stars meant better lights, but they were so bright he could hardly see the audience. He scanned the packed auditorium looking for her, hoping to spot that white blouse that stood out so well. Then he remembered it was Saturday, she wouldn't be in uniform. Disappointed that he couldn't see her, he knew it was affecting his performance. He reckoned he nailed 'I Have Loved You…' though; it felt like he was singing it to her.

After the show, the band went back to their new dressing room. Dave and Toad were enjoying the company of some groupies, but Bazza sat quietly, nursing a beer. He'd felt sure she would show up tonight. Glancing up at the clock, he realised he'd been waiting nearly forty minutes. With a deep sigh, he stood up, walked to the manager's desk and picked up the telephone. Pressing the button to connect him to the ante-room, there was a short delay then he heard Gun lift the receiver at the other end.

"Hey, man, how's it going out there?" Bazza asked.

"Yeah, alright, everything's cool here."

"Have you seen any sign of Sammie; you know, the Indian girl I was talking about?"

"No, not yet; there's no sign of her."

Bazza sighed again, "Alright, I'm gonna head back to the hotel. I'll go out the back way; I don't feel like seeing any fans at the moment."

"OK, yeah, no problem."

"But please call me there if she arrives and I'll come back. It's only five minutes away, so keep watching out for her, please; long as you can."

"Sure, man, no worries, I'll keep an eye out for her."

"Thanks, Kevin," Bazza put down the telephone, picked up his jacket and shuffled out the back door, his shoulders slumped dejectedly.

*

Sammie defied her father's orders and sneaked out to the gig. This time, she looked the part in a tight-fitting black patent-leather dress, sporting enough safety pins to give her the punk look. She blended in well with the rest of the crowd. Arriving late, she had to stand near the back and could barely glimpse the stage over the shoulders of the people in front. She tried waving to Bazza, but never managed to catch his eye. When he sang 'I Have Loved You...' though, she felt certain he must know she was there.

She stayed for the encore and joined in with the rest of the audience chanting 'more, more, more...' afterwards. When, eventually, everyone began to drift away, she battled through the throng to make her way to the dressing room where she'd first met Bazza. The girls in Electric Pussykatz, the support act, grinned when they saw her, and were plainly disappointed when she asked where The Vomix were, but they politely directed her towards the manager's office. By the time she reached the ante-room, it had been more than half an hour since Bazza walked off stage, and she was getting anxious she might have missed him. As she walked in, Gun was sitting on the desk, swigging beer from a can. "Er, hello, I was wondering if I could see Bazza please?" she asked.

"Oh yeah, little girlie, what makes you think I should let you in? He's a star now, you know; too good for a little wog cunt like you. Wait a minute," he squinted at her, "aven't we met before?"

"Er, maybe; please can I see Bazza now?"

"Ah well, there's an entry fee see, girlie."

"Oh… er… OK, how much is it?" she started to pull her purse out of her handbag.

"Ah no, girlie, it's not that kind of fee."

"What kind is it?"

He unzipped his flies and produced his ugly little cock, "You 'ave to give us a blow, little woggie, that's the fee."

"Uuughh, you're a monster," she turned to leave. She'd just reached the ante-room's outer doorway when the telephone next to Gun buzzed loudly. She stopped and turned back to watch as he hastily stuffed his member back in his trousers and picked up the receiver. She listened to one end of the conversation as he spoke.

"Yeah, alright, everything's cool here… No, not yet; there's no sign of her," he glanced at Sammie; "OK, yeah, no problem… Sure, man, no worries, I'll keep an eye out for her."

He shifted position slightly, moving the receiver from one ear to the other, so it was further away from Sammie. "Yeah, she is," he continued; "Yes, I'll make sure… Yes, boss, I'll make *really* sure… Don't worry; you can leave it to me… OK, yes, ten minutes then… Yeah, I'll tell her," he hung up the receiver and looked straight at Sammie.

"Was that…" she started to ask.

"Yeah, it was Bazza. He was asking if his mum had come to see him. I told him there was no sign of her."

"Oh," she bowed her head, unable to hide her disappointment. Her hair fell in a thick dark curtain across her face.

"Yeah, then he was asking if you were here as well. He wants to see you, but he said I had to make sure you were serious about him before I let you in. Make sure you're not messin' him around like. Wanted me to make *really* sure he did. Well, you heard him, didn't you?"

She looked up sharply. She hadn't actually heard Bazza at all, but she was too desperate to see him to care about that. She was thrilled he wanted to see her, but she knew he had every reason to be cautious. She'd heard her father giving him a hard time on the phone as she sat at the top of the stairs, crying in frustration: longing to speak to the boy she'd fallen in love with, tell him how she felt. Every time she'd tried to talk to her father about Bazza, his hand had left its painful mark across her cheek. "Sorry, father, you know best," she would mutter softly as she stared meekly at the ground, her face stinging from the blow.

Gun continued to relate his discussion, "He said he could only hang around another ten minutes, so I was to tell you to get on with it if you wanted to see him. So, how about it then? You wanna see Bazza, or go home to Daddy? Guess you might get another chance in a few months, next time Daddy lets you out. Bazza'll be a major star by then. You might get his autograph if you're lucky. So, what's it to be girlie?" he pulled his cock out again and sat on the edge of the desk, licking his lips, watching her, clearly waiting to see what she'd do.

"I *am* serious about him, I really am. I'm *not* messing him around. But I'm not touching *that!*"

Gun sighed and looked down while he replaced his member in his jeans once more. Then he looked up again and smiled, "Well, I guess there's another way you could prove you're serious."

"How? Tell me, please, I am serious about him, honest."

"You could do a dare."

"What would I have to do?" she asked hesitantly.

He laughed and reached inside his jacket. He pulled out a hand-rolled cigarette, "See this? You 'ave to smoke this, that's the dare."

"Oh, I don't smoke. My father says it's wrong for girls to smoke."

"Well, the thing is, girlie, Bazza needs to be sure you're serious about him. The only way to prove it is to smoke this. If you wanna see Bazza, that's what you gotta do."

375

She was nervous; she didn't trust Gun at all. But she had to see Bazza tonight, she just had to, or she could lose him forever. If this stupid dare was what it took, then so be it. How bad could it be? Her friend Nicky smoked. It made her breath smell horrible but, apart from that, it didn't seem to do her any harm.

"Alright then, I'll smoke it. Just for Bazza. So he knows how serious I am about him. Give it to me," she held out her hand.

"Here, let me light it for you," Gun produced some matches from his jacket. He put the cigarette in his mouth and lit it, then pulled on it a few times before handing it to her. She was a bit perturbed it had been in his mouth, but she supposed it was no worse than sharing a bottle of cola. She put it to her lips and took a tiny puff on it.

"That's no good, girlie, you need to really draw on it, suck the smoke deep inside, that's what you gotta do, or else you ain't done the dare proper and no Bazza for you."

She did as he said then started coughing and spluttering as the sweet, pungent smoke filled her lungs.

"More, girlie, go on, you gotta do it if you wanna see Bazza."

She drew on the cigarette again. It was easier the second time, she didn't cough so much.

And so it continued; every time she stopped, Gun would urge her to keep going and threaten not to let her see Bazza if she didn't carry on. After a while, she began to feel strange. The room was starting to spin, like the time she'd had half a can of cider at a school party, only much worse. She started to sway and reached out to steady herself. Accidentally, she put her hand on Gun's thigh.

He gave a low chuckle, "That's it girlie, you're warming up. You wanna give me that blow job now?"

"No, ob cord nod," she was having difficulty speaking, starting to see double; "cab I see Bazz-z-zer now?"

"Alright girlie, reckon you've proved you're serious. You can go in now."

She staggered to the door behind the desk. Opening it, she saw Dave with two peroxide blondes perched in his lap, Toad lying on the couch with a curvaceous black girl. There was no sign of Bazza.

Gun appeared behind her, laughing to himself, "Yeah, forgot to tell ya, little woggie, Bazza went back to the hotel. Hope you enjoyed the joint though. It's good stuff. Jamaican, I think."

"Join? Wha' d'ya mean, joi? I thot waz-z jus' a cigrette?"

He was laughing too much to answer. Dave looked up and responded for him, "He's given you some dope, doll. You know: marijuana. It's one of his favourite tricks. He gets girls to smoke dope just for a laugh, or maybe so they'll give him a blow." Turning to Gun, he added, "You're disgusting, Kevin, you know that?"

Her head was spinning ever faster. She had to reach out to the wall to prop herself up. She realised she'd been tricked into smoking an illegal drug. She felt angry, disgusted, and humiliated. Everyone was staring at her. They must all be thinking what an idiot she was. She had to get out of there, but she could hardly stand, never mind walk.

Gun's hand was on her breast. He started to pull up her dress, "Come on, you little wog bitch, I've given you a ride, now you can give me one."

His groping hands scared her enough to send the adrenaline pumping into her bloodstream. It gave her back some strength and she pushed him away, almost falling over as she did. She took a moment to steady herself then straightened up and marched out of the room and down the corridor.

*

The next morning, Sammie woke with a thumping headache, feeling sick. She couldn't remember much about the rest of the night after leaving the town hall; she had no idea how she'd got home. She spent most of the day throwing up. Her parents put it down to alcohol. Her mother tried to convince her father she was suffering enough and would learn her lesson without the need for him to take his belt off to her. It did no good, he gave her one of the worst beatings she'd ever had. Afterwards, he cut up her new black dress and threw it into the dustbin, "I'm not having any daughter of mine parading around like a common street walker." He grounded her for three months and confiscated her house keys.

On Monday, she begged her mother to let her stay off school. She feigned flu but, in reality, she was still suffering the after effects of the dope, combined with a colossal dose of humiliation. She took Tuesday off too. That afternoon, she was alone in the house when the phone began to ring.

"3-6-2-1," she answered as her father had taught her.

"Sammie, is that you?"

"Oh God, yes, yes, it's me, it's Sammie. Is that you, Bazza?"

"Oh my God, Sammie, I've been trying to reach you for months. I've never been able to get past your parents. Your mum's kind of OK, but your dad, he's…"

"I know… I know what they're like. I tried to reach you too, I came to the town hall on Saturday… but I, er… I…"

"Listen Sammie, I've only got a minute, we've gotta get the train. We're going to London. We're gonna be on Pop Toppers, we're recording it tomorrow night. Dickie Savage is the DJ; it's gonna be brilliant. I've managed to get you a couple of tickets; I've left them at the town hall. Just tell them you're the Sammie who came to the gig in school uniform and they'll give them to you. Please come, Sammie, I want to see you so much. I *need* to see you."

"Yes, yes, I'll come, but how do I get to you? Last time, it was… er, it was…"

"Don't worry Sammie, I'll tell everyone to let you in. You won't have any problems. Listen, I'm sorry, but I have to dash. I'll see you in London. I'm so happy I'm gonna see you again. Bye now."

As he hung up, she began working out how she was going to get to the Pop Toppers studio. She put the phone back in its cradle, picked it up again, and dialled her brother's number. He wasn't sure if going to Pop Toppers would do his street cred much good, but he agreed to drive her there. They figured the only way to get there in time was for him to pick her up from school. She couldn't risk trying to smuggle out a change of clothes so, once again, she'd be turning up in school uniform.

Her father would kill her, of course. She could almost hear him shouting, 'Keep away from those white punks,' and feel his belt across her buttocks. He would beat her soundly for this, for sure. But it would be worth it to see Bazza. God, she'd only met him for a few minutes, but she felt like they'd been together for… well, forever really.

*

Tulwar was at the school gates as Sammie ran out to meet him. She jumped into the passenger seat of his battered old VW van and leaned over to kiss him on the cheek, "Thank you, Tullie, you're the best brother ever." He grinned back at her as he handed over the tickets he'd picked up that morning then they set off into the afternoon traffic. "How long do you think it'll take to get there?" she asked anxiously.

"Should be about two and a half hours if all goes well; maybe three. I'll do my best, sis."

The tickets gave them access to the studio from six o'clock, with recording due to start at seven. They should just make it according to Tullie's estimate. She'd always looked up to her brother; she knew she could trust him. In many ways, he was a better parent than her overbearing father and browbeaten mother. They chatted easily as they sped down the motorway. She took the opportunity to confide in him, "Mrs Dobson says I should get at least six A grades in my 'O' levels. She thinks I should stay on to do 'A' levels and I have a good chance of getting into medical school."

"That's great, Sammie. I know you can do it. You were always the smart one in the family. A lot smarter than Dad, that's for sure," he laughed.

"I don't know, Tullie, Dad says women who think they can be doctors or lawyers are getting above themselves. He says they're letting their families down, 'cause they're not at home looking after their husband and children. He thinks I should train as a nurse or a secretary, and there's no point me going to university 'cause I'll be married soon anyway."

"Yeah, but what do you think, Sammie? What do you want to do?"

"I'm not sure, it's so confusing. I want to be loyal to the family like Dad says, but I want to be a doctor too. I really do. I want to care for people and look after them. Not just my husband and children, lots of people, everywhere, whoever needs help. It's what I've always wanted to do."

He laughed, "I know, I remember how you used to borrow my toys to be your patients. Well, you should do it for real, sis, you'll make a fantastic doctor. Fuck what Dad says, it's your life."

They reached the end of the motorway and made their way to the remote suburb that was the unlikely location for the world-famous Pop Toppers studio. They arrived at 6.21 p.m. and Sammie rushed inside to find Bazza, leaving Tullie to park the van.

After several minutes of frantic searching though seemingly endless backstage corridors Sammie ran into a familiar figure. It was Dickie Savage, "Hello, hello, can I help you there little lady?"

"Oh, er… hello, Mr Savage, I'm a friend of Bazza's… you know, from The Vomix? He invited me down to see him. I was looking for his dressing room."

"Now then, now then," the DJ responded in his familiar northern accent, "as it happens, you're in luck. You've found just the right guy to help you out, you see. Come with me young lady and I shall take you to your friend." He put his arm around her shoulders and led her down the corridor.

As they turned into another corridor and headed towards the back of the building, his arm slid off her shoulder and began to move down her back. By the time they reached a plain grey door at the end, his hand was resting on her bottom. The intimacy of his touch made her uncomfortable, but he was such a massive star, she felt she couldn't object.

He opened the door and gave her bum a pinch, then pushed her gently forwards, "In here, little lady." She was

382

slightly taken aback by his familiarity, but she assumed this was how stars treated everyone. Trusting him, she stepped through the door. He quickly followed, closed the door behind them, and turned the lock.

She found herself in an empty room, "Where's Bazza?"

"Oh, he'll be along in a minute, don't worry. This is where the bands come to relax before they go on stage. They can get some peace and quiet in here, you see? That's why it's a bit hidden away. You're a pretty young lady. You look like you're still at school?"

"I am, Mr Savage, I'm sitting my 'O' Levels this year. I didn't have time to change before we came down to London." She looked around. A battered old sofa ran along one side of the room. A huge mirror took up most of the wall opposite. There was an ancient radiator with iron pipes connecting it to the antiquated heating system. It was stuffy and smelly, there were no windows and the floor was bare concrete. It didn't look like the sort of place big stars would hang out. She felt uneasy.

"Are you sure this is the right place, Mr Savage? It seems a bit bare."

"Ah well yes, everyone thinks that at first, but you'll see, it's a different place once the bands get here." He sat on the sofa and patted the cushion next to him, "Why don't you come and sit here? Would you like an autograph? I'll find my pen," he started searching through his pockets.

She had to sit close to him, as he was sprawled across the middle of the sofa. She felt nervous, so she perched on the front of the cushion, her knees pressed together. He seemed to be having trouble finding his pen; he was making an enormous fuss of fiddling around in his jacket, "Ah, there it is. Damn, I've dropped it. Could you reach it, my dear, it's just behind you."

As she scrabbled for the pen to her left, the side nearest him, he turned towards her and closed his hand over hers, "No, dear, it's rolled over to the other side, I can't reach it I'm afraid."

She turned to her right to look for the pen. Such a stupid fuss, she didn't even want his autograph, she just wanted to see Bazza. She hoped he'd be here soon.

"That's it, my dear; you've almost got it, just reach back a little further."

She stretched her arm, groping for the pen. She felt something metallic on her wrist. There was a click and her hand was being pulled behind her. He tightened his grip on her other hand and pulled it towards the first. There was another click. To her astonishment, she realised she was in handcuffs. What was he doing? Before she could protest, he pushed her hard in the back, propelling her forwards. She skinned her knees as they connected with the rough concrete floor, and cried out in pain. Swiftly, he knelt behind her, put his hand on her shoulder and held her down, kneeling on the floor, as he pushed up her skirt and tore off her knickers.

"No, no, what are you doing… no… NO-O-O… Oh, God, please, NO-O-O-O-O!"

"There's no point shouting for help, little lady," he

hissed in her ear; "this used to be a recording studio. It's soundproof."

He ripped her blouse open, pulled down her bra and began roughly groping at her breast. His hand felt coarse on her tender skin. He licked the side of her neck then sucked it hard, giving her a so-called 'love bite'.

"Please, no, you're hurting me. Please stop, please."

He let go of her breast and reached behind her.

"No, oh God, please, no… please… please don't. Please no, I've never…"

She gasped at the sudden shock as she felt herself being torn open. The abrupt, violent intrusion hurt so much, she was afraid she might die. Savage held her in a vice-like grip as he drove himself into her, grunting in time with his steady rhythm. Too traumatised to speak, too stunned to scream, she found herself moaning along with him.

In the mirror opposite, she could see herself pinned to the ground by a deranged monster in the form of a man, her exposed breast bouncing up and down with each thrust of his hips. She saw the crazed, vacant, look in his eyes and the fixed grimace of his mouth. It was too awful to watch. She closed her eyes.

She tried to isolate the pain in a part of her mind where it couldn't reach her. But it wasn't just physical, like her grazed knees, he was inside her. The sheer horror of being invaded and used was so intense, so harrowing; she felt her humanity was being stripped from her, like she was nothing but an object for this abominable creature to do with as he pleased, unworthy of love or compassion.

At least it was quick. After less than a minute, Savage gave a final grunt as he spent himself within her. He released his grip, stood up, and adjusted his clothing. She knelt on the floor, panting hard as she tried to cope with the pain and shock, too dazed to move.

Before she'd had chance to recover, he grabbed her by the back of the neck and forced her to crawl across the floor on knees already sore and bleeding from falling onto the concrete. When she was close enough, he unfastened the cuff on her right wrist, hooked it around the pipe at the base of the old radiator, and locked it again.

He walked to the door then turned back, "Now don't go anywhere, little lady. I'll be back for seconds. I might try the rear entrance next time. How's about that then?" he winked then walked out, closing the door firmly behind him. Ten minutes later, he was recording his part for national television.

XXVII

BACKSTAGE

Sammie knelt on the floor, shaking and sobbing. She couldn't believe what had happened. The ache in her groin was bad, but the emotional trauma of the terrible violation was worse. She felt like a filthy, dirty animal, beaten and left to die, as worthless as her father had always said.

It was several minutes before her shaking began to subside and she started to get a grip on herself. She wanted to curl up in a ball and sob herself to sleep, like she always did after one of her father's beatings. But Savage would be back for seconds. He was going to do it again, and he was going to try the 'rear entrance'. Could that really mean what she thought?

The fear of the monster returning to rape her again gave her some strength. She took stock of her situation. She was trapped in a soundproof room, handcuffed to a solid iron pipe, unable to rise beyond a kneeling position.

With disgust, she realised there was a revolting mixture of semen and blood running down her thighs.

Was the room genuinely soundproof? He'd lied about everything else, why should she believe him? "Help, help… please help me," she shouted as loud as she could; then listened for sounds outside. Nothing: she'd have to assume the room actually was soundproof.

If she couldn't get help, her only other option was escape. She looked at the metal cuff around her wrist. It was pretty tight, but she might be able to get out of it. As a little girl, she'd had an accident riding her bicycle. Well, it was Tullie's bike in truth; her father had refused to buy her one, so Tullie had given her his old one. The problem was it was too big for her. She'd lost her balance, tipped over the handlebars and hit the ground hard. Her father confiscated the bike and beat her with his belt. When she told him her hand hurt, he'd said it was her own bloody fault and she should stop whining before he beat her again. Then he sent her to bed without any supper. The next day, her hand was the size of a balloon and a trip to hospital confirmed she'd dislocated her thumb. She was off school for days, but eventually recovered, except for one tiny thing. It was her little party trick. She could dislocate her thumb any time she wanted. She'd done it to amuse her friends for years; now she had a practical use for it.

She moved her thumb sideways and pushed it against the side of the radiator. She heard the familiar 'pop' as it came out of its socket and winced at the sharp pain. She pulled on the cuff but, even with her dislocated thumb, her hand was stuck fast. She pulled harder, but it hurt too much. She needed some sort of lubricant to ease her hand out of the cuff. Glancing down she saw the disgusting mixture dripping down her thighs. Reluctantly, she scooped some up and smeared it on her wrist, then pulled again. Finally, her hand came free.

Slowly, she got unsteadily to her feet. She took a few deep breaths then pushed her thumb back into place. It would be sore for a couple of days but that was the least of her worries. She had to get out of there before the monstrous DJ returned. She pulled her clothes back into place as best she could then stepped out of the room and began to make her way towards the front of the building.

It seemed to take an age to reach the main corridor. She was terrified she might run into Savage any moment. When she got there at last, she fell to her knees and began to sob. With the immediate danger of a second attack over, she was filled with a swirling cocktail of revulsion and shame. How could she face anyone after what had happened? She was dirty and disgusting, no better than a common street walker, like her father said. It was all her fault for getting involved with punk rockers.

But Bazza was different. His music was beautiful. And it sang to her. She needed to find him, she needed to be with him; he would help her. But would he still want her? Oh God, she hoped so. She hoped he could forgive her. She staggered back to her feet, the tears still flooding down her cheeks, and collided with the man rushing towards the stage.

"Ooh, careful da-a-a-a-arling," he grabbed onto her to save her from falling and smiled warmly into her face, displaying an enormous set of projecting teeth. If she hadn't just been viciously raped, she'd have been thrilled to realise she was in the arms of one of the biggest rock stars in the world.

"But da-a-a-a-rling why the tears; what's the matter?"

"Er, we're really late, sir," one of the minders following the star tugged on his sleeve.

The star rounded on him, "Can't you see this poor girl's upset?"

"You were due on stage two minutes ago sir…"

"Oh shut up, beefcake. This girl's in trouble.

"Now, da-a-arling, tell me what's wrong," he turned back to Sammie, still holding her upright.

"It… it… was… it was that DJ. He… he…" she put her hands over her face. She couldn't bring herself to say the words.

The star cradled her to him, softly patting her on the back, "There, there, darling, you're safe now." He gently lifted her chin, "Tell me what he did and I'll see that…"

He was interrupted by his other minder returning with a security guard, "Look, sir, we really have to go, you're almost five minutes overdue. They'll scrap your slot and give it to someone else. Security can deal with this now," he indicated the guard.

"Oh alright, Stephanie!" the star snapped. He turned back to Sammie, "You'll be OK now, darling; this man will look after you." Releasing her, he looked at the guard;

"See that you take good care of her, you hear?"

The first minder was tugging at his sleeve again. "Alright, alright, I'm going," he rushed down the corridor, his entourage in tow. "Don't stop me now," he shouted over his shoulder, laughing as he went.

"Now, what's the trouble miss?" the guard asked.

Sammie sniffed back her tears and tried to answer, but still couldn't bear to say the words. Every time she tried to speak, she broke down again. She wanted to see Bazza. She was sure he would forgive her. He would look after her, make the pain go away. She just needed to get to Bazza and everything would be alright. Finally, she managed to gather her wits enough to speak coherently, "I have to see Bazza… you know, Bazza from The Vomix?"

"Is he expecting you, miss?"

"Yes, yes, he is, yes… can you take me to him? Please? I've got to see him… please?"

"Of course, miss, just follow me," the guard led her along the main corridor, behind the performance area, then down another side corridor. She staggered after him, trying to stifle her sobs. Evidently misunderstanding the cause of her distress, he remarked, "These corridors can be confusing, miss, lots of people get lost. No need to get so worked up though. Here we are."

They arrived at a door and the guard knocked politely. As they waited, he looked at her torn blouse and bloody knees, "Took a bit of a tumble, did we miss?"

She opened her mouth to reply but was interrupted by a voice behind the door, "Yeah, who is it?"

"I have a young lady to see Mr Bazza."

"What's her name? Does he know her?"

"It's Sammie! Sammie from the town hall, the girl in school uniform, he asked me to come," she shouted.

The door opened. "Sammie, hi," it was Bazza's friend, Dave; "come in, Bazza was hoping you'd come." He ushered her into the room. "Thank you, my friend," he pressed a pound note into the guard's hand and closed the door.

As Dave turned around, she could see the shock on his face, "My God, you look a mess, what happened to you?"

She threw herself onto a sofa and put her head in her hands. She tried to speak between the painful sobs racking her body, "It was that... that... that horrible m-m-man, that m-m-monster, that... that... S-Savage... he did s-s-some, er... something t-t-to me, he... he... he..."

"It's OK, you're here now, no-one's gonna hurt you," Dave sat next to her and put his arm around her shoulders. She stiffened as he touched her but, after a moment, she relaxed and let him pull her close, finding comfort in his embrace.

"Wh... wh-whu-ere... where's Bazza?"

"He's with Grey and the new boss of the record company. They're sorting out some legal stuff on our contract. I should be with them; I just popped out to go for a pi... er, to use the bathroom. Lucky really, that's how I heard you knocking. I'll go and tell him you're here anyway," Dave got to his feet and headed for the room's back door; "you just wait there, he'll be out in a minute."

"Thank you," she sniffed.

Dave disappeared through the back door and she was alone. Still shaking from the trauma of her ordeal, she hugged herself and rocked gently back and forth, sobbing silently, tears rolling down her cheeks. So many thoughts whirled around her head. She didn't know what to do. She ought to go to the police, but she couldn't face the disgrace alone. She needed Bazza. Oh God, please let him forgive her, please let him understand she only wanted him. She was so close now; he would come through the door any second. He would know what to do, he would look after her; they could go to the police together. He would come soon and it would all be OK.

The minutes ticked by. After what seemed an eternity, the room's back door opened. Her heart leaped into her mouth. She was going to see Bazza again. But it wasn't Bazza.

A tall, thin man with long dark hair walked through the door, followed, to Sammie's dismay, by Gun. He looked different. Gone were the leather jacket and torn jeans. In their place, he wore a suit and tie, although he didn't look comfortable in them. He followed behind the tall man like a well-trained dog.

The tall man spotted her on the sofa, "Hello Sally."

"It's er... er... I'm Samaira... er, sir."

"Oh yes, of course, my mistake. You remind me of someone I used to know. You look rather distraught, Samaira; perhaps there is something we can do for you?"

"Well, sir, I, er..." she began, but the tall man cut her off as he spoke to Gun.

"Worthington, I think the young lady is in need of a pick-me-up, wouldn't you say?" Gun nodded then went to a desk on the other side of the room. He opened a drawer and pulled out a syringe filled with pale yellow liquid.

The tall man turned back to Sammie, "You've had a frightful shock. You need something to calm your nerves. I have just the thing, a highly effective medicine. You'd like something to make you feel better, wouldn't you, Samaira?"

She nodded silently. The tall man was incredibly persuasive, almost mesmerising.

"When is Bazza coming?" she asked.

"Oh, he'll be about half an hour, I expect. They're recording their piece for the show. They'll probably do a few takes. He will be so pleased to see you. You'll want to look your best for him, won't you? Let us help," he reached out towards Gun, who placed the syringe in his open palm.

"Are you a doctor?" she wasn't sure about letting a strange man give her an injection.

"Oh, much better than that, my dear, I'm a professor of chemistry. I have many decades of experience. This is just the thing you need to help you get over your unfortunate little encounter."

"I'm not sure; shouldn't I go to hospital for that, or the doctor's? I think I should go to the police as well…"

"Oh, my dear, there's no point bothering the police. Everyone knows what Savage likes to do to young girls, but no-one would ever *do* anything about it. You must understand; he's a famous, much-loved entertainer. The police are not going to pay you any attention. Spare yourself a good deal of unnecessary trouble and just forget it ever happened. Let me help you," he was preparing the syringe, squeezing the plunger to squirt a few drops into the air.

She was confused. Surely she should report Savage to the police? But the tall man was telling her not to bother. He obviously thought it was her fault; that she had brought it on herself, same as her father would if he found out. Oh God, if she went to the police, her father *would* find out. He'd be so angry. 'Dirty, second-hand goods,' he would call her. 'No decent man in his right mind will look at you,' he would say. It was like *she* was the one causing trouble. What should she do?

The tall man seemed to sense she was wavering, "You're a sensible girl, Samaira, you're quite right not to let a stranger give you an injection without seeing any credentials. Here, let me show you some identification," he pulled out a fancy-looking I.D. Card and handed it to her:

Professor Lord Mortimer
Head of Neurological Research
Royal Institute of Neurology

"You see, Samaira? I know what I'm doing," he took the card back and held up the syringe; "just take this and you'll soon feel better. The pain will go away, you'll forget all about Savage, and you'll be ready to see Bazza."

Still she hesitated. He continued, "What do you think he'd rather see: a sobbing, traumatised girl; or a happy, strong, confident girl. He'll be tired and anxious, keen to relax with you. Take this and you'll be helping him. He'll need you to be strong. You want to be strong for him, don't you, Samaira?"

He moved the syringe closer to her arm, the needle poised above her elbow. She looked down at the stunning gemstone set into the ring on his middle finger. He must be very important to have a ring like that. Perhaps she should trust him.

"Go on, Samaira, for Bazza," he urged.

Her groin ached like she'd been beaten, her knees and thumb were sore. She was in so much pain; she wanted it to go away. She just wanted to see Bazza and forget about Savage, forget her terrible shame. She closed her eyes and nodded.

"There's a good girl," Mortimer pressed the needle to her skin and pushed it into her vein. He squeezed the plunger and the medicine flowed into her bloodstream. A euphoric high washed over her. The trauma and tension dropped away. She was floating carefree, no longer bothered about her dreadful ordeal. She was vaguely aware of Mortimer and Gun leaving the room, but nothing mattered any more. This was a level of ecstasy she'd never known. She felt calm and serene, strong and impervious to pain. Time rolled by, but she was barely conscious of it. Eventually, she passed out.

Bazza returned directly to the dressing room, avoiding the back corridors open to the public. Dave had only just told him Sammie was here; the record company boss had kept them talking until they'd had to rush off to do their bit on stage, he hadn't had chance before now. Finding Gun alone, Bazza asked where Sammie was.

"Oh yeah, man, she's here alright, in the other room. But she's out of it. Totally bombed, she is."

Bazza went to see for himself. He was shocked to see Sammie slumped unconscious on the sofa, drooling on her blouse, "What's happened to her?"

"Dunno man, she's taken something by the look of it."

"But that's not like her, not like her at all, it doesn't make sense." Bazza looked closer, "What happened to her knees? Why's her blouse torn?"

"Think she fell down," Gun shrugged.

At that moment, Grey bounced in, full of enthusiasm, "Great performance, Bazza, well done. I think you'll go down a storm when it goes out tomorrow. Bound to take us further up the charts; could be top three next week." Then he spotted the unconscious girl, "Fuck, what's this? This is not good, not good at all. We need her out of here, pronto. This sort of thing can stop a band's career in its tracks. They're always a problem, these fucking junkie groupies."

"Hey man, she's not a junkie, this isn't like her," Bazza retorted.

"Alright, fine, so she's not a junkie. But we still need to get her out of here. Do you know if she came with anyone?"

"She said something about a brother, I think," said Gun.

"See if you can find him, will you?" Grey asked; "I've got to check something with the producers."

The A&R man departed, leaving Bazza alone with Sammie. He sat beside her and cradled her gently in his arms, "Come on, Sammie; wake up." She stirred for a moment and mumbled something. He wasn't sure, but it sounded like 'I love you'.

Grey returned a few minutes later, followed by Gun and a young Asian man, obviously Sammie's brother. "Oh man," the brother exclaimed, "what's happened to her? Is she gonna be alright?"

"Right you the brother then? You'd better take her home, lad, she's in a bit of a mess," Grey instructed. He turned to Bazza, "And you, you fucking genius, need to be on a bus to Glasgow in less than two hours, you start the Scottish leg of the tour tomorrow, you'd better get moving sharpish."

"Hang on," responded Bazza, "shouldn't we get her to hospital, she looks pretty sick?"

"No, too many questions, she'll be fine, she just needs to sleep it off, whatever it is."

"I don't care about questions, she's fucking sick; she needs to go to hospital."

"Look, she's probably taken some sort of drugs. There's loads of 'em about 'round here. There are guys pushing them to kids like her all the time. If she goes to hospital, she could get into a shitload of trouble and, what's more, when the press find out, it'll bounce back to you. You don't want that, especially not now, when everything's going so well. Let her brother take her home. He can keep an eye on her, make sure she's OK, can't you lad?"

"Er yeah, I s'pose so," answered the young Asian; "I don't want her to get in any trouble. It'll be bad enough when Dad sees her. I guess it'll be OK; if you're sure she's gonna be alright?"

"Yeah, sure she will, don't you worry. Now you just get her home quick as you can before anyone sees her. The police can be tough on kids like her, especially black kids; they don't need much of an excuse to push for a conviction."

Bazza watched Grey. He wasn't sure how sincere the A&R man was about Sammie's wellbeing, but it wouldn't be good for her to get a drugs conviction. He didn't want to be responsible for landing her with a criminal record. He supposed she should be OK if her brother watched her carefully. Reluctantly, he decided to go along with Grey's plan. He turned to the young man, "Well, I guess you could take her home, er…"

"Tulwar, my name's Tulwar; my friends call me Tullie. And, don't worry; I'll take good care of her. She's my little sis, I've always watched out for her. I just wish I hadn't lost her when she ran into the studio," he frowned.

Bazza could see Tullie was as concerned as he was. It helped; he knew he could trust him to look after Sammie,

"Hey man, whatever happened, it wasn't your fault. More like mine to be honest, I was the one begged her to come. C'mon, I'll help you carry her."

Grey scowled, opening his mouth to speak. "Cool it man, you've got your way," Bazza snapped, "least I can do is make sure she gets away safely. I'll be back for the bloody bus."

Bazza and Tullie carried Sammie between them, her arms draped over their shoulders. "Me van's out back, on the street," Tullie said. He laughed nervously, "Wouldn't mind goin' to Scotland meself. Get away from the bloody crap I'm gonna get off Dad for this. Still, it's worse for Sammie, she has to live with him. Least I've got me own place."

Tullie opened the back of the van. They laid Sammie on a rug and covered her with an old blanket. Bazza kissed her on the cheek, "Take care, Sammie, I love you too." Stepping back outside, he passed a flyer to Tullie, "These are our tour dates. Tell her I'll call every afternoon at four but, if I can't get her, she can try me at one of these venues. We usually get to the gig about six. That's the best time for her to call. Get her home safely, eh?"

"Yeah man, of course. I'll take care of her, you can count on it." They shook hands then Tullie hopped into the driver's seat, fired up the noisy engine, and set off.

*

Sammie woke. She felt disoriented at first but, when she glanced around and saw the back of Tullie's head, she realised where she was. For a moment, she thought everything that had happened must have been a hideous nightmare, but the ache in her groin, her sore knees and thumb, and the tear in her blouse, all confirmed it was real. She shuddered, feeling the unbearable shame weighing down on her. She couldn't face it. Not yet anyway.

"Tullie?" she called out.

"Hey sis, you're awake. You had us really worried. How are you fee…"

"Tullie, I don't want to go back to Mum and Dad's tonight. Can I stay with you, please?"

"Sure sis, if that's what you want."

"Thank you, Tullie, you're the best brother ever," she smiled for the first time since they'd arrived in London then closed her eyes and let the sound of the engine lull her back to sleep.

XXVIII

GUNSHOTS

Susan woke with the memory of being Sammie fresh in her mind. That was just a few decades ago, she would have expected to be much the same. But she'd been so different, so gullible. She'd been young, of course, but even so, it was surprising. Time and again, she'd wanted to scream at herself, 'No, stop, how can you be so naive?'

But, deep down, she *had* been the same. She had the same desire to care for people, the same ambition to be a doctor. She'd had the strength to defy her father and go to London. That was her alright; the same determination was there when it mattered. It just went to show what a difference her upbringing had made. She was the same person but, whereas in this life her father had supported her all the way, Sammie's father had terrorised her, drummed into her for years that she was worthless, second class, just because she was a girl. No wonder she'd reacted to the rape with a sense of shame, instead of the outrage and anger she should have felt. She was the victim and yet, thanks to her father's conditioning, she'd felt she was to blame.

Life as Sammie had been cruel and unfair. Sighing to herself, she wondered if Sammie's father was still alive, she'd love to give him a piece of her mind. But that would have to wait; she needed to get out of this basement first. And time was running out.

She was slowly learning how to navigate her past, although she hadn't mastered it yet by any means. She'd been trying to spend more time as Serwaah. She'd already learned something about Mortimer's motives, and she figured life as a slave might give her some ideas on how to escape from captivity. But she'd been pulled into Sammie's life instead. She felt strongly that Ben had been sharing the same vision. It had ended with her sleeping in the back of her brother's van, and she knew, with an inexplicable certainty, Ben was in a similar position now. He was close, and he was travelling towards her, she was sure of it.

Exciting as that was it meant both of them were in danger. How long did she have before Mortimer returned? Twenty-four hours, he'd said, but how much time had passed since then? There was no way of telling in the windowless basement. He could appear any minute, or it could be hours. The question was; how could she prepare for his return, or Ben's arrival, or both?

Her thumb! Her dislocated thumb! She'd used it to get out of Savage's handcuffs. My God, what an incredible coincidence: she'd dislocated her thumb when she was a little girl too. Or dislocated it *again* she should say.

Her father had taken her ice skating and she'd had an awkward fall. It hurt a lot, but she wanted to carry on; she was having so much fun and she had her father to herself for a change. When her hand started to swell though, he insisted on taking her to casualty. She was sent for an X-ray and the doctor told her she'd dislocated her thumb. Despite the pain, she was absolutely fascinated with everything at the hospital. A consultant came to see her, gave her a local anaesthetic, and manipulated her thumb back into place. She insisted on watching the whole thing and wore him out with her questions. As she was only eleven, he kept his answers simple at first, but clearly soon realised she was a bright girl with an aptitude for medicine. He gave her a copy of her X-ray to take home. Totally enthralled by the subject, she researched what had happened and learned her first metacarpal had detached from her trapezium. In layman's terms, her thumb had come loose from her wrist.

Unlike when she was Sammie, she'd never turned her injury into a party trick. Later, she found out she suffered from hypoplasia in the joint at the base of her thumb; in other words, the bones were underdeveloped. The joint had been further weakened by her accident and there was a strong risk of dislocating it again. She was warned that repeated disruption to the joint could lead to complications in later life, with a greatly increased chance of osteoarthritis. So she'd been careful, she'd taught herself to make fists if she fell, rather than putting out an open hand, as most people usually do: the cause of many dislocated joints. And she'd been successful; since her childhood accident, her thumb had remained firmly attached to her wrist.

Was it really coincidence? Had she suffered from hypoplasia as Sammie too? Did she always suffer from it, in every life? Or was there a greater force at play: destiny, fate, whatever... something that wanted her to escape Mortimer's clutches? She could see so much now, all her past laid out before her, but there was still so much to learn.

Whether some unseen force was helping or not, she needed to start working on her escape. As for the risk of osteoarthritis... if she didn't get out of here soon, there wouldn't be any later life anyway. She might as well give it a go.

She began by moving her thumb the way she remembered doing as Sammie. She pulled her hand down hard, squeezing her thumb against the metal cuff on her wrist. She could feel her joint straining; there was a surge of pain. She pulled harder, as hard as she could. The pain grew stronger, but the joint held.

Next, she tried bending her knees and letting her legs go limp. The chain on the band around her waist was slack enough for her to drop until she was putting all her weight on her wrist. It was agony, but her thumb didn't budge.

One last try, she thought. She grasped the chains on her manacles and pulled herself as high as she could, lifting her legs off the floor, holding herself up by her arms. Taking all the weight on her right arm, she wrapped the chain on the left-hand manacle around her wrist. She moved her thumb back into position and pulled her hand down as far as possible. She stayed like that a moment, holding herself up with one hand; then took a couple of deep breaths and let go. Her entire body weight came down on her left hand. She blacked out.

*

Sammie was woken by a loud banging at the front door. Sitting up, she could vaguely remember reaching Tullie's tiny ground floor flat just after midnight. She'd managed to stumble out of the van, into the living room, and collapse onto the sofa. She must have gone straight back to sleep after that, she couldn't remember anything else: but she could see Tullie had taken off her shoes and covered her with a blanket.

The banging continued. Tullie staggered out of his bedroom wearing his dressing gown and walked to the front door. She got up, pulling the blanket tightly around her shoulders, and followed him. Peering out from behind her brother as he opened the door, she saw their father standing outside with a policeman. "I've come for Samaira," he said. Then, spotting Sammie behind Tullie, he reached out to grab her arm, "You're coming with me, young lady."

She stepped back, out of her father's reach, her eyes wide with fear, "No, Dad, I don't want to come with you,

I want to stay here a while." She looked up at her brother, "Can I, Tullie, please?"

"Sure, sis, stay as long as you want. Don't blame you. I wouldn't go back there for anything," Tullie stared down their red-faced father.

"Oh, this is ridiculous," the older man exclaimed. He turned to the policeman, "Do something, she's my daughter."

"How old are you, miss?" the officer asked Sammie.

"I'm sixteen, sir."

"Are you here of your own volition?"

"Yes, sir, I want to stay with my brother."

"I'm afraid, sir," said the officer, turning to her father, "the young lady is perfectly entitled to refuse to come with you. Furthermore, I must warn you, if you try to remove her forcibly, I shall have no choice but to charge you with assault."

"Baaaaah," her father threw his hands up in the air. He scowled at her, "Fine, you stay here. You can stay here forever if that's how you feel. After everything I've done for you, this is how you repay me. Stopping out all night, behaving like a common street walker, getting up to goodness knows what. Well, that's it; you are no longer my daughter, I disown you. Don't bother coming back… ever."

"But, Dad, I was ruh… ruh…" she began, but he cut her off, refusing to listen to her now, just as he always had.

"Tulwar," he turned to his son, "you can come around to the house at the weekend. Your mother will have

Samaira's things ready for you to collect." With that, he walked away.

Sammie ran back into the cramped little living room, threw herself onto the sofa, and buried her face in a cushion to hide her tears. Tullie said goodbye to the policeman, closed the front door, and came over to kneel beside her, "Don't worry about Dad, he's a dickhead. I phoned him last night, told him you were safe and I'd bring you back today, but he started ranting on about you letting the family down, all the usual crap. I hung up in the end. Anyway, I'll talk to Mum at the weekend; it'll be alright, sis."

"Don't care," she mumbled, "I'm staying here."

He laughed, "OK, sis, you stay as long as you want. I gotta get ready for college now, you gonna be alright?"

For a moment, she thought about telling him everything: the rape, the medicine, all of it. But the disgrace was too much. She knew how proud of her he was. She didn't want to hurt him by shattering his illusions.

"I'll be fine; I just need to get some rest, lots of rest," she lifted her head and tried to smile reassuringly, hoping it would stop him asking too many questions, "thanks, Tullie."

"OK, sis, I'll leave you in peace then," he smiled back.

Tullie busied himself getting ready. By the time he was leaving the flat, Sammie had sobbed herself to sleep. He smiled down at her. She'd be alright after a good rest. She always bounced back after a beating from Dad; at least this one was only verbal. He pulled the flyer Bazza had given him out of his jacket pocket and placed it on the coffee table where she'd see it when she woke, then quietly let himself out.

*

It was early afternoon when Sammie woke again to find herself alone, still wearing the torn clothes from last night. They would have to do until Tullie fetched the rest of her things. Her head was in a whirl as she thought about everything that had happened: the rape, her father disowning her, the extraordinary feelings the medicine had given her. She looked at her arm and saw the pinprick to remind her of the experience. It would be lovely to have some more. It had made her feel wonderful. She'd forgotten her shame, felt whole again for a while. Thinking about the medicine, she began to crave it, like the way she sometimes craved chocolate, only a hundred times more.

Her thoughts turned to Bazza. She had a strange notion he'd been speaking to her; or had she dreamt it? She desperately wanted to see him again; she couldn't believe she'd missed her chance because of Savage. Oh God, she would have to explain that to Bazza. He was bound to be angry; he would be so ashamed of her. Please, please, let him forgive her, she loved him so much, she hadn't meant to hurt him. It was going to be tough facing him after what she'd done, where would she find the strength?

There was a knock at the door. This time it was gentler, less demanding. She wasn't sure if she should answer. Was it safe? Had her father come back for her? It could just be her brother forgetting his keys. It could be Bazza.

She rushed to the window and pulled back the curtain. Her heart sank with disappointment. It was Gun. She was wary of him after his behaviour at the town hall. On the other hand, he *had* helped Mortimer give her the medicine. She put the chain on the door and opened it an inch so she could speak through the gap, "What are you doing here?"

"Hi Sammie, Lord Mortimer asked me to pop by 'n see if you're OK?"

"Er, yeah, I'm alright, I guess. How did you know I was here, this is my brother's place?"

"His lordship's real worried about you. Asked me to check on you he did. Can I come in?"

She was still suspicious, "No, I don't think that's a good idea. But you can tell Lord Mortimer I'm fine, thank you."

"He said you might need more medicine," Gun produced a syringe from his jacket.

She stared at the syringe like a starving dog staring at a piece of meat. Her knees hurt, her groin was sore, her thumb ached. She needed the medicine, she needed to feel whole again, she needed to find the strength to face Bazza and tell him the truth. She took off the chain and opened the door.

Gun walked in and sat on the sofa. He patted the cushion next to him, "Come 'n sit next to me 'n I'll give you your medicine."

She was cautious; this was too much like Savage.

"No, I'll sit here I think," she sat on a hard-backed chair on the other side of the room; "but you can give me the medicine." She held her arm out.

"OK, Sammie, no problem. If that's what you want," he stood up again and moved to stand beside her; "I don't blame you not trustin' me. I was a bit of a prick at the town hall. Look, I'm sorry 'bout that. Lord Mortimer's taught me a few things since then. He's teachin' me how to act nice he is, even payin' fa' electrocution lessons so I can speak proper. I'm not gonna hurt you, honest. Here's your medicine anyway."

He held up the syringe, gave it a tap, and squeezed a few drops into the air. Satisfied, he took her arm and pushed the needle in, on the inside of her elbow, finding the vein that ran beneath. He pressed the plunger, the fluid passed into her bloodstream, and she was transported to ecstasy.

She felt the same wild exhilaration she'd felt the night before, followed by a smooth, relaxing, floating sensation. She slipped off the chair, banging her head as she fell. She didn't care, she hardly felt it. She lay on the floor, surrendering herself to the rapture.

"Thank you Kevin, I'm sorry I doubted you. You're not so bad really."

"Well, you just get better, Sammie. I'll come 'round again tomorrow shall I?"

"Oh yes, that would be f-a-a-b-u-u-l-ou-u-u-s," she drawled. As her eyelids started to droop and she began to slip into unconsciousness, she watched Gun walk over to the coffee table, pick up a brightly coloured piece of paper, and stuff it into his pocket. Then he let himself out of the flat, leaving her lying helpless on the floor.

*

Tullie returned to the flat late that night. He'd been out drinking with his mates from college. Some bloke had dropped twenty quid outside the student union, so they'd decided to make the most of their good luck. He was pretty drunk when he got in so he didn't pay much attention to the state his sister was in. He left her asleep on the floor and staggered to bed.

The next morning, bleary-eyed and hung over, he saw her still on the floor. He tried to wake her up, get her to move to the sofa, but she wouldn't budge. He was late already and she seemed to be sleeping soundly, so he put a cushion under her head, covered her with the blanket, and left her to rest. She'd said she needed lots of rest.

Sammie woke around eleven, feeling stiff and achy from sleeping on the floor. Her knees and groin were less painful but she had a bad headache and there was a mysterious lump on the back of her head. The craving for medicine was even stronger. When Gun turned up just after two, she let him in straight away and readily sat next to him on the sofa so he could give her the injection.

He held the syringe an inch from her arm and looked into her face, "There's just one thing 'fore I give you this."

"What?" she asked anxiously.

"You 'ave to swear not to tell anyone where your

medicine's comin' from. This is special stuff. His lordship wants to take care of you, help you get well enough to go 'n see Bazza. But he can't 'ave anyone knowin' 'bout the medicine, or everyone'd want some. He can't afford that."

"Yes, yes, OK, I won't say a word, I promise."

"You 'ave to swear, Sammie; swear not to tell anyone. Not about his lordship givin' you medicine or 'bout me bringin' it to you. If you tell anyone, his lordship will be very upset and I won't bring you any more medicine. Do you understand, Sammie?"

She nodded eagerly, "Yes, I understand. I swear not to tell anyone about you or his lordship."

"Are you sure, Sammie?" he pulled the syringe back a few inches, as if he was going to take it away.

"Yes, yes, please, I swear," she frantically pushed her arm forwards.

"Well, OK then," he took her arm, inserted the needle into her flesh and pushed down on the plunger; "but don't forget; if you say anything, you don't get any more... 'n then you'll never be well enough to see Bazza, will you?"

*

Tullie returned late again to find Sammie asleep. At least she was on the sofa this time. He didn't want to disturb her, so he left the lights off; he just pulled the blanket over her then went to bed. She was still sleeping when he left early the next morning, before sunrise. He left her a note on the coffee table:

Sammie,

Amazing news!

The people from the Neurology Institute were at college looking for volunteers. Most of the guys got offered £100 – but they said I had 'special aptitude' and offered me £250. They even paid me £100 in advance – cash! All I've got to do is some psychological tests – no injections or anything.

I'll be away till Tuesday. Sorry to leave you on your own so long but I could really use the money – the van needs some stuff doing and there's a few other things I need as well.

Help yourself to anything in the fridge and here's £20 so you can buy some more food and maybe some clean clothes. I'll pick your stuff up from Mum and Dad's on the way back and I'll see you Tuesday night. There's a spare set of keys in the bathroom cupboard. Hope you feel better soon.

Love, Tullie xx

Gun came around that afternoon to give Sammie another dose of medicine. He took the twenty pound note from the coffee table, telling her it was a delivery charge. She didn't object; she only cared about getting her injection.

As the days passed, she grew ever more focussed on Gun's daily visits. She hardly ate and was still in the clothes she'd worn in London. But, each time Gun came,

414

he told her she was looking better and would soon be well enough to see Bazza: so she knew she didn't need food or clean clothes, she just needed her medicine.

She thought about Bazza all the time, but she didn't know how to contact him. She thought she'd seen something with details of his tour, but she must have imagined it. She was imagining a lot of things lately, crazy things like being burned as a witch, or chained up on a slave ship. Or being raped again, only she was older and she was white. It was all like a dream, but it was so vivid. She guessed her mind was probably conjuring up such horrifying things out of guilt: to punish herself for what she'd done.

She was afraid to contact Bazza yet anyway. She wanted to see him, but she was deeply ashamed about the rape. She knew it was her fault; she had no idea how she was going to tell him. She needed to feel stronger, she needed her medicine. When she was feeling better, she would find a way to reach him. She must be getting better, the medicine made her feel so good.

Gun usually arrived about two o'clock but, on Tuesday, she was still waiting at four. She was getting desperate, pacing up and down, pulling her hair; biting her fingernails. Where was he? Why hadn't he come? How could she cope without her medicine? She had to calm down somehow. She searched Tullie's cupboards and found a bottle of vodka. She'd never drunk spirits, so she hadn't got a clue how much to put in the glass. She guessed it must be like wine. Her mother drank wine; she'd have the same amount her mother did. She found a glass, filled it with vodka, then sat down and started to drink.

It tasted awful at first, a nasty, bitter taste, but she soon got used to it. She started to feel calmer and even started to like it. She finished the glass and poured another.

*

When Tullie got home, Sammie was slumped on the sofa, fast asleep, her hair hanging over her face. She'd thrown up all over herself. He felt a moment of panic but then he spotted the rise and fall of her chest: she was breathing alright. Looking around, he noticed the empty vodka bottle on the floor. He grunted to himself, he supposed it was his fault for leaving her on her own. He laughed as he remembered his first experience with vodka, which had ended just as badly. She could clean up her own bloody mess though.

He picked up the blanket and covered her up, trying not to get too close to the vomit coating her blouse and skirt. He paused for a moment to listen to her breathing. Satisfied, he headed back out to his van. God, he was tired. He'd driven for nearly three hours on the way back from the Institute, then had to endure a lengthy lecture from his father about the way he and Sammie had behaved, how ungrateful they were, etc. "But you're still my only son, you're always welcome here," the older man concluded, then added; "I'm not having that strumpet Samaira under my roof again, though."

"Dad, I think you should..." he began, trying to defend his sister, but his father held up his hand, "I don't want to hear it. She's made her bed, she can lie in it. That's it." There was no further discussion on the subject; Tullie knew it would be pointless.

He piled Sammie's possessions on one side of the living room: four boxes his mother had tearfully handed over, "Tell Samaira I'm thinking of her... and... and I love her."

Feeling exhausted, he headed for bed, leaving Sammie sleeping on the sofa. She was still asleep when he left for college in the morning.

*

Sammie woke at lunchtime. Her head was pounding with the worst headache she'd had in her life. Her eyes ached, even her teeth. God, she felt terrible. She hoped Gun would come with her medicine today. Whatever had happened yesterday, surely he would come today. He must come, mustn't he?

She spied the boxes. She didn't have much; her father always made a point of telling her it was important not to spoil girls. According to him, girls were especially prone to becoming spoilt and could easily be ruined as a result. For years, she'd watched her brother getting far more than her and her little sister put together. It hurt to be treated as inferior, second-class, all the time; but she loved her brother, and never held it against him.

She looked down at her clothes, covered in congealed sick. Some had seeped through the tear in her blouse and accumulated in her bra. She reached in and fished it out; then, unsure where to put it, she wiped it on her skirt. She ought to wash and change. She'd do it later, when she'd had her medicine. She didn't feel up to it just now. She knew what she would do though. She started looking through the boxes for her copy of the Vomix single. After a few minutes she found it. She sat down in despair, holding the broken pieces of the record, knowing her father had spitefully snapped it in two. It wasn't enough for him that she had so little, he had to take what little she had. She began to cry.

*

Tullie's classes finished late on a Wednesday; he'd missed them last week, so he really had to go. Concerned for his sister's wellbeing, he skipped the usual drink with his pals afterwards and went straight home. As he walked into the flat, he saw Sammie sitting on the sofa, still wearing her filthy, vomit-covered clothes. She had her legs pulled up to her chest, her arms wrapped tightly around them, and her forehead resting on her knees. She was rocking back and forth, talking to herself.

"Sammie, what is it, sis? What are you saying?"

She looked up. He was shocked. She was a ghost of the Sammie he knew, thin and pale, her wild, bloodshot eyes staring from dark, sunken sockets. She shouted, "I need my medicine, he hasn't brought my medicine."

"What medicine, Sammie? Who hasn't brought it? Have you been seeing a doctor?"

"No, you fuckin' idiot, he's better than a crappy doctor, it's from... from..." she stopped, looking perplexed for a moment, as if she was trying to work something out. Then she continued, "Never fuckin' mind who brings it, you dickhead; he hasn't brought it and I fuckin' need it!"

Tullie was taken aback. This wasn't the Sammie he knew. His sweet little sister never swore, never shouted, and she certainly never spoke to him like that. What had happened to her?

"But, Sammie, if he's not a doctor how can he bring you any medicine?"

"It's an injection, it makes me feel better. I need it Tullie," she stared up at him, calmer now; her eyes pleading for his help.

"Are you telling me someone has been giving you an injection?"

"Yes, he comes 'round every afternoon. Except he didn't come yesterday and he didn't come today and now I feel worse than ever."

He knelt in front of her and gently pulled her hands towards him. To his horror, he saw the pinpricks on the inside of her elbow. Someone had been shooting her up.

"Sammie, listen to me, that's not medicine. Someone's been giving you drugs, probably heroin. Who is it, Sammie?"

She stared at him, her eyes glazing over, like she

barely recognised him. Desperate to get through to her, he continued, "It's bad stuff, Sammie; you mustn't let them give you any more. Promise me, sis, tell me you won't let them give you any more. Please?"

"Fuck off; you're as bad as Dad. I'll have my medicine if I want. It makes me feel better," she pushed him away, jumped off the sofa and rushed to the front door. She yanked the door open and ran outside into the pouring rain. Tullie caught up and tried to grab onto her, but she turned around and jammed her knee into his groin.

He fell to his knees and watched helplessly as she disappeared into the dark, rainy night.

XXIX

WISH I COULD SEE HER AGAIN

Ben was woken by the sound of al-Mansur opening the shutter, "We're just approaching An Nashash now. Kassab says we should be at Mortimer's villa in just over an hour."

"OK, thanks," Ben responded.

Still an hour to go, no need to get ready yet; in fact, it might be more useful to find out what happened to Bazza and Sammie before he confronted Mortimer. He lay back on the bench and shut his eyes again.

*

Bazza called Sammie's house every day after the night at Pop Toppers. For two days there was no answer; on Saturday, he got her father, who told him, "Go away and stop bothering us, or I'll call the police;" on Sunday, he simply hung up.

After more unanswered calls, Bazza finally got through to Sammie's mother on Thursday. "Oh, I'm sorry, dear, she isn't here. She's had to move out. Her father said so," there was a tearful sniff in the woman's voice.

"Where is she? Please, I have to know, I need to speak to her."

"Well, she was staying with her brother, but…" the woman started crying.

"But what? What's happened? Where's Sammie?"

For a few seconds all he could hear was the woman's sobbing. Then she spoke again, "She ran away last night. We have no idea where she is."

"Jesus," he exclaimed, "have you called the police?"

"They can't do anything yet. They say she hasn't been missing long enough."

"Right, give me her brother's number, I'm coming back to help."

She gave him the number. He thanked her and hung up, then picked the receiver up again and dialled. He let the phone ring for several minutes before giving up.

Pushing his way out of the phone box, he went back to the guest house where he and the rest of the band were staying. Dave was still asleep in the little twin room they were sharing. He shook him awake.

"Dave, I've gotta go home. It's Sammie, she's gone missing."

"Wha-a-a-, er… what man? You can't do that. It's a

422

big gig tonight. Grey says we might make number one if we can push…"

"Fuck Grey and fuck number one. I've got to go and look for Sammie. She's all alone; God knows what might happen."

"Hey man, you're not the only one in the band you know. We need this. You can't just go running off. Besides," Dave glanced at his watch, "you wouldn't even get there 'til midnight or somethin'. What use is that? Why don't you head back tomorrow? We've got a break tomorrow. You could go home, find Sammie, and join us in Manchester on Saturday."

"I don't know, she's disappeared, she could be…"

"Come on, man, I need you with me on stage. It's not gonna make much difference to Sammie, you won't find her tonight. And just think, if we get to number one, we could be stars. Don't you think she'd want you to be a star? How much is she gonna want you then, eh? Think about it, man."

"Well, er, OK, I suppose a few hours won't make any difference. But I'm getting a night bus straight after the gig."

"That's it man, you can be back first thing tomorrow. It'll be light 'n you'll 'ave all day to find her. I'm sure she'll be alright, man."

Bazza stayed and did the gig but, by midnight, he was on a bus back to his home town. He tried to sleep in his cramped seat, but he could only think about Sammie and worry himself sick, imagining what might be happening to her. He had no idea where to begin looking so, when he arrived early next morning, he found a phone box and tried her brother again.

"Er… hello, who is this?" answered Tullie, sounding half asleep.

"It's Bazza. Remember, we met at Pop Toppers last week. I'm back in town. Do you have any news about Sammie?"

"God, no, she's still missin'. I looked all over town yesterday, but it was no use."

"Well, two of us might do better. I'm at the bus station; can you come and meet me?"

"Yeah sure man, give me half an hour, I'll be there."

The two men who loved Sammie spent the day looking everywhere they could think of. Tullie told Bazza about the injections she'd been getting, "I didn't dare tell Mum and Dad."

"Who on Earth would do that to her? And why?" Bazza questioned.

"No idea man, she wouldn't say. Some fuckin' creep tryin' to get her to do stuff for him is my guess."

Bazza shuddered at the thought, "Well, whoever they are, we've got to find her before they hurt her any more. Where can we try next?"

Running out of ideas, they went to Skank Records' offices. Bazza was hoping to drum up some help with the search. These guys were making a fortune out of him, after all. They arrived just before six and were greeted by Gun, "Oh, hi man."

"We're looking for Sammie; have you any idea where she might be?" Bazza asked.

"Oh, er… Sammie? That little wo… er, Indian girl? Yeah, maybe; she came 'round here yesterday. She was in a right state, filthy and smelly she was. Don't know what she'd been doin'. She wanted to know if there was somewhere she could stay. I told her to go home but she said she couldn't. Said her Dad wouldn't 'ave her and her brother was gettin' too heavy. Sorry man," he looked at Tullie and shrugged.

"But where is she? Do you know?"

"Oh, yeah… well… I said she could try the company's old warehouse if she liked. Told her it'd be better than sleepin' rough if she wanted somewhere to doss. I gave her the address. Maybe she went there."

"Do you have the address?"

"Yeah sure, here," Gun wrote the address down on a scrap of paper and handed it to Bazza; "good luck man, hope you find her."

It took them almost an hour to get to the warehouse. Bazza was horrified by the thought of Sammie sleeping rough, or in some old, abandoned building. He spent the journey fretting over what she must have been through since she'd fled Tullie's flat. The nights were bitterly cold, she had no decent shelter, no warm clothing; no food. Probably no sanitation either. She didn't even have any shoes, she'd run off without them. He shuddered to think how she must be living. He prayed she would be in the warehouse when they got there, cursing the Friday night traffic slowing their progress.

They finally arrived at the gloomy old building and

parked outside. The door was open and they went in, through a small front office, into a large, empty space beyond. It was cold, damp and dusty. After a minute their eyes adjusted to the darkness and Bazza spotted a figure lying on a mattress in the corner, their back to the room. He rushed across, carefully avoiding the gaping holes where the floorboards were missing. He stood behind the prostrate figure. It was a girl with long, dark hair. Her clothes were filthy, but he recognised the school uniform. "Sammie, is it you?" leaning forward, he reached out and put his hand on her shoulder.

XXX

JUST ONE MORE

Sammie roamed the streets for hours, wandering aimlessly, lost and confused. Eventually, she found her way into a local park, where she spent the night sleeping on a bench. The bitter, icy rain persisted until dawn. She was soaked to the skin, but at least it washed most of the vomit off her clothes. She woke up shivering in the cold morning air. She needed to find Gun, she needed her medicine. If he was working for the record company, maybe she could find him there? She found a phone box and grabbed the directory. Skank Records was in the classified section: 81-83 Chamberlain Circus. She needed to get to the centre of town, but she had no money for bus fare. She looked down at her bare feet, wishing she'd thought to grab her shoes before she ran from Tullie's flat. She shrugged, there was no going back now; her medicine was all that mattered: first her medicine, then Bazza. She started walking.

Two hours later, she stood looking at her reflection in the company's office window. Her dirty, wet hair was slicked down over her head, her eyes were red, her face unnaturally pale. Her school blouse was filthy, torn and ragged, her knees covered in ugly scabs, and there was a huge crimson blotch on the side of her neck. She was a shocking sight: clearly, she was in dire need of her medicine.

Stepping carefully around some broken glass on the pavement, she entered the building. At the sight of her, the security guard jumped up from behind his desk, "No you don't, we don't want any of your sort in here."

She didn't know what sort he meant, but she needed her medicine too badly to care, "I want to see Kevin, he works for Skank Records."

"Kevin? Who's Kevin? Oh, you mean young Mr Worthington, his lordship's new assistant." The guard laughed at her, "Well, I'm sorry, but I'm not letting you anywhere near the third floor in the state you're in. You'd better leave or I'll have to call the police."

"But I need to see him, he's got my... er... er... he's got something I need."

"Something you need? Huh, I know what you're after. Out now or I'm calling the police. You've got about two minutes 'til they get here. They know what to do with little junkies like you."

He started walking back to his desk. She seized her chance and ran for the door marked 'stairs'. She reached the third floor before he caught her. He'd just grabbed her arm when Gun came into view.

"Well, well, what 'ave we 'ere; what you doin' 'ere then?"

"You didn't bring it. You know... you know what I mean. I need it so I can get better and go 'n see Bazza. Where is it?"

"What on earth you talkin' 'bout girlie?"

"Please, Kevin, you know what I need. Please, I'll do anything you want."

"Alright, you'd better come to my office," he turned to the guard; "you can leave her with me, Peterson. I'll take it from here."

The guard released his grip on her arm and headed back down the stairs. Gun led her to a nearby door and showed her in.

"So, I expect you want your medicine?"

"Yes, yes, please. Why did you stop coming? I need my medicine."

"Well, you see, Sammie; we can only give you *free* medicine for a few days. Or it wouldn't be fair to the other junk... er, patients... would it? You've 'ad all your free doses."

"But I need it, I need my medicine."

"Yeah, well, you'll 'ave to pay for it now."

"Oh, er, how much is it then?"

"Five hundred quid a shot"

"What? I can't pay that, I've only got thirty pounds in my savings account. That's not fair, I need it. You've got to give me my medicine."

"Well, maybe I could give you one more shot..."

"Yes, yes, please, one more, just one more and I'll be better, I'm sure."

"… *IF* you do me a favour"

"Yes, yes, anything, I'll do anything you want, just tell me what you want me to do."

He sat on the corner of his desk, undid his flies and took out his cock, "You know what to do."

"Uuughh, not that again"

"Fine, no medicine for you then," he made a show of putting his member back in his trousers.

"No, wait… OK, I'll do it. But you will give me my medicine, won't you?"

"Of course I will, you can trust me," he smiled.

She shivered in revulsion, disgusted at what she was about to do. But what choice did she have? She was dirty and used, no decent man would want her anyway. Her only hope was to beg for Bazza's forgiveness. She had to have her medicine to give her the strength to deal with the shame and face him. This was the only way. It would be horrible but it would soon be over. Hesitantly, she knelt in front of Gun, bent her head forwards, and took him in her mouth.

"Yeah bitch, that's it, you know what to do. Don't you fuckin' spit now. You fuckin' swallow, you little wog bitch, or you don't get your medicine."

Heeding his threat, she forced herself to swallow the vile salty liquid when it filled her mouth. She felt violated and horrid but, in a minute or two, she'd get her medicine and she'd feel better. She stood up and wiped her lips, resisting the urge to throw up. She swallowed a few more times and caught her breath.

Gun was packing himself away and readjusting his clothing. "OK, you've earned another shot," he reached into his desk drawer but, instead of pulling out a syringe, took out a pen and paper. He wrote down an address and gave it to her, "Be there at six tonight and you can get your medicine."

"But I need it now. I can't wait 'til six."

He laughed, "Silly bitch. I don't keep it here, you'll 'ave to wait. Be there at six."

She looked at the address, "That's miles away, how am I gonna get there?"

"Hmmm well, it's about eight or nine miles, I reckon. Start walking now and you ought to make it, even barefoot," he laughed again; "off you go."

She slumped despondently and turned to leave.

"Oh, and take the back stairs. It'd be better if you weren't seen at the front of the office in your state."

The address he'd given her was an abandoned warehouse on the outskirts of town. Her feet were already sore as she set off; by the time she got there, they were badly cut, torn and bleeding. She'd trodden on a piece of glass somewhere and she was limping heavily as she walked up to the old building. She knocked on the door but there was no answer. She hoped she wasn't too late, she had no idea what time it was; she'd left her watch in Tullie's flat.

She tried the door. It opened and she went inside, through the front office, into the main body of the derelict structure. She shivered in the cold, damp air, hugging herself for comfort. There was no-one here, just bare concrete walls, decorated only by fading calendars showing pictures of topless girls; and a rough, wooden floor, with many of the boards missing, and nothing but darkness beneath.

Spotting a mattress in the corner, she walked over to it, lay down, and closed her eyes, grateful to finally get some rest. She didn't know how long she slept before she was woken by the sound of a car pulling up outside. She heard doors slamming, footsteps on gravel, then voices approaching, slowly growing louder.

"… after that we'll be able to enrol you in medical school. You should easily qualify, with some assistance from me at appropriate times. Ah, here we are, she should be in here." Two figures entered the dingy room: Gun and Mortimer.

"Hello, my dear, it is lovely to see you again," the lord smiled; "young Worthington tells me you need some medicine."

"Er yes, sir, er your lordship sir, er I do, yes please, if I can."

"Of course, my dear, Worthington assures me you've earned it," he produced a syringe and passed it to her with his gloved hand; "help yourself."

"Oh, er… I'm not sure how to do it. Can't one of you give it to me? Please?"

"Well, I think it's time you learned how to do it yourself, my dear. It's quite simple really; you just need to find a vein."

She placed the point of the needle on her arm at the inside of her elbow, as she'd seen Gun do.

"Almost right, my dear, let me help you," he held the needle and guided it to the spot where her vein could be seen through her skin; "now just push the needle in and press down on the plunger. You'll soon feel better."

She did as he said and felt the familiar rush of euphoria flooding through her. Oh, this was it at last; her strength was coming back, her worries dropping away, this was heaven.

"You know, my dear," Mortimer remarked, "you've been through a tough couple of days. Perhaps you deserve an extra dose, just one more. Would you like that, my dear?"

She looked up at him and nodded her agreement.

He pulled out another syringe and held it out to her. She took it without hesitation and injected herself again. She smiled at him, "Thank you, that's *so-o-o* good."

She curled up on the mattress, allowing the waves of ecstasy to wash over her. Dimly, she heard Mortimer and Gun leave the warehouse and drive away. Slowly, she drifted into unconsciousness, and the darkness wrapped itself around her.

There, in the shadows, she lay unmoving through the long, cold, lonely night. Eventually, the sun rose and the birdsong filled the air. The warmth of the day came and went without her stirring once. As night was falling again, she remained, still lying in the same position, undisturbed by the sound of the van pulling up outside, the footsteps rushing across the room behind her, the desperate, urgent voice speaking her name.

Bazza put his hand on her shoulder. It was stone cold. With an unspeakable dread rising inside, he gently pulled her towards him.

She flopped on her back, her lifeless eyes staring at the roof. Bazza fell to his knees and began to sob, painful and hard, his body convulsing as the tears failed to come. Behind him, Tullie stood in silence, gazing in disbelief at his sister's corpse.

*

Bazza missed the gig on Saturday. He was too busy talking to the police, having volcanic arguments with Sammie's father, and getting extremely drunk. Ten days later, the news of his tragic loss propelled The Vomix to number one. They were stars.

The following night he took to the stage for the first time since Sammie's death. It was Dave who'd persuaded him to resume the tour, "Hey man, I know it's a bummer, but you gotta carry on. She'd 'ave wanted you to." They were half way through 'Wish I Could See Her Again' when he suddenly stopped singing and laid down his guitar. The rest of the band played on for a few seconds then came to a halt.

Bazza stepped back up to the microphone. "This is for Sammie," he said, then took out a knife, knelt in the centre of the stage, and cut his wrists.

Everyone thought it was a publicity stunt, even Dave and Toad. By the time anyone had the sense to call an ambulance, it was too late. Bazza bled to death on stage in front of thousands of fans.

'Wish I Could See Her Again' went platinum. So did 'I Have Loved You…' released the following month. Even 'Spit in Your Face' sold almost half a million. The Vomix's debut album stayed at number one for twelve weeks in the UK and went on to be a massive hit all over the world.

Billie made a fortune selling his story to the papers then made even more money managing 'The Betrayal'. Dave and Toad were megastars for a few years, until the acrimonious split spelt the end for The Vomix.

Dave enjoyed the fortune and fame his days with Bazza brought him, but he missed his friend more than he could bear. Years of drug and alcohol abuse looked likely to lead to an early grave but, at the beginning of the new millennium, he cleaned up his act and started touring with a new band. The highlight of his set was the slightly reworded 'Wish I Could See Him Again'.

XXXI

CONFESSIONS

Susan started to come around. She was filled with pain and anger. Throbbing pain surged through her body, but she couldn't identify the source yet. The source of her anger was clear, though. Sammie and Bazza had died tragically, needlessly, and young. Mortimer had got away with murder. It wasn't the first time; he'd murdered them many times before, in previous incarnations. But those had been centuries ago. For him, this was the same life. It seemed so recent, so connected to the present. Sammie and Bazza could still have been alive. Dave was, she knew; Tullie probably was too.

Her anger hardened and turned to determination. She had to get out of here; she had to make the bastard pay for what he'd done.

As she came to her senses, she found she was hanging by one arm, her manacled wrist bearing most of her weight. No wonder she was in so much pain. She stood up straight to ease the burden on her tortured limb. It was then she realised the pain was coming from her other arm, hanging limp at her side.

Raising her hand, she brought it in front of her face. She stared in awe. Her thumb had been wrenched from its socket, the unnatural outline of her dislocated bone showing beneath her skin. Looking to her side, she saw the empty manacle dangling beside her. Her hand must have come free when she blacked out. Glancing at the CCTV cameras, she wondered how long it had been. Had they seen? There were no lights to indicate whether the cameras were active. She could only hope they hadn't spotted her hand was out of its cuff.

Now she needed to get her thumb back into place; her hand was useless as it was. Would she be able to do it on her own, with no anaesthetic? It was a tall order, but she had to try. She reached across and put her damaged thumb in her other hand. It was hard to manipulate the bone while she was stretched in such an awkward position. She couldn't even see what she was doing. Every movement was agony. Twice she had to stop and take a few deep breaths when she was on the verge of fainting. Finally, she pushed the digit back into its socket with an audible click. The pain surged through her arm and she teetered on the edge of consciousness, but she bit hard into her lip and it brought her back.

For a minute, she stood panting, exhausted by her exertions. She held her hand up and flexed it a few times. It was painful, but her thumb seemed to be working normally; she might get chance to suffer that osteoarthritis after all. She looked up at the cameras. She knew she was pushing her luck, but she had to gamble they weren't watching. One free hand wasn't enough, she had to carry on. Turning to her right, she began unscrewing the lock on the manacle around her wrist. Once again, it was awkward and painful; her injured left hand screaming in protest as it started to stiffen. But eventually her arm came free.

She rubbed her wrists. They were sore and tender, but it was good to have the use of her hands again. Now she turned her attention to the band around her waist. That was less promising; she couldn't see any mechanism for opening it, and the chain securing it to the wall was pretty strong. She felt around the band, searching for a way to release herself. After a moment, she found a keyhole in the side. Damn, she was locked in.

If this was a movie, she'd have a hairpin that could do the job, but she only wore hairpins in surgery. Her earrings were too small as well. She wondered if she could wriggle out of the band. She pulled it upwards, but couldn't get it past her ribs; she tried pulling it down, but it lodged against the metal girdle under her skirt. She lifted her skirt and quickly confirmed what she suspected. There was no way to remove the metal undergarment; there wasn't even a keyhole this time. With a sigh, she realised she had no chance of escape.

So, what now? She'd freed her hands, but the band held her to the wall. She might delay Mortimer a few seconds, but that was about it. Still, with Ben on his way, a few seconds could be critical.

Remembering the cameras, she loosened the manacles so she could slip out of them easily then replaced her hands in them. All she could do now was to wait. In the meantime, perhaps she could learn something else from her past?

She closed her eyes and scanned the millennia. Which of her lives was likely to help? Or was there a pattern that might be useful? She focussed on her encounters with Mortimer, looking for a common theme. After a while, she realised it was staring her in the face. There it was, time and again, the same behaviour, the same obsession. She searched for when it might have begun. She concentrated hard and, in a moment, she was there.

*

Su-Chi lay shivering in the dark. Her tiny cell, deep beneath the master's house, was cold and damp, but that was not the reason she was shivering. Nor was she shivering because of the sickness that affected her when she was with child. This was her fourth time. She'd miscarried once but two of her babies had lived, a boy and a girl. She'd nursed them for forty days, then they'd been taken from her and she'd been returned to the breeding compound.

The men in the dormitory were rough, but at least their desires were natural and, as long as she co-operated, they didn't treat her badly. But now was the time she dreaded most, the early months, before her belly grew large. Each time she was with child, she was imprisoned in here, alone in the dark. But, like the cold and the sickness, the dark was not the reason she was shivering. She was shivering because she was frightened; frightened of the horror to come; she was shivering because it was time for his visit.

Her fear rose as she saw the faint glimmer of a torch approaching. As usual, he started speaking as he grew near, growing more intense as he stooped to enter the cell and began pulling on her ropes to move her into position, readying her for him to inflict his regular torment upon. She kept quiet, saying nothing in return, but she listened... and she remembered.

*

The sound of heavy locks turning pulled Susan back to consciousness. Adrenaline pumped through her bloodstream. This is it; time's up, here they come.

Mortimer, Hans, and Sun-lee entered in procession. Sun-lee was carrying the same tray bearing a flask of potion and a glass funnel. They were ready to destroy her.

"Come on, Doctor Susie, you can do it," she muttered under her breath, steeling herself for the confrontation to come. She felt certain Ben was near. She could sense his presence, and the feeling was getting stronger. She had a plan, but it was half-formed at best. She needed luck on her side, and she needed to buy time.

"Well, my dear," Mortimer announced, "I am afraid the hour has come for you to leave us."

If there was one thing countless movies had taught her, the best way to buy time was to keep the villain talking. Despite the wave of terror rising within her, she projected an outward calm; "What is this obsession you've got with me, Mamboja? What am I to you? And what's the problem with me and Bakara: why do we threaten you so much?"

"Threaten me?" he laughed; "you are merely an irritation. But one I would prefer to do without, especially now, as my plans near completion."

"What plans? Why are we a problem?"

"My plans are my affair. Suffice to say, the world is going to change in ways you could not possibly imagine. The demise of the human race as you know it is inevitable. I am simply accelerating the process and placing myself in a position to benefit."

"What process? Do you mean global warming? Are you responsible for that?"

He laughed again, "Global warming is just a symptom. The process itself is something deeper. Over the last few centuries, the Universe has struggled to produce enough souls to match the growing population on Earth. Humanity has almost bred itself to the limit; soon its numbers will go beyond what the Universe can support. Bodies will outnumber souls, creating empty vessels without a soul of their own."

"But how will that benefit you?"

"I will inhabit those empty vessels myself. In time, thanks to the steps I have planned, their ranks will swell until there are many billions, creating a ready-made army under my control. Together, we will establish a new world order and, at last, I shall be the undisputed ruler of all mankind."

"Oh, my God, you really mean it, don't you?" she stared at him aghast.

"Of course, my dear, why ever not?" he smiled.

"As for you and Bakara," he continued, "you have a capacity to be something of a nuisance. You might perhaps pose a minor inconvenience if I allowed you to join together. I would sooner not take that chance. Hence, I must now bid you farewell."

He turned to Hans and opened his mouth to speak, but she quickly interrupted, "I'm surprised you've got the balls. You usually struggle when it comes down to it. We lived together for years when I was Charlotte de Brune, and again when I was Sally Trigg. Bakara was right there on both occasions." She snorted in derision, "Honestly, Mamboja, I can't understand why you don't just kill us as soon as you find us. Or is there some reason you like having us around?"

"Not at all, my dear, I always enjoy putting an end to your pathetic little lives. But killing your earthly bodies was never my objective. It is a crude and temporary solution that leaves me with the problem of finding you again, a task that has often been tiresome and time-consuming; an unwelcome distraction from my goals.

Even now, I cannot be certain of when or where you will return, or who you will be. In the past, I always knew fate would place you in my path but, even so, it often took a long time to recognise you. Once I had identified you, it sometimes made more sense to have you under my control, where I could keep an eye on you, rather than dispose of you straight away. But, if the risk of your union became too great... well, you remember what happens then, don't you?"

She almost smiled as he confirmed his greatest fear. This conversation was proving useful, she was learning a great deal. But she had to survive to benefit. She needed to keep him talking as long as possible.

"Slavery must be helpful if you like controlling people. I bet you miss it, don't you?"

"Yes," he smiled, "they were simpler times, I must say. Naturally, I shall re-introduce the institution as soon as I am able. But there are other ways. As Samaira, for instance, you were easily enslaved with drugs; although it was fortunate your father had already conditioned you so well. I could have kept you like that a long time but, sadly, Bakara was difficult to control in that life. Even in death, as it turned out."

"So you murdered me in case we hooked up?"

"Of course, I couldn't take the risk."

"You've taken risks before though, haven't you? How did you know Sarah wouldn't sleep with Brendan before he went to Normandy? Or whether Samantha and Barnaby would wait for their wedding night?"

He laughed, "Chains and drugs are not the only ways to control people, Shebana. Social convention and religious belief play their part too. Do not judge the past by the standards of the present. In any case, you have often been watched more closely than you knew. I have a great many followers. For example, do you remember your friend Joan at the hospital in Totnes?"

"Of course, she was my best friend. I used to tell her everything."

"Exactly, including your feelings for Brendan O'Doyle"

"Yes, so?"

"Joan was operating under my instructions. As soon as you indicated a willingness to take Brendan to bed, she would not have hesitated to kill you. Luckily, you remained a loyal wife until he went to France. It saved us all a fair amount of trouble. But you see what I mean about control?"

"Sure, there's lots of ways to control someone; you're obviously quite the expert. But what about Su-Chi and Bak-Ra; you really pushed your luck there. Another two minutes and we'd have been joined together."

He was pacing up and down, clearly embracing his opportunity to show off. "Yes, that was close, I must confess," he chuckled; "well, if you must know, and you may as well since I'm about to destroy you in any case, my powers were not so well developed then. I knew I had you somewhere among my slaves, but I had no idea which ones you were. I didn't even sense what you were doing; it was only thanks to Worthington I caught you in time."

"Worthington? He was Garma?"

"Same person, different life, my dear; I'm not surprised you didn't recognise him though, a weak soul without a clear identity, did you know he was Crazy Rabbit too?"

"Hmmm, he always was a creep. Can't say I feel sorry for him after everything he did, but you've got a strange way of showing your appreciation. You don't exactly reward loyalty do you?" she glanced at Sun-lee standing with the tray and its deadly contents, listening patiently to her master's conversation.

"He'd outlived his usefulness. He was never very bright and I haven't forgotten the trouble he caused when his semen was found in your stomach. He put my careful plans at risk for a moment of personal gratification. I cannot tolerate that level of stupidity."

"My God, you can bear a grudge, can't you? That was decades ago."

"A few decades are nothing, my dear; you should know that by now. I've been tracking you and Bakara for millennia."

"Sounds like a lot of effort for a minor inconvenience," she snorted; "you're not very good at it, are you? Seems to me we always find each other anyway"

He glanced angrily at her, but resumed his pacing, evidently enjoying his captive audience, "As my powers have grown, I have become more adept at finding you. But you are right, until recently, I needed you to find each other first. The closer you got, the more I could sense you and the easier you were to find. Even then, it was often difficult to pinpoint you precisely. There were times I had you in my grasp and still couldn't tell exactly who you were. Sometimes I had to wait until you were very close indeed, the very thing I have been trying to avoid."

He stopped his pacing and turned to face her, "And that, of course, brings us to the reason we are here. All this talk of the past is most gratifying, but things are different now. This potion," he waved at the flask of black liquid Sun-lee was carrying on the tray, "means I can dispose of you once and for all. Never again will I need to be concerned with where you will appear next, or whether you and Bakara might get together before I can track you down."

Susan sensed her time was nearly up, but she had another line to pursue, and another objective to fulfil. She glanced at Sun-lee to make sure she was listening then spoke again.

"You know, I get the business about keeping us alive to control us, but I still think you've got another reason for keeping me around. I reckon you enjoy it too much. You're physically drawn to me and, every chance you get, you act on it."

He stared at her from eyes as black as coal. She pressed on, "Go on, admit it. You've always been attracted to me, haven't you?"

Laughing, he resumed his pacing, "A typical female conceit, you imagine my interest in you is sexual. I

446

have no more interest in you than any other attractive woman. Yes, you have been reasonably satisfying on occasions, but our liaisons have been no more than a means of keeping you under closer control. Any pleasure I derived was merely a bonus, you were simply an amusing plaything."

"Bollocks," she retorted, "you crave my flesh above all others, I am the sweetest fruit in all creation. Your desire for me knows no equal."

"What nonsense, you have a vastly inflated idea of your own importance, whatever gave you such ideas?"

"You did, it's what you said every night you were violating me when I was Su-Chi."

"But you couldn't speak Egyptian, how could you know?"

"I chose not to speak Egyptian, but I learned it in the compound after you mutilated Bak-Ra. I understood it alright. I understood *you* Amenemhat."

His normally pale, calm, features burned red. She wondered if he was angry with himself for getting caught out. That was good. He might be practically immortal, but he was human enough to make mistakes, and that's what angry people did.

He took a deep breath and seemed to regain some composure, then turned to face her, "Very well, my dear, I may as well admit it before I destroy you. Yes, I have indeed developed a particular taste for the pleasures of your flesh: Su-Chi, Charlotte, Sally... many other incarnations, always delightful. That time in Devon was especially delicious. I had planned to kill you, of course, just as a precaution. But it turned out that wasn't necessary, so I made the most of the opportunity; shame to waste a good plan. You were older than I usually like, but immensely enjoyable, nonetheless. Oh yes," he sighed, "you have been most entertaining, Shebana. I shall miss you."

Susan shivered as she remembered the time she'd been attacked in the darkness of the blackout. She was crying as she walked home from a late shift at the hospital, devastated by the news she'd received that afternoon. Brendan had been killed in Normandy and she felt like her whole world had collapsed. She'd been longing to be with him and had decided when he got his next leave she would throw caution to the wind and take him to bed. Now she would never see him again.

She'd turned a corner, barely able to see through her tears, and they'd grabbed her from behind. They stifled her cries for help and pulled her into a deserted bombsite where the smaller one held her down while the taller one forced himself upon her. She'd struggled against them and the tall one had struck her across the face, his ring gouging a deep scratch in her cheek. When he'd finished with her, they disappeared into the night, leaving her lying amid the rubble. Shocked and distraught, she'd staggered home, too traumatised to think straight. She'd never reported the incident; she was too heartbroken over Brendan, and had no idea who her assailants were in any case. Now it became clear, her so-called friend Joan had held her down while Mortimer raped her, and the ring he still wore had given her the scar she'd borne for the rest of her life.

Snapping back to the present, she saw Mortimer was gazing into the distance, seeming lost in his thoughts. She had him rattled, even sounding regretful; she had to press home her advantage, no matter how painful it was reliving some of her worst memories. It was the only way if her tenuous plan was to have any chance of success. She chose another example.

"So what happened with Serwaah? I was the perfect captive and you never touched me."

He looked at her with a cold smile, "Yes, I'm sorry to say I missed you that time. I was close, but I picked the wrong sister. By the time I realised my mistake, you were lost somewhere among the cargo. Still, I found Bakara and eliminated the threat; and Fremah was pleasurable enough for a while."

"Yeah, and some thanks you gave her," Susan looked at Sun-lee as she spoke, "keel-hauling her 'til the sharks got her. That's some way to treat your lovers." Pursuing a hunch, she turned back to Mortimer and continued quickly, "I'm surprised you never had a go at Sammie, you had plenty of opportunity."

"Oh, my dear, how little you know, even now. My followers are not just servants, they are my vessels. I can enter their bodies and experience what they experience, just as if I were there myself. Good practice for when I have an army to control. Mr Savage was one of my favourites; I enjoyed many fascinating exploits through him. But the sweetest of all was the time we had you," he stared at her like a ravenous predator eying a meal; "such a pity you escaped before we could return for seconds."

She shuddered. The memory of what Savage had done was bad enough, but now she knew there'd been two of them. She'd suspected as much, but it was still a horrible feeling to hear it confirmed. She hesitated a moment. She needed to get back on the offensive. She hit back as best she could.

"Huh, so it was some kind of vicarious rape then? You didn't even have the balls to do it yourself. No wonder you never had the guts to go for She Wolf. I'd have slit your throat and you knew it."

"Ah, yes, you were quite impressive as She Wolf. It took me a long time to realise that was you. I was planning to let Crazy Rabbit soften you up before I took you myself. Alas, it was not to be. Well, my dear, remember it well, that was the last time you defied me. It will never happen again." He turned to his waiting henchman, "Would you get the lady ready please, Hans."

Hans stepped up to Susan and took a firm grip on her chin, forcing her head back so her mouth would be ready for the funnel. She clenched her fists to make sure her hands didn't slip out of the manacles. She could have pulled them free, pushed Hans away, but that would do no good. She needed help to accomplish her plan, and there was only one way she stood any chance of getting it.

"Is that it then? You're just going to destroy me now?

After everything we've done together? Don't I mean anything to you? Haven't I given you a lot of pleasure?"

Mortimer laughed, "Yes, my dear, you have given me a great deal of pleasure," he stared ravenously at her again, "I have always enjoyed *fucking* you."

She twisted her head in Hans's grip and looked at Sun-lee, "But you're still going to kill me, aren't you? It doesn't bother you that we've shared a bed, that you've had many years of pleasure from my body? We've even been married."

"I'm sorry to disappoint you, my dear, but no, it doesn't bother me at all. I may have enjoyed your body on a few occasions, but I have never hesitated to dispose of you when necessary. Now I have the power to dispose of you for good and, if you think for a second the pleasure I have taken from you might stop me, you are very much mistaken."

Susan watched Sun-lee as Mortimer spoke. The other woman's mouth dropped open as she stared aghast at her master. Susan knew she was hitting the mark; she just needed to goad him on a little further.

"Sure, yeah, you've disposed of me a few times, but that's never stopped you fucking me first, has it? What about those nights before you burned me alive when I was Samantha Parsons?"

"Yes, that was absolutely exquisite, I must admit. The anticipation of your impending death in the fire made those nights in your cell all the more satisfying. Then watching you burn... and oh, how you burned... Yes, tasting your flesh then watching it roast... what could be sweeter?"

"So, why not now then? Don't you want another go? One last shag for old time's sake? I've learned a few tricks since I was Sally."

"Ha! I'm sure you have, Shebana. The kind of tricks you would try to use to get the better of me. I know how much stronger you are now. You are severely misguided if you think I would be foolish enough to take that risk."

"So you'd fuck me again if you weren't worried I might escape?"

He gave a manic laugh as he stared gleefully at her, "Oh yes, indeed, Shebana, indeed I would. I would fuck you senseless, like I have many times before and then, when I was done with you I would still happily destroy your body and consume your soul."

"Yeah, I thought so," she responded, still looking at Sun-lee.

His smile faded, "Enough of this pointless repartee, I have enjoyed reminiscing with you, Shebana, but your time is up; Sun-lee, the potion please." When his assistant failed to move, he turned and followed Susan's gaze. Sun-lee was staring at him, her mouth gaping open, a look of abject horror on her face.

"Sun-lee… **Sun-lee**… **SUN-LEE!**" he had to shout to get her attention. Finally, she moved forward with the tray shaking in her hands and placed it on the floor next to Susan. She picked up the funnel and reached upwards, moving it slowly, but inexorably, towards Susan's open mouth…

An alarm rang out, almost deafening in the confined space of the basement. One of the computer screens flickered into life, displaying an armoured personnel carrier approaching rapidly across the desert.

Mortimer crossed the room in three quick strides and sat in front of the newly activated screen. "Hans, man the weapons," he shouted. The henchman released his grip on Susan and took a seat at one of the monitors. He flicked a switch and brought it to life.

Sun-lee put down the funnel and stood uncertainly next to Susan, watching the others at the controls.

With Mortimer and Hans distracted, Susan pulled her hands free and reached down to grasp the metal band around her waist. She spoke quickly to Sun-lee, "You heard him. I've been his plaything many times in the past. He still wants me, even now, but he's happy to destroy me all the same. What do you think will happen to you in the end? Help me and I'll help you. Can you get me out of this?"

Sun-lee hesitated, looking from Susan to Mortimer and back again.

"Remember what happened to Worthington," Susan urged; "you know he'll do the same to you, he doesn't care about you; he doesn't care about anyone. This is your only chance, Sun-lee; release me and we can escape together."

Closing her eyes, Sun-lee took a deep breath. "OK," she nodded. Opening her eyes again, she glanced at Mortimer then reached into a pocket in her tunic, took out a small key and inserted it into the metal band. With a click it sprang open. Susan was free.

"Come on," Susan grabbed Sun-lee's hand and ran for the open door.

Mortimer spotted the fleeing women, "Get them, Hans, I'll deal with this."

They got through the door ahead of Hans. Susan saw a staircase a few yards away, on the other side of the corridor, and ran for it. They charged up the first flight of steps and turned the corner then Susan stopped, waiting for the henchman. As he appeared, she brought her knee up sharply into his groin. He staggered back and fell down the stairs behind him. She grasped Sun-lee's hand again and they continued their rush upwards. After climbing three more flights they came out in the villa's lobby and Susan was somewhere she recognised at last. Still running, she pulled Sun-lee towards the back of the villa. The alarm had stopped and she could hear Hans lumbering up the stairs. He'd recovered quicker than she expected.

The women burst out into the open at the rear of the building. Susan saw a pair of headlights a few hundred yards away. She felt certain it was Ben. She ran towards the oncoming vehicle. Glancing back, she saw Hans had reached the back door of the villa. He crouched down, pulled out a gun and took aim at her. She put her head down and ran faster, dragging Sun-lee along with her.

There was a loud 'whoosh' as a rocket soared over their heads and the dark desert was lit by an almighty explosion as the APC blew up in front of them. At the same moment, the sharp crack of a pistol sounded from behind. Sun-lee staggered and collapsed into the sand at Susan's feet. She rolled over and stared at the sky with unseeing eyes. Susan released the dead woman's hand and ran on towards the flaming wreck of the APC. The front of the vehicle had been obliterated. No-one in there could have survived. She ran to the back. The rear doors had been blown open. Someone was inside.

Ben staggered to his feet and saw her, "You... you're..."

"Yes, I'm OK, come on, quick," she grabbed his hand and pulled him out of the APC. They ran into the desert night together.

XXXII

TOGETHER AT LAST

S usan was exhausted. They'd been running through the desert for what seemed like hours. She'd long since used up the burst of adrenaline that had helped her escape. The sand dunes were hard going, especially barefoot. She had the wretched metal girdle to contend with as well, although it was a lot better than the last one the bastard had trapped her in. When they came across a small hollow, she just had to sit down.

Ben ran on a few paces then stopped and turned around. He scanned the horizon behind them then came to join her. She was panting hard. "You've done well," he said, "we've covered around five or six miles, I reckon. I think we can afford a brief rest. They don't seem to have followed us; probably waiting for daylight. We'll need to find cover before dawn." He glanced at his watch, "that's about another four hours.

"How are you feeling, er... er..." he laughed

nervously; "I'm not sure what I should call you: Susan, or Sarah, or Sally, Shebana, Charlotte, Sammie… I mean, who are you? Who am I for that matter?"

She studied his face as she caught her breath. So, this was, quite literally, the man of her dreams, the man she was destined to be with. It seemed strange and yet she knew it was true. She got her breathing under control and smiled at him, "Well, I'm Susan this time, and you're Ben. Let's stick with those names, shall we?"

"Er, yeah, OK then Susan. So, are you alright?"

"Yeah, I'm fine; I just need a quick break."

"OK, good," he sat next to her. He frowned, as he noticed the mark on her cheek left by Mortimer's ring, "You're hurt, did he…"

"It's nothing," she said, fingering the mark; "that's the worst he did, I was lucky."

They sat in silence for a minute, until Ben said, "You know, it's weird, I hardly know you as Susan, but I feel like I've…"

"Loved you since the dawn of time?" she interrupted. They both laughed.

"Yeah, I know," she continued, "we don't really know each other as Susan and Ben, but we've been together a long time, a *very* long time."

"But never completely *together* as such," he added; "at least not as man and woman."

"No, we never have been, have we? Mortimer, Mamboja, or whoever you want to call him has seen to that."

457

"You know why, don't you?"

"Not exactly: but it seems to be his greatest fear, and he's gone to enormous lengths to stop us. Do you know why?"

"Well, er… according to Del Rivera, if we ever get together, er… you know, consummate our relationship, we'll become a twin soul. Then we'll be the only ones who might be strong enough to stand up to Mortimer, stop whatever he's doing. That's why he's always kept us apart. Now he's planning something big and he wants us out the way before we can fulfil our destiny. But we've got him now, haven't we? He's slipped up this time."

"What do you mean?"

Ben stood up and began loosening his belt, "I'm sorry this isn't very romantic, but we need to do this as soon as possible."

"Whoa there tiger," she laughed. She lifted her skirt to reveal her metal underwear, "I'm afraid you're going to have to wait."

"Shit, not again, I don't believe it. My God, have you been carrying that bloody thing the whole time since…"

"Oh yes," she nodded.

"Blimey, you've done even better than I thought." He frowned, "Well, we've gotta get it off. I mean, you know what we need to do, don't you? We have to; it's the only way we can beat Mortimer. Del Rivera said he started the Black Death, and now he can destroy souls. God knows what he's up to this time. We've got to stop him. I'll find a rock and we can smash that wretched contraption off."

"I don't think we should do that. It ended pretty badly last time, don't you remember?"

"Oh shit, yeah, you're right," he sighed; "I guess we'll have to wait a bit longer. That fucking bastard gets us every time. What a tragic life... er, lives, we've had; never together, never happy."

"Well, there was that time on Lesbos."

"Yeah, we were happy then, but it was the only time."

"No it wasn't. We were happy again. Here, let me remind you," she put her hand on his forehead and transported him over three centuries back, to a hot little island in the Caribbean.

*

When the ship finally reached land, the sailors dragged the prisoners to the slave market and put them on the auction block, one by one. Some had already been sold before Serwaah got there, but she saw the white men haggling over Baako. She knew some of their words now and, from what she could tell, they seemed eager to buy him, despite his mutilation. In fact, many of those bidding appeared to see it as a virtue. Perhaps they believed castrated slaves would be less trouble, easier to control.

There was less haggling over the women. The only ones who attracted much interest were the pretty young girls. When her turn on the auction block came, Serwaah was petrified. The white men prodded and poked her, groping her breasts and her womanhood. It was horrible but, when the bidding was over, she realised she had been bought by the same man as Baako. Whatever torments lay ahead, at least they would be going to the same place.

They were taken to the plantation in different carts. She watched Baako being led in one direction, while she was taken to a wooden hut at the back of an enormous white house. She spent the night shaking in fear, terrified of what the white men were going to do to her; she hadn't forgotten the things Fremah had told her. But, in the morning, the white men took off her chains and led her to the big house, where a black girl called Daisy, who could speak the white men's words, gave her some strange clothes to wear.

Over the next few days, Daisy showed Serwaah what she was expected to do. It was light, easy work, not difficult once she learned how. She had to help clean the big house, change bed sheets, and serve the master and his family their food and drink. The white people called her Dolly, which was apparently meant to be her new name. She didn't understand why they couldn't use her proper name but, apart from that, she was treated far better than she had expected.

Sometimes though, when she was in the top part of the big house, she could see the other slaves out in the fields. They were not treated well. They toiled in the blazing sun from dawn to dusk every day, with the overseers' whips always at the ready. She knew Baako was somewhere among them and her heart ached for him. Every night she lay awake for hours, praying she might somehow be able to see him soon.

It was almost a month before her prayers were answered. The other house slaves were getting excited; they kept talking about 'First Saturday'. Daisy explained this meant the master would allow them to spend an evening with the field slaves.

Serwaah was trembling in anticipation as she walked down to the compound, following the others. As they approached, she scanned the faces of the waiting people, searching anxiously for her beloved Baako. At last she saw him. She ran to him and threw herself into his arms, tears of joy running down her cheeks.

They embraced for a minute then he led her to a tiny hut where they sat side by side on his bunk. "How are you, my love?" he asked.

"My heart still bleeds for Fremah and Kofi, and for Afia and the others who were lost. But I am well treated here and the work is simple. How are you, my love?"

"Our work is hard in the hot sun every day. But, if you work well, you do not suffer the overseer's whip, and the day passes."

He looked aside and fidgeted uneasily. She sensed he had more to say, "What is it, my love?"

"Danquah is here."

"Oh, that is good, my brother is here too, I did not know. How is he?"

"He does not speak to the rest of us; he is the overseer's favourite and spends most of the time with him, even at night."

"Oh, I see," she looked away, filled with an odd mix of

feelings. She was glad her brother was well, but disturbed to hear of his behaviour. She would not care if he chose to sleep with a man for love, but sleeping with one of the white devils to gain favour was another thing. After a long silence, she looked back at Baako, "Are you healed where you were cut, my love?"

"Yes, I am healed, but I am not a man any more," he looked down in shame.

She put her hand on his arm, "You will always be my man. You do not need a cock and balls for me to love you."

He wiped his eyes, trying to hide his tears, "You are wrong, Serwaah; you are a beautiful woman. You should find a proper man to please you."

She put her finger on his lips, "Hush, my man, there is no-one could please me more than you." Removing her finger, she bent forwards and kissed him on the same spot.

For the next three years, they saw each other once a month. They hugged and kissed, talked and laughed. Sometimes, the master let the house slaves stay in the compound until morning, and they lay in each other's arms all night. They lived for the times they had together, and pined for each other when they were apart.

They often saw Danquah, but rarely spoke with him. As well as enjoying the favour of the overseers, he had become the self-appointed compound guard, helping to enforce the nightly curfew. He eagerly reported transgressors and watched with glee as they were brutally punished. Serwaah felt a residue of familial affection for him, but otherwise he was universally hated. The other slaves called him the white man's dog.

By this time, she had learned much of the master's language. One day she overheard a conversation that chilled her to the bone. The master had decided to sell half the plantation to his neighbour. Half the field slaves would be sold too. She was horrified. Baako could be sold off and taken away. The neighbour's slave compound was only three hours' walk from the master's house, but it might as well be on the moon as far as she was concerned. She would never see Baako again. She couldn't face that, she couldn't live without him. Not after everything they'd been through.

She threw herself onto her bed that night, desperately wanting to weep. She'd lost so much, surely please not Baako too. The tears began to rise inside, but they were halted by the familiar voice within, 'Not yet, Serwaah, not yet.'

In the morning she woke with a new determination. She had to be with Baako, whatever it took. She knew what she had to do. As well as the language, she'd learned a few other things while she'd been working in the master's house. She'd learned there was an island across the ocean where all people were free, whatever the colour of their skin. She'd learned there was a man called Daniels who would take people to this island if they paid him in silver. There was plenty of silver in the master's house. If she gave him enough, Daniels would take them to the island of freedom. Then they could be together.

A few days later, it was the night before First Saturday. Just after dark, she sneaked down to the compound and made her way to Baako's hut. He was startled as she entered. She put her hand over his mouth and whispered quickly, "Shush, my love, it is only me. We must leave this place. The master is selling half the slaves. He will sell you, I know it, and I will not see you again. I could not take that, my love; we must flee so we can be together. I will be back tomorrow and you need to be ready to leave. We will go straight after curfew, when there is no-one around to see us."

She removed her hand, allowing him to speak. "But, if we are caught, we will be punished. I could not bear to see you tied to the whipping post, it would kill me," he whispered back.

"We are dying here already, my love, a little every day. If we are caught and punished we only die sooner, but if we get away, we live. We must try, my love, I cannot live without you."

He nodded, "You are right, my love, I could not live without you either. I will be ready tomorrow."

She kissed him long and passionately then disappeared into the night.

The following afternoon, she stole two silver candlesticks from the dining room. She took a sheet from the laundry and placed them in it, together with her few pieces of spare clothing, and a small carved wooden warthog Baako had made for her the year before. She made a bundle of the whole thing and tied the sheet in a knot. At sunset she walked down to the compound with the other house slaves. When they asked her what the bundle was for, she smiled coyly, "It is for pleasing my man." The other girls laughed.

She went straight to Baako's hut and found him waiting with a bundle of his own. His was much smaller, wrapped in an old shirt. She sat beside him and they held each other tight until the bell sounded to signal curfew. "Come, my love," she urged; "we must find this man Daniels. He will be in the town in a place called the tavern. If we walk all night, we can be there by sunrise."

They left the hut and began making their way out of the compound, keeping to the darkest corners, well out of sight. Baako carried Serwaah's bundle, which was much heavier than his own, and she carried the lighter one. When they reached the high wooden fence at the edge of the compound, he placed the heavy bundle on the ground and climbed over. Then he turned around and reached out for Serwaah to pass both bundles to him. She threw his light bundle over the fence and he caught it, then she reached down to pick up her heavy bundle. Lifting it high above her head, she had almost passed it over when someone grabbed her from behind and flung her to the ground. The bundle fell and burst open, scattering clothes, candlesticks, and a small wooden warthog at her assailant's feet. She looked up and gasped as she saw her brother standing over her.

"Out after curfew, attempting to escape, and stealing the master's silver," Danquah laughed, "they will wear out the whip on you, little sister."

"Please, my brother, come with us. There is no life for any of us here; we can be free, there is an island across the ocean. The white men will n…"

Danquah slapped her across the face then took a handful of her hair and began to drag her away.

"Leave her alone," Baako hissed from across the fence.

"Oh, I see you have your pet eunuch with you. What will you do pathetic eunuch? I expect you wish you were still a man now?"

In one swift movement, Baako leaped over the fence and launched himself at Danquah. The white man's dog gave his sister a kick in the ribs then whirled around to meet Baako's challenge. The two of them fell to the ground, wrestling each other. They rolled in the dirt again and again, both trying to gain the upper hand.

Serwaah got to her knees, "No, please, Danquah, Baako, my brother, my love, please don't." She tried to pull them apart but Danquah pushed her away violently. She landed hard and lay gasping on the ground, dazed and winded.

The two men fought on, rolling over many more times until eventually Danquah managed to get on top. He straddled Baako's chest, his hands around his throat, and began to throttle him.

"No please," Serwaah begged. She tried to pull Danquah off but again he pushed her away. She floundered in the dirt and, scrabbling around, her hand fell upon one of the candlesticks. She picked it up and crouched behind her brother.

"Please, Danquah, get off him," she begged. He squeezed Baako's throat tighter still. She closed her eyes and swung the candlestick. It grazed the back of her brother's head. He turned and stared at her, "You sting like an insect, sister. I will deal with you next." He returned his attention to Baako, pressing down with renewed vigour.

Baako's eyes rolled upward, he was moments from death. Serwaah raised the candlestick high and brought it down as hard as she could. There was a crunch as the back of Danquah's skull gave way. He rolled off Baako and lay dead on the ground beside him.

Serwaah stood up quickly and dropped the candlestick, staring in horror at her brother's lifeless body, "No, no… oh, my brother… no-o-o-o-o-o… what have I done?"

Baako sat up, wheezing and panting, as Serwaah knelt and took Danquah's head in her hands, "Oh, my brother, why wouldn't you stop, why did you make me do it; why, my brother why?" She bowed her head, on the point of tears as, once again, her grief threatened to overwhelm her. Then, abruptly, she let go of her brother and stood up. She lifted her chin, stared into the distance, and softly muttered, "Not yet."

When he'd recovered his breath, Baako gathered together the bloody candlestick, its companion, and the other contents of Serwaah's bundle, and replaced it all in the sheet. He knotted it together as before and dropped it carefully over the fence. Serwaah was still frozen to the spot. He took her hand and pulled her gently forwards,

"Come, my love, I know you mourn him. Whatever his faults, he was family. But we must go now."

She looked up at him, put her hand on his cheek, and stared into his eyes, "You are my family now. You are all the family I have and all the family I will ever need."

They climbed the fence, collected their bundles, and ran into the night. After an hour or so they slowed to a walk but kept going in the direction of the island's only town. As the sky began to lighten before dawn, they were lying near the top of a small hill overlooking the harbour.

"Now we must find the tavern," she said.

"How will we know this man Daniels?"

"He has a patch across one eye and a long red beard; that is all I know."

They moved stealthily down the hill, keeping to any available cover. It was quiet so early in the morning so they had no trouble. When they hit the outskirts of the little town, they moved through back alleyways, gradually working their way towards the centre.

Serwaah sniffed the air and pointed to their left, "It is this way."

"How do you know, my love?"

"It has the same smell as the master's cellar, the smell of the firewater they drink at night."

They found the building the smell was coming from and approached the rear. They crouched behind some barrels and paused, wondering what to do next. If they went inside to find Daniels, they'd soon be spotted as runaway slaves. That would spell disaster. But, without going inside, how would they find Daniels? How would they get to the island of freedom?

A man emerged from the tavern. He didn't have an eye patch or a red beard. He went to the far side of the yard and urinated against the fence. Then he belched, spat, and walked unsteadily back inside.

"We are in the right place," Serwaah declared, "but I do not know how we will find Daniels."

A few minutes later, a large black woman came out into the yard. She busied herself with some chores for a while then stopped and looked at the stack of barrels.

"I hears ya breathin'. Ya best come out where I can see ya."

Slowly, Serwaah and Baako came out from behind the barrels and cautiously approached the woman. Serwaah spoke to her, "Pardon us, lady, we looks for Daniels. Can ya show us where is Daniels?"

"I ain't no lady, girl, but I can soon show ya Daniels. Follow me."

The woman led them around the side of the tavern. The alley opened onto the town square and the woman pointed to the middle, "There's Daniels; he been there a couple o' months now."

In the centre of the square stood a gallows where a tattered corpse swung slowly back and forth on a rope. A big crow pecked at one eye socket, the other had the ragged remains of a patch. A few wisps of red hair could still be seen on the corpse's chin.

"He got caught smugglin' runaways like you. Don't

ya fools eva stop 'n tink 'bout all da trouble ya makes for us all?"

"Please, lady, my man gonna be sold. We only run so we together. We don't want make trouble."

"Hmmm well, ya made it all the same," the woman looked them up and down, as if assessing what she should do with them; "which plantation ya from, chile?"

"We from Miller plantation, lady"

The sound of an approaching horse and cart interrupted the conversation. The woman quickly ushered them back down the alley to the tavern yard. She opened the door to a small outhouse and showed them inside. "They be lookin' for ya soon," she whispered; "ya better hide in here for now. Daniels is gone, but I tinks I knows anudder way to help ya. Wait here 'n I'll be back for ya later."

They crouched in the corner of the tiny outhouse, clinging to each other, shaking in fear every time they heard the slightest noise, terrified of being discovered and the dreadful consequences it would bring. As the hours passed slowly by, Serwaah's anxiety mounted. She was plagued by doubts. Could they trust the woman? Why was she helping them? Would she betray them? How was she going to help them anyway? And when was she coming back?

As her doubts and fears whirled around her head, she thought about Danquah too. She was filled with remorse, but not regret. What else could she have done, he would have killed Baako; she had no choice. Even so, she was deeply troubled. She'd killed her own brother; she was a murderer with blood on her hands. How was she going to live with herself? And what must Baako think of her? That was what worried her most.

Time dragged by in their little wooden prison. It grew hot and uncomfortable but they didn't dare move, or even speak, as there seemed to be a constant procession of people outside. Mostly it was just men from the tavern, relieving themselves against the fence, but, late in the afternoon, there was more of a commotion.

"You there, woman, have you seen two young runaways? A girl and a boy both about twenty years old; she's a housemaid and he's a field slave. They've run away from the Miller plantation. There's a reward for their capture."

"No sir, massa, I ain't seen no runaways," it was the woman who'd helped them.

"What's in that shed there?" the unseen voice demanded.

"Oh nothin' massa, jus' some supplies for the tavern; salt pork, molasses, beans 'n stuff."

"Open it up, I need to check inside."

"It's jus' some supplies, massa; it's awfa messy 'n smelly…"

A third voice interrupted the discussion, "Sir, we've just had word the runaways have been spotted near King James's Point. The captain wants us to check it out right away."

"Very good, corporal, let's go"

The sound of footsteps marching away was followed by a blessed silence. Baako and Serwaah breathed a sigh of relief. They huddled together, still terrified of being discovered, but at least their doubts about the woman's intentions had been dispelled.

A few hours later, as it began to go dark, the woman returned. She had two grey blankets, which she handed to the runaways, "Wrap these 'round you, chillen'; ya'll be harder to see. Now, follow me."

She led them through a maze of alleyways and eventually down to the harbour. She took them over a gangplank onto a ship lying at anchor. They made their way down deep inside to a tiny storeroom. The sound of rats scuttling away in the darkness could be heard as they entered.

"Well, it ain't no palace, chillen', but ya'll be safe in here. Ma sister's son, Toby, is a cabin boy. He'll bring ya some food and water. Won't be much, but ya'll get to Hingland halright, I reckons."

"Thank ya, great lady, ya has saved us," Serwaah bobbed her head and smiled. She untied her bundle, reached inside and pulled out one of the silver candlesticks. She offered it to the woman.

The woman gently pushed the candlestick back, "Hell, no, girl, I get caught wit' dat an' I'm up there wit' Daniels. Ya keep it, chile, ya gonna need it. An' don' go showin' it no-one else, neither."

"But why you help us, lady? Why?"

"Ha! It's a long story, chile; let's jus' say I ain't got no love for dem Millers. Now ya keep quiet down here an' ya'll be halright. I gotta be goin' now," she turned and left, taking her lamp with her, leaving Serwaah and Baako alone in the darkness.

The ship set sail the following morning. It was cramped and uncomfortable, and they both felt terribly sick the first few days. But it was a better journey than their last voyage. They slept a lot of the time, dozing in and out of consciousness, barely able to tell if it was night or day in the darkness of the little room. As promised, Toby brought biscuits and water most days and, occasionally, a few scraps of half-eaten meat or fruit. His visits punctuated the monotony of their isolation and gave them their only sense of time passing. They spoke in whispers now and then, but tried to stay as quiet as possible. Serwaah thought more about the blood on her hands, constantly worrying what Baako must be thinking; but she couldn't face the idea of raising the subject while they were trapped in the tiny storeroom.

They crossed the ocean for the second time in their lives and, eventually, the ship came to rest. They could dimly hear the distant sounds of seagulls and shouting men. A few hours later, Toby appeared and led them up to the gangplank. They could barely walk after being confined in the storeroom so long. As they left the ship, Toby said, "Here you free. This is Bristol, Hingland. Law says you free here." They thanked him for his help and he disappeared inside the ship.

It was dark and still on the dockside. They realised it

must be the middle of the night, so they found a secluded spot behind a warehouse and settled down to sleep. The air was cold, but they kept each other warm. When the first rays of the rising sun woke them, they looked around to see people of every hue already hustling and bustling back and forth in the early morning light. Some were dark-skinned like them. No-one was in chains.

Leaving the dock, they wandered the streets of the amazing city. It was gigantic, far bigger than the town they'd escaped from. In the afternoon, they found a shop filled with silver and gold. They went inside and showed the man the candlesticks Serwaah had taken from the Miller house. He gave them a huge bag of coins in exchange.

With a few of the coins they bought food and clothes and found a room at a tavern. When night came, they lay like spoons in the enormous feather bed, Serwaah's back against Baako's chest. He put his arms around her and held her close. She knew she should be happy. Finally, after so much pain and sorrow, they were safe. But guilt clung to her like a dark cloak, she felt bad that she was alive and free when so many others had perished or were still enslaved. Worst of all was the blood on her hands, her brother's blood. She could take it no more, she had to know.

"Baako, my love," she whispered; "can you still love me after what I have done?"

"What do you mean, my love?"

"I killed him, I killed my brother, I am a monster, a murderer; how can you love me now?"

He turned her around to face him, kissed her on the lips, and hugged her closer still, "Serwaah, my love, you saved my life, you did what you had to do. It wasn't murder, it was mercy; it was the bravest thing I have ever seen. You are not a monster, it is the white men who took us that are monsters; it is they that brought evil upon us, they that killed Kofi, Fremah and the others, and they that darkened Danquah's heart and turned him against us. They are the monsters, not you. You are a hero. Of course I still love you; I love you more than ever."

His understanding and forgiveness overwhelmed her, they enveloped her with warmth, just like the arms he held her with, and dispelled the dark cloak of guilt that had been weighing her down. At last, her heart accepted it, they were safe, they were free; all the horrors of so many years were behind them. She closed her eyes and felt the tears begin to rise; tears of joy mixed with sadness, tears of relief mixed with hurt. The familiar voice spoke within her, 'Now,' it said; 'now it is safe.'

For the first time since the white men had come to their village, she began to cry. Baako held her tight as her tears became a torrent and she buried her head in his chest. She sobbed and wailed; weeping her heart out for everything they'd suffered and everyone they'd lost. It lasted all night until, as the dawn lit the room, her shoulders stopped heaving and she lifted her head. Her eyes were red but she gave him the brightest smile he'd seen for years, as bright as when they first met, and she said, "Now we are free, my love, now our life begins."

After a few weeks walking around the city, learning how life went on there, they found a more permanent place to stay and decorated it with reminders of their African homeland. Pride of place in the centre of the mantelpiece was reserved for the little wooden warthog. One evening, Serwaah picked up the ornament and examined it closely. It gave her an idea.

The next day they bought some wood and Baako began carving animal figures. A few days later, Serwaah set up a stall by the docks where she could sell the little wooden models to children of grand ladies and gentlemen passing by on their way to far off places. In time, she also sold jewellery and other things, and they made a good living.

As the years went by, she often thought of the people they'd lost, but only with love and affection. It seemed her tears had washed all the anger and despair away and given them a fresh start. She never heard the strange inner voice again but she didn't forget the strength it had given her when she needed it most. One night, many years after they'd arrived in England, she told Baako about the voice. He nodded in understanding, never doubting her for a moment. "Do you think it might have been my father?" she asked.

"Perhaps, but I think it more likely it was you. You are stronger than you know, my love, you always have been."

They couldn't have children of their own but, as time

passed, they became 'aunt and uncle' to many of their friends and neighbours' children. Their home was always filled with laughter, not to mention an endless menagerie of pets of every description.

It seemed as if they grew happier with every passing year. She was all he wanted and more. He never stopped being grateful to wake up every day, see her beautiful smile, and feel the power of her deep brown eyes pulling him towards her, just as they had always done. He, in turn, was the centre of her world, all that she desired, and her love for him grew deeper every day. Despite his mutilation, he pleased her more than any other man ever could.

They lived together for over forty years. When their time eventually came, they both died peacefully in their sleep, him first, then she followed just two weeks later. She couldn't wait to be with him again.

XXXIII

THE GULLY

en woke to see Susan smiling down at him. He felt refreshed after experiencing their life in Bristol in the eighteenth century. "Thank you, that was wonderful," he smiled back at her.

"You see, there have been happy times."

"Yeah, in the end, although we went through hell to get there"

"Doesn't everyone, one way or another?"

"Hmmm, not like that, I hope," he glanced at his watch, concerned they might have lingered too long in the hollow, but quickly realised he'd only been out a few minutes, just long enough for Susan to get the rest she needed.

She saw the look, "Surprising isn't it, we can live for years in the past while only minutes pass in the present. Still, I suppose we should keep movi…" she stopped and cocked her head to one side. There was a faint sound, but growing steadily louder. They climbed out of the hollow and saw a light in the distance. The source of the sound became apparent. A helicopter was fast approaching, and it was fitted with a searchlight for scanning the desert.

"It's Mortimer, or Hans," she said; "they're looking for us, we need to hide."

"They're probably following our footprints. I know an old army trick that might work, what we need to do is…"

But she was off and running, "Follow me, I know a place."

She led him to a steep-sided gully, surrounded by cliffs. The ground was solid rock, so they were able to cross without fear of leaving footprints. She took him to the far end and pointed to a hole in the cliff, "We can hide in here."

"It's tiny."

"The entrance is small, yes, but it leads to a big cave underneath. There's plenty of space."

"But, how do you know?"

"I've been here before. We both have. Let's get inside and I'll show you."

They crawled through the tiny opening then made their way down the side of the cave. It was pitch-black inside, but Susan found her way easily, she knew every step. Remarkably, Ben discovered he knew the way too, instinctively finding the hand and footholds as if he'd made the descent many times before.

Finally, they reached the floor of the cave. She took his hand and led him to a small niche in the side of the chamber. There was a layer of fine sand on the floor, which meant they could sit in comfort.

"So, when were we here before?" he asked in a low whisper. They might be hidden from sight, but he knew how sound carried in the desert. He couldn't hear the helicopter now, it may have landed and Mortimer or his henchman might be out searching for them on foot. They could be perilously close for all he knew.

"It's easier to show you," she said. Once again, she placed her hand on his forehead and transported him far back in time. But, this time, not far in distance.

*

The two tribes were camped either side of the oasis. Despite their bitter enmity, neither group was prepared to move. Both were determined to spend the hot summer months there, even if they had to share it with the other. There was an uneasy truce and Maalik gave strict orders no-one should speak to any of the other tribe.

Most of Basira's days were taken up by chores but, whenever she had any free time, she liked to go to the gully. It was a charming, secluded spot, where she could sit in the shade of the solitary tree and be alone with her thoughts. It felt like the only place she could truly be herself. At fifteen, she was on the cusp of womanhood, but wanted to stay a child. She was betrothed to Maalik's son, Khalifa, and in no hurry to marry him. He was pleasant enough, but she found him incredibly boring. Her father was excited about the wedding though. Marrying his daughter to the sheikh's eldest son would enhance his standing immeasurably.

One afternoon, she arrived at the gully to find a boy her own age sitting on the rocks. She watched him a few minutes as he idly threw stones at a spot on the other side of the gully. She thought he was handsome, but he must be from the other tribe, so she was forbidden to speak to him. There was nothing to stop her smiling, though.

She slowly walked across to the boy and gave him her brightest smile. He smiled back. She supposed he was probably forbidden to speak too. Hopping up onto the rocks, she sat beside him then picked up a stone and copied what he'd been doing. A game developed between them: he would throw a stone then she would try to hit the same spot. They would both cheer if she managed to get close, or laugh if her stone struck far away.

The cheering and laughter went on for a while until it started to get dark. She got up, smiled at him again, and turned to leave.

"Wait," he spoke at last, breaking the silence, "what is your name?"

"I am Basira," she blushed, feeling a thrill as she realised she was disobeying Maalik's orders by speaking to the boy.

"I am Sabri. Will you come here again, Basira? Perhaps tomorrow?"

"Perhaps," she responded, then turned and ran all the way back to her father's tent.

It was three days before she had another chance to visit

the gully. Her heart sank when she saw Sabri wasn't there. He must have given up on her. Curse it, why had she been so non-committal? That had been stupid, she should have told him the truth; that she would be back when she could. If only she'd been able to come sooner, but her mother kept giving her extra chores. Her youngest brother was teething and things were a little fraught in their tent. As the eldest daughter, she was expected to wash and cook for her father, uncle, and brothers, so she'd been working from dawn to dusk. Now she'd missed her chance to see Sabri again, it was so unfair. Feeling dejected, she tried shouting in the hope he might not be far away, "Sabri, are you here?"

Suddenly, a deep, booming voice filled the air, "Who disturbs the peace of my gully. I am angry."

She span around in circles, looking for the source of the mysterious voice. She heard laughter; evidently someone was enjoying her confusion. After a minute, Sabri appeared from a tiny opening in the rocks at the end of the gully, "You are so funny, Basira. You were looking everywhere for the cave monster."

Now she was laughing too, "Where were you? Do you have a special hiding place?"

"Yes, let me show you."

He led her through the tiny opening, down into a large cave beneath. As they descended, their eyes adjusted to the dim interior. He stood on the floor of the cave with his arms outstretched, "What do you think? I found it yesterday while I was waiting for you."

"It is magnificent, it is like a palace."

He gave her a mock bow, "My gift to you, my princess; your very own palace." They both laughed again.

"Look," she pointed at a niche that held a layer of fine sand suitable for a cushion, "that can be our throne room. Let's sit in there."

They sat and talked for a long time, telling each other about their families, their lives in the tribe and many other things.

"But soon I have to marry Khalifa. Everything will change."

"When will that be?" he asked.

"When the summer is over I will be sixteen. Then we will be married."

"That is a great pity. You deserve someone better, someone who loves you."

She looked down, "You are kind, Sabri, but it is my duty; I have no choice."

A gloomy silence fell over them. Perhaps feeling her sadness, he put his arm around her shoulders. She leaned into him, comforted by the caring warmth of his embrace. He gently lifted her chin and looked into her eyes then bent his head and kissed her softly on the lips.

For the next two months, they saw each other as often as they could. They sat in the cave and kissed, or talked about everything happening in their lives, and everything they wished could happen. By the end of the summer, Basira knew she was in love. The thought of marrying Khalifa was breaking her heart, and she knew Sabri felt the same.

"I cannot do it. I will tell father I refuse," she announced one afternoon.

"But what will happen? He will be very angry. Are you sure you want to face his anger?"

"Yes, I am sure. He cannot make me marry Khalifa, I want to marry you."

"I want that too, but our people do not even speak to each other. How can we marry?"

"We will find a way. I will tell father and he will have to let us. What else can he do?"

"When will you tell him?"

"Tomorrow; I will tell him tomorrow. Then I will meet you here afterwards. Now I must go; it is almost sunset," she kissed him on the lips and started to leave but he held her hand and gently pulled her back.

"Be careful, my love. Do not underestimate your father's anger," he held her close and kissed her tenderly; "I love you so much, please take care."

The following day, she screwed up her courage and went to see her father. She was anxious about his reaction; she knew he would be angry. But she was excited too. It would be difficult at first, but once her father accepted she was in love with Sabri, she would be free to see him more often and, hopefully, marry him soon. She prayed her father would see the happiness their union would bring to the family and how she would make him proud by giving him fine grandsons with Sabri.

"May I speak with you, father?"

"I am busy, child, it will have to wait."

"Please, father, it is important," she could see no sign of anything he might be busy with.

He sighed impatiently, "What do you wish to speak about?"

"I cannot marry Khalifa, father."

"What?" his anger was immediately aroused; "what do you mean? This marriage was arranged long ago. You are marrying Maalik's son, don't you understand what that means for our family… for me? You would dare to disrespect your father… and the sheikh? I will hear none of it, you will marry Khalifa."

"No, father, I cannot, I am in love with another boy."

"In love? *In love!* Who is this other boy? When have you met any other boys?"

"His name is Sabri, father. I meet him at the gully. And I love him."

"Sabri? I don't know any boys called Sabri. There is no-one called Sabri in the tribe."

"He is from the other tribe, father, from the other side of the oasis."

Her father began to shake, his face turned red, his eyes bulged. He gulped, seemingly unable to speak. After a few seconds, he regained some control and started to shout, "*The other tribe!* That is forbidden. Have you any idea how much shame you have brought on this family? I cannot believe what I am hearing. You dishonour me. You dishonour our family. You dishonour our tribe."

"But father, I love him, I cannot marry Khalifa because I love Sabri, I must…"

"Silence," he struck her across the face with the back of his hand, knocking her to the floor. She lay stunned, her ears ringing. She was shocked and frightened, she had known her father would be angry but she never imagined it would be as bad as this. He stood over her, shouting, "Meeting a boy from the other tribe in secret behind my back, betraying me, betraying the family, you have ruined everything you disgusting little whore." He kicked her in the stomach, winding her badly, then bent down and pushed his hand inside her robe, roughly probing her most intimate region, "Praise Allah, at least you are intact, that is something to be thankful for. There is only one thing to be done."

Grabbing her by the hair, he dragged her across the floor into the main body of the tent; ignoring her desperate gasps as she tried to regain her breath. He shouted for her uncle, Karim, and her eldest brother, Hasib. She was still lying, stunned and winded at his feet, when they arrived. He spoke to them urgently in hushed tones. Then the three men turned her on her stomach, pulled her hands behind her back, and bound them to her feet. Her brother fetched a sack, and they bundled her in, tying it closed. "Hasib, tell Maalik we will meet him in the gully. We will do this in the place she chose to dishonour us," her father informed the others.

Inside the sack, Basira began to recover from her father's blows. She struggled against her bonds but soon realised it was useless. She tried to shout, but the sack muffled her voice. Her mind raced, wondering what her father was going to do. Would he beat her, perhaps whip her even? Why had he sent for Maalik? Was he planning some sort of public humiliation to prove his loyalty? What if they banished her? She was afraid to think what form her punishment would take, but what terrified her was the thought of not seeing Sabri again. Whatever they did, however much it hurt; she could take it as long as she could be with him afterwards.

Peering through the sackcloth, she could just make out enough to see Hasib returning. As soon as he was back, the men carried her out of the tent and tied her to the back of a camel. Hasib led the animal while her father and Karim marched alongside. She tried to speak to her father as she bounced inside the sack, begging his forgiveness, asking what he was going to do to her. "Be quiet, you filthy whore," he snapped, giving her a vicious slap on the head to emphasise his point.

At the gully, they took her down, pulled her out of the sack, and dragged her to the solitary tree where she loved to sit in the shade. They tied her to the trunk, stretching her arms around it in front of her. Her father ripped open the back of her robe, exposing her naked flesh. Straining her neck to see behind her, she watched him go to the camel and pull his riding crop from the saddle. "Father, please, I have done nothing wrong. I cannot help loving Sabri. We have only kissed, nothing more."

"Silence, harlot, you have done much more. You have brought dishonour on our family," he turned to her brother; "Hasib, muzzle your whore sister." He handed the boy a short length of rope. Hasib walked up behind her and stretched the rope across her mouth, tying it tight behind her head. When he had finished, he turned to leave but suddenly stopped, bowing low. "He's coming," he whispered urgently.

Basira looked over her shoulder to see her father and uncle also bowing low as Maalik strode towards them, his long black robe flowing behind him. Her fear heightened at the sight of the sheikh. He had always scared her. She remembered the time, many years ago, when he had come to see her father. The men had talked for a while then she had been told to stand in front of Maalik and let him examine her. He had touched her in places that made her feel ashamed then pronounced, "I will not take her myself, but she will make a fine wife for Khalifa."

Repulsed by Maalik's touch, she was relieved he did not want her for himself. His parting words meant little to her then, but came back to her now, "See she remains pure. Any threat, no matter how small, must be dealt with at once. I will hold you responsible, Walid."

"Yes, my lord," her father had grovelled before Maalik, just as he was doing now.

"All is ready, my lord. She has been tempted, but she is still pure, I swear it. I will beat some sense into her, you will see. She will not stray again; she will be an obedient wife for your son. How many strokes do you advise my lord? Twenty? Thirty?"

"It is too late for that," Maalik responded, "she has

dishonoured the tribe; she cannot be my son's wife. She has lost her ird, she is worthless now," he picked something up and held it out to Basira's father; "you know what you must do."

Her father stared at the object in Maalik's hand, "Er, yes, er… yes, of course, my lord." He dropped his crop and took the object, then beckoned to Hasib, calling him over. "You heard," he handed the object to Hasib; "you gather more, Karim and I will get her ready."

Basira was shaking as her father and uncle untied her from the tree, turned her around, and tied her again, facing outwards, with her arms stretched painfully behind her. They passed another rope across her forehead and tied it around the tree, holding her head firmly in place.

Hasib was stacking rocks in front of her. She stared in horror at the growing pile as she realised what they were going to do. She was trying to speak, to beg for her life, but the rope in her mouth stopped her forming coherent words. Surely they wouldn't? Surely they just wanted to scare her? Oh please, don't let this be it, she needed to see Sabri, she loved him so much, it couldn't end like this.

Her father and Karim crossed the gully and stood behind Hasib just as he finished his work. The three men looked expectantly at Maalik. "You may begin the punishment," the sheikh declared.

Basira shivered. Terror coursed through her body like a bolt of lightning. Tears flowed down her cheeks, not just from fear, but also despair, knowing she would never see

Sabri again. 'Goodbye my love,' she thought, and braced herself for what was to come.

Each of the executioners picked up a rock and threw. Hasib missed altogether; Karim hit her in the chest; her father's rock hit her in the face, crushing her nose and sending blood flooding down her throat. They all picked up a second rock and threw again. Their collective aim improved. She took a blow on the forehead that stunned her; another rock broke her jaw and smashed out most of her teeth.

The stoning continued until they'd exhausted their ammunition. There was a pause while Hasib collected the rocks. Basira was barely conscious, but her ragged breathing echoed in her ears and the intolerable pain coming from every part of her body told her she was still alive. Through eyes blurred and misty from the blood dripping into them, she watched her brother restoring the rock pile. As soon as he was finished, they began again.

When the rocks had been thrown a second time, Maalik walked across to examine her. She was battered and broken, more a mass of bleeding flesh than a living girl; but she was still breathing. He looked closely at her. One of her eyes was gone but she stared back at him from the other, out of a jumbled mess of blood and bone. "That's one I owed you," he hissed; "there will be more." Then he turned and addressed her father, "I think that should be enough. We can leave the birds to finish her. Would you agree?"

"Er, er… yes, of course; that would be best… I agree."

Maalik strode away. Her father ran after him, extolling the virtues of her sister, imploring the sheikh to consider her as a match for Khalifa. Karim and Hasib led the camel away. Basira was left alone, with nothing but her pain and the tortured sound of her breathing for company. She slipped in and out of consciousness, edging closer to death, but she clung to life with a single thought: she had to see Sabri one last time.

*

Sabri arrived in the gully at the usual hour, excited to see Basira as always, but filled with anxiety as he worried about her planned confrontation with her father and speculated how it might have gone. He stared in astonishment at the gruesome figure tied to the tree, wondering who it could be, what they had done to deserve such a fate. Then he looked at its feet and saw Basira's sandals. The shock hit him with the sudden ferocity of a desert sandstorm. His blood ran cold. He fell to his knees in front of her and began to wail.

She coughed and he realised she was still alive. Quickly, he untied the ropes binding her to the tree and her bloody body fell into his arms. He sat cross-legged on the ground, hugging her to his chest, "Oh Basira, my love, what have they done to you."

She made a gurgling sound as she looked up at him with her remaining eye. He bent down and kissed the tattered flesh around what was left of her mouth, even the teeth that had made up her lovely smile were gone. He sat back, her blood coating his lips, and whispered, "I love you, Basira."

He sat there the rest of the day, and through the night, holding the bloody mess that had been the beautiful girl he loved. She probably died soon after he arrived, but he wasn't letting go until he was certain.

By sunrise he knew she was gone. He took her to the cave and carried her down to the little niche they had shared so often. He laid her at the back and covered her with his robe. "Now you can be in your palace forever, my princess," he gently kissed her broken forehead then climbed out of the cave.

XXXIV

THE CAVE

Ben woke feeling completely disoriented. He searched his mind, trying to recall where he was. Slowly, it came back to him. The cave; yes, of course, he was in the cave by the oasis. But when was it? And who was he?

He sensed a presence next to him in the darkness, "Who's there?"

"It's me, Susan. You're back in the present."

"Oh, yes... right, yes... God, it feels so strange... I mean, we were just here. I, er..." he reached behind him and felt something jagged. It was a bone, a broken rib bone. "That's..."

"Yes, there you are, right where I left you."

"You mean this has been my tomb for... for I don't know how long?"

"About six hundred years, I reckon. Not every day you get to visit your own tomb."

"God, that's freaky. That's my skeleton lying there. That was me, I was Basira. Those bastards stoned me to death; my own family. They treated me like an animal, like a possession to be bought and sold, just 'cause I was a girl. They didn't care what I thought or anything. It was terrible."

Susan laughed, "You don't see things from a female perspective often, do you? That's been a woman's lot throughout most of history. Things have really only just started getting better."

"No, you're right," he frowned; "I do seem to be a man most of the time. I've been wondering about that. It seems a bit odd. I mean, if we *can* change then surely it ought to be fifty-fifty."

"Well, from what I've seen, every soul can be born as either a man or a woman and can happily change gender from one life to the next. But there are some, like us, who have a preference. You tend to be male, I prefer to be female. Despite some of its drawbacks," she chuckled.

"But why; like you said, women have had it pretty tough."

"Being a woman just seems right. I've been a man, but I don't think it suits me. And yes, it's true, women have often been badly treated, but it does feel good to be a woman. Plus, best of all, women can bring life into the world, which is just the most phenomenal thing. I'm glad I'm a woman now, anyway," she smiled.

"Why?"

"Well…" she tossed her head. At that moment, the moon rose above the cliffs and cast its light through the entrance to the cave, illuminating her golden hair as it swirled around her. 'My God, she's stunning,' he thought, almost as if seeing her for the first time. He stared at her in the moonlight. She stared back with the same intensity. Both had the same reaction. They lunged forward with all the passion and hunger twelve thousand years of anticipation could create. They kissed so hard their lips bled. Their hands explored each other's bodies; they began to pull off each other's clothes. His lips moved down to her breasts, her hands were running across his chest and buttocks.

He pulled back and whispered hoarsely, "But we can't, you've got that damn contraption on."

"No, we can't. But there are other things we can do," she pulled him close again.

*

As the first light of dawn filtered through the cave's tiny entrance, it found them lying naked in each other's arms. Almost naked, one thing separated them: her metal underwear.

"So, I guess it's true then," he said.

"What's that?"

"We are meant to be together."

She laughed quietly, "Yes, I guess we are."

"Do you think we're safe here? I mean, if we can remember this cave, won't Mortimer remember it too?"

"I don't think so, he was never here. Maalik never came closer than the tree."

"But he'll remember the gully. Surely he'll figure out we must be somewhere close?"

"We'll be OK for a bit, today at least. I can't explain it, but I can sort of shield us while we're in here. I don't think I can keep it up for more than a day, but we're safe for now."

They lay in silence for a while, enjoying the comfort of each other's bodies and the peace that came from knowing they belonged together. At last, she looked up into his face and asked, "How much do you remember?"

"You mean about the past? Past lives?"

"Yes, what have you remembered?"

"Well, er… let me see," he thought for a minute. "Starting most recently, back in the '70s I was Bazza, the guy from The Vomix," he shook his head in amazement; "I can't believe I wrote those songs. Pity I don't get the royalties," he grinned briefly then suddenly frowned; "you were Sammie, of course. My God, you had a bad time there; I wish I'd…"

"It's OK; you didn't know what was happening," she squeezed him tight; "go on, what about before that?"

"Well, you were Sarah the nurse and I met you in three different lives: little Brian, who died in hospital; Brendan, who died on D-Day; and Billy, who died at the Somme. Before that, I was…" he went on to recount the lives he'd experienced since his crash in the Highlands, until he'd gone back as far as he could; "… then, right at the beginning, we were Bakara and Shebana, drowning on the beach. Well, Mamboja drowned us. Or Mortimer,

I mean. He always gets us, one way or another, doesn't he? Anyway, that's the lot, that's what I've seen so far. How about you? Have you seen it all?"

"Most of it, I think; there are a few blanks, but they're short. I don't think there are any lives missing. I haven't experienced it all yet, but I can sort of 'see' it, if that makes sense? It's like looking down on a vast expanse of land from the top of a mountain, only it's time, not land, thousands of years laid out before me."

"That must be amazing."

"It is, yes, truly amazing. Dozens and dozens of different lives, in different places, being different people, and I can visit any of them. Anything except this life, oddly," she frowned and a look of sadness passed briefly across her face before she continued; "but so many memories, so much experience, it's all there if you know how to look. Everything you've ever learned, every skill, craft, piece of knowledge, you can recall it all. And the people you've known, people who've been dead for centuries, millennia, you can bring them back to life in your mind. It's wonderful, Ben, it's like time travel."

"Except you can't change anything"

"Just as well," she shrugged, "it would be chaos. You'd never know where you stood."

"I suppose not. I wish I could change some of it though," he sighed. "So, is there much I haven't seen?"

"Oh yes, lots, although you've seen most of the recent stuff"

He laughed, "By 'recent', you mean a few centuries?"

"Yes," she laughed with him, "well, it's all relative when you've been around for nearly twelve thousand years."

"Phew," he whistled, "it's just incredible. I'm still struggling to believe it."

"I know. It takes some getting used to," she smiled warmly.

"And you can do kaetchemos now."

"Kaetchemos?"

"Yeah, er, that's what Del Rivera called them. It's like a trance where you can relive the past, same as when you dream, except you're awake. Del Rivera put me in a few of them. Only he couldn't choose where I went. You seem to be able to."

"Yes, I guess I can," she suddenly sat up; "you know, I hadn't questioned it until now. I learned how to navigate my past while I was chained up at the villa. I didn't have much else to do and I thought I might find out something useful. After we escaped… well, I didn't even think about it, to be honest, I just knew I could take you where I wanted. I acted on instinct." She slowly shook her head, "I suppose some of Mortimer's powers must have rubbed off on me."

"Or he's awoken powers already within you."

"Hmmm, maybe I am a witch, after all."

"Well, if you are, you're a good one," he sat up and kissed her again, holding her close, gently caressing her soft skin.

After a while, she pulled back and looked deep into his eyes, "We have to go back, you know."

"*Go Back!* You must be joking."

"We have to go back and confront Mortimer. There's no point in running."

"But surely we should get away… find someone to take that thing off you… become a twin soul, like Del Rivera said. Then we can deal with Mortimer. We should confront him when we're strongest, that's our best chance."

"Think about it, Ben, eight hundred years ago, he made a device even the best locksmith in the country couldn't open. Now he's learned how to defy death and consume other people's souls. Just how secure do you think he's made this bloody belt?"

"Well, I don't know, there must be someone who can help. I've still got friends in the army, we could…"

"Look, we've seen it before; this thing would kill me in the end, like when I was Charlotte. Even if there was anyone who could get it off, Mortimer would probably track us down first."

"I thought you said you could shield us?"

"In here, for a day or two, yes, but this is a special place. Once we leave, he'll start to sense us. He'll find us, he always does. He'd catch us unawares and have his chance to destroy us. Even if he only killed us, it would give him decades to pursue his ambitions without interference. We can't take that risk. He told me his plans are nearing completion. This time will be worse than the Black Death. He's going to create an army of soulless monsters to enslave the human race. We have to go back, Ben; we have to stop him now."

She'd spoken firmly, with hardening resolve, but she looked aside, and softly added, "Or at least we've got to try."

"OK, yeah," he nodded, "I guess you're right, we have to go back and deal with him." Then he too looked aside and lowered his voice, "I can't say I fancy our chances, though. I don't think we've ever beaten him in a fair fight. And there's something Sleeping Bear said…"

"We've got no choice, Ben, it's our destiny; we're the only ones who can do it," she hugged him tightly. "We *have* beaten him, anyway. I beat him when I was She Wolf; you told me you'd seen it."

"Yes," he laughed, "but you only beat him 'cause that other girl flashed at him…"

"That was Del Rivera."

"What? Really?"

"Oh yes, that was him, helping us out. He was Frances, or Feathered Dove, as she later became. He's helped us many times, or at least he's tried. He was Captain Smith in the First World War; he was poor, brave, Fremah when we were taken as slaves; he was my sister Florence in the twelfth century…"

"Florence? I thought he was the locksmith, how can he have been Florence?"

"No, he wasn't the locksmith, he was definitely Florence."

"But I was married to her, we, er… we…"

"Yes, I know," she laughed; "takes some getting used to, this reincarnation thing, doesn't it?" She stopped and thought for a minute before continuing, "Anyway, who says it has to be a fair fight? I think I have something that might help."

"What do you have? You ran from the villa with nothing but the clothes you were wearing. What can you possibly have?"

"Ah yes," she chuckled, "well, I've been here before, you see."

"Yes, I know, you left me here six hundred years ago."

"Oh, I've been here more recently than that. Do you remember when you were Captain Basil Cunningham? You died at Isandlwana fighting the Zulus?"

"Yes, I remember," Ben felt his stomach where the assegai had plunged into him.

"And I was Lieutenant Sebastian Barnes. We loved each other, but never dared admit it?"

"I know; I'm sorry."

She smiled, gently resting her hand on his cheek, "Don't be sorry. Those were different times; it wasn't an easy thing to admit then. And we were both equally to blame. The point is, after you were killed, I had to find a way to hide my grief. I couldn't show my feelings to anyone; I was expected to carry on as if you were just another fallen comrade, even though my heart was breaking. So I joined the Royal Ordnance Archaeological Unit. We travelled all over the world. It was the distraction I needed. A few years after you died, we went on an expedition to the Scottish Highlands, where we recovered some early fourteenth century artefacts, including a remarkably well-preserved claymore, painstakingly wrapped with a great deal of care before it was buried. Instantly, I knew there was something special about it. I could feel a certain, er… power, within it. I took a risk and smuggled it away from the unit. My next posting was to the Middle East, a remote corner of the Ottoman Empire where we had permission to do some excavations. Something drew me to this cave. I climbed inside and found the skeleton behind us. I touched it and I knew… well, not everything… but enough. I had the claymore in my tent and I…"

Breaking off, she turned around then started digging into the sand beneath Basira's skeleton. After a moment, Ben began to help. He felt something cold and metallic. He pulled it from the sand and found himself holding an ancient sword, a Scottish claymore, almost five feet in length, four inches wide by the hilt, tapering to a vicious point at the tip. His fingers tingled where they touched the sword; his head began to spin…

XXXV

AN ORDINARY LIFE

Bryce had fought with Wallace from the beginning, back when they were just a band of outlaws. He fought with him all through the war and stood beside him when he was defeated at Falkirk. He went into hiding with him and privately wept when he was captured and executed. He escaped from the English and fled far into the north, where they couldn't follow. Or, at least, they wouldn't. They knew they weren't safe.

He tried to settle down to an ordinary life, eking out a meagre existence on a croft by the sea. But his days with Wallace filled his dreams every night. He heard stories of the Bruce's rebellion in the south and considered joining him. But he wasn't sure if he trusted the new king. Bruce had sided with the English before. The whole thing seemed to have petered out now anyway.

At least there was Sionag to distract him in the daytime. She was his neighbour's daughter and the most beautiful thing he'd ever seen. Her long, flowing hair was a vibrant red; her emerald-green eyes seemed to see into his soul. Whenever she was near, he would find an excuse to talk to her. He had charged the English cavalry armed only with a dagger; he had climbed cliffs a thousand feet high; he had faced the most extreme dangers imaginable; but he couldn't find the courage to ask her to step out with him. Her smile reduced him to a blushing boy; her very glance thrilled him to the core. He was hopelessly in love. But he was thirty-four years old and she was what, perhaps twenty at most? Why would she have any interest in him?

He sighed. It was hopeless. Any day now, she would find a boy her own age and that would be that. He should find himself an aging spinster or widow. He needed to be more realistic about his prospects.

On a sunny morning in the autumn of 1306, he was digging in the field by the beach when he saw her coming by with a basket of mussels. "Mistress Sionag, I trust yae are well this fine morning?"

"Why, aye, I am most hearty thank yae, Master Bryce. And how dae I find yae?"

"Oh, er… very well, thank yae."

She started to move on, but he was desperate not to let her go, "Will yae be at kirk on Sunday, Mistress Sionag?"

"Waell, of course, Master Bryce, where else would I be on the Sabbath?"

"Aye, of course… er, aye, so will I."

She smiled at him, "And will yae be at the ceilidh on Saturday, Master Bryce?"

"Oh, er, waell, I dunnae ken, I dunnae always feel like that sort of er… waell yae ken, A'm nae very guid at dancin' and er…"

"Waell it wud be a great shame if yae didnae come. A'm sure I cud help yae wi' the dancin' if yae wanted," she smiled again, so warmly he thought he might melt, then she turned away and continued up the beach, skipping along beside the waves.

On Saturday afternoon he washed his clothes in the sea and went for a swim. Dried off and dressed in his freshly cleaned garments, he set off for the village just before sunset. He arrived as it was going dark and entered the village hall as the ceilidh band began to play.

The dancing was subdued for the first hour until Tam, widely regarded as the neighbourhood rogue, produced a meat stew and a barrel of whisky. The stew was the best thing Bryce had ever tasted. Washed down with copious amounts of whisky, it was like nectar from the Gods.

As soon as everyone had eaten their fill, the dancing resumed, now far more energetic than before. Bryce was content to sit and watch the rest of the village enjoying themselves, until Sionag came over to him. "Are yae ready fae me tae help yae wi' the dancin' now, Master Bryce?" she smiled down at him as she stood with her hands clasped before her, swaying gently from side to side in time with the music.

"Er, I… I…" he stammered, but she reached down, grasped his hand, and pulled him to his feet. As his ear reached her lips, she whispered, "Come wi' me, ma brave sir, I will show yae how tae dance."

They danced for hours. He staggered as best he could, clumsily at first, but grew better by the minute with her tuition. She adeptly avoided his wayward feet and gradually coached him to step more gracefully. By the time the band was playing the last reel, they were moving in unison.

The ceilidh came to an end and the revellers began to drift away. "Wud yae like me tae help yae tak yaer faether hame?" he asked, looking across at the old man, who had drifted into a drunken stupor.

"Och, dunnae warry aboot him, he'll find his way; yae can walk me hame tha," she stuck out her arm for Bryce to take and they strolled out of the hall together. They walked in comfortable silence, their path lit by starlight and the luminescence of the sea. Finally, they reached the little house where she lived with her father.

"Waell, I bid yae guid night, Mistress Sionag."

"Are yae nae gonnae kiss me then?"

"Waell, I, er... I, er... I wud like tae, aye, er... but am I nae a bit auld fae..."

His modest demurral was silenced as she reached up, grasped his face in her hands, and pulled his lips down to hers. She kissed him long and passionately. When she finally released him, she said, "Yae silly mon, A'm yaers if yae wan'. Here fae the askin' if yae wan' me," she turned her face slightly downwards and looked up at him with her sparkling emerald eyes; "I will see yae at kirk tomorrow."

She held his gaze for a moment then skipped away into the darkness and disappeared inside her tiny house.

Bryce walked slowly back to his neighbouring croft, thinking long and hard about what she'd said, and what it meant for them both. In the morning he set off early, ready for Sunday worship. He knew people in the village whispered behind his back, saying things like, 'He's dangerous, he was in the war.' He knew there would be a lot of opposition; her father would probably be against him most of all. But he'd made a decision and he was determined to see it through, no matter how much it would hurt if it went wrong.

Throughout the service, Bryce and Sionag exchanged furtive glances across the crowded pews. Whenever he caught her eye, she smiled broadly back at him, her eyes twinkling in the light streaming through the stained glass windows, her hair glowing like fire.

Finally, the service was over and the congregation filed out into the bright autumn sunshine. Bryce was a minute behind Sionag but, as soon as he got outside, he made his way to where she was standing next to her father. He glanced nervously at the old man then took her hand in both of his and got down on one knee, "Mistress Sionag, will yae…"

He stopped as he heard the familiar but unexpected sound of armed cavalry approaching. He stood up and turned to see Lord MacFinnan and six of his castle guard riding towards the kirk. Had the laird recognised him as a rebel? Had someone informed on him? If he was arrested for treason, anyone with him would be in danger. Quietly, he moved away from Sionag and her father, to the edge of the crowd.

MacFinnan and his men rode into the kirkyard, trampling the flowers lying on some of the recent graves. The laird held up a hand and the column came to a halt facing the anxious villagers.

"Three calves are missing from my prize herd. Does anyone know their whereabouts?" MacFinnan demanded.

A few people murmured and glanced around at each other. No-one dared look at Tam. Now they knew where the meat in the stew had come from… but they were too loyal to point the finger. Tam turned his face to the ground.

"Very well, you have taken three of mine; I will take three of yours," MacFinnan turned to the captain of his guard; "put three of them in irons and take them to the castle."

The captain and his men dismounted, then moved forward and seized three people from the crowd.

"No, you fools, not decrepit old men and ugly crones," MacFinnan snapped, "take what matters to them most, take three maidens."

The guards released their captives and seized new ones: Imogen, the baker's daughter; little Ailsa, just sixteen, and recently engaged to Red Willie … and Sionag.

The crowd pressed in around the unfortunate girls. The guards pushed them back hard, hitting out at anyone who tried to interfere. There was much snarling and muttering but everyone fell back. Each guard carried a lethal claymore battle sword, a weapon so mighty it had to be wielded two-handed to be effective. Few men could hold it in a single hand for long. By contrast, the villagers had been forbidden to carry weapons since King Edward had taken control of Scotland and, although Bryce knew Tam, Red Willie, and a few others had daggers hidden in their socks, their tiny blades were no match for the claymores.

He tried to reach Sionag, but he couldn't get through the throng that separated them. He cursed himself for leaving her side; he thought he'd been doing the right thing, but instead he'd abandoned her when she needed him most. Finally breaking free from the crowd, he came face to face with one of the guards, a big, ugly man with a dark beard. Evidently sensing trouble the guard drew his sword and levelled it at Bryce's chest. Bryce stepped back and held his arms out by his sides in a gesture of surrender. There was nothing he could do... for now.

As the armed men put the girls in iron manacles, MacFinnan declared, "I take these maidens as compensation for my stolen cattle. For each calf returned to me, I will release one of the maidens. You have until sunset tomorrow. Then the maidens hang."

The guards tied ropes to the girls' manacles and attached them to the saddle on one of the horses. MacFinnan took his place at the head of the column then led it away, with the captive girls pulled along at the rear. Imogen and Ailsa were crying, while Sionag stared at

Bryce, her eyes filled with a sadness that struck deep into his heart.

As soon as MacFinnan and his men were out of sight, the crowd rounded on Tam. "Yae took them bloody calves, didnae yae?" demanded Imogen's father.

"A'll kill yae," Red Willie lunged at Tam, ready to punch him in the face.

Bryce pulled the boy back, "There's no use us fightin' among oorsells, we hae tae save our womenfolk." He stared down the angry mob, waiting for the fire in their hearts to subside enough for them to see reason. Then he turned to the thief, "Now, Tam, jus' tell us wha' yae did wi' the laird's cattle. Did they aw gae in the stew?"

"Aye," confirmed Tam, staring at the ground, "we ate 'aem aw last night, aw trae of 'aem. A'm sarry, I didnae think anythin' like this wud happen."

"Nae, yae didnae bloody think at aw, did yae? Now ma sweet lassie is gonnae hang 'cause o' yae, yae bloody thievin' fool," the baker's anger had turned his face a bright crimson.

"Look, A'm sarry. I said A'm sarry, didnae I? Wha' dae yae wan' me tae dae?"

"A'll tell yae wha' yae can dae; wha' we are aw gonnae dae. We are gonnae git the lassies back," said Bryce.

"How we gonnae dae that?" asked Red Willie.

"Yae aw gather as many weapons as yae can. Knives, clubs, rakes, wha'ever yae can git… swords if yae hae 'aem. Meet me at the castle at low tide tonight. We are gonnae break in and free the lassies," Bryce faced the gathered crowd, scanning the faces of the men, trying to look each in the eye in turn. Some met his gaze with chins raised, ready to fight alongside him; others avoided his stare and looked at the ground. In a corner of the kirkyard, an old man sat with his head in his hands, his scrawny back heaving as he sobbed. Bryce went over and put a hand on his shoulder, "We will bring her back, Alistair, I promise yae." Sionag's father stared up at him, his red-rimmed eyes streaming with tears. There was blood running from a gash on his forehead, where a guard had hit him as he tried to pull the man away from his daughter. The old man gulped and nodded but couldn't find the strength to speak.

Bryce began to stride away. "And where are yae garn?" Red Willie called after him.

"Tae git ma sword, then tae the castle; A'll meet yae there later."

*

Bryce headed for nearby Beinn Dearg. He climbed the hill for over an hour, coming eventually to a secluded spot hidden among the crags. Kneeling on the ground, he dug into the peaty soil with his bare hands until his fingers touched cold steel. As he pulled his mighty claymore from the earth, he felt the strange mixture of fear and excitement that always came before battle. He'd missed that feeling, even though it was the prelude to pain and death. He'd never enjoyed killing for its own sake, but fighting in a good cause sent a thrill through his veins. Wallace had been a good cause. This was an even better one. He would fight to the death to free Sionag, hopefully with the help of the village, alone if he had to.

Shortly after sunset, he waded across the loch to the island where MacFinnan's castle stood. At high tide, this crossing was impossible; at low tide it was an easy paddle. Just now, the water came up to his chin, and he had to be careful not to lose his footing in the strong current, nor to make any splashes that might alert the castle guards.

Reaching the island, he could see the castle was heavily guarded, but he knew from experience there was always a way in. He circled the tiny island and found it: a small, unguarded, gate on the far side, hidden from view on the loch shore.

Entering the castle, he made his way stealthily through the interior, occasionally hiding in the shadows as a sentry passed by. Eventually, he found the dungeons. He ached to go to Sionag, but he could make out the profiles of several guards in the dim light. He hid behind a corner and, as his eyes adjusted to the darkness, took stock of the situation.

The girls were chained to the wall, hanging by their arms. Imogen and Ailsa were slumped forward, their heads bowed, chests heaving as they wept. Sionag held her head up, watching her captors.

Thick iron bars separated the girls from three guards sitting around a table. A further two stood either side of the door to the girls' cell. All five wore battle armour. The two at the door had a claymore at their side; the three at the table each had one within easy reach.

Counting the sentries he'd passed made a total of at least eight armed guards defending the dungeon. Combining this with the narrow passageways and tiny entrance gate meant a direct assault would be suicide for the men from the village.

He considered his chances of freeing the girls on his own. He could probably dispose of the guards by the door before the others had time to react, and then maybe take out two more, but five? And that was assuming the guards were of average ability. It only took one to be more skilled and he would almost certainly be defeated. Even if he succeeded down here, he would still have to fight his way past at least three sentries on the way out. No, it was too risky. He was willing to die for Sionag, but not before she was safe.

Reluctantly, he decided to find another way to save the lassies. He looked at Sionag. The simple green dress she'd worn to kirk was torn. He could make out a bruise on her shoulder and a large, red mark on her face, beneath her eye. It looked like she had put up some resistance before they chained her to the wall. Glancing at the largest of the guards at the table, Bryce recognised him as the ugly brute he'd encountered earlier. His looks had not improved; there were three parallel scratches across his cheek, undoubtedly Sionag's work. Good for her. Looking at her again, he felt sure she was staring back at him, but she couldn't possibly see him in the dark passageway, could she?

He began to turn, ready to leave. The tip of his sword scraped the wall. The big guard squinted into the darkness in Bryce's direction and started to rise to his feet. At that moment, Sionag began to scream at her captors and all eyes turned to her. Bryce could scarcely believe the savagery of the abuse pouring out of her sweet mouth. She *had* seen him, and she was giving him the diversion he needed to creep away unnoticed. He nodded in acknowledgement, then turned and made his way out of the castle.

At low tide, Bryce watched from his hiding place in the bushes near the base of the castle as a group of villagers silently crossed the shallows. He was disappointed to see only eight in the party. Red Willie led, followed by Tam, and Imogen's father. Limping along at the back, on unsteady old legs, was Alistair. Five of the group had knives, two had clubs, none had a sword, and Alistair had nothing at all.

"Where are the rest?" Bryce demanded in a whisper.

"They wudnae come, the cowards," hissed Red Willie.

"Wha' are yae daen here?" Bryce asked Alistair, who could barely walk, never mind fight.

"A'm here fae Sionag. Dunnae try tae stop mae."

"Waell, aw right then, I understand, but stay at the back when the fightin' starts."

"Yae'll nae put me at the back, laddie; tha's ma wee lassie in there," the old man fixed Bryce with a stubborn stare and he knew any further discussion would be pointless.

"Aw right, listen everywan," Bryce began; "the lassies are in the dungeon. They are tae heavily guarded fae us tae git tae 'aem. We've gae wan chance an' tha's when they bring 'aem oot tae the scaffold in the courtyard. We will hae tae hide 'til then, an' then storm oor way in, straight up the main steps. Tha' will nae be easy, but A'll lead the way. Now aw git some sleep if yae can, an' make sure yae are waell hidden, it will be dawn soon."

The villagers took cover in the bushes. Bryce inspected everyone's position to make sure they wouldn't be seen when the sun came up, then found a place of his own and settled down to wait.

The day passed agonisingly slowly. His back began to ache from lying on the rough ground so long. He must be getting old; he never had this problem when he was with Wallace. He daydreamed about past glories: the raid on Scone, the victory at Stirling Bridge, storming the castle at Duncrennan… and many others. As the long afternoon finally drew to a close, he watched land, sea, and sky changing colour while the setting sun slowly dropped towards the horizon, bestowing its warm glow on everything. Just as the fiery orb touched the ocean at the entrance to the loch, he heard the sound of chains. The lassies were being brought up from the dungeon.

"This is it lads, git ready," he whispered; "but keep quiet 'til I gae the word."

The villagers moved into a crouch, ready for the attack. They heard a loud voice coming from inside the castle.

"His mighty grace, Lord Duncan James Edgar MacFinnan, appointed by divine right of His Royal

Highness, King Edward, governor of these lands, hereby decrees, inasmuch that he has rightly and justly taken these three maidens of the parish of Lochpool in place of his rightful property unlawfully taken from him by persons unknown, and inasmuch as said property has not been returned to his lordship by this, the appointed hour, that said maidens' lives and liberties are now forfeit, and proper and just punishment for the crime shall be carried out on their persons. Maidens of Lochpool, you are hereby condemned to death by hanging, sentence to be carried out forthwith."

"Wha' the hell did aw tha' mean?" whispered Red Willie.

"It means the lassies are in place an' we dunnae hae lang," Bryce replied; "aw right lads, this is it, on the count of trae; wan… tae… trae… CHARGE!"

The villagers burst out of the bushes and ran for the castle steps. Bryce was in the lead, his claymore held high. Red Willie followed close behind, dagger in hand, then Tam, also carrying a dagger, Imogen's father, wielding a club, the other villagers, and lastly old Alistair, limping along at the rear.

The men guarding the entrance were taken by surprise and slow to react. They turned to face the oncoming assault and began to descend the steps towards them, but they were unprepared and out of formation. Bryce thrust his claymore into the first man's throat before he had chance to raise his sword. As the man fell to the ground, Bryce pulled his sword free and swung it at the next one in his path. The second guard had his sword raised high, ready to bring it down on the assailants. Bryce plunged his claymore into a gap in his armour and he too fell to the ground. Two more now stood ahead of Bryce, blocking his ascent. He ran towards them and continued fighting his way upwards, but the speed of the attack began to slow.

As Bryce engaged the guards, the other villagers rushed to join the battle. Red Willie moved fastest. He put his dagger into a guard's eye before the man could turn towards him in his heavy armour. Willie's victim fell over the side of the steps and lay dead on the ground below. Another heavily armoured guard lumbered towards Willie, but the boy quickly sidestepped him and ran through the main gate.

The guard Willie had evaded continued down the steps towards the other villagers. He swung his sword at Tam but the thief dodged beneath it and followed Willie. Next came Imogen's father, swinging his club at the guard's head. This time, the guard was swiftest and put his sword through the baker's chest. The baker collapsed in a heap, clutching his wound, gasping for breath. The mortally injured man blocked the other villagers' path and the guard turned his attention to Bryce.

Still fighting the others in front of him, Bryce was unable to bring his sword to bear in time as the man who'd struck down the baker aimed his weapon and pulled back, ready to drive it into his side. The man lunged forward, his blade heading straight for Bryce.

From out of nowhere, Alistair jumped into the path of the sword, taking it in his shoulder. The startled guard stepped back in surprise, pulling his sword free. He teetered on the edge of the steps. Alistair leaped at him and they both fell to the ground.

The other villagers were now able to move forward. Two of them attacked the guard on Bryce's left, allowing him to focus on the one to his right, pushing him up the steps with the ferocity of his offensive.

But the villagers were poorly armed and inexperienced in combat. One of them soon took a fatal blow to the chest. The guard was getting the better of the other man too, sending his dagger flying into the bushes below, and forcing him to his knees. The guard raised his sword above the kneeling man, ready to strike him down.

Bryce saw his comrade's predicament. Facing the man to his right, he took a pace back, dropping onto a lower step, then thrust his sword upwards, deep into the man's groin. Swiftly pulling the claymore free, he swung it at the guard to his left, hitting his neck with such force he was decapitated.

Stepping over the headless body, Bryce picked up the dead man's sword and handed it to the kneeling villager. "Here, use this, Fearghas," he smiled.

"Thank yae… er, aye… I will."

With the guards outside the castle now dealt with, the raiders broke through into the courtyard. They were greeted by a harrowing scene. In the centre stood two wooden posts, eight feet high, a crossbeam spanning the gap between them. Sionag, Imogen, and Ailsa were standing on a narrow bench beneath the crossbeam. Each had her hands bound behind her back, and a noose around her neck, tied to the beam above.

A cleric stood to the right of the scaffold, a scroll in his hands, obviously the man whose voice the villagers had heard. MacFinnan stood on the other side, behind six armoured guards with their swords drawn, facing the villagers. A seventh guard was wiping his bloody sword on the back of a prostrate figure in front of him. Tam was dead.

Far to the right, Red Willie was facing the captain of the guard. Willie had his dagger drawn; the captain had his claymore raised towards him. The body of another guard lay behind Willie.

Bryce assessed the situation. The cleric was no threat. Willie could take care of himself. That left him and three inexperienced villagers against seven armoured guards and MacFinnan. "My kind of odds," he said under his breath, then shouted, "Come on lads, charge!"

Dodging to the right of the foremost guard, Bryce thrust his claymore at the man who'd killed Tam, finding a gap in his armour and pushing the sword deep into his chest. As he twisted the blade, he noticed with satisfaction it was the big thug with the scratches on his face. The man collapsed to the ground. He wouldn't be beating any more maidens.

Advancing towards the scaffold, Bryce raised his sword high and, with one swing of the mighty weapon, he split the next man's head in two. Then, sensing someone behind him, he whirled around, hacking into the neck of another man, killing him instantly.

Looking back, he saw one of the villagers was down, but Fearghas and the other survivor, Hamish, were still in the fight, each now armed with a claymore. Hamish was fighting ferociously, pushing back two of the guards. Fearghas was desperately fending off one man and another, the one who'd just taken down a villager, was about to join the fray. Bryce paused a moment, uncertain whether to go to Fearghas's aid, or circle behind the scaffold to get to MacFinnan. The matter was soon decided as Red Willie came flying out of nowhere, leaped onto the back of Fearghas's would-be assailant, and slit his throat.

'My God, if we'd had Willie at Falkirk, Wallace would be ruling Scotland,' Bryce thought. He turned and made his way towards the scaffold. The cleric had fled, leaving no-one between him and MacFinnan. The laird was not wearing armour, but he had a mighty claymore to match Bryce's own and held it ready before him, prepared for battle.

"Let the lassies gae an' yae live," Bryce shouted as he reached the side of the scaffold, opposite MacFinnan.

"Never! They are my property now. Their lives are forfeit," MacFinnan placed his foot on the rickety wooden bench and gave it a push. The girls cried out in alarm as the bench rocked, threatening to topple. They had to fight hard to keep their balance, save themselves from falling. The laird laughed at their distress; he stared at Bryce, "I knew you were here, I thought this might flush you out. Now let us see which one you care about most."

Bryce started to run, heading straight for Sionag, furthest from him. He felt like he was wading through a bog; everything seemed to slow down. He watched helplessly as MacFinnan raised his leg, aimed his boot at the unstable bench, and kicked it over.

The girls screamed as they dropped, but their cries were cut short as the nooses tightened around their throats. They swung on the ropes, legs kicking, gasping for breath. Bryce leaped towards Sionag. He passed his sword into a single hand and grabbed her around the waist with his other arm, hoisting her up. He turned just in time to parry a thrust from MacFinnan. "So, she is the one," snarled the laird.

As Bryce fought back, he saw Red Willie move like lightning. The boy jumped at the last guard standing between him and Ailsa, took him down with a quick slice of his dagger, then used the man's falling body as a platform to leap high into the air. He cut through the rope above Ailsa's head and held on to her as the two of them fell to the ground together.

Fearghas and Hamish were trying to fight their way through to Imogen. The two remaining guards stood in their way. Fearghas fell with a wound to his arm, leaving Hamish alone.

Bryce had to work hard to keep MacFinnan at bay. Although he was the superior swordsman, he was hampered by the need to hold Sionag up. The laird was furiously hacking and lunging at him. He could feel himself tiring. The claymore was meant for two hands, he wouldn't be able to keep this up much longer. He made a sharp thrust at MacFinnan's stomach and the laird fell back a few steps. It gave him a brief respite. He twisted around and swung his sword at the rope above Sionag's head, cutting her free. Letting her fall to the ground, he quickly turned back to face his opponent.

MacFinnan's sword, meant for his back, plunged into Bryce's chest. He knew immediately he was a dead man walking. The sword had ruptured his lung; he would drown in his own blood within the hour. MacFinnan smiled, gloating in triumph, "Thank you for pointing Shebana out to me, I shall enjoy her company before she hangs."

Bryce stared back at him. He didn't understand everything MacFinnan was saying, but he knew well enough he was threatening Sionag. He'd be damned if he'd let the monster win. He wasn't finished yet. His eyes reduced to slits as he firmed his resolve. Clenching his teeth, he grasped the blade of MacFinnan's sword in one hand, pushed down hard with his feet, and propelled himself forward.

MacFinnan's smile faded. He tried to pull his sword free but Bryce held it firm as he advanced towards him along the blade. "Guards, take this man down," the laird shouted, but the last of his men were busy with Hamish and Willie.

Bryce pushed forward again, feeling the sword emerging from his back, protruding almost a foot. He let go of the blade and grabbed MacFinnan's wrist, holding him fast, "I hae yae now, yae bastard."

With a final push, he brought his own weapon to bear. "A'll see yae in Hell," spitting blood into MacFinnan's face, Bryce thrust his mighty claymore through the laird's dark heart.

MacFinnan fell, already dead. Bryce collapsed beside him, the laird's sword impaling him through the chest. He lay in the dirt gasping for breath as blood began to flood his lungs. Sionag crawled to him, her hands still tied behind her back, "No, no, no-o-o-o-o! Ma love, Bryce, ma love, dunnae leave me, I love yae."

He let go of his sword and reached up to touch her cheek, "A'm sarry ma love, I dunnae wan' tae leave yae either, I love yae tae. But yae will hae tae be strang. Be strang fae me, ma love. Live a guid, lang, happy life. Fae me"

She leaned down and kissed him on the lips, tasting his blood, then lay next to him, their faces an inch apart.

A few feet away, Hamish and Willie finished off the last of the guards. Willie climbed up to the crossbeam and cut Imogen down. It was too late; her lifeless body fell to the ground. Ailsa was sobbing with a combination of horror and relief. The injured Fearghas found a knife and cut the rope binding her hands then knelt behind Sionag and cut her free too.

Sionag got to her knees, wrapped her arms around Bryce, and cradled him to her. She started weeping, and her tears mingled with the blood spilling from his mouth and chest. The mixture of blood and tears flowed onto the ground, forming a crimson puddle that slowly expanded and reached the claymore lying at Bryce's side.

Struggling for breath, he somehow found the strength to speak, "Tak ma sword, sweet Sionag, tak it and sell it. It is worth a few crowns, it will set yae up. Tak MacFinnan's as waell. Och look, here's ya…"

He started coughing, unable to finish. She looked around to see her father staggering across the courtyard. The old man was bleeding from a wound in his shoulder but otherwise seemed unharmed. He knelt beside her, "Och lassie, it is wonderful tae see yae." He reached over to Bryce and took his hand, "Bless yae, laddie; bless yae. Yae hae saved ma precious lassie. May aw the saints sing yae tae yaer seat in Heaven."

Bryce tried to reply but only managed a few coughs and splutters.

"Save yaer strength ma love, dunnae speak nae mare," Sionag gently lifted his head and kissed him again. She smiled down at him through her tears, "A'll see yae again wan day, dunnae warry."

"Aye," he whispered.

She sat with him in the courtyard as he slowly ebbed away. The sun went down, the air grew cold, and so did he.

*

At low tide, the small group of survivors filed out of the castle. Fearghas and Alistair, both injured, led the way; Sionag and Ailsa followed, carrying Imogen between them; Hamish and Willie carried Bryce at the rear, his claymore and MacFinnan's wrapped in a blanket and balanced on his chest. They crossed to the shore and made their way home to the village.

Sionag couldn't bear to sell Bryce's claymore, but she knew she couldn't keep it either. They buried it with him, still bearing the stain of his blood and her tears, far up on the slopes of Beinn Dearg.

She did sell MacFinnan's sword, and got enough to start a new life in Inverness. Before she left, she stayed to watch Willie and Ailsa marry in the kirk on Christmas Day. She smiled at the young couple's joy, but cried to herself later.

In the New Year, Alistair's health began to fade. She held her father on his death bed as he slipped away, just as she had held Bryce. She never forgot his final words, "Mak it worth it lassie. Hae a guid life fae Bryce, and fae aw the others tha' died tae save yae. Bless 'aem aw."

After the funeral, she packed her belongings, ready to leave the village. She'd heard MacFinnan's cousin was on his way to take over the castle. She wanted to be away long before the new laird arrived. The night before she was due to depart there was a knock at the door of her tiny cottage. She thought it might be Willie and Ailsa. She had decided to give the croft to them and they would be moving in next week. Perhaps they needed to check something before she left?

Opening the door, she was surprised to see Fearghas. It was pouring with rain and he was soaked to the skin, so she asked him in straight away.

"Wha' brings yae oot on such a night, Master Fearghas? Yae'll catch cold in this dreadful rain."

He stood in front of her, looking down at the floor, his bonnet clasped in both hands before him. In the firelight she could see the anxiety in his face. She also saw how awkwardly he held his injured arm. It had healed since the battle at the castle, but it would never be quite the same, he would never regain his full strength.

"Mistress Sionag, I… er, I…"

"Wha' is it Fearghas, wha' dae yae wan'?"

"I… er… waell, yae see, er… Bryce, he saved ma life. I wud be dead if nae fae him. An' I ken he loved yae an' yae loved him. An', waell, er, A'm nae Bryce, A'm nae e'en half the mon he wa'. But I dae think he wud hae liked it if yae had somewan tae look after yae. So I wa' wonderin' if yae wud like me tae come wi' yae tae Inverness? Just tae look after yae, I wudnae expect anythin' else o' yae, if yae git ma meanin', Mistress Sionag."

She paused a moment then stepped towards him. She put her fingers under his chin and gently lifted his face so she could look him in the eyes. Then she kissed him lightly on the cheek. "Sweet Fearghas, I cannae think o' anythin' better, or anythin' Bryce wud hae liked mare. If yae can accept tha' a part o' ma heart will always be his then I wud be glad tae hae yae look after me. In fact," she softly touched his injured arm, "we can look after each other."

Sionag and Fearghas left for Inverness the next day. They married two years later and raised a fine family. She learned to love him and he adored her, but they both understood part of her would always belong to Bryce. As Fearghas often said, "I think part o' me belangs tae him tae, lass."

XXXVI

DESERT CROSSING

B en sat on the floor of the cave, studying the ancient sword he'd once wielded so skilfully. They'd slept a few hours after experiencing life as Bryce and Sionag and now the midday sun was shining through the entrance. The light was strong enough for him to make out the stain covering the middle part of the blade. Although it had faded to an ochre colour, he knew it was his blood mixed with Sionag's tears. A second stain covered a few inches at the tip. That was MacFinnan's blood, or Mortimer's. The three of them had all stained the sword. Perhaps more than any other object in the world, it embodied their spirits, the 'trinity of souls' they had become. Could this be why it held a strange power?

"So, are you suggesting we storm into Mortimer's villa and attack him with this?" he asked Susan.

"Not exactly, but, as you can tell, the sword has a special significance. I'm sure it has a role to play. You beat him with it once, after all. And it's been soaked in our essence."

"Our essence; what do you mean?"

"Our fluids, my tears and your blood, mingled together, have lain on that sword for seven centuries. Perhaps it's the closest thing we have to the union that will make us strong enough to challenge Mortimer. It has to mean something."

"Maybe, but I can't see a sword being much use against a rocket launcher."

"You forget, he doesn't want to kill us, he wants to consume our souls, or at least destroy them. He could have killed me easily, but he didn't because he knew he'd have to face us again in our next lives. He won't want to take that risk."

"Hmmm, yes, I suppose that gives us a tactical advantage. We can use that. But we need some kind of plan. I still don't think a direct assault is going to work. He has weapons, twenty-first century weapons; no doubt he'll have guns…"

"Yes, Hans has a gun; he killed Sun-lee with it. We'll need to be careful with Hans. I've realised who he is, or who he was, to be more precise; he's almost as evil as Mortimer."

"Why, who was he?"

She told him and Ben shuddered in revulsion, recalling the horrendous atrocities perpetrated by the despicable man she'd just named, one of the most abominable figures of the twentieth century.

"But, how do you know?"

"I recognised him. I was reliving my life as Sarah Wilkes. I was at the cinema with that bitch, Joan…"

"I thought she was your friend?"

"Huh… yeah, so did I, but that's another story. Anyway, we were watching a newsreel and there he was. It was so obviously Hans. The glasses are gone and he's more thickset, but the mannerisms are the same. And the eyes… they're the same chilling, evil, dead eyes he had before, devoid of humanity or compassion. It's him alright."

"Well, I suppose it makes sense. He has the same blind devotion to a fanatical maniac, the same lack of morality; I guess you must be right."

"I am, make no mistake. And it means we know what he's capable of. He's utterly ruthless. Don't underestimate him, Ben; he won't flinch at anything."

"No…" Ben frowned; "well, we'll probably have to deal with him before we can get to Mortimer, so that needs to be a key part of our plan. And the bastard will undoubtedly have more help by now. He may not want to kill us, but he'll have the firepower to stop us. Tell me everything you know about the villa, especially the events last night, before you escaped."

Susan described her experiences at the villa, what she could remember of the layout, the contents of the basement, and everything that had happened during her captivity, culminating with the final moments before she fled.

"As I suspected," Ben concluded, "it's pretty well fortified. A direct attack would be futile."

"So, do we approach at night? Take him by surprise?"

"I don't know; that security system of his is top notch. From what you tell me, he saw the APC coming long before we got there."

"But if it's just the two of us, sneaking up on foot, how could he see us?"

"Oh, believe me, there are systems that can spot a single intruder, on foot, in total darkness, over a mile away. And we can safely assume he'll have the best there is."

"So, we can't attack, and we can't sneak in, what can we do?"

"Well, how about this…"

As he explained his proposal, he couldn't help feeling it was suicidal. But then, as he reminded himself, dying wasn't the problem. She suggested a few refinements and they spent a long time discussing a host of alternatives and contingencies. At one point, they heard a helicopter, but it was far away. Later, there were distant, muffled voices and they tensed, fearing the worst. But the voices slowly faded and they resumed their deliberations; although they were careful to whisper softly.

Eventually, they settled on a final plan they felt had the best chance of success; albeit a slim one. He glanced at his watch, "OK, it's almost four; let's get some sleep before we set off."

He lay down and closed his eyes but, before he could drift off, he felt her hand caressing his chest. "Are you sure there isn't a better way to pass the time?" she asked.

*

Leaving the cave at sunset, they took the claymore and one other, somewhat unusual object, with them. Susan led the way to the oasis where they'd lived six centuries before. They drank from the pool and ate some fruit then Ben made a makeshift bag out of his shirt. "Energy and moisture," he pointed out as he placed more fruit into the bag. He also took a few lengths of reed and slipped them into his pocket, "We may need these too."

They walked north, following a GPS app on Ben's phone that showed the way to the villa. After a few hours, he suggested they take a rest. They sat next to each other in a sheltered dip between the dunes.

"I thought it was cold at night in the desert," she said. "Not here."

"Pity, I was looking for an excuse for you to hold me."

He laughed, "We don't need an excuse." He wrapped his arm around her and pulled her close.

"Do you think Mortimer will send the helicopter tonight?" she asked.

"I don't know. He might. But he'll probably expect us to be heading away, not back towards the villa."

"Unless he senses us approaching; I told you, I can't shield us everywhere, the cave was special."

"Hmmm, well, if he knows we're coming, he can just sit back and wait, can't he? He won't need the helicopter. Anyway, we'll hear it coming miles away; it's the least of our worries. Shall we go over the plan again?"

They ran through the plan a couple of times then got to their feet, ready to resume the long trek, but Ben hesitated.

"Susan?"

"Yes?"

"Look," he sighed, "there's something I haven't told you. It's something Sleeping Bear said. I've been thinking it over. I think it means one of us isn't going to make it."

"Why, what did he say?"

"Well, I didn't take it seriously at first, but he was right about the marriage of stars and finding you among the sick, so I…"

"What did he say?"

"He said I would lose you seven times. And the thing is I've been working it out and… Shit, the fucking helicopter."

The faint 'whump whump' sound could be heard, far in the distance. But it was getting louder by the second. "Quick, run back along our tracks, I know a trick," he urged.

They ran a few hundred yards back the way they'd come then he dropped to his knees and pulled her down next to him, "This is a good spot." He quickly dug two small, shallow trenches within the area already disturbed by their footprints. "In here," he said, "we'll have to hide beneath the sand."

"They look like graves"

"Don't worry, I've done this before," he assured her.

"But how will we breathe?"

He smiled and pulled out the reeds he'd taken from the oasis.

They lay under the sand as the sound of the helicopter grew ever closer, reaching a deafening climax, almost as if it was hovering directly overhead. Ben started to fear they'd been discovered. Then it moved away and the sound gradually faded until he could hear it no more. When he was reasonably certain it was safe, he sat up. He looked around and saw a distant light moving away from them. Breathing a sigh of relief, he pulled Susan up beside him, "OK, we can carry on. We were lucky; I don't think they spotted our tracks. They're heading south, looks like he hasn't sensed us yet," he smiled again.

She pulled him close and kissed him passionately on the lips then moved back a few inches and stared deep into his eyes, "I don't care what Sleeping Bear said, we're in this together; we're going to do this together, and we're gonna survive this together; right?"

"Yeah," he stared back at her; "yeah, er… right."

But, as they resumed their journey, he couldn't help thinking about Sleeping Bear's prophecy, 'I was killed at Isandlwana, so I lost her there. Then I was Billy and I died again, so that's twice. Then…' Every time he thought about it, he became more convinced one of them was going to die; they weren't going to survive this together. And, for the one who perished, it was going to be horrific, worse than anything he'd seen before.

As the anxiety built within him, he glanced across at Susan, walking next to him. She smiled reassuringly, almost as if she could read his thoughts. He returned her smile, hoping he looked more confident than he felt, but inside he kept running over the times he'd lost her since that night with Sleeping Bear... and he couldn't get them to add up to seven.

*

Susan looked at Ben walking beside her and saw the falseness in his smile. She frowned, something wasn't right. He was anxious, she supposed. Even if he was a professional soldier, they were still facing enormous risks. He probably knew better than she just how slim their chances were. As they marched towards the villa under cover of darkness she hoped, against all odds, their crazy plan might somehow succeed.

Hours later, they reached the top of yet another rise in the seemingly endless dunes and saw the villa's lights a mile away. Ben turned and pulled her down into the sand, "OK; it's game time." He knelt behind her, his claymore in hand. "Take off your blouse and put your hands behind your back," he ordered.

XXXVII

CONFRONTING A DEMON

Susan could feel the heat of the rising sun on her exposed skin as she staggered over the rough terrain. Ben had torn strips from her blouse to tie her hands behind her back, leaving her wearing only a bra and skirt, and making it hard to keep her balance as they made their way across the desert. He marched behind her, his sword pointed at her back. Looking up at the roof of the villa, she could see the rocket launcher aimed in their direction, cameras tracking them... machine guns too. They were about a hundred yards away when a burst of shots hit the sand in front of her and they came to an abrupt halt.

"Stop," Hans's voice boomed from the speakers on the roof.

"I want to speak to Mortimer," Ben shouted back.

After a long silence, a reply came from the speakers, "Yes, Major Carlton, this is Lord Mortimer. There is no need for you to shout, the external microphones are quite sensitive. So, tell me, major, how may I help you?"

"The doctor here's been tellin' me all kinds of mumbo jumbo about souls and reincarnation and all that rubbish. I don't know what to believe, to be honest. I've had some strange dreams, it's true, but some of what she says seems a bit far-fetched to me. She claims you want to destroy us, some kind of weird black magic thing to stop us being together. She believes all that nonsense. Maybe you do too. Personally, I think it's a load of bollocks. The point is… I ain't gonna die for it. So, I've been thinking; and it seems to me, if you want to stop us getting together, you only need to get rid of one of us, right?"

There was another long interval before Mortimer spoke again, "Go on, major, I'm listening."

"Right, so here's the deal. You only need one of us, so take her, you can have her. Do what you want with her, I don't care. Just leave me out of it. Let me walk out of here and I won't give you any trouble. I'll leave you in peace, not a word to the authorities."

Ben paused, waiting for a reply, but there was nothing but silence from the speakers.

"Do we have a deal, Mortimer?"

Susan turned and hissed at Ben, "What are you doing, this isn't what we planned. And why the fuck am I tied up? It was only supposed to *look* like I was tied up. I can't get out of this stupid fucking army special knot you've done. Let me go *now!*"

"Look, I'm sorry, but I told you, I hardly know you. I might have known you in the past but, in this life, we're practically strangers. It's this life that matters, here and now, and I just want to get on with mine. One of us is going to die today, I'm sure of it, and I'd sooner it was you. Nothing personal, sweetheart, but that's how it is."

"Uuughh!" she screeched and spat in his face; "you fucking, devious, shitty little bastard, I thought I could trust you, I thought you loved me. I can't believe it! After all we've been through, you betray me like this? And what we did in the cave; did it mean nothing to you? Were you just using me to pass the time?"

"It was nice, I enjoyed it, but it's not worth dying for," he prodded her in the thigh with his sword, drawing blood; "now, eyes front, let's see what his lordship has to say."

Susan faced the villa again, a look of desperation on her face, blood trickling down her leg. She watched the silent speakers, waiting to hear what Mortimer decided.

"Your little squabbles are most amusing, major," the lord said at last; "I'm glad to hear that you, at least, have seen sense. Very well, you are right, there is no need for any unpleasantness between you and I, the doctor alone will be sufficient. Bring her to me and I will let you walk away unharmed. You have my word."

Ben tapped Susan on the hip with his sword, "You heard him, you bitch, get moving."

She walked on, Ben following close behind. They were fifty yards from the villa when Hans appeared and trained his gun on them, "Keep coming, major, I will tell you when to stop."

Susan was crying now. She stumbled, collapsing onto her knees, "Please, Ben, please don't make me do this. He'll destroy me. He won't just kill me, he'll destroy me forever. You haven't seen; you don't know what it's like. Please, you can't."

Ben reached down and pulled her back to her feet, his face grim. "Rather you than me," he pushed her forward and she staggered on towards Hans.

When they were twenty paces away, Hans said, "Alright, major, that's close enough. Send the doctor to me now."

Lowering his sword, Ben stepped up behind Susan. "Go," he commanded, pushing her forward again. She almost fell, struggling to keep her balance with her hands behind her back, but she steadied herself and crossed the last few yards to where Hans was waiting. He grabbed her arm in a painful, iron grip, spun her around to face Ben, and shouted, "OK, major, thank you for bringing the doctor to us. You have been most helpful." He gave a cold smile beneath his emotionless eyes, "You can go now."

Ben turned, as if to walk away. Hans raised his gun and pointed it at Ben's back. Susan could see he was aiming at the base of Ben's spine, where the bullet would cripple him, but not threaten his life.

Suddenly, Ben stopped, holding up his empty left hand. "Actually, before I go…" he turned back to face Hans, who swiftly lowered his gun.

"I just wanted to ask," Ben continued, taking a slow, careful step towards Hans, "I mean, ask if you can remember," he took another slow step, "if you can remember all those terrible things you did," another step, "I mean, were you really him?"

"Really who, major?" Hans had his gun pointed at the ground, clearly distracted by Ben's question.

Ben took another step, "You know, in your last life, were you him?"

"Who, major, who are you talking about?"

Ben stepped forward again, "Were you really Heinrich Him…"

'Heinrich' was the signal. As Ben spoke the name, Susan pulled her hand free from the slipknot and whirled around with the object they'd concealed within it held firmly in her grasp. She plunged the jagged, broken, rib bone, Basira's rib bone, broken when she'd been stoned to death, into Hans's eye. He screamed and staggered back, clutching his face.

Ben raised his claymore and charged. He crossed the short distance in a couple of seconds, paused to gather himself then thrust the sword into Hans's stomach. He twisted the blade. It was a mortal wound.

"Seig heil, you bastard"

Hans collapsed onto his knees then toppled forwards and lay spread-eagled in the sand. Ben bent down, plucked the dying man's gun from his twitching fingers and handed it to Susan, "Can you shoot? You weren't so good when you were Sebastian."

"Never suits me well, being a man," she aimed the gun at Hans's outstretched hand and blew a hole in his palm; "you forget, I am She Wolf."

Ben smiled, "So you are. Come on, let's go." He held out his hand for her to take and they ran to the villa's back wall together then began to make their way towards the rear entrance. "Stay close to the wall and we should be safe. He might not want to kill us, but he could take us down if he wanted. You deserve an Oscar by the way, that was brilliant."

"You too, you almost had me convinced when you stabbed me in the leg. We didn't rehearse that bit."

"Bit of improv. Sorry; thought it might be more persuasive."

"Well, the cat's out of the bag now. I think Mortimer knows we're in it together."

He pulled her to him, hugging her tight, "We are, but I'm still worried one of us isn't going to make it. I've worked it out, I..."

She put her hand on his cheek and kissed him softly, "Shhhh, we'll make it, both of us. And, anyway, even if we do get killed, we can find each other again. We're going to be together, Ben. If it isn't this life then so be it, but we *will* be together."

"Unless he destroys one of us"

"Look, we know what we have to do. He can shoot us, stab us, whatever, dying isn't a problem. We just need to make sure he doesn't use the potion on us. We agreed, didn't we?"

"Yeah, I know," he sighed, "we kill ourselves first if we have to. Christ, I hope I don't have to kill you though; I don't know if I could."

"You would if you had to, Ben. You're strong, you can do it. And besides, we've killed each other before."

"When was that?"

"Long time ago, I'll show you one day," she kissed him again then took a step back and smiled, "but let's not give up on this life yet. I'd rather have you now if I can," she gave him a wink then turned and continued creeping along the wall towards the villa's back door; "come on, have a little faith. We're the saviours of the Universe, remember."

*

Ben followed close behind Susan, thinking how incredible she was and hoping, if one of them had to die, it would be him. He'd wait thirty years for her if he had to, he'd wait sixty, he'd wait a thousand, but he couldn't lose her, he just couldn't take that. Never mind Mortimer, if she was destroyed, it would destroy him anyway.

She reached the door first. It had been left open and she was about to enter, but he gently pulled her back, "Careful, it might be guarded." Cautiously, he took up a position to one side of the entrance and peered around the doorframe.

Two sentries were guarding the staircase leading down to the basement. They wore full body armour and helmets equipped with bullet-proof visors, leaving few vulnerable spots for a shot from Hans's pistol. They were armed with semi-automatic machine guns, which they had trained on the rear entrance. But, instead of aiming high, towards the body of anyone entering the villa, the sentries had their guns pointed low, towards where the legs of an intruder would be. The reason for this quickly dawned on him.

"There's two armed guards," he whispered, "but you were right, it looks like they're under orders not to kill us. You stay here, I'll deal with them."

He took a few paces back then ran at the open doorway and hurled himself through. He dived onto the floor of the lobby then somersaulted forwards, gambling the sentries were too afraid of Mortimer's wrath to fire at him as he tumbled across the floor. Unable to shoot without risking a mortal wound, they would be frozen in indecision.

It seemed to work. He rolled across the floor without a shot being fired. Springing to his feet, he thrust his sword through the nearest man's throat. The other sentry struggled to bring his weapon to bear, firing at the ground, just missing Ben's foot. Ben whirled around and plunged his claymore through a gap in the man's armour, deep into his chest.

The guards collapsed, dead before they hit the floor. Susan ran into the lobby and joined Ben next to the dead men, "Should we take their guns?"

"No use, look," he picked up one of the weapons and showed it to her; "digital safety catch, locks as soon as the grip is released. We can't fire them without the code. We'll have to stick to the plan."

"I see," she frowned. "Well, at least this one works," she held up Hans's pistol. "Alright then, let's do it," she turned towards the stairs; "it's this way."

"Wait a minute," he pulled a packet of chewing gum from his pocket and offered it to her; "want some?"

"Er... maybe not just now."

Smiling, he popped a strip of gum into his mouth. He chewed for a minute then walked slowly across to one of the huge, gold-framed mirrors and smashed it with the hilt of his sword. As he bent down to pick up a broken shard, she cautioned, "That's seven years' bad luck."

"I've had twelve thousand already," he laughed; "I think I can cope with another seven." He took the gum out of his mouth and used it to attach the shard to the tip of his sword. Holding the weapon aloft, he nodded, "OK, ready now."

She led the way down the stairs. At the bottom, he signalled her to stand against the wall, a few feet from the open control room door. He stood between her and the opening then slowly manoeuvred his makeshift mirror into position. The first thing he saw was a flask of black potion sitting on a desk beside the wall. Then, adjusting the mirror, he saw Mortimer standing in the middle of the room, flanked by two guards with machine pistols aimed at the doorway, ready to shoot them down as they entered.

"There's no point hiding in the corridor, major, I can see you on camera," Mortimer shouted.

Ben looked up and saw a camera on the other side of the hallway, pointing straight at them. He swung his claymore and cut the camera in half. Sparks flew and the mirror shard went spinning through the air to shatter against the wall at the end of the passage.

"Most impressive, major, but I still know you're there. What happened to our deal? Just hand over the doctor and you're free to go."

"No deal, your lordship," Ben shouted back.

"As you wish, major," Mortimer replied.

Ben turned and whispered to Susan, "Come on, just as we practised in the cave. Are you ready?"

She nodded, "As I'll ever be."

He gave her a quick hug then dropped onto his hands and knees. Behind him, she did the same. Looking back at her, he whispered, "Three… two… one… go!"

They burst into the control room, Ben leading, his claymore gripped in one hand, followed quickly by Susan, clasping Hans's gun. The guards stared at them in astonishment as they scrambled across the floor.

"Aim carefully, I want them disabled, no shots to the head," ordered Mortimer; "remember: if you kill one, you take their place."

Like their comrades in the lobby, the guards froze in confusion, clearly terrified of making a mistake and killing one of the attackers. Rising to a crouch, Ben slashed the nearest man's legs from under him. As the guard fell, he put his claymore through the man's throat. Susan lifted Hans's gun and shot the other guard in the shoulder. The man dropped his pistol and fell back.

Ben and Susan got to their feet and started to close in on Mortimer. He backed away towards the far end of the room. Susan pointed the gun at him, "On your knees, you bastard."

Mortimer smiled and clasped his hands together in front of him. He stretched out his finger and tapped the face of his watch. A loud buzzing came from the belt under Susan's skirt. She dropped the gun and fell to the floor, writhing in agony.

Ben rushed at Mortimer, his claymore held high above his head, "Stop that, let her go, or I swear I'll cut you in half." As he passed the wounded guard, the man grabbed his ankle, tripping him up. Ben fell forward onto the floor. He twisted around and put his sword through the guard's chest but, by the time he'd regained his feet and turned towards Mortimer again, the dark lord was holding a claymore of his own.

"You are not the only one to retrieve an old weapon, major. I bought this back almost two centuries ago. It has tasted your blood before. Now it will taste it again."

Ben glanced at Susan. She was lying on the floor, gasping for breath. The electric shock had hurt her badly. He turned back to Mortimer, "I seem to recall I killed you that day, Mortimer, or should I say MacFinnan?"

Mortimer laughed, "Yes, you did. Well, you were probably the best swordsman in Wallace's army, after all.

But it cost you your life, didn't it? In any case, I don't think you did so well last time we fought, did you, little Bartie?"

"I did well enough to give you that scar, and I learned a few things after that, I can assure you."

"Hmmm, yes, well…" Mortimer briefly touched the scar on his forehead, then grasped his sword in both hands; "you may have been pretty good in 1306, you might even have been back to scratch by Waterloo, but you're not Bryce or Bartie now. When was the last time Ben Carlton wielded a sword before today?"

"Never, but I'm ready to give it a go."

Ben lunged at Mortimer with a ferocity driven by centuries of anger and frustration. But the lord easily parried his clumsy thrust and swiftly counter-attacked. Within seconds, Ben was desperately holding Mortimer back, the lord's blade an inch from his face. With a colossal effort, he managed to push Mortimer away and went back on the offensive.

The fight raged back and forth. Ben was strong and energetic but Mortimer was still a practised swordsman. Taking out the guards was one thing, this was quite another. Ben sensed Mortimer was toying with him, just as he'd done two centuries ago. He feared he would soon be overwhelmed.

Then something began to change. He started to move instinctively, as if he'd been fighting with the claymore all his life. Old skills from his time as Bryce were returning. Gradually, he got the measure of his opponent and started forcing him towards the corner.

Mortimer was falling back step by step. As he drew level with one of the desks, he reached out to a computer screen and swept it towards Ben's face. Ben ducked and the screen bounced harmlessly off his shoulder, but he was thrown off balance and Mortimer slashed at his forearm. Ben lost his grip and his sword went skidding across the floor.

Pouncing forward, Mortimer sliced across Ben's calf. Ben fell to his knees. The lord smashed the hilt of his sword into Ben's solar plexus, leaving him gasping for breath. Standing over Ben with the tip of his sword resting on his abdomen, Mortimer smiled in triumph, "One quick thrust through the gut into your spine will disable you. You should live long enough for me to consume your soul. With you gone, I will have chance to enjoy some quality time with Shebana. I think I will keep her as a pet for a while before I destroy her. It might be rather fun," he turned to leer lasciviously at Susan... just in time to see her coming at him with Ben's claymore in her hands.

"No you fucking won't, you bastard."

Mortimer quickly raised his sword and easily fended off Susan's thrust. He responded with a low cut aimed at her thighs and she jumped back to avoid his blade, giving him space to advance. He continued to attack and she slowly gave ground, backing away towards the desk where the evil black potion sat waiting to claim its next victim.

As she retreated from his onslaught, he taunted, "You must be tiring, my dear. These swords weigh over six pounds. I don't believe I've ever seen a woman using one before. They're not really designed for the weaker sex."

But, as Ben watched, he could see Susan's confidence was growing. She was developing an affinity with the weapon in her hands. The strange power flowing from the sword connected her to Bryce, giving her the strength and skills she needed. As she evaded another of Mortimer's ripostes, she retorted, "That's always been your weakness, Mamboja."

"What's that, my dear?"

She took a step back and momentarily dropped her guard. Just a little, but it was enough. She smiled as Mortimer took the bait and lunged towards her. Swiftly, she brought up her sword, parried his thrust and plunged the claymore deep into his stomach.

"You've always underestimated the power of a woman."

Mortimer dropped his sword and fell to his knees, clutching at his wound. Thick, dark blood oozed slowly through his fingers, unnatural looking blood, completely unlike the blood of any normal person.

Ben staggered to his feet and hobbled across the room. He picked up Mortimer's fallen weapon and stood beside Susan. He placed the tip of the sword on the lord's chest and prepared to finish him.

Mortimer looked up with eyes that were almost black, "You can't win, Bakara; you will never win. Her belt is tuned to the rhythm of my heart. If my heart stops, the belt activates and the poison will be released. She will be dead within a minute and her soul will be destroyed forever. I win, Bakara, I always do. I always will."

Ben hesitated, not knowing what to do. Next to him, Susan put the claymore down on the desk and picked up the potion. As Ben let the sword in his hand begin to drop, she grabbed Mortimer's hair and pulled his head back. Jamming the flask into his open mouth, she screamed, "Fuck that, you bastard, you're not going to win this time."

Half the potion had emptied into Mortimer's mouth before he lurched backwards and knocked the flask away. The flask flew sideways and smashed against the wall. Mortimer stumbled to his feet, clutching at his throat. His face turned bright red, his eyes burned brighter still. Smoke came from his mouth, his nostrils, his ears, and began to rise from his clothes. He staggered around the room, arms flailing; then fell to his knees again in the centre of the floor.

"I won't... I can't... uuughh, er, aaaghh... aaaghh, I will be... I will be... ba-a-a-a-a..."

He collapsed forwards, his clothes on fire. More smoke emerged from his mouth to join the rest and form a cloud that glowed and pulsated, brighter than anything Ben had ever seen. Yet somehow it was dark as well. It was bright black. It drifted slowly upwards and passed through the ceiling, disappearing from sight.

Mortimer's body continued to burn. Ben took Susan's hand and began to lead her out of the control room. They'd almost reached the door when a beeping noise started coming from her belt. She lifted her skirt and they both saw a small red light flashing in time with the beeping.

The beeping and flashing were getting faster. She

looked at him with tears in her eyes and tried to manage a smile, "At least we got him this time. Hopefully, he won't be back. I love you, Ben. I'm sorry we didn't get to stay together long." She knelt down and bowed her head, "You know what you have to do. Be quick, I'm ready."

For a moment, he simply stared at her, a look of horror on his face. Then he gulped and nodded, "OK... I, er... OK..." He slowly raised Mortimer's sword high above her neck.

"Quickly, Ben, thirty years is better than forever. Hurry."

As he looked down at her, he felt overwhelmed by love and grief. An iron resolve suddenly overtook him, "Screw that, we've had enough tearful farewells. Not this time." He dropped the sword and knelt beside her, "There has to be a keyhole or something. If I can find the keyhole, maybe we can find the key."

"There's nothing, Ben, I checked it before."

"His watch then," Ben looked at Mortimer's burning body. The watch was on fire, sparks flying from its shattered face.

"Damn it, there's got to be something." He ran his hands over the belt, "Did you check everywhere?"

"I think so, I..."

The beeping and flashing were almost continuous. There were only seconds left.

He pushed his hand between her thighs. He felt a slight indentation in the belt, next to her crotch. It was an odd shape, not like a keyhole, more like a...

"His ring!" Ben jumped to his feet. He picked up Mortimer's sword and ran towards him. The heat was intense, every part of the lord's body was ablaze, but Ben could see the ring was still intact. He swung the sword, slicing through Mortimer's fingers, then reached into the flames and grabbed the digit bearing the ring.

Dropping the sword again, Ben folded his hand around the burning finger to extinguish the fire and ran back to Susan, urging, "Lie on your back and open your legs." He knelt in front of her, Mortimer's dead finger in his grasp, and pushed the star-shaped ruby into its slot. As the beeping became a single tone, he twisted the gem. A click came from the belt and it sprang open. He dropped the finger and pulled the vile contraption off her. A split second later, as he held the belt in his hands, only inches from her flesh, there was a second click. A vicious needle coated in black liquid sprang up from the base.

Throwing the belt to the side, Ben pulled Susan up onto her knees and threw his arms around her, "Oh, thank God, thank God you're alright. I love you, Susan, I love you too."

They knelt on the floor of the basement, holding tightly on to each other, crying tears of joyful relief. Mortimer's body burned for a while then the flames flickered out.

*

Susan spoke first, "Come on, it's more comfortable upstairs." She got to her feet, took Ben by the hand, and pulled him up after her. She led him out of the control room, up the stairs to the lobby, where she sat him down on a sofa so she could tend to his injuries. As well as his wounds from the swordfight, he'd burned his hand in the fire. But there wasn't anything she was too concerned about. "Nothing life threatening, major," she smiled, "but we ought to get you bandaged up all the same."

She used a piece of broken mirror to cut some strips off a curtain then sat next to him and set about binding his wounds.

"Er, sorry if I was a bit rough when I was checking the belt," he said; "er… I was in a bit of a hurry, you know?"

"That's alright," she laughed, "I think Mortimer's severed finger between my legs was the worst part. What made you think to look there anyway?"

"A hunch," he shrugged; "it's where people often put things they don't want anyone to find."

"Huh, good hunch," she looked up and stared into his eyes, "you saved me, Ben; you saved my soul. Thank you."

"Well, er, I… well thank God Sleeping Bear was wrong, anyway."

"How do you mean?"

"He said I would lose you seven times and there've only been six."

"Six?"

"Yes, I lost Sebastian when I died at Isandlwana; I lost you three times when you were Sarah, and then I lost Sammie. Oh, and the one I always forget is Sally. You were still alive when Sleeping Bear made his prophecy, so I lost you when I died at the Alamo. That makes six. According to him, I was supposed to lose you again. I was convinced one of us was going to die. I hoped it would be me, but when that damn belt started beeping I was afraid I was going to lose you. It was like destiny stacked against us all over again."

She smiled and put her hand on his arm, "But you *have* lost me seven times since you met Sleeping Bear. You've missed one out. In 1898, when you were a little boy growing up in a tiny house in the Rhondda, a baby girl was born next door. That was me, but when I was a few weeks old, I was taken sick. My parents couldn't afford to pay for a doctor, so they were relieved when a certain Doctor Mortimer offered his services for free. You can guess the rest. Anyway, that's your seven."

"Well, that explains it then. Bit of a relief in a way; but yet another example of the evils he was capable of. I wonder what exactly his big plan was."

"Fuck knows; something to do with accelerating the end of the human race as we know it and creating an army of empty vessels to help him rule the world. It was all to do with overpopulation. It is worrying that he said it was inevitable though, maybe we should warn someone?"

"Yeah, but he was mad, I'm not sure if we need to take his ravings seriously."

"Hmmm, I don't know," she stared out at the desert, frowning as she thought it over.

"Uuughh," she shuddered, shaking the thought from her mind. She returned her attention to Ben's wounds,

"Thank God he's gone anyway. Whatever his plan was, I reckon he'd been working on it a long time. You know how I saw Hans in that newsreel?"

"Yes," he nodded.

"Well, Hans was standing with the other party leaders at the front of the balcony. But behind them at the back was another figure. It was pretty blurry, I couldn't be sure, but…" she looked up from her bandaging, "I think it was Mortimer."

They sat quietly as she finished putting the makeshift bandages in place, each of them trying to digest the implications of what she'd just said. When she was finally done, she turned to face him, "Do you think he could have survived? His soul, I mean?"

"No, he burned up from the inside like the others, he couldn't have survived."

"But where did he go? He just floated away. Can we be sure?"

Her question hung in the air for a long time. Then she sprang to her feet, smiled down at him and, in a perfect Irish lilt, said, "Now be sure to get those changed at least twice a day, you hear." She took his hand and led him upstairs to the opulent guest bedroom where she'd been staying just a few days before.

They stood together in the centre of the room, holding each other close. They kissed long and passionately until she pulled back, panting from the ecstasy of their lovemaking. She tossed her golden hair then stared into his eyes and smiled broadly, "So, are you still in a hurry, tiger? You seem to have got my knickers off, after all. Would you like me to lie on my back and open my legs again?"

"Whatever you want," he smiled back.

They fell onto the bed and began to pull each other's clothes off, feverishly, lustfully, and yet gently too. Their naked bodies crashed together in heated excitement and, finally, they joined in the union destiny had waited almost twelve thousand years for.

Sometimes people say 'the Earth moved'. For Susan and Ben, it actually did.

EPILOGUE

THE BEGINNING?

It was a fabulous day; the kind of day sensible people stayed outdoors, enjoying the weather. The sun did not just shine; it beamed down on the pure golden sands of the beautiful beach and the soft, lapping waves of the turquoise sea making its way gradually into the secluded bay. Only complete fools or those with urgent work to do would be inside on a day like this.

Two children were playing on the beach: a boy, about four years old, and a little girl, slightly younger. They were good friends already. In fact, they'd been more than friends for a long time.

Khulekani watched the children adoringly. They were perfectly safe. The UV filter in the giant dome above would protect them from harmful radiation. She saw her son, Bafana talking to her friend's daughter, Sybella. The dark-skinned boy seemed to have a protective instinct towards his little friend with the long, blonde hair and stunning, crystal-blue eyes.

This was such a fantastic resort, Khulekani thought. An interesting place too. She'd read somewhere they'd recently found traces of an ancient culture, nearly twelve thousand years old, which had occupied the area. She had no idea how they worked these things out, but apparently the inhabitants had worshipped the sea and made human sacrifices on this very beach. She shuddered at the thought of the poor victims being staked out on the sand, waiting to drown.

'Relax,' she told herself, such horrors were a thing of the past. Nobody was making human sacrifices in 2117. 'One planet, one nation, one people,' that was the world philosophy now, just as President Carpenter had said in her inaugural speech so long ago. The terrible wars and ecological disasters of the mid-twenty-first century were fading into history, and humanity had been enjoying a new era of peace and prosperity for decades.

From the corner of her eye, she saw another family arrive on the beach. They also had a boy with them, white-skinned with long, dark hair, a few years older than her son.

The new arrival ran across to the other children. He spoke to them for a moment then pushed Bafana down onto the sand. As Bafana lay on the beach, the stranger grabbed Sybella by the hand and started to pull her away.

And so it began again.

COMING SOON...

THE SECOND INSTALMENT
IN THE SOULS SERIES...

DESTINY OF SOULS

CHAPTER 1
CHAMPION OF THE EMPIRE

Susan stood in the centre of the arena, her bronze battle axes held at her sides dripping with the blood of the fallen gladiators strewn around her, each of them killed with a single strike.

For the first time in her life, she was able to glory in her womanhood. Her new leather tunic, splattered with her opponents' blood, displayed the contours of her body. She wore it proudly in the sure and certain knowledge she was as good a warrior as any man.

She stared up at the despot who'd condemned her to death, lifting her chin in open defiance. "Octo!" declared the emperor. She steeled herself for her next challenge, knowing it would probably be her last.

Check www.bayleytheauthor.com for details of publication and availability, and to read the rest of Chapter I.